Is Nothing Sacred?

by
Walter von Wegen

Published by Buchholz Press
Knoxville, Tennessee

Is Nothing Sacred?
by Walter von Wegen

© Copyright 2005, Walter von Wegen

This book is a work of fiction. Names, characters, places and incidents are either products of the author's unabridged imagination, or are used fictitiously. Any resemblance to actual events or locales or persons, living or dead, is entirely coincidental.

ISBN: 0971108722

Cover: David R. Willie
Interior: Bob Spear

Printed in the United States of America
10 9 8 7 6 5 4 3 2 1

Published by Buchholz Press
Knoxville, Tennessee

For: Professor Francis R. Ginanni and Mike Clopton

Acknowledgements:

Many thanks to:
my family,
David and Erin Willie,
Laurel Boyd
Angela McCallum
and all the fine folks at 391

cover designer: David R. Willie—www.goacme.com.
Editing and interior layout: Bob Spear—Heartland Reviews
www.heartlandreviews.com

In memory of Lee A. Carr

Farewel happy Fields
Where Joy for ever dwells: Hail horrours, hail
Infernal world, and thou profoundest Hell
Receive thy new Possessor: One who brings
A mind not to be chang'd by Place or Time.
The mind is its own place, and in it self
Can make a Heav'n of Hell, a Hell of Heav'n.

John Milton, *Paradise Lost* (1667)

"They that can give up essential liberty to obtain a little temporary
safety deserve neither liberty nor safety." – Benjamin Franklin,
Historical Review of Pennsylvania, 1759

"After one look at this planet, any visitor from outer space would
say, 'I want to see the manager'." – William Burroughs

Prologue

New Years Day, 2044

THE NEW YORK CYBERPOST
Jet Liner Shot Down, Crashes in Harbor

Yesterday morning, New Yorkers again awoke to the sound of heavy artillery, as the .909 caliber cannons mounted atop the Empire State Building shot down an explosives-laden, stolen jetliner that was aimed to crash into it. A New York Mayor's Office spokesperson said this morning. "The cannons atop the World Financial Center were definitely a help." Empire officials added, "It's great to have those National Guard personnel around to help with the heavy artillery."

The jetliner, which was stolen or hijacked (depending on which source we talked to) from a Boeing service hangar in Maine, did not apparently have any passengers other than the hijackers themselves, FBI officials said this morning.

~ ~ ~

Venice

Early Thursday morning on January 1, a severed head was reportedly seen bobbing in the waters of the Rio Orsolo, amongst the gondolas, not far from the Piazza San Marco. It was found in an area illuminated under the city lights, more or less well preserved in appearance. The shocked gondolier, who found it at about 6:30 a.m., immediately phoned the *Polizia Municipali* on his mobile phone.

About 600 meters northwest through Venice's serpentine alleyways, *Ispettore* Brezzi answered the call at the modest police headquarters that occupied several side rooms in the elegant white palazzo at 4137a Riva del Carbon, south of the Rialto Bridge adjacent to the Grand Canal. Wind gusts lashed the steel bar-and-mesh-covered windows outside as Brezzi reluctantly took the call. He had been hoping for a quiet morning on duty, as he was alone in the office this particular morning.

As he listened to the gondolier's peculiar and somewhat incoherent tale, Brezzi, a medium-sized man with a neatly-trimmed blonde beard and a round face, tapped his fingers impatiently and secretly wondered if he should hang up, as it was probably a prank. But, when he did a search on the desk computer, the caller's account came on-screen, and Brezzi saw it was indeed a registered gondolier, one with very few complaints from the tourists. *Scacia, that was his name...*

He reluctantly concluded there must be something in it. Even a hung-over gondolier had better things to do on the morning after New Year's Eve than to phone in a prank like that.

Brezzi got to his feet slowly, as he too had been celebrating last night. His newly acquired seniority meant not having to do 'idiot night' duty, which had meant patrolling up and down the Grand Canal for drunken tourists who fell in the dark jade waters off the Piazza San Marco.

Even better, he no longer had to cart off the idiots who blew off their fingers by holding on to firecrackers too long. He had done enough of *that* in his earlier years.

He rubbed his sore belly ruefully, and then oh-so-slowly pulled on his dark blue police parka. He walked out the double front doors and saw the winds were already fierce at 7 a.m. this morning, especially for anyone travelling by *Polizia* boat, which were tiny and open, except at the back where the arrested or injured had to be transported.

Normally, he requested a driver from the motor pool, but Brezzi knew none were available, as they had all been on duty the night before. He didn't really want to go out on the water with his stomach the way it was, but it was either that or go on foot, which meant prolonging the agony.

Accepting the inevitable, he kept his grumbles to himself. He stepped out on the thin bobbing wooden pier in front of the building and took boat number seven. It wasn't really an official police speedboat, because it was really meant for ferrying important mainland people around for visits to guarantee next year's budget, but it would have to do. All the regular patrol boats had been felled by a mysterious engine computer virus that stubbornly refused to be cured.

He cursed when he slipped momentarily as he set his damp shoes on the polished wood deck. He stepped back, then gingerly set one foot on the deck, testing it a moment before climbing in.

At least this boat had the most powerful engine, he reminded himself. If nothing else, he could take it out later and do some marlin fishing around Malta later in the month.

He punched in the right PIN code on the first try, much to his surprise. The engine started up readily and he set off, noting that the waves were especially choppy. He didn't bother turning on the siren or the flashing blue lights. The Grand Canal was bereft of traffic this morning. The normal Vaporetti lines would not start running again until the afternoon, and only a masochist would hire a gondola at a time like this.

He turned the boat towards the dock. *What the hell am I doing?* he asked himself as he almost steered straight into the wooden posts silhouetted against the few damp rays of sunlight peeking through the clouds.

He found a vacant docking post in front of the Calle Vallaresso and pulled in. Again he cursed the lack of a partner, not only because it was against police rules to venture out alone, but also because getting the boat tied to the mooring post was proving to be a real pain in the ass because of the wind and the waves.

On the fourth attempt he succeeded in getting the rope around the slippery post. He leaned over and switched off the motor. He got out carefully and walked past Harry's Bar without looking. He didn't need any reminder of last night. He was one of the lucky few who didn't have to pay full price for the overpriced drinks there. This morning, he wasn't feeling so lucky.

After a cursory glance in both directions, he crossed the chic shopping arcade on sal. San Moise before going right on Calle San Selvadago.

Immediately, he saw the cluster of straw-hatted gondoliers huddled at the canal's edge. Their clouds of cigarette smoke were rising, like from row upon row of skinny, black-clad smokestacks. The mustard-yellow façade of the Hotel Cavaletto reflected on the rippling waves, making him feel queasy for a moment. He stopped to regain some composure. He noticed that some hotel guests were already peering down from their windows, and he knew he would have to hurry before the hotel owners and the reporters came.

Upon seeing his uniform, the gondoliers turned expectantly as one. "*Ispettore*, here is the..."

"...severed head. I know, *signori*. I took your call," answered Brezzi wearily. He bent over laboriously to have a look.

At least it wasn't a joke, he thought. The head was bobbing in the jade green canal waters and bumping up against the stern of one of the gondolas, the face reflecting ghost-like on the boat's shiny black finish. He took a closer look. Male, Caucasian, bald, grey hair turned mostly white. Nose like a hawk, pasty complexion. Brezzi estimated the victim was in his mid-to-late fifties. He snapped some digital photos of the head in the water for the crime scene report and made a note of the water temperature.

The gondoliers crowded around. The smell of nicotine made Brezzi instantly nauseated.

"Stand back!" he snapped. "I can't do anything when you stand around like that!" They moved back quickly.

He looked at each face slowly. "Did any of you touch the head?"

"No, *Ispettore*. We did as you said," replied one, the tallest of the group.

"Well, good! Now help me to fish it out. I want to avoid touching it," said Brezzi, looking at the one standing closest. "Give me your oar."

The gondolier, a thin young man with a van dyke beard and stooped shoulders, shrugged and handed his oar to Brezzi.

7

Brezzi carefully prodded the head with the tip of the oar before deciding to push the flat blade under the head. The head bobbed worryingly for a moment, but didn't tip off the blade.

Before the gondolier could object, Brezzi succeeded in launching the head in one smooth motion out of the water and into the back of the gondola, on the canvas-covered platform the man used to stand on when ferrying customers.

"Hey! That's my gondola you... you ruined!" he shouted angrily, gesturing wildly.

"*Stai zitto!*" snapped Brezzi, waving at him to be quiet. "We'll get you a new tarpaulin from our stockroom. Besides, I need this tarp now to take the head to..." he grimaced, "...*head*quarters." He began unfastening the small tarp and picking up the corners carefully, grateful that his all-too-persistent hangover was limited to his head and not his hands, which were steady enough.

It was then that he noticed the gold wire-rim spectacles hanging from one ear. He paused for a moment. *Was this a joke after all?*

No. The head was real, he could see that, especially at the point below the larynx where it had been cut off. The blood vessels, the red muscles and grey-green severed tendons at the bottom of the neck were all too convincing. *This guy had a really short neck*, Brezzi noted, *like a hunchback.*

He also noticed the death stare, the double chin and the medium-sized, nondescript mouth, slightly open. The teeth especially caught his attention as the water ran out of the mouth and throat cavities—a slight underbite for sure, but every tooth was white and perfectly in a row, something still unusual in many parts of Italy and Southern Europe.

Brezzi thought silently for a moment. *A celebrity? A politician? A foreigner? Perhaps...*

He looked over at the gondoliers, "Are you *sure* nobody touched it?"

"*Si, Si, Ispettore!* Nobody!" they all chorused. Brezzi wasn't really sure if he believed them. He took a few more head-on shots to get a good image of the face.

Suddenly aware of the time, he quickly pulled up the corners of the tarp and stood up, dropped the head into the official evidence container, the largest he'd been able to find, short of a full body bag. He sealed it carefully and began making his way back to the police boat.

Then he stopped and turned suddenly, surprising the gondoliers, "Hey, I want all of you to come to the *stazione* today and tell me what you saw and when!"

An angry chorus of protest arose.

"Hey, *stronzi di merda, non mi rompete le palle!*" barked Brezzi. "It's New Year's morning! How many customers can you possibly miss out on?"

Chastened, they looked at each other and shrugged.

"Besides," added Brezzi, permitting himself a rare grin, "look at the bright side. Once word gets around, you'll have *lots* of extra customers, all who want to see where the famous floating head was found!"

With that, he hurried quickly away, grateful to get out of smelling range of the tobacco smoke. He crossed the shopping arcade quickly, glad that it was empty for the moment.

He let out a loud curse as his toe caught a raised cobblestone in the middle of the walkway. He stumbled, almost sending the container with the head rolling into the side of a building.

Quickly recovering, Brezzi hurriedly twisted his way through the canvas-covered scaffolding along the side of the Palozzo Barozzi, which had suffered considerable flood damage in the heavy rains a month ago. He felt a foul mood coming on, as his headache grew worse.

Nothing made him more irritable than getting a faceful of smoke, especially in the morning. He couldn't understand why all the gondoliers in Venice seemed to be chain-smokers. Most of the tourists who could afford the exorbitant gondola rates were Americans, and *they* rarely were smokers. Why would an amorous couple hire a gondola, only to get cigarette ashes drifting into their hair, just because some idiot couldn't control his habit for half an hour? Momentarily forgetting the severed head, Brezzi shook his own in disbelief.

Walking up to the boat, he took the container and set it back in the covered back section, out of view. As he set it down carefully in a corner of the cramped cabin, a thought suddenly occurred to him. He fished out the digital camera. "Were you an American, *Signore Testa?*" he asked the digital image of the head.

Silence. Brezzi felt somewhat unnerved by the expressionless half-smile and dead eyes that seemed somehow to be looking at him.

~ ~ ~

By mid-afternoon, Brezzi was exhausted. News of the head had spread-like wildfire. The phone hadn't stopped ringing ever since he had taken *la Testa* over to the local coroner's office.

For all its fame as an ancient port to the world, Venice was really just like a small town, once you took tourists out of the equation. And that was the problem that worried everyone—if the tourist stayed away, there would be no one left to pay.

The two major newspapers, *IL GAZZETTINO* and *la Nuova Venezia*, had sent reporters for exclusive interviews. RAI Uno and Due had sent television crews. Now Brezzi faced a highly agitated group of men that included the proprietors of the Luna Baglioni, Grand Hotel dei Dogi, and the Ca del Borgo, all major luxury hotels.

Brezzi tried to bring the meeting to order. "*Silenzio! Silenzio! Basta, sta zitto un po', no?*" (will you please shut up?)

Signore Bresco of the Baglioni was getting on Brezzi's nerves in particular. "The head, the head it is..."

9

"Dead." said Brezzi flatly. "And that's *all* I know about the damned thing. We've only just started on this case, and already you want a suspect behind bars. This is not the movies. The coroner's report will be done by next week, by then I should know something. Until then..."

"But our customers, what about our customers?" they all chorused.

Brezzi motioned emphatically for quiet by slapping the podium. *"Tacete! Tacete!* Quit worrying—how many tourists speak or read fluent Italian?"

The hoteliers all looked at each other and shrugged. "A few, perhaps..." said Bresco meekly.

"Exactly. So don't get your panties in a wad. Besides, this is January, it's freezing cold and all your precious tourists will be here in time for *Carnevale*..."

"You'd better have this case solved by *Carnevale*, Ispettore!" remarked Bresco tartly. The others nodded. *"Si, si!!!* By *Carnevale!"* They kept repeating this as they departed.

Signore Bresco gave him a particularly withering look as he walked out.

Brezzi watched them go out the front and turn right on to Riva del Carbon. "Too bad they don't keep walking straight ahead-into the goddamn Grand Canal..." Brezzi said to no one in particular.

"They're right, you know."

Brezzi turned around, surprised to see a familiar figure in a dark suit standing behind him. "Ispettore Murano, I didn't see you walk in."

"I didn't want to draw attention to myself. You, my friend, have your hands full." Murano rubbed his hands together and blew on them. He was a thin, weather-beaten man of about 50 with a pencil-thin moustache and sparse grey hair combed back. "Of course, the whole *Polizia Municipali* has responsibility—but *you*, my friend are the focal point. If *you* solve this, you will be a hero. But if you *don't*..." he shrugged and held up his hands.

Brezzi sat back down in his chair, then turned to his former mentor. *"Si.* But what can I do? We are but a tiny side office in the Piazzo Loridan. You know how I have to ring the police in Mestre all the time because we don't have the facilities—especially for a possible serial killer."

"Yes, but Henri, everyone won't see it that way, they'll all scream 'excuses, excuses!' If you don't solve this one, it'll cost you your job for sure. Those people have the real power here."

Brezzi nodded, grimacing.

Murano took a sip of espresso, then looked up. "Serial killer? What makes you think this is the work of a serial killer?"

"Okay, okay, maybe not a serial killer—but a professional, none the less. Someone with a surgeon's precision."

"Well, keep that in mind—but don't tell anyone until you have something concrete."

"I know, they'll laugh in my face if I say something about serial killers. They'll think I've been watching too many Martin Scorcese films on cable

TV. What was the name of that one killer in *Badlands*?"

"Charlie something." Murano smiled. "Only in America could something like that happen..."

"*Si*." Brezzi put his shoes on the radiator. "I hope, only in America."

"But Henri, one thing..."

"What?"

"Get your facts straight," Murano gave him a sly wink, "Scorsese didn't direct *Badlands* , Terence Malick did."

Brezzi gave him a withering look. "Nobody likes a smart-ass."

"Everyone's a smart-ass nowadays," Murano laughed. "Henri, the rules have changed—you're in show business now, like it or not. Better get used to it..."

~ ~ ~

The coroner's report was disappointing: cause of death–unable to be determined. The report recommended sending the head to a bigger facility with more resources.

After carefully re-packing the head in a thermopack 'cold box' normally used for dry ice transport, Brezzi strapped it to his little-used Vespa motor scooter that he kept parked in the garage near the Vaperetto dock at Fondamenta San Chiara and took it to the big *Polizia Municipali* station on the mainland to ship it to Interpol headquarters in Lyon for analysis. He had immediately ruled out any of the Venetian-based shipping companies because he knew all too well how quickly gossip spread.

It took him considerable time to convince the aging *Ispettore Generale* with the carefully waxed moustache to send it overnight without personally inspecting the contents.

By the time Brezzi got back on the Vespa and strapped on his luminous *Polizia* helmet, the sun had already set, leaving the now-cloudless sky to fade into many stars and a full moon.

He looked up momentarily upon hearing an approaching airliner lining up its approach. Unlike most tourist areas, Venice had only a small airport, with only a few international flights. Brezzi had always had a yen for flying, and he loved to watch the planes take off and land. Encouraged by the unusually balmy winter night, he decided to indulge this whim and take the 'scenic route' past the runways.

He was only half a kilometer away from the terminal when his Vespa suddenly died and coasted to a halt. *Cazzo! Out of hydrogen again!* He knew all the local H2 stations would be closed at this hour. *Oh well, I'll just have to take the Vaporetto back from the airport.*

He rolled the scooter into the mostly empty parking lot after much exertion, and then set off for the south end of the 'arrivals' terminal where the *Vaporetti* were docked.

The airport was nearly empty, with only a lone currency exchange booth open for business.

The customs officer with the police dog recognized him and waved. Brezzi nodded and the dog growled at him. A planeload of disembarking passengers began walking through the doors, on their way to clear customs. As a matter of routine, Brezzi walked along with them, inspecting each one cursorily.

Suddenly, a small man broke from the line and vaulted the ropes, running madly for the exit. The customs officer let the dog loose. Brezzi instinctively pulled his gun out and took off after the man.

Almost immediately, Brezzi was out of breath and knew the chase was hopeless. He went down on one knee, aimed and fired at the fleeing figure. The gunshot echoed through the almost deserted terminal.

To his amazement, the man grabbed his buttock and fell to the ground. Puffing heavily, Brezzi got up and ran again. He slid to a halt, straddled the man and pressed the gun barrel against his neck.

The customs officer, also badly out of breath, came up. "*Grazie*, Ispettore. You probably saved my job." The dog made a whining noise behind them.

Keeping his eyes firmly on the fugitive, Brezzi grinned, "Most likely, Cippolina. Perhaps you should spend more time in the fitness room, like our friend here."

Cippolina eyed the skinny fugitive and shook his head, making his double chin wobble. "I think it would take more than that. This one is probably a pro. He looks like one of those Serbian criminals, the ones they hire 'out West'."

Brezzi raised an eyebrow and nodded thoughtfully.

As he did, the first Paparazzi snapped his picture.

That was the photo that appeared on next morning's front page of the *la Nuova Venezia*.

~ ~ ~

Brezzi threw the paper in the trash the next morning. He walked into the study and sat down heavily on the sofa.

His wife Sophia looked at him sternly. "You're complaining again, Henri" she said flatly.

"But I haven't even *said* anything!" exclaimed Brezzi irritably.

"It's written all over your face. Go look in the mirror."

Brezzi walked over to the hall bathroom and switched on the light. His still-youthful face was indeed creased with frown lines. He sighed and closed his eyes.

She came over and caressed his neck. "At least the news was favorable. Hero policeman captures suspected fugitive."

"This is just the beginning. This could go on for months." He made a face. "Those bastards in the press won't stay favorable for long. I got a bad feeling about this head case. You'll see, they'll forget all about the 'heroic act' by Wednesday afternoon."

"Henri, bad temper is a terrible waste of energy. Let's go out tonight and eat somewhere nice."

He rubbed his eyes as she massaged his forehead. He looked up. "It will have to be on the mainland. Everywhere I've been today, people have been asking about that damned severed head. I could barely get my groceries through the crowd at the check-out."

"I know. It's all my first-grade students want to talk about in class. Little Marco Cippolina came up to me during storytelling hour and asked if there was a Grimm's fairy tale about Little Red Riding Hood and the severed head."

Brezzi laughed out loud, then caught himself. "Oops, I'm sorry."

She smiled and rolled her eyes. "Better get used to it, Henri. That's what television does to people. You know that, but you've never been on the other side of the cameras before. You've only had to keep the Paparazzi away from the celebrities. Now it's your turn. *Our* turn, actually."

"Can I quit and go join one of those 'Survivor' games on a desert island somewhere?"

"You don't want to give up, Henri, not *now*. It's not your nature—you know that."

Brezzi turned and walked back to the sofa. He was silent for several moments.

"Do you still want to go out?" he asked.

"Yes, my dear. Let's not make our home a dungeon. But let's not go to the mainland—there it will only be worse. Yes, the Paparazzi will be waiting." She shrugged, "But, it's better to be pestered by people you've known all your life—at least *they* wait until you're finished *eating*."

Chapter 1

THE NEW YORK CYBERPOST
ECSTASY NOW LEGAL!!!

Today the FDA announced the approval of the drug MDMA, better known by its street name Ecstasy. The drug is to be used for psychiatric treatment of depression, especially in conjunction with cancer treatments.

MDMA's road to legalization has been a rocky one, as agency approval was repeatedly delayed by legal roadblocks resulting from the substance's illicit past. The substance, first invented in 1910, was originally intended as a treatment of psychological anxiety, a condition that has been constantly on the rise since then, as evidenced by rising suicide rates.

The most substantial hurdle was because nobody legally owned the patent, which was long expired by the time the substance was banned in the 1980s. This resulted in a fierce legal battle, whicheventually was resolved when production rights were granted to all four remaining pharmaceutical giants.

"VIAGRA FALLS" TO STAY

A federal judge ruled yesterday that the re-named Niagara Falls cannot revert to the original name because of the still-valid sponsorship contract with New York State, despite intense local pressure. "Renaming the Falls saved the state from bankruptcy," said judge Charles Nockenwelle, "and although Viagra and all other 'erectile family' drugs have been banned in the meantime, the contract itself is still binding, for the remaining 20 years."

Monday, January 4:
It was unseasonably warm, almost shirtsleeve weather. The magnetic Transrapid commuter train whooshed past over Captain Richard Hayte's head, but he took little notice. He was too busy munching on a fortune cookie, from his second box of the day. He wadded up the tiny paper inside

and threw it away without looking at the fortune. Instead, his gaze was directed at all the Smash bars that had sprung up along 95th Street in the last few years since that big case broke.

A few passers-by recognized him and nodded hello. Hayte nodded back and half-smiled. It wasn't like he could be invisible anyway. He was clad conspicuously in an iridescent purple and yellow L.A. Lakers warm-up suit. He thought about putting the hood up over his head but decided it was too warm.

Hayte towered over most who greeted him. He was 6 foot 8 and a half but looked taller.

Despite his notoriety, he still liked to go out to prowl around. It kept his instincts fresh, even if his cover as a plainclothes detective had been blown for once and all three years ago by the headlines.

Hayte and his colleagues, Donohue, Shrini, and Dietrich, had come within a hair's breadth of being booted off the force until the New York Times Sunday Edition published a story about their bravery in chasing down leads in cases involving disappearing teens, a series of car viruses, and a new street drug called Smash.

Then the long-running TV news magazine *60 Minutes* ran a segment on them all.

Since then, their whole situation had been turned on its head. Now they were collectively known as the 'Sewer Squad', in honor of all the time they spent chasing a terrorist gang leader through the sewage system in Harlem. There was even talk of book offers.

They were all taken off of the suspended list and put in line for promotions.

After that, the proceedings had become something of a cause célèbre, which meant Hayte was constantly recognized when he was out and about. Now that he worked behind a desk instead of undercover, that wasn't such a handicap. It made other things difficult; however, as he liked to mull over things instead of constantly having to say hello to strangers who recognized him. Today he was thinking about the big move ahead.

Harlem... What does it really mean to me, anyway?

Hayte was glad he had not been forced to go to another city. He had spent his entire professional career, hell, the bulk of his adult life here. It would've been like cutting off his past and starting from scratch. *Hell, this place owns my ass,* he thought to himself as he brushed past a gathering crowd at the corner newsstand.

And yet, he *was* leaving, to move to Greenwich Village. It felt a little like going to another country.

He felt instinctively for his keys, the remembered he had just finished giving them back to the landlord for the last time.

He looked around with mixed feelings. This would be his first real night away from the old 'hood, and he wasn't sure how he felt about it.

He descended the stairs to the subway that would take him to the

Village for the night. Or so he had thought, because the subway entrance was padlocked shut. *Son of a bitch...* Then he remembered that the subway was still flooded.

He went back up to call a cab with his tiny mobile phone. The connection was horrible, but at least he got through to the cab dispatcher.

He smiled again with some satisfaction. *Nowadays the cabs will pick up African-Americans. Poetic justice indeed that Whitey has to beg for service...*

The ride cost him $50. As he handed over the fee, he remarked to the driver "Not hurting for business, are you?"

The Pakistani at the wheel grinned and spoke in a clipped accent. "No, not at all since the subway flooded! I'm in a whole new tax category this year..."

Hayte couldn't resist saying, "Better watch out—I hear cab driving is pretty risky in white neighborhoods."

The cabby winked. "Don't worry—I got a new Paralyzer under the seat—and I got a permit too, officer! I saw you on television!" He waved and pulled away from the curb.

Hayte turned and stared at the row of unfamiliar pastel-colored facades on West Houston Street, near Bedford Street. *Gentrified. Everything here...*

At least I can afford it on a Captain's salary.

He sighed and went up to the brightly-lit doorway and punched in his new entry six-digit code. He had to enter it three times before he got it right. It beeped and the front door popped open. He looked at it skeptically for a moment before walking in. *This is gonna take some getting used to...*

The elevator had an 'out of order' sign. *Funny how it was working when they showed me the place...*

He sighed and took the stairs up to the sixth floor.

There, he fished out a chip key. The apartment door slid open without him pushing it.

Hayte walked in, ducking to clear his head. He silently watched to door slide shut behind him.

He sat down in the recliner and picked up the remote control. An extra-long Murphy bed swung down from a black metal console on the opposite wall.

He took his shoes off, lay down on his stomach and was immediately asleep.

~ ~ ~

A feral scream sounded in the night.

Hayte work up. *What the hell is that noise...* He sat up groggily and corrected himself: *noises?*

Putting his ear to the wall, he listened for a moment.

Not torture, though, he realized gradually as the bare walls came into focus in the darkness. *Lots of moans, from the sound of it. Sexual moans, but they were strangely clipped… mechanical.*

He looked at the clock. 4:02 a.m.

He thought about calling to complain, but decided it was too much trouble. He sighed, rolled over and pulled a pillow over his head.

~ ~ ~

Hayte got up the next morning still feeling tired. Try as he might, he couldn't stop yawning. Even the morning coffee failed to stem his stupor. He shook his head. *Maybe it's just that I can't get used to not being in Harlem…*

He shaved and plucked carefully at the ingrown hairs on his chin. Picking up his watch, he slipped it on and checked the time. The display told him his blood was again running low on electrolytes. He frowned and fiddled about with the 'mode' key until the time was displayed. He sighed, knowing he had a van full of boxes to unload.

Looking out the window, he was a bit surprised to see the rental van was still where he had parked it. No signs of broken windows or vandals.

Amazing how street crime has dropped since Smash was legalized…

He got dressed and went downstairs. Walking across the street, he checked to make sure there weren't any parking tickets. There weren't. He rolled up his sleeves, unlocked the van and picked out some boxes to carry up.

Puffing heavily up the stairs, Hayte carried the first batch of boxes in and began setting them down in front of his door. *Six months away from the gym, and already I'm out of shape…*

After pushing them inside with the side of his foot, he left the door open and went back down.

He passed a rotund man going up, swearing the whole way. "Goddamned elevator breaks down every damn week!"

Hayte frowned as he slid past. "Oh, *that's* good to know…"

The man looked at him. "Hey! You're new here, ain't ya?" He wiped his bald pate and pointed to the elevator. "You can bellyache all you want, but it don't do no good. That damn elevator breaks down every fucking week!" He leaned closer. "Hey—you look familiar. You ever been on TV?"

Hayte hesitated, then nodded reluctantly.

The man's small puffy eyes widened. "Yeah! I know you, you're one of them cops that…that…" he waved his finger, "*yeah*, that busted that Smash ring!"

"Not *busted*." corrected Hayte. "Nobody was ever arrested. We were the ones that found there was no way to ban it…"

"Because of *where it comes from!*" The man laughed loudly and slapped Hayte on the back. "Man! I can't thank you enough! You and your pals turned my line of work into a gold mine!"

Hayte raised his eyebrows. "And what business is that—a Smash bar, perhaps?"

"Naw, I'm in Adult Entertainment—I direct and do soundtracks! My name's Stanley, Stanley Bialystok, by the way. You may have heard of me!" He extended his hand.

Hayte shook it awkwardly. "Hi. I'm Capt. Richard Hayte…" He paused for a moment, then a light went on inside his head. "Was that *you* I heard in the middle of last night? You film here in this building?"

Stanley's eyes widened in surprise. "Oh! Geez, I'm sorry 'bout the noise. That was the soundtrack I was working on. I got an editing studio in my den." He rubbed his eyes. "I was up most of the night—I got a deadline hanging over my head. I had to fly in a few sampled moans and groans into a soundtrack due last week."

"A *few*? It must've lasted *at least* an hour…"

"Hardly. It was only a few seconds, we just did some loops. The sequence, that is…" Stanley rolled his eyes. "Gawd, it was hell! The same samples, over and *over* again. There was this gawdawful click that I had to edit out—150 times!"

Perplexed, Hayte wrinkled his forehead. "That sounds like way too much trouble, considering the audience."

Stanley shook his head emphatically. "Not any more—high tech sex is *en vogue*. To you—or not you *personally*, but to the *viewer*, all that THZ-Dolby surround stuff is neat, but for me it's a real pain in the ass—if you don't place the sound precisely in the right spot, or *spatial area*, it sounds like a couple of ventriloquists having orgasms from different fuckin' rooms!"

"I had no idea the audience was so discriminating." Hayte said dryly.

The sarcasm was lost on Stanley. "Oh *yeah!* Reality is *in*—and the more realistic, the better! All ya hears about is L.A. and their great adult film industry. Well, fuck 'em! The Big Apple has plenty of sex, and we're gonna show them how it's done!"

Hayte suppressed a laugh. "Are you, now."

"Yeah—Hey! You wanna come to a session and see for yourself?"

Caught off guard, Hayte could only say, "Uh, maybe later…"

"Aw, don't be such a puritan! You'll be fascinated! I fucking guarantee it! I'll come by tomorrow morning, and we'll go straight to the studio."

"But tomorrow's *Sunday*."

"Sunday's my *fun*day!" winked Stanley. "See ya tomorrow, bright and early! Hey—let me tell you something else—this session tomorrow is real cutting edge stuff! It's only a matter of time—and government approval—before we put the first 'tactile stimulation' devices on the market." Stanley held up his hands, made a loop with the thumb and index finger of his left hand and then stuck his other index finger through it. "You'll be able to feel *exactly* what the actors are feeling."

Hayte thought for a moment. "Have you thought about handing out condoms before each showing?"

Stanley chortled and slapped him on the back. "Ha! That's GREAT—hand out condoms! I LOVE it!"

Hayte took his hand slowly out of his jacket pocket. *Jesus,* he thought to himself, *you were just about to shoot a guy for slapping you on the back.*

Puzzled, Stanley looked him over. "You were *serious* about the condoms?"

~ ~ ~

By noon, all the boxes were upstairs. Hayte's muscles ached, but he didn't stop to rest, because the van had to be back at JFK airport by 1pm.

Scrambling through side streets and running a few red lights, he got the van back to the rental agency with five minutes to spare. Now he could relax on the way back on the airport shuttle. Or so he thought.

He walked down the steps to the subway entrance, but it was padlocked.

No subway service, Hayte reminded himself for the umpteenth time. *Damn this fucking flooding!*

That meant another fifty dollar cab ride. He felt like hitting something. Then he remembered the Connecticut Limo service. *That would take me back to Manhattan, at least. And it would save me twenty-five bucks…*

~ ~ ~

The 'limousine'—in reality a stretched minivan—pulled away, leaving Hayte in front of the former Rudi Juilliani High School. The school had had to be closed five years ago in the wake of the huge outbreak in teenage shootings at Metropolitan New York schools. The $3.4 million facility was brand new at the time, so it was quickly converted into a NYPD district precinct that acted as a kind of liaison between Mid-Town Manhattan and Harlem.

Hayte took the steps two at a time, the big slabs of marble leading to the domed entranceway. He cursed as he abruptly stumbled on the top step.

His shoe size was only 12-1/2, otherwise he would've had trouble getting on the police force in the first place. His feet were almost too big to operate the gas and brake pedals in most police cars, even in the ultra-modern Mercedes S-Types most of the force now used.

As he went down the hall to Plainclothes Dept., he had to squeeze his way past a group of Interpol Exchange cops going on their orientation tour. Hayte noticed the guide spoke English with a heavy Asian accent.

Hayte greeted the fat desk sergeant at the main security desk. "Anything new, brother?"

"Same ol' same old, brother," grunted the round-faced sergeant named Mathers. He had pale freckles dotting his medium-brown skin. He nodded toward the departing Interpol tour. "Just another group of Interpol cops that can't speak good English."

"A few do, though" said Hayte, looking back over his shoulder.

"Yeah, a few..." the sergeant agreed. "That one guy from Italy, what's his name? He was sharp as a tack."

Hayte nodded. "Yes, he was. Say, anything else going on that I should know about?"

"Naw, not much..." grunted the sergeant, taking a wad of memos off the bulletin board behind him and tossing them in the trash. "Just the usual art wackos from the Village requesting to come by and visit the temp cells." He was referring to the team of performance artists from Greenwich Village who wanted to come in and computer map all the cells and record all the ambient noises—all as part of a Guggenheim Foundation project to stage an updated version of Dante's *The Divine Comedy*.

Hayte grinned, "Never thought we'd need a waiting list to go to jail..."

The sergeant let out a laugh. "Maybe we should all sign up."

Hayte trod past the stairways leading to the temporary jail cells built in the cavernous basement which was originally designed to be a gym for 1500 students.

The cells were temporary because below them, there were two levels of underground parking for the squad cars. As a gymnasium, there was no need to install soundproofing materials.

Three years ago, Amnesty International had paid a surprise visit and filed a lawsuit with the 11th Circuit Court alleging that the constant comings and goings of squad cars at all hours constituted a gross violation of the prisoners' rights.

It made Hayte laugh every time he thought about it. "Sonic terrorism," they called it. Now the cells were labeled 'temporary', and no suspect could be held there longer than 48 hours without being transferred. To Riker's Island, which most felt was much worse, especially after it was privatized.

Hayte went back to his cubicle and switched on his terminal. He winced when he saw there were 731 messages in his 'in' box. *Only three days out of the office, and just look at them all...*

He sighed and began to sift through them. Most were bulletin board posts about the Phantoms case. No encouraging news at all.

Word on the street had it the Phantoms fancied themselves to be reincarnations of the Jesse James Gang of the Wild West. *Except that this gang didn't ride horses, at least not the flesh and blood kind*. In fact, nobody knew exactly *how* they moved, because no one had ever seen them actually escape the crime scenes. They brazenly came in unmasked, but none had ever been arrested previously or positively ID'ed from mug shots. Their MO was to attack like a virus, sweeping in and out of NYC banks and financial institution, then leave without a trace.

Hayte felt very fortunate to not be involved with the Phantoms case, the bulk of which was being run by the Domestic Terrorism Squad of the NYPD. Hayte had refused all entreaties to join, pleading that he couldn't attend Law School classes at night and take the rigorous Anti-Terrorism training courses at the same time. Now that law school was over, most of his time was spent studying for the bar exam.

He also had little desire to chase the Phantoms all over Manhattan—or cyberspace, for that matter.

He sifted quietly through the rest of his messages. He rubbed his eyes and started to close his mailbox. Then one at the bottom caught his eye.

It read simply, "Meet me 2Night@PickledApe? Perry."

"Don't mind if I do..." Hayte smiled to himself.

~ ~ ~

The sign at the door read "Unload gun and remove ski mask before entering."

Hayte strode into the darkened cavern that was the front bar.

Just as his eyes started to adjust to the darkness, the room morphed into a large wrestling ring, and two large wrestlers appeared on either side of him. One had tattoos etched on a lumpen shaved head, the other had corn-rowed hair and what looked to be a long strand of braided beard hanging from the chin.

The first wrestler charged to his left, causing Hayte to step back. The other one slam-bounced off the ropes, then was picked up and thrown down to the mat, causing the whole room to vibrate menacingly.

It was only in mid-leap that Hayte recognized both were holograms.

The tattooed one grabbed the opponent's ear and was poised to bite.

In a flash, the referee intervened. "LADIES, LADIES!! *Biting* means *instant* disqualification! *And* a life-time ban!"

The two contestants stomped off to their respective corners to sulk.

Hayte took advantage of the lull to slide off into the back room, an exact replica of the old Max's Kansas City club.

The hulking doorman nodded at Hayte's badge and jerked a thumb over his shoulder. "Your partner's over there."

Hayte immediately recognized Donohue's spiky blonde hair and wiry frame. He walked over with a grin and slid into the corner booth. Donohue was wearing his usual denim shirt, coat and jeans. To Hayte it looked like he'd been drinking for some time.

"Hi Perry!" He took his partner's outstretched hand. "Long time, no see..."

"That's for sure," agreed Donohue, inadvertently knocking over his beer.

"Nice move, Spilly Boy..."

"You should know, Mister Klutz!" Donohue looked at Hayte's Los Angeles Lakers outfit and sneered, "Rich, why do you wear that Lakers shit?"

"Just to piss you off, *partner*..." grinned Hayte.

Donohue shook his head. "If you weren't so damn tall, somebody would've stuck a knife in your black ass for wearing that 'round Manhattan."

Hayte looked over the seedy surroundings. "Mmm, not in this *fine* neighborhood, Perry. Why *do* you like this place so much?"

"Dunno," grinned Donohue. "Nostalgia, maybe. The lesbian wrestlers remind me of Officer Patrovsky."

"Yeah, except she's hetero..." smirked Hayte.

Donohue grimaced. "*Unfortunately*... Anyway, I hear she's now in the SWAT team."

"Good place for her," agreed Hayte. "Maybe she'll shoot down a Phantom or two..."

Donohue took a big gulp of beer. "That would save us all some trouble. Glad I don't have to deal with that."

Hayte ordered a whiskey. "Which do you mean—Patrovsky or the Phantoms?"

"Both."

Hayte noticed the bank of TV monitors mounted on the wall. The cameras were pointed at the patrons in the front room, not on the wrestlers. The views rotated back and forth. After a while, Hayte found the constant motion made him slightly nauseous.

Noticing Hayte's discomfort, Donohue remarked, "You'll never make it as a surveillance specialist, Rich."

"Luckily, I won't have to. It reminds me too much of Las Vegas, Perry..."

"Good place to look for suspects." admitted Donohue. "I miss the old underground gambling halls." He downed his beer and quickly changed the subject. "Rich, I never see you around any more. How the hell you been keeping?"

"OK, I guess. Between law school and everything, I got my hands full,." he admitted.

"*Jesus*, Law School... I never thought of you going over to the other side."

"The *other* side? Perry, where do you think *you're* gonna be in 20 years? It's not like there's any clear career path in Plainclothes, and you know it."

Donohue spread his hands. "OK, Rich, I admit it—you *are* right. I don't have a clue where I'll be in ten years." He ran a hand through his sandy blonde hair, cut short and showing gray at the temples. "At the moment, it's like being at a poker table where all the cards are printed in invisible ink."

"Perry, that's exactly why I decided to go in this direction. The NYPD pays all my tuition at City U—which is amazing, considering what law school costs—*and* they'll pay for my bar exam, provided I take it within the next two years. I want to take it this spring, ASAP. I figure the NYPD's always gonna need cops who know courtroom law. I bet I can keep working until that new mandatory City retirement at 75—you know it's still only 65 for detectives. Even the best cops burn out eventually."

"Working 'till 75? Sheesh!" Donohue shook his head. "Remember, that's only if your voice holds up."

Hayte nodded soberly, "You got that right…" He reached in his shirt pocket for a throat lozenge. There weren't any left. "None of us are getting any younger."

"You got *that* right. I really wonder about this mid-life crisis shit, if there's something biological behind it…" said Donohue.

"Maybe so, but that's not why I'm studying law."

Perry's tone grew more animated. "Yeah, but it seems like everyone I know is going through this. Maybe it has to do with us outliving our original intended lifespan of 40 years. We're thwarting the laws of nature—*and* paying the price."

Hayte laughed out loud. "What—is Perry Donohue saying there's more to life than just casual sex?"

"Smart-ass!" Donohue pretended throwing his beer at him. "Maybe there is, but sex is still great. For now, anyway…" He took a swig of beer, grimaced and pushed it away. "I can't believe I still drink this stuff."

"Face it, Perry, you're a conditioned animal, like the rest of us. Age grows in inverse proportion to flexibility. Change upsets the balance of things."

Donohue dropped his voice. "Speaking of… what's your take on our new police chief? I'm getting real weird vibes off of him."

Hayte shrugged. "Shabazz? I hear he's all right—for a Muslim…" he made a face. "Other than that, I don't know much about him."

"What's a Muslim doing in the NYPD?"

"Perry, you should know already. You Irish crackers did the same damn thing—you join the force to gain respect." Hayte ordered another glass of whiskey. "Hell, it's just the same deal with the Muslims. Shabazz is the first to make chief, though. You gotta read the writing on the wall, man. The main thing in the NYPD today is diversity—it's all the Mayor's Office talks about now. That's also why we got all those Interpol exchange programs with Europe and Africa."

"I thought about doing one of those, heading off to some exotic locale, maybe Europe, but really, my place is here in New York." Donohue looked at his erstwhile partner, "But, *you* in a *courtroom*? Rich, don't you miss the action *a little*? All those things we went through together?"

"In the sewers and junkyards of Harlem, you mean?" Hayte let out a loud laugh. "Yeah, I miss bumping my head on sewer concrete—that damned Smash case was just about the death of me." He pointed a long bony finger at Donohue. "Perry, *you're* lucky you're only five-foot-one…."

"Fuck you, Rich, and I'm actually five foot-three *and a half!*" He winked to show he was only half kidding. "Ain't *my* fault you're six-foot-nine— you should go and slap yo' mama for taking all those anabolic steroids during pregnancy!"

Hayte grinned. "I wish I could've met *your* parents, Perry—I bet they were so *tiny and cute!* Bet I could've picked 'em both and put em one under each arm! Hey, stop that!" he yelled as Perry playfully began swatting him on the head with a rolled-up newspaper.

"Yeah, I'll stop!" Donohue smiled broadly. "I'm ruining a perfectly good newspaper on that nappy hair of yours!" He stopped and flattened the paper on the table. "Real paper newspapers are pretty damn rare these days—look at all the grease spots from that Lucky Tiger hair gook..."

"I better call it a night, Perry. I got my couch session tomorrow morning, first thing—and I don't want to be hungover."

Donohue looked up, perplexed. "Your 'brain drain' session? I thought you were going on vacation this week."

Hayte nodded. "I *am* going on holiday—but I still got to go to my 'brain drain'—unless you leave the country for your vacation, it's still mandatory. After the second appointment, you can do sessions online, but the first time has to be in person. I got *another* new therapist."

"I don't know how you put up with it, Rich—I had to look outside the program to find one I could live with...." Donohue stirred the ice in his glass. "Hope this one's better than your last one..."

Hayte smiled and rolled his eyes. "Yeah, you got that right. All that prayin' and shit before our sessions—that got on my nerves, big time." He finished his drink. "Well, see ya, partner. Let me know what happens while I'm gone."

Perry raised an eyebrow. "Gone? Where are you headed—Florida?"

"*Florida?!* Naw, man, that's Cracker country..."

Donohue laughed in response. "Yeah, right. Cracker country..."

Hayte continued, "I'm actually not taking a real vacation, I'm moving—to Greenwich Village."

"No shit?! The *Village?* You, Harlem Hayte, a Village person? That does *not* compute!"

"Better adjust your parameters, you Irish Cracker." He turned to leave. "See ya, Perry."

"See ya, *Homeboy.*" grinned Donohue.

Chapter 2

Monday, February 8

Hayte hesitated for several moments in front of the therapist's door without knowing exactly why.

"I got a funny feeling about this…" he said under his breath, then he stepped up to the dark mahogany door and knocked.

A crisp female voice answered, "Come in."

Hayte peered around the door, instantly knowing what he would see, but hoping he wouldn't. White, female, early 30's. *Very attractive and… Jesus, a blonde. Why does the Department always pull this shit on me?*

His face must have betrayed his thoughts, as she immediately said, "Come in, Captain. Don't be so shocked—a woman *can* be a good psychiatrist too, you know." She extended an elegant hand. "The name is Duchamp, *Doctor* Duchamp. Please, take a seat."

Hayte nodded sheepishly and stretched out his long frame on the couch. "Sorry 'bout that, Doctor. It's… just past experience…" He tried to avoid staring at her legs.

She pointed a light pen at her palm-top's screen. "You have a lot of past experiences, Captain. I see I'm the fourth Police psychiatrist you've had."

He nodded. "Uh-huh. The last one was a Jesus freak, the one before that was a kindly old gent—he suffered a stroke, so the hospital put him on life support without asking his family. They are still fighting the court system for legal euthanasia, like what they got in Holland."

"You mean *The Netherlands*." she said sharply.

"Sorry." He tried not to stare at her breasts.

"Just so you know the difference. It's like saying Texas and the USA are the same thing." She absently twirled a flaxen lock, showing off her perfect nails. "Anyway, Captain, what about your first psychiatrist?"

Hayte let out a low whistle. "Miss Schaffley. She was a special case."

Dr. Duchamp arched her elegant eyebrows. "How so, Captain?"

He folded his arms behind his head and leaned back. "Well, she was attractive, raven-haired, highly intelligent and…" he looked up for emphasis, "genetically re-engineered."

She looked over the tiny computer screen at him. "Oh *really?*"

He tried to avoid staring at her green eyes. "...yes. Miss Schaffley was a 'product' of GeniTech, that big company that pioneered the anti-HIV gene modification."

She looked skeptical. "Please explain just what you mean by the term *product.*"

"She... her biological aging mechanism was genetically frozen—switched off. She was engineered to look thirty years old for the rest of her life, however long that might be—somehow, except for her hands, which looked like old leather. That's why she always tried to hide them."

"Really. How interesting!" She absently glanced at her nails.

He looked at her penetratingly. "More interesting than you know. Ageless beauty does have its price."

Duchamp looked at him with a quizzical expression. "Really?"

"Really." Hayte nodded, "Schaffley was more or less indirectly responsible for the murder of our then-police chief Hershey. He was sexually harassing her, so she told her 'friends' at GeniTech. The next thing we knew, his brains were splattered all over his apartment at the Dakotas. It doesn't take a genius to figure it out—but we never could find enough proof to make a case against the company. We weren't even able to find a possible trigger man. We had to rule it a suicide and shut the case."

She raised her eyebrows. "*Company* assassins? Isn't that a little far-fetched?"

Hayte smiled faintly to himself. "No comment."

She shifted in her chair and re-crossed her legs. "Let's talk about something more here and now, shall we? Tell me about yourself..."

"It should all be in my dossier, isn't it?"

"It is, but I'd like to get something more. Something from a fresh perspective..."

"Sure, like what?"

She brushed a stray strand from her mouth. "I don't know, maybe your musical tastes..."

"All right." Richard chuckled softly. "I like old punk music, really obscure stuff... Groups you've probably never ever heard of..."

She looked at him disbelievingly, "Captain, let me get this straight—a six-foot-nine African-American likes *white music*? How did *this* get started?"

"Hard to swallow, huh?" Hayte grinned from ear to ear. "But it's true. I got into that kind of music when I'd visit my uncle in Detroit. He had this huge digital collection he inherited from *his* dad, who used to play that kind of music in a band called the Gories."

She made a face. "I can imagine what *they* must've sounded like..."

"Maybe. They were really garage-y. But they were good. And when I found out what *their* influences were, it led me to a whole sub-culture I never even knew about. But most people don't remember that music used to have a culture of its own, today they all think songs are just ad jingles for products. It is exactly *that* understanding of music and its culture which helped me as a detective to understand all these underground youth cults that spring up in New York and then die out again. Hell, my biggest success, the Smash case, came out of knowing that. Remember when the city was overrun with gangs of white kids?"

She tapped the pointer absently on her knee. "Oh yes, I think I remember that..." She caught a glimpse of the wall clock. "Oh! I'm so sorry. We'll have to save that for next time. Can you come the same time next week?"

"If I have to, yes." Hayte sat up. "These sessions are still mandatory, right?"

She laughed. "I'm afraid so, Captain. Only your Chief and the IT staff are exempt from psychoanalysis." She made a note in her planner.

Richard paused at the door. "And the staff at the Coroner's."

She looked up, "Ehh, I don't think I want to analyse *them*. People who deal with dead people are *creepy*."

~ ~ ~

Venice, February 9:

The rain came in torrents, lashing the wire mesh on the *Polizia Municipali* HQ windows and causing the old hand-blown glass windows underneath to vibrate dangerously.

Ispettore Brezzi slammed down the phone in disgust.

Murano looked up. "Nothing from Interpol?"

"*Nothing*." Brezzi ran a hand through his thinning blonde hair. "No headless torsos have been reported anywhere within a two thousand kilometer radius, excluding Algeria and the former Soviet Bloc countries. They are now making inquires in Moscow. And they say the police in Algeria won't even answer the phone."

Murano drummed his fingers. "Is it possible that the head came from Algeria? They slaughter each other for breakfast."

Brezzi frowned. "I don't think so. The head was definitely Caucasian. They say there have been no reports of any murdered tourists or diplomats from either Europe or America for almost 14 months." He got up and walked to the window. "They think Moscow may be the key—but there have been so many Mafia killings there over the past 50 years, no one may ever know for sure."

Murano mimed dancing a jig. "That'll make the hoteliers *very* happy."

Brezzi massaged his forehead and nodded. "*Si*. Very happy indeed. They'll simply accuse us of being incompetent and go marching over to the *Carabinieri*—if they haven't already."

"I got news for you, Henri. They already *have*. That idiot Crespo has been going round and promising a quick resolution sometime within the next week."

Brezzi slammed a fist down on the desk. *"Ma dove hanno la testa? Crespo—that testa di cazzo?* Oh Lord, that fuzzy-headed idiot will drag every wino he sees on the street into the interrogation chamber and beat a confession out of them!"

"Which is why you can't wait for Interpol to solve your problem, Henri. *Carpe diem*—you have to use your own grey cells—you can't expect anyone else to do it for you."

Brezzi waved his arms around the room. "But we don't have the necessary equipment here! We *can't* solve this on our own!"

"And *that's* exactly what Crespo and all the Carabinieri will say." Murano walked over and looked Brezzi in the eye, "You have to *ask* for help. Is there anyone you know personally in Lyon?"

Brezzi shook his head. "Nobody. *Nessuno.*"

"What about somewhere else—London?"

Brezzi shook his head again. *"Nessuno."*

Murano absently threw a wad of paper in the direction of the lone wastepaper basket. "And in *America?*"

Brezzi suddenly sat up. *"Si!"*

"Si?" Suddenly hopeful, Murano took his feet off his desk.

"Si!" Brezzi punched the air in triumph, "I did that exchange program for Interpol in New York! I could call them!"

"Do you remember the name of anyone, Henri?"

"Yeah, yeah! Let me see…" Brezzi started rummaging around his desk drawers.

Murano frowned at him. "Still don't use that computer for stuff like that? Henri, what's it there for?"

"Big paperweight," Henri triumphantly produced a tattered address book. "Aha!" He looked at the clock, "What time is it in New York—7 or 8 in the morning?" He started dialing.

"I don't know." Murano shrugged and pointed to indicate that he was going out for a patrol on the harbor.

Brezzi nodded his acknowledgement from his desk and continued trying to place his call.

It took four or five times to get past Telecom Italia and connect to the switchboard overseas. The automated voice droned in his ear "If you know the extension you want, dial it now." He punched in the four digits nervously, not knowing if they were still valid.

A bored voice answered. "Hello, NYPD Plainclothes, Lower Manhattan precinct, Capt. Donohue here."

"Perry! *Ispettore* Henri Brezzi here—I am calling from Italy…"

Donohue almost spilled his coffee in surprise. "What the hey—Brezzi?"

"Si! Perry, how are you?"

"Henri! Damn! How the hell are you? Jeez, it's been…"

"Five years, I think. A hell of an education, you said."

"Aw man, I can't believe it's *you!* You still in Venice?"

"*Si*. How are you, Perry?"

"To be honest, Henri, I'm real stressed. We got a gang of terrorists called the Phantoms that have been hitting banks all over Manhattan—and they keep escaping without a trace. It's not my case right now, but I got a bad feeling it will be soon."

"Sounds not good. Maybe I picked a bad time to call..."

"That's OK, Henri. I could use a distraction. You want to come to New York again?"

"Yes, but not right now. I got a favor to ask, Perry..."

"Sure—what've you got? Problems with *Americano* tourists? Someone you want me to check out?"

"One tourist in particular. I think you say 'he lost his head'..."

Donohue sounded interested. "Went nuts? Shot up a McDonalds or something?

"I mean *literally* lost his head—we found it floating in a canal off the Piazza San Marco—no body. Looks like it was cut off by a surgeon, real clean slices at base of neck. White male, bald, hawk-nosed, glasses, age between 50 and 65..."

"No shit? This ain't some kind of Italian April Fool's joke, is it?"

"No, it happened on New Year's Eve, Perry. That's too soon for April Fools, even for us. I passed it on to Interpol, but so far they got nothing. Some big noise at Interpol says the victim may be from East Europe or Russia, but me, I don't think so."

"Meaning you got no proof."

"No proof, but I *think* he was American. North American, maybe. I don't know—eh, something about the way he looked, his glasses..."

"A severed head with *glasses*?"

"Yes. Bifocals, wire rims." Reading off his notes, Brezzi read out all the details.

Donohue listened attentively, every now and interrupting with a question. "So you think the victim was American?"

Brezzi paused, then said, "Yeah. I don't know *why*, but something... eh, I could send you some digital 3-D photos."

"Tell you what, Henri—send me a normal photo over the InterPoliceNet to my office, and I'll get someone to look into the matter. You got e-mail?"

"Yeah. I don't like it, but I got it. I'll send it along right now."

"I'll be waiting for it. I'll let you know if we turn up anything, all right?"

"OK, Perry."

"And Henri, don't wait five years to call back, OK?"

Brezzi laughed.

~ ~ ~

Later that same day:

Donohue opened Brezzi's e-mail attachment and looked at the images.

"Jesus, what an ugly mug... would've put me right off breakfast if I'd seen that floating around my neighborhood," he muttered to himself.

He closed the file and forwarded it to Missing Persons. As he did, an idea occurred to him. He opened the US State Department website and went to their Americans Missing Abroad page.

He soon wished he hadn't. "What kind of mutants are we sending overseas?" It was the ugliest collection of overweight people he'd ever seen. He scanned a few of the individual statistics. Most of the missing were in the over-400 pound category. Fortunately, none were from New York City. *Only the slim survive in the Big Apple...*

A beep signalled an incoming message. Donohue opened his mailbox. The subject line said it all: John Doe #45-2043. The head was now the 45th unidentified corpse this year according to Missing Persons. Brezzi's head was yet another anonymous victim that matched no records and that nobody had reported missing.

Donohue closed the message without noticing the lines at the bottom that stated that the Missing Persons search had been abnormally terminated after only .11 seconds, with no explanation given.

~ ~ ~

Rose Monday, February 15:
Venice was shrouded in dense fog, which the weak morning rays had not penetrated. Thousands of ghostly masked figures glided past noiselessly in their elaborate costumes, perched on gondolas or atop the multitude of bridges across the islands.

Inside the *Polizia Municipale* entrance hall, Brezzi patted his ample belly with satisfaction. "You see that?" he pointed outside at the *Carnevale*-goers and the packs of Japanese tourists pursuing them, "Signore Floating Head had no effect on tourism. I called every hotel personally—all are booked up."

"You mean, *I* was right" countered Murano, stubbing out his cigarillo. "I told you before, Henri, the paparazzi get bored and move on to the next embarrassment. So I won—where are the Cuban cigars you promised me?"

Brezzi slapped himself on the forehead. "Shit. I forgot. I..." He cocked an ear. "I hear something. Some people coming—a group, maybe."

Murano peered out the front door. "It's Bresco, Capelli and the rest of the hoteliers!"

"Quick! In our costumes!" yelled Brezzi. They dashed back in the police office and began donning the rest of their disguises.

As the hoteliers spilled through the entranceway and marched into the now-vacant office, two figures costumed as Marquis de Sade and Cardinal Richelieu slipped out the back way and boarded a waiting gondola, which then blended into the fog amid the ethereal shapes of other Carnevale revelers floating up and down the Grand Canal.

Chapter 3

NEW YORK CYBERPOST
The Same Old Song is G-O-N-E
Commentary by Paul O'Neill

They say music ain't what it used to be. Once upon a time, music was made for its own sake, and songs were created to celebrate love, the joys of life, or to be used as pointed social commentary.

No more. Nowadays, every song on the Hot 100 is a product of advertising agencies, designed to sweeten the pitch for diet pills, running shoes, pimple creams and even multi-colored condoms.

Heaven forbid we should have any kind of art without product placement. The notorious rapper, Crap Daddy, regales us with the shape, color and size of his bowel movements, but it's not outrage he's peddling: his latest album, The Big Dump is a joint project between P&G and Galaxo-Vivendi cannily calculated to promote laxatives and adult diapers.

Even the grand old tunes are saddled with this pseudo-subliminal baggage. Think about it: when's the last time you heard a song that doesn't have a Madison Avenue link? Every single kind of Campbell's soup has its own jingle, many of which are old Beatles tunes owned by a company subsidiary that bought the rights after Michael Jackson self-destructed 30 years ago.

What's next? Beethoven promoting bathroom tissue? Mozart hawking mouthwash? ClearRadio playing "The Ketchup Song" 24 hours a day?

It makes the music lover in me very sad. But more than that, it makes me ask: what are the values of this 21st Century American society? Is money the only thing that matters?

Manhattan later that same day

Descending the stairs from his apartment along the Brooklyn-side, East River shoreline, Donohue looked at the overcast skies and grimaced.

Then a shrill, evil whistle started. He immediately put his hands to his ears and ran back inside.

He had forgotten today was a Noise Day.

On official Noise Days, all New York City residents were required to wear hearing protection outside the home or office. It was one of the few laws with almost 100% compliance, and no extra money was needed to enforce it. The horribly shrill, high-pitched whistle took care of all that.

The whistling was created by the combination of two factors: the first was the high winds from Canada that meteorologists blamed on the melting polar ice caps. The second reason was more local in nature: the swanky new architecture of the much-ballyhooed new Norton-Humes monstrosity built up in Midtown—something went horribly wrong with the building's complex window system, which was designed to heat and cool the interior without a central climate control. Whenever high winds hit Manhattan, the result was an unbearable 120-decible banshee shrieking that defied description. On Noise Days, the Mayor's office could dependably expect a deluge of complaints from as far away as Jersey and East Long Island.

Swearing a mile a minute, Donohue ransacked his closet for his hearing protection. He fumbled with the clumsy old-fashioned yellow headphones. At least his official police headset did fit perfectly under the headphones.

Back outside, Donohue stepped gingerly onto the row of two-foot high temporary wooden platforms laid end to end on the sidewalk, which was presently invisible under about six inches of opaque brown floodwater.

The stench made him queasy. Not for the first time, he cursed global warming, the mayor and anything else that drew his ire. Right now he hated the floodwater the most. Every day, he had to go searching for higher ground to park the police car. Now the waters had reached the sandbags along Marcy Avenue.

Normally, it was not allowed to use police cars for commuting and personal use, but the NYPD had finally relented after threats of a combined police and fire department strike when the floods were at an early peak. Perry knew all too well that he was personally liable if the car got damaged by the high water.

It was still better than paddling a rubber raft through the flooded subway tunnels, where there was still considerable danger of electrocution from the large number of third rails that hadn't been disconnected from the power grid in time.

Word had it that City Hall was about to give up hope of getting all the water out and instead only pump out selected areas. All connecting tunnels to the boroughs would be blocked off and subway service would be resumed only between Midtown and Wall Street.

The whistling dropped a note and then stopped. Donohue heaved a sigh of relief and took off the headphones. The platform ahead had flipped over, so he had to wade through the remaining water in his knee-high rubber boots. He grimaced as he stepped into the water and the cold seeped through his toes. *Gawd, what a mess.* He sloshed up the hill to the car.

He crumpled up another parking ticket on the windshield and was about to get in when he remembered to turn back the odometer. *Don't want to get into any more trouble...*

Things were bad enough as it was. Once underway, he found he made little progress in all the traffic on the streets that were still passable. The traffic reports said both the Brooklyn and Manhattan bridges were crammed. Not only cars but also pedestrians pulling makeshift rickshaws were vying for space in the cold rush hour morning drizzle.

Donohue decided the Manhattan bridge had the better chance of emptying out before nine a.m., which was when he was due in for work. He edged the two-toned white and blue Mercedes forward slowly in the throng of cars and people.

As he sat immobile on the bridge, right at the top of the arch, he was tempted to don his personal MP7 player again and try to find an updated traffic report on the radio, even though he could be fined if caught wearing one while driving. NYPD squad and unmarked cars no longer had car stereos or personal navigators, a policy put into effect after the 'mad car' virus epidemic five years ago.

He rummaged around in his kit bag on the vacant passenger seat. He could only find his miniature police headset. *Damn it!*

Just then, the police radio blared into life. "Calling car 829, Capt. Donohue, are you there?"

He replied wearily, "Donohue here."

"We got an XR-549 at the JP Morgan-Chase Bank on Broadway. Please respond immediately."

"A robbery in progress? Sorry, no 'can do'. I'm stuck in rush hour traffic on the Manhattan bridge, midway past the second trestle—and nothing's moving!"

A new voice came on, a woman's. "Perry, just flip on the hazard lights and park the car on the sidewalk. Await further orders."

Donohue was surprised to hear Lieutenant Shrini's voice. "What's the deal, Shrini? Must be a *big* bank robbery!"

"It is, Perry. The Phantoms have struck again, and this time they've taken hostages! Just park the car where ever you are and get to railing, *now.*"

"Will do," said Donohue, resignedly. He donned his police headset.

Shrini's voice crackled in his miniature earphones. "Oh, another thing—Perry, you got your SWAT gloves with you?"

Donohue fished the heavy leather studded gloves out of the kit bag.

"Yeah! What for?"

Shrini laughed. "You gonna do some climbing, Perry! Over."

"Shrini—whaddya mean? Over?"

The radio remained mute. Donohue resisted the urge to hit something.

Instead, he flipped on the hazard lights, shut off the engine, shifted to neutral and opened the door. He scrambled for traction as he pushed the heavy car over to the curb .

The richshaw driver in front of him, a heavyset bald man with one bushy black eyebrow stretching across his fleshy forehead, turned and yelled at him. "HEY BUDDY! THIS AIN'T A FOOKING PARKING GARAGE!"

Ignoring him, Donohue continued pushing the car onto the curb.

"HEY COPPER—I'M *TALKIN'* TO YOU! ASSHOLE!"

Without a word, Donohue rolled the car onto the man's foot. The man's voice went up an octave. "HEY ASSHOL—OWWW!! YOUR CAR'S ON MY FOOKIN' FOOT..."

Attracted by the commotion, the other passers-by started encircling them, yelling and cheering. Donohue calmly turned to the man and folded his arms. "I'll make you a deal, *pally*. You quit calling me an asshole, and I'll release the parking brake and let this car off your foot."

The rickshaw driver stared daggers at him.

"C'mon, deck his filthy pig ass!" yelled a bystander.

"Yeah!" yelled another. "Do it!"

The rickshaw man took a swing, but Donohue was well out of reach. He snarled at Perry,

"Hey, copper, I could scratch and dent the shit outta your car..."

"And I can take my billyclub and smash the shit outta your bald *head*." Donohue tapped his thigh with the club for emphasis. "Well, dirty little rickshaw *boy*, what's it gonna be?"

The bald man tugged futilely at his trapped foot. It wouldn't budge. He looked at Donohue savagely. "OK, copper, *okay*. You gotta deal."

"Now say 'please'."

The man's entire head went brick red. Through gritted teeth he spat out, "P-L-E-A-S-E! Wit' fuckin' *sugar* on top!"

Donohue released the parking brake. "See what a little courtesy does for you?"

"Fuck you" said the man, hopping on one foot. "You're gonna pay..."

The rest of his reply was drowned out by the sound of helicopter blades above. Above the din, a megaphone crackled into life. "Attention! *CAPTAIN* DONOHUE!"

Surprised, Donohue waved acknowledgment. He recognized the voice as belonging to Lt. Snipes from the SWAT team. He looked up.

A big N.Y.P.D. Anaconda helicopter began to hover over the bridge, some 100 feet above the top span. Snipes leaned out and yelled, "GRAB HOLD!" A steel cable spilled out of the sliding door, stretched taut and plummeted down, scattering people in every direction. The end landed with a smack on the canvas roof of a convertible. Donohue saw it was a safety hoist used in sea rescue operations.

He ran over and strapped the belts around, then tugged on the cable. The helicopter began to rise, taking Donohue with it, swinging like a pendulum.

Too late, Perry realized he had forgotten to put the police car's parking brake back on. He gestured frantically with his one free arm, but to no avail. He looked down and watched helplessly. His car begin to roll off the curb and down the opposite slope of the bridge, scattering rickshaws and other cars in its path like real-life dominos.

As he was being pulled into the chopper, he could see a dizzying sea of angry faces yelling things he couldn't hear over the rotors' noise.

Reeling Donohue in like a prized marlin, Sgt. Snipes' ebony face was split in a wide grin. "Lookie here what I caught! 'Doberman' Donohue strikes again! Looks like you found a way to cure your little traffic problem!"

Perry climbed into the vacant seat and first unbuckled the cable, then strapped himself in the chair. He pointed down. "Man, it *ain't* funny—that angry mob will tear my Merc to pieces!"

"We got you covered, Pee-Wee. We dispatched Lt. Shrini on a moped to pick it up and bring it back. She can pack the moped in the trunk." Snipes pointed down. "See?"

The helicopter circled back around. In the distance, Donohue could see a tiny uniformed figure get in the Mercedes and switch on the flashing lights. As the view receded in the distance, Perry saw the car begin to move, again scattering people in its path.

He turned around to Snipes. "Looks like you got all the bases covered. So why do you need me?"

Snipes shrugged. "You remember the Phantoms, don't you?"

Donohue did. "Does that mean I'm assigned to the case now"

Snipes smiled wanly. "Looks like it..."

Donohue grimaced. "Which Chase bank are they holding up?"

"The one on Broadway!" yelled Snipes, strapping himself back into his seat. He motioned for Donohue to do the same.

Perry complied, then tapped Snipes on the shoulder, "*Which* one? 623 Broadway or 525 Broadway?"

"Six-two-three!" yelled Snipes.

Perry placed his hands together under his chin and frowned. "You got any more details?"

Snipes nodded. He yelled in Donohue's ear, "Three gunmen, all with machine pistols... and possibly grenades too! We estimate a total of 30 hostages! They—the Phantoms, they're being interviewed live on VNN right now if..."

Donohue broke in, "Forget that! We gotta cut all power to the building immediately! Water, electricity, *everything*." He reached for the 'transmit' button on the headset Snipes was handing him. "This is Captain Donohue—who am I talking to?"

A reedy voice answered, "Lieutenant Melchers, Cap'n."

Fighting nausea as the helicopter climbed relentlessly, Donohue spoke slowly. "Melchers, listen good—we gotta shut off all utilities to the building at the crime scene immediately! Cut off all communications with the outside world."

"Will do, Cap'n."

"Another thing, Melchers—patch me over to Lt. Shrini as soon as she clears my car out of the mess on the bridge..."

Snipes turned and said, "you can do that on the ground, Captain. Pilot says we can drop you in Central Park and West in about ten seconds—here, better hook back up to the drop cable..." He handed Donohue the straps.

Without another word, Donohue began strapping himself back onto the cable. He risked looking out through the open side door. There was rapidly-approaching patch of green that he assumed was Central Park.

He didn't like what he saw. Brown puddles everywhere, big ones resembling the sinister oil slicks off of Rockaway Beach.

Snipes grinned. "I promise we'll try to set you down on a green patch, Captain!"

Controlling his stomach, Donohue nodded grimly.

Snipes smile faded. "Easy, Captain. Helicopters are cruel beasts—but it'll soon be over."

The pilot called out, "Ten seconds!"

Looking closely, Donohue could see the ripples from the rotor blades dance across on the standing water.

Snipes tapped on Perry's shoulder. "Are you ready?"

"YES!" snapped Donohue.

Snipes slapped him on the back. "NOW!"

Donohue jumped out. He felt himself swinging back and forth like a pendulum as he plummeted. The cable suddenly yanked back with a jolt, then played out slowly until he was around five feet above the ground.

Perry undid the belts and dropped to the ground. His feet sank up to his ankles in the watery turf. The helicopter roared off, sending a hail of debris swirling around him.

Grimacing, he extracted one boot, which almost came off as the ground sucked back. Looking up, he silently cursed at the now empty sky. *Nothing but goddamned ugly rainclouds*, he noted. He made his way to the nearest walkway, taking care not to sink any deeper into the slime.

Shrini came running up, her short legs pumping furiously, as Donohue made his way to the sidewalk. "Perry! We got Con Ed to switch off the power..." She brushed off a stray strand of black hair that had found her mouth.

"Damn, Shrini, you got here faster than the chopper!"

Shrini's grin was like a beacon in her dark features. "Had to drive on the sidewalk sometimes!"

"What about the water and gas to the building?"

"Already called, they said it would take another five minutes. Here's where we cross—the van is over there!" she pointed over the narrow divide.

They crossed the street, dodging taxicabs at random. At the van's door, Donohue stopped and said, "Nobody has answered my question—why *me*? I've not even been formally assigned to the Phantoms case."

"Chief Shabazz wants to speak with you about that, Perry. He's online and *waiting*."

Donohue frowned. "I don't like the sound of that…" He reluctantly stepped inside the van. The computer monitor was on. Donohue switched his headset to 'receive' and said, "Captain Donohue here."

Chief Shabazz's ebony visage appeared onscreen. "Glad you could make it, Captain. I'm here to tell you, as of now, *you* are in charge of the Phantoms case."

Momentarily forgetting he was talking to a computer display, Donohue spread his arms, nearly poking Shrini in the eye in the process. "Why me? The Phantoms are Folger's case."

"Not any more" said Chief Shabazz. "I've taken Folger off the case—you're our expert on Domestic Terrorism—you proved you know your stuff in the Smash case. It's all yours. Just be sure you let Melchers know when you arrive. I've put Folger on indefinite leave."

Donohue tried to keep the sarcasm out of his voice. "Thank you, Chief."

Shabazz's voice boomed over the headphones. "Capt. Donohue, one more thing. You are not to use tear gas or bullets inside the bank's premises."

"What do you mean, we can't use tear gas or bullets? I thought it was a bank robbery, not a museum heist!"

Shabazz's voice betrayed his irritation at Donohue's tone. "*Wrong*, Captain. It's a real elaborate set-up, more like a museum than you would think. The main lobby is lined with display cases of rare coins. Medieval shields, personal artifacts of King Louis XV, ancient spears and swords—the place is about as opulent as the Met. Just follow orders, Captain."

His visage vanished, now replaced by a test screen.

Shrini nudged Donohue sharply in the ribs. "Congratulations! Now get your finger out of my eye!"

"Sorry." Perry dropped his hands to his belt and began nervously fingering the loopholes. A thought suddenly occurred to him. "Medieval shields, coins… Shrini, does that sound like a bank to you?"

Shrini pointed to her screen. "It *is* a bank, Perry—just look at the circular customer service area in the middle—it's equipped with bullet-proof Lexan shields."

"Wait—if they had Lexan all around them, how did the Phantoms take them hostage?"

Shrini's voice was grim. "First they took customers at gunpoint and then they threatened to execute them if the tellers didn't come out."

"One thing technology can't overcome—a ruthless criminal..." He turned to Shrini. "And we're dead sure it's the Phantoms who are doing this bank heist?"

Shrini nodded. "Dead sure. They identified themselves on VNN."

"In that case, we need to go into overdrive. They're notorious as being the most high-tech bunch of bank robbers ever ..." He nervously ran a hand through his hair, then put a hand on her shoulder. "Shrini, what I need is for you to jam every means of electronic communication the Phantoms have to and from that building—the fiber optic stuff, mobile phones, all satellite links with the Internet, everything! Can you do it?"

She nodded again. "It'll take a while. What's your plan?"

"We got to cut off all their links with the outside—make *us* the only path to the outside world."

She nodded.

"Another thing," he took the e-key out of her hand. "I'll have to drive while you do the jamming with the gear in the back-we don't have much time."

She arched an eyebrow. "Okay... but drive slowly, *please*? I can't type in commands if I'm being thrown to the floor all the time."

Donohue started the engine and pulled out rapidly before remembering. He slowly turned and headed down Broadway with the siren off.

Shrini called out. "The TV networks are screaming about the power cut—they were right in the middle of a VNN interview with the ringleader..."

"Put out a press bulletin—tell 'em the floodwaters were leaking into the power grid—that'll shut 'em up!" He leaned on the horn to disperse the crowd of onlookers in front of the police barricades blocking off Broadway at the crime scene.

Donohue carefully slid the van between the gap in the barricades and pulled up next to the multitude of police vehicles already inside.

The van came to a stop a block away from the bank.

Donohue stepped out of the van. He leaned back inside and commented, "At least the wind has finally died down. My ears couldn't take much more."

"I know what you mean. That horrible shrieking and whistling..." Shrini suddenly stopped talking and listened on her headset for a moment. "Perry—we got a big problem—the robbers say the hostages are locked in the safe—and if the power isn't switched back on, they'll suffocate!"

Perry said over his shoulder, "We can turn the juice on, but only short blasts. Every thirty minutes or so—keep it irregular. Turn it on—but only for short bursts of about a minute or so! That'll send enough air in, but it won't be long enough for the Phantoms to set up any communication links! And it'll make the power outage story more believable."

She gave him the thumbs up sign.

He walked up to the main barricades, which were barely withstanding the crush of reporters climbing all over each other to get a closer look.

Even on his tip-toes and his elevator shoes, he couldn't see over the crowd or even estimate how far it was to the barriers ringing the crime scene.

He cupped his hands over his mouth. "MELCHERS! ARE YOU THERE?"

No one responded. He briefly thought about trying to club his way through, but the sight of all those cameras stopped him.

He shouted again. "POLICE! COMING THROUGH!"

None of the reporters even so much as turned around. *Sometimes, being Plainclothes does have disadvantages...*

He tried again, this time, flashing his badge. "HEY! LET ME THROUGH!!"

A towering brunette woman turned around and looked down at him. "Oldest trick in the book, pal." She guffawed, then turned back. She nudged her cameraman. "Get a load of the pip-squeak behind us..."

The cameraman grinned and said in a low voice. "Someone should arrest him for impersonating a boy scout..."

Angrily, he stormed back to the van and threw open the sliding door, causing a startled Shrini to knock her keyboard off the shelf and draw her gun. "Jesus, Perry! Don't *do* that! You scared me half to death—I almost shot you in the forehead!"

"Sorry." He waved an arm at the throng in front of the barricades. "I can't even *get* to the crime scene."

"You don't have to. I can show you the inside from the cameras—I got scans of the robbers while the power was still on. Here, the images are saved on the hard drive."

Donohue rapidly scanned each camera view. "Only three gunmen, as far as I can see... they're herding hostages into... looks like the safe..."

"Not the cash safe, Perry. The safety deposit box one."

Donohue nodded, "Uh-huh... Looks like the entire back area of the ground floor is sealed off."

"Yes—the entire back was sealed off with steel doors when the alarm was triggered."

He switched to another camera view. "Wait a minute—what about the fire escapes?"

"No. They're not sealed, that's against regulations. The SWAT team's got those covered, though. Perry, we're switching on the power again..."

Just then, the intercom blared, "Melchers reports a group of reporters tried to break into the crime scene..."

Shrini rolled her eyes. "Great..." She switched to live pictures and stared at the screens as the images suddenly went fuzzy. "Dammit, Perry, something's wrong!"

Donohue tapped her shoulder. "Lemmie check something." He got out the back and saw immediately that a huge plastic bag had blown against the antenna panel. He tried to grab a corner, but his arms were too short. Annoyed, he patted his belt until he found his big white billyclub.

He stood on the bumper and finally managed to drag the bag within arm's reach. He grabbed it and wadded it in his coat.

"Better!" yelled Shrini from inside, "*much* better!"

~ ~ ~

The apprehended journalists, about 75 in number, didn't say a word, just stared ashamedly at the ground like chastened schoolchildren.

Melchers screamed at them, "You IDIOTS! Do you *know* how close you came to being *shot?*"

The reporters remained silent.

Melchers' face was beet-red. "You're just a *Goddamned nuisance*! We're confiscating all your credentials and equipment—*and* consider yourself lucky that's ALL we're gonna do!" He gestured to a husky policewoman who looked to be all muscle. "Officer Patrovsky, get all their shit and take it downtown!"

Melchers then walked over to the SWAT man guarding the group and said in a low voice. "When she's done—get 'em *all* outta here."

Patrovsky dumped the last press ID into a large plastic bag. The SWAT man nodded. The journalists left without a word.

~ ~ ~

The journalists walked back to their respective camera crews.

"Man, we were lucky not to be hauled in..." said the VBS correspondent, a medium-sized black man in a flashy pin-stripe suit. "Or be shot by the cops..."

The petite brunette VNN reporter next to him smiled wanly. "Tell me about it..." she said, shaking her head. "Hell, we could've been shot by the bank robbers too..."

He nodded emphatically. "Can't imagine what came over me..."

She started to walk away, then turned around suddenly. "Bernard? Your name *is* Bernard, isn't it?"

Bernard nodded, "Yup. Bernard Duncan. And you're...?"

"Zane, Zane Lewis. Bernard, do *you* recall exactly how the stampede started?"

He thought hard for a second. "There were a few in front that must've started the whole thing—next thing I knew, we all were going in. Why?"

Zane frowned, "Dunno, it just seems funny, somehow. I mean, we're supposed to be pros, and a pro wouldn't ever have done something like that, I mean, not as a *conscious* decision."

He shrugged. "We're pack animals. If anyone gets the jump, we all gotta go for it. It's our *job*."

"Did you recognize any of the first ones, the instigators?"

"No… can't say that I did." He shrugged, "There're so many cable and Internet networks, it's impossible to keep up with who's who any more…"

"Yeah, but… this bugs me. I mean, we violated basic *common sense*. I'd sure like to know just who started this." Zane reached in her purse and pulled out a card, "Here, Bernard—take this and call me later tonight. I got a feeling there could be a story here. Wanna work together on this?"

"Good idea." Bernard half-smiled and took the card. "Yeah, I think you're right. I'll give you a call tonight."

~ ~ ~

Back in the surveillance van, Donohue and Shrini resumed their scanning of TV traffic. Shrini changed to the broadband satellite channels.

A man's narrow face appeared onscreen. "We demand 3 millions dollar and escape car…"

Donohue snapped, "How come this asshole is still broadcasting? I thought we had all the power off!"

Shrini clicked on another display. "We *do* have a total blackout—and jamming too. This must be coming…"

"From outside." said Donohue grimly. " Or it was taped beforehand. This whole thing is beginning to stink…" He paused, then keyed his headset microphone. "This is Captain Donohue calling SWAT Commander, Commander do you read?"

A sonorous voice answered, "Commander Chambers here—we copy, Captain."

"OK, listen up—I want you guys on full readiness. You may be storming the building in ten minutes. You got that?"

"Got it, Capt. Just say the word."

Perry turned to Shrini. "Listen, is there any way to do another 30 second power burst and access all the surveillance cameras again?"

"Just a second." She clicked on a screen. "OK. We got 28 cameras, Perry."

"I just need views of the ground floor—mainly the lobby and the back area."

Furrows appeared in her wide forehead. She squinted at the display. "It's possible. We got 10 cameras in those areas to choose from."

"Can we save those to the hard drives without wiping the earlier photos?"

"Yes. It'll be pushing things to the limit, but I'll compress the old ones and transmit them to the White Elephant first. Give me a sec."

Donohue leaned closer and unsnapped the clip on his shoulder holster. "OK—here's what I need for you to do. In two minutes, open the taps and scan all the cameras I point to." He pointed to the diagram onscreen. "I need images from here, here and…" he tapped the camera positioned above the passage to the safety deposit boxes, "especially *here.*"

Shrini reached down and re-activated another laptop. "Good thing I keep everything on standby…" she muttered.

"Why doesn't this van have the virtual headset display monitors?" snapped Donohue.

"You want cataracts in three years?" retorted Shrini. "Brain cancer in ten? *I* don't!"

She logged on to the ConEd system and tapped her fingers impatiently. "Come on, come on… There! I'm in." She turned to Perry. "OK, power 'on' in T-minus 60 seconds! Perry, get ready to click on the camera icons you want…" She handed him the keyboard and moved to the laptop. He nodded, his face blue in the light of the screen.

They were now sitting back to back in the cramped van. She nudged him in the back. "30 seconds…"

Donohue blew on his palms and rubbed them together.

Shrini nudged him again. "Go!"

Perry felt his fingers on the mouse move agonizingly slow. The pointer jerked awkwardly from icon to icon in the diagram.

Another nudge from Shrini. "Power 'off', Perry. What have we got?"

He rubbed his eyes. "Let's have a look."

The first image appeared onscreen. Donohue clicked on the next view. And the next. Sweat began running down his face. He started cursing silently, then keyed his microphone, "Chambers—send in the SWAT team NOW!"

Chambers responded evenly, "We're going in, Capt."

The first wave of SWAT personnel stormed the building, and every news camera outside zoomed in on the action.

Two perfectly synchronized rows of riot gear-equipped cops crawled about the building's parameter below window level, until they reached the big glass revolving door in the center.

Then, the rows disintegrated in perfect sequence, as each officer hurtled through the emergency entrances on either side and found something to crouch behind.

A deathly silence crept in. The first few SWAT personnel peered over their overturned desks

The front of the bank was a complete mess. Glass cases lay overturned, broken shards lay everywhere on the tiled main floor. Some were even sticking up like dragon's teeth out of the French blue carpeting in the customer service area.

Cautiously, a first officer advanced to the next row of desks, combat boots crunching on the broken glass. The others began to follow suit, always in groups of threes. Row by row, they advanced.

On the far left, an officer kicked a metal trash bin across the center aisle.

It clattered over the white tiles, scattering its contents.

Then it lay still.

Another stood up and swung her attack rifle in all directions.

Next to her, Chambers hissed "Patrovsky—Get DOWN!"

"Sir," she flicked up her face shield, "the bank is deserted—except for *us.*"

Chambers opened his mouth, but thought better of it. He stood up and looked around.

One by one, the others did the same. Some started photographing the scene.

Chambers keyed his mike. "Capt. Shrini—do the surveillance cams show anything?"

"Just a bank full of SWAT personnel-and broken glass. And it's *Lieutenant*, actually, Commander..."

"OK, Lieutenant." Chambers turned to the others. "Listen up—we got an 'all clear'—Patrovsky, get away from that ATM!"

"Sorry sir," said Patrovsky sheepishly, "I just remembered I needed lunch money..."

"Getting your prints all over it, wrecking evidence!"

She shook her head emphatically. "Sir, I doubt it—we just did a quick spray-down on everything computerized a moment ago—everything came up negative!"

Just then, Donohue's voice come over their headsets. "Chambers, *what about the employees? Are they still locked in the safe?*"

"Yes, Captain, looks like they are. The floor is empty and the safe is shut."

Perry responded, "Go see if there are any employees on the upper floors—otherwise, they're all crammed in that one safe!"

Chambers yelled to the others, "OK, listen up! We got employees to rescue! Everybody, go to Attack Plan C—but leave your weapons on standby! We're going to do a full building search, floor by floor!"

Instantly, the room was a swarm of blue riot uniforms flowing in beautiful precision. The stairwells became a river of blue, marching upward.

The radiowaves crackled with activity. "First floor reporting in—empty!"

A few minutes later, "Second floor reporting in—empty!"

Back in the van, Donohue turned back to Shrini. "I got a feeling all the employees are stuffed in that safe. Are you sure about the total number?"

She squinted at the readout. "About thirty, according to the personnel records the bank provided."

Donohue grimaced. "Shit. Turn the power back on..."

She did so, lightning fast. "Everything on—no, wait—the ventilation system's not responding for the deposit box safe!"

"Oh shit! It wouldn't be ventilated anyway, would it?"

Shrini thought for a second. "Yes, it would. They got nozzles the diameter of a penny, feeding in at floor level. I've got Central Dispatch on stand-by, Perry—do you wanna talk to them?"

Donohue nodded. With two clicks she connected them. Without introduction, Donohue started immediately barking out commands to the central NYPD dispatcher.

"This is Captain Donohue calling HQ, HQ, do you read?"

"We copy, Captain," said a clipped voice over his headphones.

"We got approximately 30 bank employees trapped in the bank safe—actually, the deposit box safe. We need either the bank's safe codes or..." he paused for breath, "the detonation squad to come blow the steel doors off their hinges."

"We'll get on it, Captain."

Removing his headphones, Donohue turned to Shrini. "No use in me sitting here, wasting time. I think I'll take a look inside, see first hand what's there."

Shrini agreed. "Yeah. I can radio you when HQ calls back."

Donohue got out and walked rapidly, but slowed his pace as he approached the gaggle of reporters again. They were still ringing the crime scene parameter like an impenetrable fence of flesh.

After noticing how tall most of them were, Donohue impulsively got down on all fours and started crawling, right behind the ones at the back. A fat woman screamed "Hey!" as he went right under her skirt.

"Sorry..." he looked up briefly, "I lost my contact lens!"

Loudly, he kept repeating "Sorry—got a lost contact! Sorry! Oops!" A wave of bodies parted nicely on either side. Some reporters even got down on all fours to help with the search.

Donohue quickly reached the front and tried to vault the crowd barriers. He made it on the second try.

"Hey! Did you find it?" someone called out. Donohue ignored the question and walked purposefully to the building.

Chambers spotted him and waved him over. "Captain, we think we've made contact with the bank employees..."

"How?"

"They've been answering our taps."

Donohue keyed his headset mike. "Shrini, did you get that? The employees are alive."

"Got it, Perry." Her voice crackled over his earpiece. "Still waiting for HQ to call back."

Donohue turned to Chambers. "Alright, let's take a look at it. Is the path clear?"

Chambers nodded towards the back. "See the wheelchair ramp?"

Donohue raced over to it. A group of cops were clustered around the massive steel door, their riot face shields up, sipping coffee. They looked him over with interest.

"No, I did *not* bring doughnuts!" snapped Donohue. They looked disappointed.

Ignoring their reactions, Donohue went up to the touchpad that controlled the safe's door. A black sergeant holding a machine pistol said, "Captain, there's nothing we can do without the access codes."

Donohue looked at him from the corner of his eye. "You sure they're OK?"

The sergeant shrugged. "The employees? Yeah, I tapped with my gun muzzle on the door shield, and we *think* we heard a response." He frowned. "But it's hard to know for sure through all that metal, Captain."

Donohue got down on all fours and looked round the perimeter of the door. "How much metal are we talking about?"

Chambers came over. "That's got to be a good sixteen inches, Captain, if not more."

Donohue peered round the edges of the door. "Can we insert an air hose somewhere?"

"It's airtight, Captain. We *need* those access codes."

"*Great...* So let's *get them*," Donohue snapped.

"We're working on it—we got calls placed to their central headquarters. The problem is that the local bank manager is locked inside," Chambers tapped the safe with his baton, "and his boss is on holiday in the Lower Antilles and hasn't checked his voice mail in weeks."

"*The Lower Antilles?* Didn't they have all those shark attacks last week or the week before?"

Startled, Chambers said, "I didn't know about that, Captain. That might account for the delay..."

Donohue keyed his headset mike. "SHRINI! You there? Yeah—does anybody else in the goddamned New York banking industry know the access codes to the deposit box safe? Yeah... I'll wait."

He paced around nervously. A minute passed. Now finished with their sweep of the upper floors, the remainder of the SWAT team came over and formed a semi-circle around the safe entrance.

"What's the situation in the rest of the building?" queried Donohue.

Patrovsky flipped up her riot mask and snorted, "Scared the shit out of three floors' worth of cowardly accountants. Most of them were cowering behind their desks when we came in. The rest of the floors were deserted."

Donohue turned to Chambers, "Why didn't those accountants phone us about the robbery when it actually started? We might've been able to catch the robbers red-handed!"

Patrovsky answered. "They said they didn't even know something was wrong until the TV crews showed up outside."

"Jesus!" Donohue shook his head.

Chambers nodded, "And by the time it *was* phoned in to us, the whole shebang was already on the air."

Donohue keyed his microphone again. "Shrini? Any luck?" After a moment he slammed a fist against the safe door. "DAMN!" He turned back to Chambers. "We got to bring in the Detonation Squad!"

The SWAT team started cheering and giving each other high-fives. "YEAH! BLAST THE FUCKER!!"

Over the headphones, Shrini broke in, "Perry, this just came in—the bank's board held an emergency meeting a few minutes ago and they want to forbid the use of explosives on the safe-they say the damages would force closure of the location."

"Screw 'em! I got thirty or more employees and customers locked in that safe—and they're likely to suffocate real soon. Call in the Deto Squad!"

The SWAT team roared its approval.

Shrini's voice sounded agitated. "I've just located the Detonation Squad—but it'll take at least half an hour to get them back over from Jersey..."

Donohue was apoplectic. "What the hell are they doing *in Jersey?*"

"Part of the budget cuts. They're on loan to Newark International Airport—the General Accounts Office says it saves bundles of money."

"Jesus!" Donohue rolled his eyes. "Can they bring enough explosives? We need a lot of very high-grade plastic EXP stock, at least 15-20 kilos."

"Let me check." Shrini sounded less than convinced. "They say they've got the explosive, Perry. They say they're approaching the Holland Tunnel right now—which means we won't be able to contact them again until they come back out on our side..."

"Why?" demanded Donohue.

Chambers broke in, "All that anti-terrorist shielding destroys all wireless reception in all our underground tunnels, and even on the subway."

Donohue began nervously fidgeting with his holster. Then his expression brightened, "What if we can *call* someone inside the safe—maybe one of them knows the codes..."

Chambers shook his head. "We tried that already, Captain. The safe walls stop all outside carrier signals from penetrating."

The minutes began to drag. The donut delivery man showed up with armfuls of boxes and the SWAT team swarmed all over him, each taking a box.

Donohue paced from one end of the lobby to the other, glass crunching under his boots in a slow rhythm as he fingered the snaps on his holster. Munching donuts slowly, the SWAT team sat and followed his path.

Chambers nudged the sergeant. "Jesus, look at 'em bobbing their heads back and forth..."

The sergeant grinned, "Yeah, like they're watching a slow-motion tennis match..."

In the middle of his tenth lap, Donohue stopped and keyed his mike, "Shrini! How much air do they have left?"

In the scan van, Shrini looked at her readout. "We're down to less than 10 minutes of air, Perry. The Detonation Squad should've already made it to the scene by now..."

"Tell me about it," snapped Donohue irritably, "Where the hell are they?". Melchers came and tapped him on the shoulder, "Captain, they *are* here, but they cannot get in—those TV reporters out front are blocking the way..."

"JESUS!! THAT TEARS IT!!" Donohue stormed outside, pulled out his Magnum .555 and went into firing stance. All TV cameras immediately focused on him as he systematically shot out their TV spotlights and deflected satellite antennas, one by one. Horrified throngs of reporters and their technicians began trampling each other in their panic.

All 210 TV and Cybernet news stations on the scene switched back over to live coverage as Donohue continued his target practice, only stopping once to quickly re-load.

Then he stopped. He calmly stepped through what was left of the crowd, smiled and beckoned to the jet-black NYPD Detonation Squad van to approach the bank. As helicopters overhead relayed the pictures to the public, the van rolled slowly in, making more crunching noises as it rolled over broken spotlights and boom microphone rigs. A dropped TV camera lodged in the undercarriage, trailing sparks in the growing shadows as the van rumbled up to the front doors of the bank.

The Detonation Squad stepped out in cool precision and filed into the bank.

Melchers walked up to the squad commander, a squat Bangladeshi with coke-bottle glasses, and pointed out the correct vault. "Sir, it's the deposit box vault—over there, to the left."

Commander Nehru was not pleased when he saw it. He put his hands up and said in a clipped accent, "Oh no, not *another* round vault door!" He turned to Melchers as Donohue came back, "Do you know what will happen if we need to blow the hinges off?"

Donohue broke in, "Commander, just do it—we only got seven minutes of air left in that vault, and I don't want it full of dead bodies!"

Nehru glared at him. "And what about a roomful of squashed policemen?" He gestured wildly with his arms, "That's door's gonna roll like a son of a bitch when we blow it off its hinges!"

Donohue keyed his headset mike to 'intercom' and yelled, "EVACUATE THE PREMISES—IMMEDIATELY!!! THAT'S *AN ORDER!!*"

Startled, the SWAT team looked up from their seats, some with mouths full of donuts or coffee.

Perry waved his arms at them. "I said *EVACUATE*—NOW!!! OR GET SQUASHED LIKE BUGS!"

In a flash, the SWAT team cleared out in a cloud of plastic cups and donut wrappings.

When Donohue turned back around, Nehru was already calling out orders in his clipped accent. "Now, place 4.5 kilos of explosive just below that steel plate—the door pin is right below it, and we want the pin to fragment cleanly the whole length. Fencher, you do the same with the top hinge—you're tall enough to reach it if we drag that desk over..."

Four burly men in black dragged the heavy desk over as he was speaking. Fencher climbed on it and was just able to reach up and slap the explosive on the top plate. Nehru looked at the men and gestured, "Now drag over all the other desks and form a barrier to stop the door when it comes off..."

Donohue interrupted, "Do you think it will stop the thing from rolling?"

Nehru snapped, "Not bloody likely, not with a 10-ton steel door! But it might slow it down enough to *not* blow through the back wall into the next building!"

Perry grimaced, "Oh..." Another thought occurred to him. "Where are the detonation wires? We only got 120 seconds left..."

Nehru grew more irritable. "NO WIRES! Where have you been, the 20th Century? We use electromagnetic pulses to trigger explosives—always have!" He shooed Donohue away, "Now, *please* stop looking over my shoulder—I got no peripheral vision and you standing here really distracts me!"

Melchers broke in, "What about inside? Won't the hostages be killed by the blast?"

Nehru turned livid. "NO CHANCE! The blast is directed outside—AT US! Now, go outside and *LET ME WORK!*"

Perry looked at his watch. "We got 30 seconds, Nehru."

Nehru brandished the small remote control detonator at Donohue. "Which gives *you* 20 seconds to get *your butt* out of *here*, Captain!"

Donohue folded his arms. "Not me. I'm staying."

"Suit yourself, Captain *Pancake*," snapped Nehru, holding his thumb above the button, "five, four, three, *two...*"

The blast drowned out everything. The floor shook like an earthquake and bits of false ceiling rained down in a huge dust cloud.

Donohue opened his eyes just in time to see the massive steel locking mechanism come flying past and smash through the plate glass façade a few feet away. The door glowed red at the edges and began to roll, snapping off its hinges cleanly. With every roll it hopped suddenly as it ran over its hinges, teetering to each side, shaking the ground.

It slammed deafeningly into the far wall, shattering the pile of desks in its way like matchstick figures, then it careened into the main cash safe door with a thundering clang and came rolling back, weaving and wobbling threateningly.

"Aw shit!" yelled Donohue and Nehru, not knowing which way to run as the door loomed massively over them. Perry collided with Nehru, knocking Nehru's glasses flying. They both fell in a heap.

The door lost momentum and fell over on its side, rotating on its round edge like a gigantic warped coin, making a 'whomp-whomp-whomp' sound until it thudded to a stop.

Slowly the view returned to vertical as Nehru found his glasses.

"Shit, that was close!" said Donohue, rubbing the bump on his head.

Nehru glared at him with his one remaining open eye, "Next time, when I say 'go', you should leave, Captain!"

Donohue decided not to punch him. Nehru's left eye was already swollen shut and would probably have been black if his skin color were not so dark.

As the smoke cleared, the first hostage, a portly middle-aged woman with beehive hair and broken spectacles, poked her head out of the deposit safe. Her mouth fell open. "Oh, my *goodness!*"

Chapter 4

The evacuation of the hostages was finally proceeding smoothly. Armed with the personnel list provided by Shrini, Melchers was checking off the names of each employee as they tottered unsteadily out of the blackened hole that once had been the entrance to the deposit box safe.

Donohue began to get uneasy. Sensing something wrong, he stopped Melchers and motioned for everyone to be still. He moved slowly to the center of the chamber and stood, alert. "I hear something. In the corners of the safe, something is *hissing*..."

Melchers was nonplussed. "What is it? I don't hear anything..."

Donohue said "Shh!" He went inside and walked over to the far corner of the safe. He bent down. There was a compact oval bundle wrapped in what looked like burlap. Donohue prodded it tentatively with his boot. On the burlap there was a crudely-stamped 'K'. He crouched down for a closer look. His eyes widened. "Melchers! Forget the list—get everyone out *now!*"

Instantly, the SWAT team formed a chain and swiftly herded the rest of the employees out.

Perry quickly scanned the safe's parameters. He called out, "We got similar objects in each corner of the safe—look!"

Melchers came in and looked over Donohue's shoulder. "What? Explosives?"

"Not exactly..." Perry frowned. "I think it's..."

Melchers ran out, leaving Donohue to stare intently at the objects. He keyed his mike. "Shrini—are you there?"

"Still here, Perry. What's up?"

Donohue spoke softly. "I just found four, repeat four, oblong objects at each corner, and each is wrapped in what looks burlap. If it's what I think, then inside the metal is coated with an inert substance... and that will either melt or evaporate, causing the stuff to explode when it reacts with water..."

Melchers rushed back in. "I got a fire extinguisher!" He was very out of breath.

"No—*don't!*" Donohue grabbed his arm. He turned the extinguisher over in Melchers' hands "Do you see this? It contains *water!*"

Melchers looked at him uncomprehendingly. "Well, *yeah*... but..."

Donohue left him standing there and went over to the far corner. He keyed his mike. "Bring in the Detonation squad back here—this looks like real weird… and tell them to hurry!"

The SWAT captain came on-line. "Captain Donohue, can you switch on your headset video camera?"

"Yeah, just a sec," Donohue reached for the switch on his belt. "Can you see what I see?"

"Yeah" said the SWAT man. His voice took on a puzzled tone. "That's a chemical symbol stamped on the wrapping…looks like something outta high school…"

"Chemistry class!" broke in Donohue. "It's raw potassium, and once the inert substance melts away, it'll combust big-time!"

The SWAT captain's voice distorted over the headset, "Donohue—if you're right, air wouldn't be enough to make it explode. It needs something like… water."

Melchers' face went pale. He set the fire extinguisher down and closed his eyes.

Looking back at him, Donohue suddenly had another thought "Oh shit…." He keyed the mike again. "Shrini, Shrini—are you there?"

Her voice was steady. "Right with you, Perry."

"Check the building diagram again and tell me if the water sprinkler system includes the safety deposit box area!"

A few seconds later, she came back on the line. "It *does*, Perry…"

"Shit!" hissed Donohue. "That means there must be a timer or a detonation device somewhere else in the building, ready to trigger the sprinklers on! Shrini—where's the control system to the sprinklers?"

Shrini radioed back, "That'll be in the basement, Perry!" Donohue ran out and looked frantically for the door to the basement. After trying three doors, he found it. He yanked on the handle, and fortunately it opened.

He was just about to descend the stairs when Shrini radioed back. "Wait, Perry! The whole sprinkler system is automated!"

Donohue keyed his mike again, "Which means what? No power, no sprinklers? No, that can't be right!"

Shrini looked at the diagram. "You're right—it's on a second circuit. I bet it's…"

"Solar powered." said Perry, grimly. "Which means we can't cut the juice or override it. Once the potassium starts reacting with the water vapor in the air, that'll trigger the sprinklers, and the whole place will go up like a rocket." He looked at all the trashed Medieval artifacts outside, in the main lobby. "Wait—I got another idea!"

He grabbed the bronze shield that a Phantom had obviously wedged between the elevator doors to bend it into a 'U' shape, kicking at the elevator and wiggled the shield loose. The elevator shut immediately.

Donohue immediately radioed again. "Hey, Nehru! Get your Deto Squad over here on the double! I need you guys to form a line from the safe to the front door!"

The Detonation Squad came running back in, still clad in their black helmets and face shields. Donohue immediately made them form a line. "Alright! You're gonna form a relay—we're gonna run a 'hot potato' relay with this shield here—we got four heavy payloads we gotta pass till you get to the last man—and that man has to run it out to the street with a partner who will lift up the subway grating so he can drop it in the vent! Got that?"

"You can't do that!" objected Nehru. "That will blow up the subway!"

Donohue shook his head, "Fuck it, man—it's flooded already! It'll blow up and out like Old Faithful—now, let's *GO!*"

Without waiting for Nehru to answer, Donohue ran inside the safe, taking the shield with him. In one smooth movement, he scooped the first bundle and passed it to the first Deto Squad man, who grunted with the unexpected weight. Under Nehru's disapproving eyes, the bundle was passed from man to man until Ferris, the last man, grabbed it and shoved through the glass revolving doors. His partner Parker raced out in front of him and just managed to get the heavy grating up enough to let the bundle slide in the opening. Ferris then dropped the grating and they got away just before the geyser shout up 40 feet in the air, taking the grating with it.

The grating fell to the pavement with a horrible clang.

"QUIT WATCHING AND PASS THE SHIELD BACK!" screamed Donohue. "WE GOT THREE MORE TO GO!"

Ferris and Parker raced back to the line and passed the shield back. Donohue scooped the bundle up and passed it along.

Again, the two men raced out and dumped the bundle down the vent. Another big flash, followed by a geyser. This time, the men didn't turn around before they dashed inside and passed the shield back.

Donohue grabbed the shield and ran back inside the safe. Shield and bundle made their way down the human chain. In tandem, Ferris and Parker raced outside with the bundle, but as Parker was passing the shield to Ferris, he slipped and fell. "SHIT!"

Ferris just managed to grab him just before Parker tumbled down the vent. The shield slid down the subway vent. The explosion instantly knocked them both off their feet and the geyser drenched them.

"You son of a bitch!" Nehru angrily turned to Donohue. "You nearly killed two of my men!" He stormed off without waiting for a reply.

Melchers came up. "That was close, Captain..."

"You don't know how close, Melchers. I was just about to deck his ass..." Donohue put his hands on his hips. "Are all the hostages out of the building?"

Melchers said, "Affirmative, Captain. We're bringing in some vans and ambulance to take 'em all to Beth Israel Hospital, just to be safe." He pointed at the safe. "Is that the last of the booby traps?"

Donohue nodded. "I hope so—let's do a last inspection, just to be sure. We're gonna need some more pictures anyway" They stepped over the debris and Donohue began taking digital images. They were so intent on their work that they didn't notice that the SWAT team had gone off in search for more coffee. The Deto squad was already driving away.

When Melchers and Donohue came out of the bank safe, the press had returned, complete with lights and microphones.

"What's all this shit?" demanded Donohue, "Where's the SWAT team? I want EVERYBODY OUT—NOW!!!" He rushed toward a TV camera and put his hand over the lens.

That was the image 145 million viewers saw worldwide an instant later.

Donohue fought his way back through the crowd and got in the surveillance van. He sat down heavily in an empty seat and put his head between his knees. "Gawd, I am exhausted. Shrini, you would not believe what I just went through to get those hostages out..."

"I saw it all, Perry" said Shrini, grimly pointing to the monitors "... and so did Chief Shabazz did, too. He wants to talk with you. *Now.*"

From the monitor, Shabazz's voice boomed, "Captain Donohue. This is your chief speaking. As of now, you are suspended without pay until your case is heard by the Board of Commissions."

Donohue was stunned. "*What?*"

"You heard me, Captain. You are suspended immediately."

"This *can't* be happening..."

Chief Shabazz's visage frowned down at him. "It *is* happening, believe me! The Phantoms slipped through *your* hands, Capt. Donohue. They outsmarted *you.*"

Donohue sat back up angrily. "Wait a minute! This case was dumped in my lap at the very last minute—you can't hold me responsible!"

Shabazz almost laughed. "Oh, yes I *can*... and you'd better believe the press *will*. Get ready!" His face faded from the screen.

Shrini shook her head, "Perry, I'm so sorry..."

Donohue waved his hand dismissively. "Forget about it—it's not your fault. But the worst thing is, I *think* I know how they did it."

"Did what?"

"Escape. I can't prove it yet, but sloppy NYPD security has a lot to do with it, that's for sure."

"You know I'll help back you up on that, Perry—but you had better have every detail down pat, otherwise, you'll get eaten alive."

"I know, believe me." Donohue turned to go. "Look, I've got to get outta here while I still can walk without falling over. Can you drop me off? I need to go home and recharge my batteries. I'll call you later, OK?"

Shrini's face still showed concern. "All right, Perry—but don't wait too long. You know what tomorrow's papers will be like."

With a grimace, Donohue nodded. Shrini started the engine and began to pick her way out of the crime scene as the first fire engines made their way into the area.

~ ~ ~

When he got home, Donohue leaned against his front door and let out a long sigh. He turned all three of his dead bolt locks, then wearily went over and unplugged his phone and answering machine, ignoring all the messages already on it. He lay down on the couch, closed his eyes and was immediately asleep—forgetting completely about the tiny cell phone in the pocket of the shirt he had flung over the armrest.

Chapter 5

NEW YORK CYBERPOST
Denmark Takes On America In Court!

Denmark is reportedly ready to file a landmark lawsuit against the American government for having triggered the current flooding crisis by permitting drilling in the Great Alaskan Wildlife Preserve 40 years ago.

Those first five drilling rig collapses have been widely seen as the root cause of the current Polar Meltdown which has seen great expanses of land disappear under sea waters-including 89% of Greenland - a territory of Denmark.

Venice, February 17 - Ash Wednesday:
Brezzi had just come in from all-night patrol when a loud series of knocks disturbed his concentration.

He looked up, just in time to see an unwelcome visitor come strutting in, an emaciated figure with a cigarette wedged firmly between his rubbery lips. *Cazzo, it's Crespo.*

Brezzi didn't even have time to react as the small Carabinieri officer rudely slammed a large wrapped package on Brezzi's desk. "What the fu..." said Brezzi, startled.

Crespo grunted through a cloud of smoke, "Aren't you gonna *thank* me? This package came for *you*. It was sent *to the wrong address!*"

Brezzi waved the smoke away. "Thanks a lot!" Here's a Euro for the delivery!" He held out the coin between his thumb and forefinger.

Crespo sneered and slapped the coin back in Brezzi's shirt pocked. "Better save it for a rainy day, *Bambino*, when you're out begging on the street! After I solve the mystery of the severed head, your ass is *history!*" He stalked out, but the door stuck and he couldn't get it shut. "Next time, give them the *right* address, you moron!" he yelled from the hall.

Back from his patrol, Murano walked in. He looked at Brezzi, winked and disengaged the door-stop. The door slammed shut. He shook his head at Crespo's departing figure outside, "Dumber than a bag full of hammers, that one." He walked over to Brezzi's desk and looked at the package curiously. "Aren't you going to open it?"

"In a minute" Brezzi took a sip of coffee. He looked at the stamped instructions on the side. "Keep Refrigerated." he read aloud, "Maybe it's that French wine I ordered the other week—but I don't know why they sent it here."

Murano pretended to be outraged. "You drink *French* wine? Sacrilege! Italian wines are the best in the world!"

"Franco, how do you know if you don't ever try French wines?"

"When you've tasted perfection, why bother looking elsewhere?" retorted Murano.

"Suit yourself." Brezzi grabbed a pair of scissors and cut through the plastic holding the invoice. A look of horror crossed his face. "What?! It's from Interpol! What the hell..." He took the long stilletto he used for opening letters and slit the packing. He slit the packing tape and opened the box. "Shit! *Shit! Testa di cazzo!*" He pulled the plastic bag out.

Even Murano was shocked. "They *sent* the head *back*?!"

"Yes! Of all the idiotic things to do..." Brezzi opened the bag and stared in disbelief. "Jesus Christus—they put *lipstick* on it!"

Murano couldn't keep from laughing. "How did they make him smile like that?"

"I don't know—it's like a bunch of kindergarten children!" Brezzi started waving his arms frantically and pounding the desk, "This was VALUABLE EVIDENCE!! CRAP! CRAP! Mother of GOD!"

Murano turned the head over. "I *like* the eyeliner..."

Brezzi turned to him in a tantrum. "Get *serious!* What can I *do?* We can't keep it *here!*"

Murano smiled ruefully and set the head back in the box. He patted Brezzi on the shoulder, "Henri, you're a good policeman, but you shouldn't get so excited. Look, I got to go outside and have a smoke—I'll be back in a minute." He went outside while Brezzi paced furiously.

A few minutes later, Murano returned. "Henri, for God's sake, *sit down!*"

Brezzi obliged and cradled his head in his hands. He looked up. "Franco, I'm sorry. But this case is getting to me."

Murano smiled reassuringly. "Well, *don't* panic. *Every* problem has a solution."

Brezzi looked at him. "And what's the solution to... this?"

"Well, Henri, you're always *bragging* about that king-size *freezer* of yours at home. Now you can put it to good use!"

"I can't do *that*—unless I want a divorce! Be serious, Franco!"

"I *am* serious. All right—*think!* Where can we find deep freezing facilities?"

"*Si*—deep freeze! I got an idea!" Brezzi started dialing. Then again and again. He slammed down the receiver in disgust. "Busy!"

Murano sipped his espresso. "Welcome to Italy...and Telecom Italia."

Brezzi looked up. "Franco, do you ever wash that coffee cup?"

Murano smiled. "I don't *have to*. After a while, it's self-cleaning!"

Brezzi grimaced, then dialed again. "*Ciao*, Ispettore Brezzi here..."

~ ~ ~

"*Si! Grazie... Ciao!*" Brezzi hung up the phone with satisfaction.

Murano looked at him. "Problem solved?"

"Yes. For the time being. A local butcher's shop will keep it overnight, no questions asked. But what to do after that, I just don't know..."

"Why not call that friend in New York back, send him the head?" Murano made a face and poured out the dregs of his cup. "Wait—first you better find a way to ship it."

Brezzi nodded approvingly. He quickly opened the Yellow Pages and started dialing.

~ ~ ~

Thursday Morning, Feb. 18:

"*Cazzo!*" Brezzi yelled, slamming down the phone again. "*Nobody* will ship it—yesterday, I tried every private shipping company, then all hospitals and the Red Cross, and now even the United Nations. They all said to call Interpol. Franco, that head won't keep long at the meat packing place and I can't trust anybody. What am I going to do?"

Murano stretched and yawned. "That New York detective you know, why not invite him over here—I mean, even New Yorkers like to be tourists *some*time."

Brezzi's face got hopeful. "Franco, you're a *genius!*"

Murano tapped the desk, "Like I said, Henri—you get too excited. Calm down, and you can think better."

"I *try*. But, Franco, tell me your trick—how can you *be* so stoic?"

Murano refilled his espresso. "Simple, Henri. I am an old man. I've seen just about everything. But you know what the best thing is?"

Brezzi looked at him quizzically. "No. What?"

Murano looked up to the heavens. "It's very simple. I have only *two* more months, God, just *two more months* to retirement..." He sauntered across the chilly hall for another espresso as Brezzi dialed again.

~ ~ ~

The cell phone vibrated in Donohue's pocket, waking him in the middle of a really good sex dream. "God damn it!" he yelled disgustedly after the 15th ring. He fished out the cell phone and glared at it, now silent again. He reached over and hit the display button on his portable clock. The luminous image flashed on the far wall in 3-D: 2:36 a.m. He groaned. The phone started ringing again in his hand. He turned on the lights, unfolded the earpiece and said "*What?*"

"Perry, that is you?"

"Huh?! *Henri,* what the hell do you want?"

Brezzi sounded agitated. "I am *so* sorry about the time, but I got a big... what's the word—*emergency.* Can you get your police analyze the severed head for me?"

"I thought Interpol was looking into it..."

"Something funny happened—*they sent it back.* After smearing it with lipstick."

"*What?*"

"*And* if we *don't* get it analyzed quick, we gonna lose a lot of evidence. I can't trust Interpol any more, and the *Polizia Nationale* says it's a local case, so *they* won't take it, so *you* are my only chance. Can you help me?"

Perry winced and squirmed in his chair. "Uh, I dunno..."

Brezzi's voice became even more pleading. "It would really help me. Can you send a courier to pick up it?"

Donohue was silent for several moments. He pulled out his pocket diary from his overcoat and switched it on.

Finally he said, "Can I call you back, Henri? I may be able to come over myself—I've never been to Italy, and I got some vacation leave..."

"*Great!*" Brezzi's voice distorted in Perry's ear. "Your ticket will be waiting for you when you come to work—I just sent the order off."

"Aw geez, Henri, you don't have to pay for it..."

"It's worth it, Perry. It may save my job. *Ciao!*" The line went dead.

Donohue stared at the phone for several moments before slowly folding it and setting it down. He switched off the lights, leaned back and closed his eyes. *What the hell, maybe I could use a break from this Phantoms shit...* He drifted off to a restless sleep.

Chapter 6

NEW YORK CYBERPOST
PHONE-ZAPPING *LEGAL!!*

Yesterday the US Supreme Court delivered a shock verdict, a unanimous ruling approving anti-terrorist phone zapping—with immediate effect!

Phone-zapping involves delivering an unexpected mega-volt electroshock via phone connection to anybody caught in the act of phoning in a bomb threat, regardless of whether mobile or fixed phone lines are used.

A New York Port Authority official commented, "[the ruling] is wonderful—all our problems can be solved with the push of a button!" Another unnamed official added, "The only thing better would be a camera to watch 'em fry!"

Mobile Phone Plague Continues

Hackers have recently managed to infect mobile phones nationwide with a virus known as 'Blazing Saddles'. The virus, which spreads every time the mobile is used, erases all pre-programmed 'ring samples' and replaces them with a sonorous farting noise that is so far impossible to eradicate. The virus was discovered last week, after a chorus of embarrassing noises threatened to drown out presentations at a proctologists' convention in Madison Square Garden.

Friday morning, February 19:
"*WHAT!?*" Chief Shabazz yelled to nobody in particular. He was alone in his office, reading his e-mail, when he came across Donohue's request for vacation leave—effective immediately. The message added that he had not taken any vacation for the past three years and that, according to union rules, he was entitled to it, even at short notice.

"That S.O.B!" Shabazz got up and raced down the stairs to Donohue's office. It was still littered with printouts and mug shots of the Phantoms.

"I'm gonna kill him," muttered Shabazz, glaring furiously at the empty chair. "His cracker ass is toast..."

~ ~ ~

Meanwhile, Donohue boarded the noon flight to Paris-De Gaulle, where he would change planes to Venice. His mobile phone was switched off and resting at the bottom of his carry-on bag. He knew it was a big risk, but he felt he had little alternative. Besides, he reasoned that it might be better to call Shabazz after he landed at Charles De Gaulle airport, after the Chief had had some time to calm down.

He closed his eyes an hour after takeoff and slept through dinner. When he woke up again, the sun was rising as the plane flew across Ireland.

He began to get worried after the fifteenth hour in the air. Normally, the huge 1000-passenger planes took only 12 hours to get over the Atlantic— or so it said on the holographic movie display on his headset, when he clicked on the 'info' channel. He took his headset off and glanced at his watch nervously, watching the light blue 3-D hologramic numbers pulse on the black background in time with the Cesium World Standard Clock in the World Financial Center atrium.

An annoying cycle started. The plane would slow noticeably, change direction and pick up speed again. Each time the plane slowed, Donohue started zipping up his travel case, only to stop again when the plane gained altitude again. It was when he looked out the window and saw the same pattern of city lights pass by for the third time that he figured he had better find out what was going on.

He flagged down a stewardess. "Excuse me, Miss? Could you tell me why the delay? I have a connecting flight to make."

The stewardess shrugged. "Sorry sir, we haven't heard either. Sir— you cannot use your computer now, I'm sorry."

Donohue shut the palmtop with a sigh. He pointed to the 'fasten your seatbelts' sign, "Uh, is it OK to use the bathroom? If we stay up much longer, I'm going to burst."

Just then, someone else tapped on her shoulder and she turned around.

Taking his cue, Donohue flipped off his belts and set off down the aisle. Seeing he was unnoticed, he quickly squeezed into the tiny WC. He put the toilet lid down, propped a foot on it and began dialing his mobile.

A sleepy voice answered, "Shrini here. "

"Sorry to wake you, Shrini—it's Perry."

"Oh *great*, so I'm on call around the clock—just for *you*..." He heard her sigh. "What can I do for you, Perry?"

"My plane to Paris has been going in circles for hours now—and they won't say why! I got a connecting flight to Venice that departs in... yikes!— only 20 minutes from now!"

"No problem, Perry. I don't need sleep anyway. I'll do a little digging and send a message to your portable."

"You're a princess, Shrini."

"Uh-huh, Perry." She hung up.

Five minutes later, as he walked down the aisle and sat back down in his assigned window seat, his palmtop vibrated twice, in short bursts. He opened it discretely and double-clicked on the message. His eyes widened as he scrolled down.

Perry, here's the situation: All Paris airports were ordered closed after 4 pm. local time, effective immediately. There is a curfew after nightfall—swarms of wild bats are attacking the whole city, and there is too much danger of jet engines ingesting the bats and crashing. All night flights are being re-routed to either Amsterdam Schiphol or Frankfurt am Main. Yours will land in Frankfurt in about 2 hours. From there, you are on your own, as there won't be any connecting flights until tomorrow at the earliest.

Sprechen Sie Deutsch, Perry? They do have rail links.

Good luck!

Shrini.

He cursed under his breath and snapped the palmtop computer shut. He closed his eyes wearily. *Here's my chance to 'experience' Europe…by rail.*

~ ~ ~

Saturday, Feb. 20:

The plane touched down at 10 p.m. local Frankfurt time. Donohue heaved a sigh of relief and began to stretch, glad to finally be back on solid ground.

He was among the last to leave the plane. *Jesus—800 passengers, and every fucking one of them has to screw around with their carry-on luggage for 10 minutes before getting off the plane…*

The corridors to customs seemed endless. No moving sidewalks, just golf carts pushing people out of the way to ferry green-uniformed police back and forth. He was tempted to find a service door, sneak in a storage room and lay down against his carry-on bag.

Finally he saw the customs booths in the distance. Upon seeing that the non-EU Citizens' line was nearly empty, he ran past several throngs moving slowly ahead of him and held out his passport to a granite-faced official, who barely glanced at it before indicating he could pass.

He took his passport from the official and walked through passport control—moments before a tide of Eastern Europeans from another flight descended on the area. He watched in horrified fascination at the way they pushed and shoved each other out of the way, while the bored-looking customs officials very slowly and painstakingly checked all the passports being waved furiously in their faces.

Perry turned to go and almost ran straight into the muzzle of an Uzi submachine gun. "Sorry," he mumbled to the towering airport security guard.

The man didn't even acknowledge his apology. Swallowing his irritation, Donohue looked around and noticed many other guards carrying the same weapon. He looked around at all the marble and granite floor surfaces and thought to himself, *Jesus, I sure would hate to be around when you boys actually do shoot—the ricochets would slaughter everyone…*

He was walking over to baggage pickup when he felt something bump him repeatedly on his ankle. It was his motorized suitcase, which had located him before he could locate it. He went quickly through the 'nothing to declare' line, his suitcase contentedly whirring along behind.

It took him another half an hour of going in wrong directions to locate the train station. He ran across it accidentally as he went through what he had thought was the wrong set of sliding doors.

The ticket windows were all closed for the night. Disheveled travelers clustered around a huge pillar-shaped ticket automat in the center.

He watched several other passengers buy tickets, but when he went up to the monstrous thing, he saw he had only bills, no change, and there was no change machine anywhere. The automat did not accept credit cards, at least as far as he could tell.

A sympathetic old lady smiled at him and made change so he could buy a ticket. "I always feel sorry for you Americans," she said with a slight accent.

Donohue was startled. "How did you know I was American?"

She smiled, revealing incongruously even, very white teeth. "That 'lost puppy' look—I see it all the time when I go back to Europe. You don't speak any foreign languages, that's obvious. Where do you want to go?"

"Uh… Venice."

"Oh my, you *are* lost. She smiled again and pointed to the sign, "Better take this train—it's a S-Bahn, and it will take you to the main station. There you can get a ticket for a *Nachtzug*, a night train. The ticket sellers speak English. Better hurry, the trains stop running soon."

Donohue nodded his thanks and ran to the S-Bahn, getting in just before the doors shut on his suitcase.

The S-Bahn train was ancient and dirty, its orange seats long since faded to dingy brown. Sticky beer stains covered the plasticised floor covering , which was beginning to peel in places. Graffiti covered most of the windows. The door to the toilets flapped open and shut as the wagons wobbled. When Donohue thought about relieving himself, he looked in and was greeted by an overflowing toilet with no seat. Waves of stench wafted out. He decided instead to wait until the main station.

The S-Bahn jolted to a halt. "*Frankfurter Hauptbahnhof, bitte alle aussteigen. Dieser Zug endet hier,*" announced a coolly automated female voice.

Not understanding a word, Donohue followed the rest of the passengers out. By now, his bladder was tormented by every step he took.

In the big domed Hauptbahnhof, which reminded him of an enormous metal and glass aircraft hangar, he frantically searched between the trains for the WC sign. He peered down the badly-lit passage that looked to be the main entranceway. Between the two central pillars, a group of bizarre-looking young people were sitting cross-legged in a circle. Each was waving the palm of their right hand in their own face and making a low whistling sound. The paused for a moment, then repeated the gesture in unison. And again. Perry wondered silently if he had stumbled into an adjoining insane asylum.

There—a sign above a staircase leading down. The WC was hidden behind a international press kiosk between the open lobby and the train platforms.

The stairs were not lit, and he stumbled and nearly fell twice as he wobbled down the narrow staircase with his suitcase in hand. Four flights of stairs more, and he was finally there. He fished out the unfamiliar coins out of his pocket. Coin after coin went in the slot, but the turnstile wouldn't budge. He saw there was a gatekeeper behind a glass booth. Donohue went up to the man and pointed to the coin in his fingers. The man held up five fingers in reply.

Donohue's mouth opened in disbelief. He fished out a penlight and shined it on the metal plate above the coin slot and saw it was no mistake. *Five fucking Euro to use the toilet!?*

It took him three tries to get his suitcase through the turnstile in front of the bathroom. He went up to the stand-up urinal, unzipped and began relieving himself. He was startled to feel drops hit his head.

Puzzled, he looked up. Water was dripping from an exposed light fixture. His eyes widened in shock. With a loud curse, he almost amputated himself in his haste to zip up.

He angrily picked up his suitcase and looked for the exit. There were no signs in English. The turnstiles blocked him from going out the way he had come in.

He went to the gatekeeper's glass window and tapped on the glass. "Excuse me—do you speak English?"

The gatekeeper shook his head and went back to reading his *St. Pauli Szene* skin magazine. Donohue stomped back to the bathroom. Seeing no exit there, he came back out again and stared daggers at the gatekeeper.

Several minutes passed. Trains rumbled past overhead.

Finally in exasperation, Donohue vaulted the turnstile and then snuck the suitcase out below it. The gatekeeper stared at him like he was some kind of space alien.

When he got back to the platforms, he looked up at the big sign and saw there was only one train that was headed to Italy—and it departed in four minutes. He ran to the ticket office, which luckily was still open and paid with a credit card without questioning the outrageous price.

He ran up to the train and managed to board a luridly-painted wagon moments before the doors shut. Finding an empty compartment, he shut the sliding door behind him, sat down and closed his eyes—without even noticing the *faux* leopard-skin seats at first. He looked around, perplexed. *What the hell is that smell—incense?*

Two garishly-dressed young women poked their heads in the compartment. The tall one, a dark skinned beauty with longish bright blue hair and Polynesian features, asked, "*Möchten Sie heute abend ein Paar Madels zum geniessen haben?*"

Not knowing a word of German, Donohue smiled and shrugged. They came in, sat down opposite him and closed the sliding door.

Donohue was intrigued by their garish outfits. "Do you speak English?"

"Of *course* we speak English!" they said in unison, "We're *prostitutes!*"

The second girl, who had a lovely milky-white complexion and short orange hair, switched on the portable boom-box radio that was tilted crazily on the seat. An old Byrds hit was playing, "I Knew I'd Want You". "I'm Jodi," she said, "and this is Linda."

Finding them both irresistibly attractive, Donohue could not help staring. He noticed Jodi had iridescent green eyes that went well with her hair color.

Seeing his look, Jodi smiled knowingly and began caressing Linda slowly. "*Schatzi*, your breasts are getting *bigger…*"

Linda smiled and began gently tweaking Jodi's nipples, which now poked their way through her shiny skin-tight black top. "No, Liebchen, it's *your* breasts that are bigger!" She started French-kissing Jodi and rubbing first her own crotch and then deep between Jodi's legs, which were now spread to reveal a few orange pubic hairs poking out of her ultra-short hot pants.

With one eye on Donohue, Linda started to pull off Jodi's top, but stopped just after the nipples, which were bright pink at the edges of her bullet-shaped tips. She held out a hand to Donohue, "200 Euro for the show, then we do you sandwich-style."

It was all Perry could do to keep from dropping his wallet on the floor as he fumbled with the unfamiliar bills. Jodi's petite brown hand plucked out two of the orange ones and handed them to Linda, who smiled and ran them over her now-exposed labia before tucking them in a large purse. She quickly pulled down all the folding seats to form a big lay-down bed. Linda pulled out a big green towel and spread it like a picnic cloth.

Then, with a florish, she pulled off Jodi's top and skirt and then her own, shaking her breasts in joy. Linda began rubbing Donohue's crotch slowly with both hands, then unzipped him and slid his penis between her soft breasts. Then Jodi nibbled on Linda's ear and said, "The strap-on?"

"Yes! The strap-on!" Linda reached in her purse and produced a fearsome black dildo that, upon exposure to light, began to pulse and glow like a Siamese Fighting Fish.

Jodi quickly wrapped the tiny clear elastic bands around her full buttocks and mounted Linda, sliding the now-deep purplish phallus in with an exquisitely moist slurping noise that repeated with every thrust in and out.

Jodi continued French-kissing, then reached out and expertly grabbed Perry's penis and scrotum, placing her index finger on his anus as well. "Put your *geiler Schwantz* here—right on my lips, make the meat in our sandwich!"

Perry found himself in a perfectly-synchronized three-way pumping cycle of bouncing breasts and buttocks. Donohue looked up and saw the ceiling was mirrored. He found himself enjoying the visuals immensily, as each girl alternately deep-throated him, then ran her lips up and down, riding his penis like a quivering popsicle.

His eyes crossed as his ejaculation went all over the big green towel spread over the seats.

A slight tapping noise on the sliding noise made him focus again. He slid the door open a fraction, "Huh?"

A woman conductor was standing there, holding out her hand. The door slid open. She didn't even blink at all the nudity. "*Zugestiegene, bitte die Fahrkarten.*"

Donohue lunged for his trousers. "I... I don't speak any German..."

"Ticket, please" she replied coolly. He pulled his out and she stamped it. "Now, take your cloth-his and go to the next wagon."

He hurriedly gathered his clothing and stepped into it. The girls blew him a kiss as he stepped out and said in unison, "*Tchüss!*"

Further down the hallway, another passenger stumbled out of a neighboring cubicle, his chubby face read and sweating. "Who-eee!" the man said to no one in particular.

Donohue looked at the man and took in his thinning blonde hair, Bermuda shorts, brightly-colored t-shirt with the Lone Star logo and strap-on wallet carrier around his beer gut. There was no question in Donohue's mind. He said to the man, "You American?"

Surprised, the man turned and looked at Donohue. "Yeah! How'd you know? You, too?" He held out a fleshy hand, "Starkwell, Charlie Starkwell's the name, selling potency drugs is my game! Thank God Viagra's still legal overseas!"

Donohue took his hand and shook it firmly. "Perry Donohue. Pleased to meet you, Charlie."

"The pleasure's *all mine!*" Starkwell laughed loudly at his own joke, then paused to look Donohue over, "So Perry... what do you do for a living, if I may ask?"

"NYPD."

"Ho-ho-*ho!* A cop in the Bordello Wagon! Welcome to Europe, my friend!"

"Bordello Wagon? So that's it!"

Starkwell let out another guffaw, "You *didn't* know? Didn't you notice the writing on the side of the train, or the nameplate on the cabin you just walked out of?"

Donohue peered up at the small gold plate on the now-closed sliding door. It read "Girl Sandwich Delight."

A slim, elegant hand tapped Starkwell on the shoulder. "Sir?"

"Huh?" Starkwell looked startled, "Oh yeah—my hat—thank you, honey..." He proudly put the puce-colored Tirolean hat on his head. "Look like a real native, huh?"

Donohue looked at him dubiously. "Uh, sure..."

Ignoring the response, Starkwell continued, "Yeah, the bordello on wheels concept is 'bout the only thing that saved the Deutsche Bahn—the German National rail—from going el broke-oh! Way back at the turn of the Millennium, they were in real bad shape..." he waved his arms expansively as they walked to the next wagon, "now they're not only privatized but actually *rolling* in cash, stockholders are lining up—they got a 14-year waiting list to buy shares. Ya have to wait for someone to OD on Viagra and have heart failure to get a chance at buying!" Noticing Donohue's look, Starkwell added, "It doesn't bug you that Viagra's still legal over here, right?"

"Naw." Donohue grinned and looked over his shoulder, "Well, that's not the *only* thing here that ain't legal stateside..."

"Rejoice and partake, that's what I say!" Starkwell held up a hand as they passed the WC, "Can you wait a sec? I gots to pee like a racehorse..." He ducked inside as the door slid open automatically.

When he re-emerged, Starkwell was flapping his hands spasmodically. "Goddamn Deutsche Bahn—spend all this *Geld* on super-hi-tech trains, but can't be bothered to re-fill the soap dispenser or the paper towels..."

Donohue nodded at the bright purple window curtains. Starkwell grinned, "Good idea!" and wiped his hands dry.

They entered the bar area, which was filled with cigar smoke. "Here, let's get a booth," said Starkwell, "I feel like a double martini—a *real* martini, not any of that sissy Italian stuff..."

The train lurched sickeningly. A huge, horrible squealing filled their ears and pierced through their skulls. Shatterproof plastic whiskey bottles and cups flew everywhere. Donohue was thrown forward into Starkwell's mammoth gut.

The train finally screeched to a halt with a final lurch. "Get... off... my...nuts..." gasped Starkwell.

Donohue stood up on wobbly legs. "Sorry...Charlie... What the hell was that?"

Starkwell took a deep breath, sat back up and opened the window. "I bet I know," he said, still white-faced. He pointed at all the flashing lights and police swarming over the dark forested hillside next to the train. "Yup! Damn art terrorists again!"

"What?!" Perry stuck his head out for a look.

"Art terrorists." Starkwell rubbed his sore belly. "Good thing this didn't happen when I was still in the Bordello—heard a couple of shoe salesmen got instant vasectomies last month when that happened before..."

Donohue slid the window shut. "So this *has* happened before? Is this an organized terrorist movement?"

"Oh *yeah!*" Starkwell nodded emphatically. He turned and ordered a martini. "Make it a triple, pal! OK?"

He turned back to Donohue and said, "Yeah, those bozos make life-sized paper mâche statues of famous politicians and celebrities, then they go and tie them to randomly-chosen high-speed railroad tracks, usually only a couple of minutes before the train comes."

"So why *stop* the fucking train if it's only paper mâche?"

"Because you'd wipe out *half* of the world's prominent art collectors in the process, that's why!" Starkwell took a big gulp of gin and chewed on the olive. "Those fuckers will fight to the death to get their hands on a genuine effigy that's been tied onto the tracks—they can sell them for *millions*—the last one went for $25 million, or so they say." He swished the martini in the plastic cup and grimaced. "Jesus—putting drinks in shatterproof plastic makes sense from an insurance standpoint, but it sure don't *taste* right..."

Chapter 7

Donohue bid Starkwell farewell in Munich and boarded the last train to Venice half an hour later. By the time he boarded, he was shivering visibly, as he hadn't bothered to take winter clothes. The train, an old EuroCity, was in ill repair and not well heated.

He was visibly disappointed to find the Alps shrouded in impenetrable fog, so he quickly opted to pull down the window shades in his individual compartment and unfold the Murphy bed built into the compartment. He closed his eyes and dozed off immediately, despite the train's electronic hum fading in and out.

At about 5 a.m., he felt hands probing his ticklish stomach. *My waist pouch,* he realized with a start, sitting up suddenly. The would-be thief let out a yell and ran out before Donohue could get a good look at his face. After stalking the corridors without success for half an hour, Perry gave up and took to the toilet.

As he sat down to do his business, something unusual in the waste paper slot caught his eye. "What have we here?" he said to no one, bending over for a closer look.

He fished it out of the wadded up plasticene hand towels. His eyes widened as he examined it more closely. It was a folded up New York Times printout about the last Phantoms robbery.

Immediately, Perry ran down the hall to his compartment, fished out a plastic evidence bag from his suitcase and just managed to beat an old woman back into the WC. "Sorry! Forgot something—out in a second!"

The old lady said something rude and struck the door with her cane as he closed it.

Donohue ignored her for the moment and got down on his knees to look for anything else. In the bottom of the bin, he found a small bundle wrapped in cellophane. He quickly stuffed it in his bathrobe and made his way out of the cramped WC. The old woman glared at him for a moment and muttered something in a foreign language. Perry waved at her dismissively and entered his compartment, locking the door behind him.

He unrolled the bundle and switched on the light. The paper unfolded to reveal a Italian passport. Perry was tempted to throw the newspaper clipping away, but something told him to hold on to it. He folded the paper back up and put it in the plastic bag. He took another small plastic baggie out of his shaving kit and put the passport and its wrapper in it.

He took his trousers off and wadded them up under his head. He stuck his waist pouch under his armpit, lay down and switched off the light. He fell asleep immediately.

It was late morning when the train crawled to a stop. Perry raised the window blind and saw a snow-capped mountain range half-hidden in the distance by fog on his left. The terrain around was much flatter now and seemed strangely familiar. *Reminds me of… Florida, all these swampy areas… all that's missing is the Spanish Moss hanging off the trees…*

Putting his trousers back on, he stepped out of the compartment. The weather-beaten station sign said Mestre. A few passengers trickled off as the rain started falling more heavily. With a jolt, the old train started up again. Hesitantly, the train edged out on a narrowing peninsula. Donohue wondered belatedly, *Am on I on the right train?*

He felt relieved when the Venezia sign slid into view. Still, he was surprised at how provincial the train station looked and how old the other trains were.

Outside, the drizzle continued. It felt good to stretch his legs, but his motorized suitcase was having difficulty with the cobblestones. With a sigh of annoyance, he switched it off and picked it up. The weight almost dislocated his shoulder. He wrestled it down the steps and over to a long line of other tourists standing sleepily along the Fondamenta Santa Lucia. The line led to a small white wooden booth. He thumbed through his Venice guide and recognized he was at the Vaporetto ticket office.

When his turn came, he leaned forward and said, "Do you speak English?"

The portly man with the small moustache shook his head. "No, *Signore*."

Donohue flailed through his guidebook, looking for the glossary. After what seemed like an eternity, he was haltingly able to say, "*Scusa, un biglietto linea uno?*"

The man smiled, took Donohue's proffered 20 Euro bill and slid a ticket under the glass. There was no change.

Perry briefly thought about angrily demanding his change, but thought better of it after seeing a Vaporetto boat pull up to the dock. With a grunt, he grabbed his suitcase and wrestled it over the wooden planks to the boat, which was just about to pull back out again into the greenish waters. He jumped onboard and just managed to keep a grip on his suitcase.

There were no empty seats, so Perry stood at the rail and watched the ancient buildings go past. The Rialto Bridge came and went. As time dragged on, he began to get nervous. He checked each stop against his guide, looking for the right one but not finding it. As the Piazzo San Marco came sweeping into view, he cursed inwardly. He would have to take another boat back, as this boat didn't dock at the stop he needed.

He stepped out onto the corrugated steel ramp and was relieved to see that the boats going the other way also docked there. Looking at the Piazza, he was shocked to see that, beyond the end of the dock, the street and waterfront was submerged in high tide. Gondolas floated in a line as far as he could see, seemingly moored to nothing. In the plaza itself, he saw a long line of tourists gingerly making their way across the wooden floodwater scaffolding to get to the cathedral.

After marveling at this for a moment, he found an empty seat under the white awning at the dock's end and listened to the rain hit the metal. The fog and rain got heavier.

A fat, hairy, middle-aged transient was sitting to his left, beneath a no smoking sign. The man kept putting his fingers to his lips in a daze. Donohue looked closer and realized the man was holding the stub of an unlit cigarette and sucking on it compulsively.

Donohue was grateful when the Vaporetto came into view. The wind was starting to make him shiver. He quickly got on and hoped no ticket-taker would appear in the crowd on board.

Seeing one at the other end of the cabin, Donohue quickly made his way to the gate and got off on the next stop. He decided he would find the hotel on foot. He looked round and noticed nobody else had gotten off on that stop—a bad sign. It looked to be a little-used one, with no clear way out.

Feeling weak from not having eaten breakfast, he set foot on the slick cobblestones that seemed to flow endlessly on the narrow streets between the crooked buildings.

After heading up several dead-end alleys, he began to feel rather like he was trapped in an indecipherable maze. The heavy fog and mist didn't make things easier. His arms ached from lugging the overfilled suitcase, its wheels spinning uselessly on the uneven cobblestones.

Sea water seeped in and out of the slits etched along the walkways' edges. He took care not to step in the puddles or drag the suitcase through them. The suitcase occasionally tipped over when he cut a corner too close.

Perry grew more impatient, looking in vain for any semi-familiar street name etched in the buildings, anything that corresponded to what was on his now-damp map. He squinted and looked at his surroundings. *I'm lost. At least the wind has died down...*

He stumbled from a tiny alleyway that was partially blocked by floodwater platforms and found himself wide slate-stone square. He made a beeline for a shuttered newspaper stand a few meters away, hoping to identify the spot.

It was when he unfolded the map once more that he noticed there *was* wind, but it didn't bother his contact lenses. This was puzzling...

He looked around the square. He saw a side street with a stand-in café. He suddenly realized he was ravenously hungry. He went inside.

Fortunately, the woman behind the counter spoke English.

It took three helpings of pizza to stop his stomach from growling. Feeling rejuvenated, he resumed his search for the hotel.

As it turned out, he was only a few meters away from the hotel. It looked so different than how he had pictured it, back when he had found it online in that cyberbar in Brooklyn. But now that seemed ages ago.

The Christmas lights seemed especially incongruous in the elegantly decaying surroundings. He lugged his suitcase up the agonizingly tiny stairs and pulled open the heavy door.

The lobby was cramped but warm. The girl behind the counter spoke some English, Perry was pleasantly surprised to learn. The girl stepped out from behind the counter and pointed, "Your room is of another house. Eh, follow me."

She led him down another series of narrow, catacombed streets and across several small bridges. Just before the street dead-ended, she stopped and opened an elaborately carved oak door. They stepped into a narrow foyer lined with massive oak beams and a glass door leading out to a side canal. Donohue was startled to see a gondola come sweeping past and disappear just as quickly.

His room was on the top floor, she informed him. As they went up the tiny winding stairs, he struggled to keep pace with her. The sides of the roof were only inches above his head as they walked down the small hall. When she opened the door for him and handed him the key, he thanked her, collapsed on the flimsy bed and fell asleep.

~ ~ ~

When Perry awoke, it was dark. He sat up and switched on the light. There was no clock. He stretched and looked around. His door was still open. He quickly got up and shut it. He was relieved that all his belongings were still intact.

Because the roof's angle cut drastically into the room's dimensions, he saw the only window was almost at floor level. He lay flat on his stomach to open one side of it and poked his head out. A few people passed through the tiny square below. A church bell started ringing in the distance. He closed his eyes and counted silently. Must be 7 pm. Too late to call Brezzi. He decided to take a walk to clear his head.

His room had no bathroom. He found the community WC at the end of the hall. He stared blankly for a moment at the bidet nestled alongside the toilet. He had to duck to take a piss in the tiny confines.

Outside, the drizzle had stopped. He descended the winding steps and went back the way he thought he had come. As he rounded the corner of the Calle le Botteghe, a sharp gust of wind hit his face and he winced instinctively, then blinked in surprise. No pain from his contacts. He looked around, puzzled. People hurried past the big church that dominated the square. Then he realized what it was that seemed so unusual. *The city has no cars; ergo, my contacts don't hurt!*

To his jaded urban ears, the ambience felt very strange and somehow eerie, despite all the people walking by and talking.

He followed a group of tourists for a while, then veered into a small shop to buy beer for the night. He correctly assumed it would be overpriced, but by now he was past caring.

At that point, he realized he was lost. He reached in his back pocket for the map, then remembered he'd left it in his opened suitcase.

The beer bottles clanked in the paper bag as he retraced his steps.

Another arcing alleyway, lined with unused wooden platforms, past a few art galleries and delicatessens, and he was there. Those crazy Christmas lights were a welcome sight. He stopped and watched them as they switched on and off in sequence, creating a motion like neon swallows in the darkness. It made him dizzy after a while.

Then the rain came back. He quickly went back inside.

As he trudged up the winding stairs and past the upstairs dining room, he resolved to go to police headquarters first thing in the morning.

~ ~ ~

By noon the next day, Donohue was really lost and growing more irritable by the minute. He had combed the main islands of San Marco and Castello the whole morning without success.

His guidebook was apparently incorrect—every time he pointed to the listing for the police, people shrugged and shook their heads.

In every building he was sent to, his questions were greeted with blank stares or incomprehensible attempts to tell him something.

He was walking slowly back to the Rialto Bridge and had just paused to peer up a small alleyway when he caught a glimpse of the blue *Polizia Municipale* boat going up the Canal Grande. He immediately broke into a run, slipping frequently on the slick cobblestones. He only narrowly avoided crashing into a large group of Japanese tourists on a wooden bridge. He desperately sought to find his way to the canal walkway. He saw several possible ways, all choked with tourists.

The cobblestones continued to abuse his foot arches. He slid to a stop and peered around the next corner. He dashed into the Calle Carbon, where tourist traffic was noticeably lighter.

Aha! At the end of the street was a group of four blue-suited policemen. Donohue came running up as they dispersed, two boarding a patrol boat attached to a blue and gold mooring pole, the other two going inside a weather-beaten building with a marble façade and windows covered in rusted wire mesh.

Donohue bent down and caught his breath for a moment before he went in. There were no signs. He looked around the roomy, high-ceilinged hallway for some kind of familiar symbol. Moments later, he noticed the tiny police shield on the first door to his right. He knocked and peered in. "Um, excuse me..."

"Perry Donohue, Welcome to Venice!" said Brezzi, grinning widely. "You made it!"

"Henri! Good to see you!" Forgetting his fatigue for the moment, Donohue shook the proffered hand with enthusiasm. "It took me *forever* to find this place..."

Brezzi looked nonplussed. "Really? Why didn't you call 113 and just ask?"

"With *my* Italian? Oh, *please!* There's no way!" He held up his tour book "When I looked you up here, I got sent to a place called Cah-bin..."

"*Cazzo!* You mean the Carabinieri? Those idiots—what did they say?"

"They looked at me like I was from Mars..."

"They don't like to acknowledge we exist." Brezzi rolled his eyes and muttered something else into his coffee.

Donohue cupped his ear. "Pardon?"

Brezzi flinched. He shouted "DON'T DO THAT!"

"Do *what*, for Christssake?" Donohue looked annoyed.

"Touch your ear! NEVER in Italy..."

Perry raised his eyebrow and repeated his gesture. "Like this?"

"Yeah—*that!*"

"I don't get it—what's the big deal—it just means I can't hear you..."

"Perry, you're in *Italy*, not '*Little* Italy'," Brezzi shook his head emphatically. "*Here* it means you think I'm a homosexual and you're looking for action!"

"Yeah? As NYPD Gay Squad commander 'Miss Clint' Pierce would say, 'Don't flatter yourself, *bitch!*'"

Brezzi looked at him. "Huh?"

"Never mind, Henri. Inside humor. Anyway, I'm just glad to finally get here." He walked over to the window. "You'd have a great view, if it weren't for this wire mesh. What's it for? Burglars?"

"No, much worse—those *maledetti* pigeons! You wouldn't believe how much they shit!" Brezzi went over to Murano's desk and coaxed a couple of coffees out of the ancient machine. He brought a cup to Donohue. "So, Perry, how is Europe... so far? This is your first trip overseas, no?"

"Yes, it is. It's been an ordeal." Donohue grimaced at the memory. "My plane was re-routed to Frankfurt, Germany because Paris has been plagued by..."

"Ah yes, the vampire bats at night. I heard about those," Brezzi nodded. "So you flew in from Frankfurt? You should... eh, called me from the airport."

"Naw, I had to take a train 'coz it was so late when I got in to Frankfurt. I flew on one of those Supersonic Airbuses they got now, got to Frankfurt late at night. Went through hell to find the main train station and take a piss... Then I got on some wild-ass train to Munich that got delayed by the some group that puts statues on the tracks..."

His mouth full of coffee, Brezzi tried not to choke from laughing. "Yes, yes! I know them—the Bader-Neuschwanz *terroristi*, the types who make those huge paper mâche caricature statues of important world leaders! The videos are world-famous!"

"Really? They make videos?" Donohue shook his head, "Well, it must have been spectacular to see that train come to a dead stop, 'coz it threw me halfway down the dining car..."

Brezzi laughed. "What? That's so typical of the Germans! We never for that stop *our* trains! Why? Because they're never on time!" He laughed loudly at his own joke. "And they always try and arrest the art dealers! Such stupidness—we let them fight for a while, then chase them off. They do more damage to each other than we could, anyway."

Donohue looked at him. "What do you mean? You got the same problem here?"

"*Si!* The gallery owners here always fight over the sculptures—there was almost a mini riot in Mestre a couple of months ago. Those statues are a huge collector's item, especially the ones pulled off of bridges—the more danger involved, the more money they get for the piece. The train slows for five minutes, tops, then everything is fine. We only have to make sure they don't get too crazy when they fight over the damn thing and get run over by the train..."

"So they *really* fight over the damn things? Someone told me that on they way here, but I found it hard to believe. How much do they sell for?"

Brezzi drew imaginary numbers with his fingers. "Oh, a lesser one, anywhere from two hundred thousand to eh, five hundred thousand Euro, maybe...*But*, a *really* beeeg star, possibly twenty or fifty million, according to the grapevine."

"Wow..." Perry was intrigued, "Tell me about the big fight in Mestre."

"The mini-riot? We had sixteen gallery owners fighting over a paper mâche Pavarotti—the thing was enormous, as you can imagine—and four collectors got knocked down by the locomotive. Fortunately the train got slowed in time, they only got bumped around a bit."

Donohue sat down and poured another cup. "In the US of A, the lawsuits would be flying..."

"Italians, we know the consequences, you get a little too crazy, you gonna get hurt. Nobody goes to court."

"Somehow, I like that way better," Perry smiled. "I got a lot to learn about Europe, I can see that already."

"So, Perry," Brezzi prodded him playfully, "anything about *Venezia*—sorry, Venice, that surprises you?"

"Yeah..." Donohue flared his nostrils unconsciously. "I expected it to be a lot *smellier*..."

"The city, or the people?" Brezzi eyed him expectantly.

Donohue laughed, "Both. I also expected everyone here to have garlic breath."

"You Americans! Always think Italians are compulsive wine and garlic eaters. Go to Vienna, my friend. Austrians are the *worst*."

"Austrians? *Really?*"

Brezzi's grin got wider. "Really. They all think *knoblauch*—garlic—that it is some kind of miracle cure for old age—totally wrong, I must say—but they swallow it in capsule form like candy... I had to go to Vienna last year for a three-week Interpol conference on clone organ trafficking, and *Mio dio*, it was horrible! At 7 a.m. on the U-Bahn—sorry, subway—it was a nightmare! Entire trains full of people with stinky—*stinky* breath! *Ma che schifo!*"

"But Italy is famous for garlic..."

"For using it in *cooking*, Perry, not as a *compulsion!*" retorted Brezzi.

Murano walked in. "Ah! So your American friend is here," he said to Brezzi in Italian. "Go, take the afternoon off—I can handle things while you're away."

Brezzi thanked him and turned to Donohue. "Come, Perry, I have the afternoon off." They went outside. Donohue squinted as the sun peeked through the clouds. "What shall we do, Henri? Act like tourists?"

"Later, Perry. I need to get this head situation fixed, once and for all. I got a pack of very nervous hotel owners breathing down my neck, and nothing to show for almost five weeks' worth of investigation. If I don't solve this murder before *Pasqua*, it'll be *my* head that is found floating in these waters."

They got in the patrol boat and Brezzi started it. Perry shouted over the engine noise as they pulled out, "When is *Pasqua*, anyway?"

Brezzi steered the agile boat into the main line of traffic, following a small freighter. "Uh, what do you call it in English—ah! Easter."

Donohue shook his head. "When is it this year? I never know. Kinda like Daylight Savings Time—nobody knows when that starts either..." He looked down the unfamiliar waterway. "Where are we headed, by the way?"

A big gust of wind caused the bow to rise. Brezzi shouted, "To the mainland. I had to store our 'package' there, to keep it away from the neighbors! You'll see."

~ ~ ~

They pulled up to the pier. Brezzi jumped out and tied the boat to a dilapidated mooring post. "It's over here," he said, pointing to a warehouse.

Donohue looked skeptical. "A meat packing place?"

"That is right! I didn't think you understood Italian, Perry!"

"I don't, but I sure remember that smell. Reminds me of Lubbock, Texas. I had an uncle who used to work in a slaughterhouse there."

Brezzi knocked on the door, said a few words in Italian and indicated to Donohue to wait. Brezzi went inside. After a few minutes, he re-emerged, clad head to foot in full thermal gear, and beckoned for Donohue to follow. Brezzi winked, "You need formal wear to go inside, Perry, just like those exclusive restaurants on Broadway…" He indicated another thermal outfit hanging next to the freezer door.

"I bet it's 'one size fits all'," muttered Donohue darkly. He took the bulky suit off the hook and struggled to put it on over his street clothes. It was about three sizes too big. He tightened the belt loop as far as it would go. Brezzi motioned for Perry to follow, then walked into what looked like a meat locker. Donohue stepped inside.

It was a meat locker.

Brezzi was nowhere to be seen. Livestock carcasses hung everywhere. Donohue peered around the frosty confines. He noticed another heavy door behind some hanging poultry. He heard the sound of something being lifted. Feet clattered on a steel ladder. A conveyor belt started.

Even though he was clad in the insulated suit, Donohue still had to tap his feet to keep warm as he waited.

The door budged and groaned, then popped open, sending a fine mist of ice crystals flying. Brezzi finally appeared, carrying what appeared to be an oversized translucent white plastic paint container. Perry noticed a reddish blob in the middle. Brezzi set it down and shrugged apologetically. "Sorry, Perry. It was the best we could do. I was lucky to find this meat packer on the mainland, a guy who wouldn't ask too many questions." He set it down with a soft 'thud.'

Donohue opened the top. "*Jesus!*"

Brezzi said dryly, "I thought the lipstick was a nice touch."

Donohue gingerly shook the head out onto the stainless steel table.

Brezzi tapped the head with his gloved forefinger. "Let's say you're right about this guy being famous or something. I'd say he was either in business or… politics."

Donohue looked at him doubtfully. "You think so?"

"Yes, Perry, I think so." Brezzi rolled the head over, exposing the severed neck muscles. "See here? That's a silicon chip!" he pointed triumphantly. The enlarged the image to reveal a tiny rectangle sewn under a loose flap of skin close at the base of the neck.

Donohue's eyes widened. "Well, I'll be! Our man's been uploaded into Virtual Space!"

Brezzi nodded approvingly, "Like Berlusconi."

Seeing Donohue's puzzled look, Henri laughed. "I don't expect

Americans to remember Italian prime ministers—we've had so many, more than a hundred since World War II."

Donohue's eyes got even wider. "You got a *virtual* Prime Minister?"

"*Ex*-Prime Minister," corrected Brezzi. "Berlusconi was PM twice, the last time at the turn of the Millennium. But he was also owner of a media empire, including three TV networks and lots more, Internet, virtual gladiator shows and so on. When his health began to fail, he had his personality uploaded to a big computer, right when the technology was new, and then he willed his entire fortune to his virtual self."

"Bet that caused a stink with the relatives..." commented Donohue.

"In the whole European Union. The Central Court in Brussels had to rule on it. But Berlusconi eventually won, long after his physical body was buried at sea. So now the Virtual Berlusconi still runs his companies and still makes tons of money, so everybody's happy. I've even heard rumors he bought out the Mafia's monopoly on garbage collection in South Italy."

"Too bad we don't have any rumors about this guy here," said Donohue. He carefully took a smudge of the lipstick on a piece of sulfur-free cellophane and put it in an evidence envelope. He turned the head over slowly and laid it back on the examining table. "I'm no expert, but it looks like it's still in remarkably good shape, considering..." He bent closer and examined the face. "You're right, Henri, he does look American." He ran a gloved finger over the frosted and hairless forehead. "Somehow, he looks familiar, but I can't place the face."

Brezzi raised his eyebrows. "He can't have been a movie star, not with that face."

"Movie star?" smirked Perry, "Ha! We don't have any more flesh-and-blood ones—where you been, Henri? They're all computer-generated now, or re-animated 'oldies' from the 1940's like Humphrey Bogart. The real ones priced themselves out of the market 5-10 years ago. They are still on strike, as far as I know."

Brezzi looked up in surprise. "*Really?* I never watch movies, so I never noticed. America's such a crazy place..." Brezzi put the head back in the container.

They stepped outside and took off the outfits.

Brezzi said "American or not, we can't keep him any longer. Today I must take him back to the Stazione. " He picked up the container and they walked back to the boat.

~ ~ ~

Brezzi stepped off the boat. Donohue glanced at the carton. "Too bad we couldn't take those insulated gloves with us. That thing's *cold.*"

"I think I got some fur gloves." Brezzi went inside. He came back with only one pair. "You can have these, I'll use the rubber gloves, Perry." He put them on and Donohue did the same. "Here, I carry it inside."

"I'll help." Donohue grabbed one end and they took it inside quickly. They set it on Brezzi's desk.

Brezzi cleared papers out of the way. "I don't think it will fit in the fridge."

"I need to get this to New York before any more damage occurs." said Perry. "Can I use your phone?"

Suddenly hopeful, Brezzi asked. "So you *can* take it with you?"

"Yeah, but it will have to be on the sly. Here's what I'll do: I need to get my flight re-routed so Chief Shabazz—my boss—won't catch up with me before I sneak the head to our lab. You're with Interpol, right? Can you write a letter to the airline as an official Interpol... uh, official, vouching for me?"

Brezzi looked shocked. "You're *not* with Interpol?"

"Nope." Donohue shrugged, "Never thought I'd need to be." He looked at his watch. "Shit—forget it, we don't have enough time. I'll have to bluff my way through."

"Are you sure? I could have the papers ready by tomorrow," said Brezzi.

"That's too late—I need to be outta here by tonight, or Shabazz will really have it in for me. I want to be already in the office, working away when he comes stomping in and yelling for my head—pun intended."

"Here, look at this." Brezzi handed Donohue a plastic card.

Donohue squinted at it. "Your old Interpol exchange student card? What good would that do me? Besides, it's got your photo..."

"That one does, this one has *yours*," grinned Brezzi, as a new card popped out of the ancient pneumatic card printer next to the coffee machine. "As acting chief, I'm allowed to give temporary cards to my staff." He took the old card and gave Perry the new one. "Congratulations on your promotion. See? It really *does* pay to be a member. Just take it with you. And work a bit more on your Italian accent..."

"*Grazie*, Henri." Donohue pocketed the card. "Now, all I need is to get my plane ticket."

"Here, take my phone." Brezzi handed it to Donohue. "Just call the airport here. We have most of the major airlines."

Perry tried the first three listings in the phone display. "Jesus!" He clapped the phone shut.

"What?"

"They all have automated menus—in Italian!"

"What did you expect? Here, let me do it." Brezzi took the phone. Impatiently, he tapped his fingers as the options menu droned on in his earpiece. Finally, he exclaimed, "Ah!" He held up a hand-held touch-tone pad, punched the code and held it to the earpiece. "I can't believe they put 'menu in English' as option '39' on the language menu, right after Bulgarian..."

He tapped in several more commands, then handed the phone back to Donohue, who mimed along with the recorded message, "Please hold the line, your call *is* important..."

After several minutes, Donohue began yelling again. "Goddammit!" He jabbed angrily on the touch pad buttons.

Brezzi looked over Perry's shoulder. "What's wrong now?"

"Fucking automated menus! Where's the goddamned pound key?"

"There," Brezzi pointed to a tiny button on the side. Donohue jabbed at it unsuccessfully. "Goddamn it, Henri! Can't you Italians make proper touch pads?"

"It's a GE," said Brezzi dryly. "Here, let me do it." He took the phone and touch pad and then jabbed the pound button with a paper clip. He handed it back to Donohue.

Twenty minutes later, Donohue was finally able to get a live operator. "I don't believe it—a *live person actually works* here!"

The phone operator laughed politely, "Yes sir. Can you hold?"

"NO! I CAN'T!! DON'T HANG UP!!!"

"Sir, will you *please* stop shouting?"

"This is Captain Perry Donohue, of the New York Police Department. I *need* to make some changes to my return flight ticket..."

"Sir, what changes do you need? Normally tickets are non-exchangeable."

"This is official police business. I need to leave a day earlier and I have cargo that needs to be deep-frozen, preferably in liquid nitrogen."

"Sir, we normally need special authorization..."

Donohue said, "Lady, this is Interpol business, and any delays coming from your side may aid terrorist networks. Time is of the essence!"

"Sir, first we normally need formal authorization from the US Consulate in your area..."

"Then connect me with your boss," said Donohue, taking the phone with him into the bathroom.

Five minutes later, he re-emerged and handed the phone back to Brezzi, who raised an eyebrow. "*And?*"

Perry smiled in relief. "I *think* it's all worked out. I said we had vital evidence to take to the FBI. I hope I can slide through inconspicuously—because I'm facing a shit rain for coming over here and abandoning the Phantoms case..."

Brezzi held out his arms. "Perry, why not let me help out? Maybe the Phantoms also operate overseas. I *do* owe you a favor..."

Donohue looked bemusedly at all the antiquated equipment in the office. "Henri, I don't want to piss you off, but do you really think you have the equipment to hunt down the most high-tech gang in the world?"

"You have all that high-tech stuff in New York, but it hasn't helped you so far. Our technology may be old, but at least I know how to work it."

Donohue shrugged. "Oh hell, why not? I'll send you the whole file if you want. You got UPS in Italy?"

Henri rolled his eyes, "Perry, we even got FedEx..."

Donohue rubbed his eyes. "Too bad all you can't figure out the time difference between Italy and New York..."

Henri suppressed a grin. "That really did bother you?"

"Yeah, you roused me out of a sound sleep. Why didn't you just send me a voice mail message over the Internet?"

Brezzi shook his head. "Perry, I got five different e-mail accounts, all with different passwords, and I can't remember any of them... Except the one I share with my wife, she always knows it. But she wasn't home then."

Donohue laughed. "I got the same problem. It's a hell of a lot easier to pick up the phone."

Brezzi put his hands to his face, "And all those instant message providers want you to sign up for e-mail first—with a password that is 15 letters or longer."

"Doesn't the Venetian Police Dept. have its own secure server?"

Brezzi shook his head emphatically. "We have to share one with the Carabinieri. Talk about insecure—those idiots wouldn't know a security leak if it came up and pissed on them."

"Speaking of..." Perry walked over to the tiny bathroom next to the closet. He reached in the cabinet and pulled out a roll of toilet paper. "I don't know how you Italians cope with this."

Brezzi tilted his head. "What's wrong with it?"

"You could mistake it for sandpaper..." Donohue pulled off a piece and mimed sanding the wall.

Brezzi smiled lopsidedly. "Perry, I'll let you in on a big secret. *Spit on it* first before you wipe." Seeing Perry's look, he added, "*Really*. It's not like you'll infect your..."

"OK, *okay*, I get the idea!" Donohue walked to the window and looked out. He watched a few boats go past "I'd like to come back someday, Henri, but as a tourist. But I'm bringing my own toilet paper, first."

"And leave what behind? Your underwear?" Brezzi fired back.

Perry waved at him to be silent. He pointed out the window. "Henri, who is that group of men approaching here?"

Brezzi looked out. "*Cazzo!* The hoteliers! They want to know about the head!" Brezzi ran around, gathering up all of Donohue's things. "Perry—quick, you got to leave—go now and take the head out the side door!" Brezzi grabbed the container with the head, handed it to Donohue, then rushed him through a pair of connecting offices to the back entrance. "Perry, as soon as you know—eh, something, you—eh, call me, OK?"

"Yeah, I'll do that Henri," Donohue untangled the sleeves of his coat as he put it on. He grabbed the thermal container and took off down the alley.

~ ~ ~

The Vaporetto boat maneuvered into the dock and unloaded its passengers. Donohue kept a firm grasp on his suitcase as its motorized wheels clicked and rotated uselessly in the air. Suddenly, he realized he was missing something. He looked frantically around.

He started yelling "*Wait—Aspetta! Aspetta!*" as he desperately dashed back and jumped on the Vaporetto and almost fell on the slippery deck, right before the boat was about to pull out again. The gate attendant started yelling at him and gesturing as Donohue ran back in the covered cabin.

He ran back out with the thermal container and smiled apologetically. The attendant put a hand to his forehead but opened the rope gate again anyway.

Donohue went to the information desk and pointed to the container. "*Parle ingles?*"

The man nodded curtly. "Si."

Donohue flashed his badge and Brezzi's Interpol credentials. "Do you have cold storage?"

The man looked puzzled "*Non lo so...* eh, maybe."

Donohue mimed shivering and the man looked more confused. Perry thumbed through his guidebook. "Eh... *Freddo... mettere in cella frigorifera,*" he gestured, indicating the container.

"Ah!" the man pointed to the container. "On the plane?"

Donohue nodded. "*Si!*"

The man summoned two uniformed customs officials, who came up and turned the container over with dubious looks. They conversed with each other in rapid-fire Italian and were just about to open it for a look. The second man opened up a penknife and made to slit the packing tape. A third man came over to look. Nearby passengers waiting to check in luggage began craning their necks.

Donohue felt his heart racing.

"Ah! Ispettore Brezzi!" said the first, pointing to the return address label.

Donohue nodded back with relief and pointed to the label. "Si! Brezzi!"

The three men escorted Perry to the front of the queue amid protests from other passengers, where he signed several unfamiliar documents. Then the container was handed to the airline security and his baggage was checked in without hassle.

Donohue was among the first to board. Mindful of the airline's rules, he switched off his cell phone. He was delighted to see his ticket had been changed to first class.

As he settled into the oversized chair and looked out the window, he could see Brezzi waving frantically in the departure gate. He smiled and waved back.

~ ~ ~

Brezzi came storming in the police station, slamming the door. "*Cazzo!*"

he yelled, causing Murano to spill his coffee. He looked at Brezzi inquisitively. "What's wrong?"

"I forgot to tell Donohue about the man I shot in the airport!" He looked at the old rotary phone on his desk, sighed and rummaged around in his desk for his mobile. "I hope I can reach him. I don't want to leave a voice mail message."

"*Capito*," agreed Murano, mopping up the rest of his coffee with a cloth. Brezzi began dialing.

An hour later, he hit the redial button on his mobile phone for the umpteenth time. "*Merda!* No answer. Why is it I always remember things too late?"

Murano shrugged. "Perhaps you have too many things in your head? Send him an e-mail."

Brezzi said "Ah!" He pulled out his mobile phone again, took a pen and started laboriously tapping in a short missive.

~ ~ ~

Perry almost missed making his connecting flight because fog delayed his takeoff from Venice for 90 minutes. He had to rush from one end of Paris-Orly to the other, only making his plane with two minutes to spare.

The return flight from Paris was bumpy. Perry began to regret not having forked over the extra $400 to fly Mach 10 and arrive Stateside in roughly 35 minutes. He rued it even more after he spilled red wine all over himself and a couple of neighboring passengers.

It took eight napkins to clean up the mess. For the rest of the flight, he would be tormented by the wine fumes.

He had a bulkhead seat next to the urinals. Throughout the flight, streams of people went in and out of the toilet. He began to wonder, *what happens to all that waste water?* He knew damned well he'd never seen a plane hooked up to a sewage pump.

He daubed up the last of the wine from his seat. He retrieved his CD player. Ancient by today's standards, it was the one device that would still work if it got wet. And it wouldn't get fucked up with every direction change the plane made or fade in and out when the solar flares kicked in. One huge blast of static on a flight to Nashville had been enough for him to chuck his satellite radio in the trash.

He set his watch to Eastern Time and reclined his seat. *Best not to worry about US Customs until the plane landed...*

Chapter 8
NEW YORK CYBERPOST
Insecticide ban upheld

The US Supreme Court ruled against the pesticides industry yesterday, saying the 5-year-old FDA emergency ban on insecticides was "absolutely necessary to preserve life on Earth as we know it." Chief Justice James "Jack" Osborne sided with the majority in saying "any further damage to the ozone layer would cause catastrophic climate changes and destroy the worldwide insurance industry in the process." He added, "Americans will simply have to find other ways to control household and outdoor pests. We are the world's most innovative land, and I have every confidence we will find an alternative solution very soon."

Leading pesticide officials were not immediately available after the ruling, which came at the surprising time of 12:39 am this morning.

Monday evening, February 29, 8:30 pm:

The massive plane set its wheels down in Baltimore with a jolt, waking Donohue from his slumber. He felt badly jet-lagged as he righted himself. Squinting in the momentarily intense glare of the interior lights, Perry saw a strange sparkly substance all over his shirt. It took several moments before he realized he must have been drooling all over his shirt and it had crystallized as it dried.

Before the plane had finished taxiing back to the terminal, he was up and already walking to the exit door. He flashed his badge at the sour-faced stewardess. She was obviously not impressed by his unshaven, rumpled appearance. "Sir, please remain seated until the plane is docked."

Perry asked, "Can I get the container I put in cold storage now?"

She eyed him coldly. "Sir, you have to wait. It has to go through customs first."

Perry pointed at his badge, "I have no time for that. This is official NYPD business, lady."

She burst out laughing. "In *Baltimore?!* Aren't you a bit out of your jurisdiction, shorty?"

Perry briefly considered popping the buttons on her blouse.

The exit door opened, saving Donohue from further humiliation. Without another word, he stormed out. She called out behind him, "Have a *nice* day, sir!" and reached back to pick up the phone to security.

Donohue raced out, pushing past the other passengers and rushing to a men's room.

Perry sat in a vacant bathroom stall and began thinking furiously. He knew that his NYPD badge would carry no weight with US Customs. *This could be a huge dilemma...* Best to leave the head unclaimed, he reasoned. He flushed, washed his hands and walked back out.

It was then that he saw the three dark-suited men walking in a pack towards Customs.

Oh shit. Has to be FBI... Donohue tried to appear nonchalant. Without any concept of what he was looking for, he began looking for something, *any*thing that looked like a way out of the mess he could see coming his way.

He had to slow down several times to avoid drawing looks from all the National Guardsmen patrolling with dogs. The whole scene seemed reminiscent of an old war movie.

Just as he was just about to really panic, he spotted a UPS counter up the corridor.

He walked straight up to the employee door and muttered, "Sorry I'm late," at the desk help as he went through the service door.

As he had guessed, the locker room was close by. He went in and was pleased that the room was empty. He reached in the laundry bin and grabbed a uniform with 'small' written on the tag. He quickly put it on and dumped his old clothes in his carry-on bag. The trousers started to slide down his waist before he remembered to retrieve his belt. The uniform was not a great fit and it stunk, but it would have to do.

The only thing missing was a hat. He looked around, hoping to spot an extra one.

Grabbing a chair, he stood on it and peered over the lockers. *There!* And it was adjustable. *Elvis be praised!*

Stepping out of the locker room, he saw a table with the familiar mobile tracking device-cum-signature pads. He quickly grabbed one and hooked it to his belt. He grabbed his carry-on and slung it across his back.

He ran back out into the main airport corridor and was lucky enough to hitch a ride on a cushman cart heading back to the boarding gates. He clambered on and stuffed his carry-on under his legs.

Donohue turned and said "Thanks!" to the driver, a dangerous looking 300 lb. Samoan, who nodded and asked, "Where ya headed, buddy?"

Pulling the borrowed UPS cap down low over his face, Donohue said, "Good question. I got a last-minute overnight package to pick up from a incoming flight from Paris..."

"Yeah? Which airline?"

Donohue told him as they rode past the pack of FBI men walking rapidly in the same direction.

The Samoan pointed to a short corridor on the right. "I'll drop you off over by the employee lounge. It's right next door to the International Flights terminal."

Donohue thanked him and jumped off, carry-on bag swinging dangerously. He looked through the big bay windows of an unused gate and saw a group of foreign airline insignias. He quickly found the crew door. He tried the knob and was shocked to find it was unlocked. He raced through and ran down the portable stairs to the tarmac. As luck would have it, he found himself among the jets from the correct airline. He quickly glanced around. The FBI types weren't in evidence. Yet.

He dodged the baggage wagons going past and walked quickly to a baggage specialist wearing the airline's uniform. "'Scuse me—is this the flight from Paris? I got a special pick-up to make."

The specialist nodded, "Yup, that's the one—whatcha looking for?"

"Deep freeze container, has 'medical samples' stickers all over it."

"Oh yeah—I just saw that one—we had to set it aside for Customs..."

Donohue tapped the hand-held signature pad, "We already got the OK from Customs—it's a rush-rush delivery, has to be delivered by 10 tonight..."

The man looked at his watch. "That's cutting it *real* close—it's 9:20 already." He pointed to a parked baggage cart that was fully loaded. "There! I see it on the upper rack!"

Donohue ran over and reached up to slide it off. The carrier came over. "Sure you can handle it?"

Perry grunted and heaved the container on his shoulder. "Sure, no prob. Thanks a lot!" He ran and jumped on the back of a passing cart.

Luckily the driver was unaware of his presence, as the piles of baggage hid Donohue nicely from view. Knowing that he was carrying too much, Perry quickly stuffed his carry-on in a gap between two soft-sided suitcases and wedged himself against the container to keep it from falling off.

He stole a glance behind and quickly ducked down—right as the first FBI man went up to the same baggage specialist. He saw the specialist point in his direction as the cart rounded the corner to the baggage load-in area.

Donohue jumped off as the cart slowed, leaving his carry-on on the cart. He would have to claim the carry-on and his suitcase later.

He dashed up a portable staircase and ran inside to the main terminal, slamming the door behind him in his haste.

He set the container down and bent over, totally out of breath. It was then he noticed he had stepped into a totally alien environment. An art exhibit? He was surrounded by podiums filled with rows and rows of what looked like white plaster beanstalks of differing sizes. The spotlights set on the floor softly illuminated them, casting silhouettes on the white walls. Looking down, he saw small name plates at the base of each 'stalk'.

He heard footsteps coming up the aluminum steps, jarring him back to reality. He shouldered the container again and raced out of the room, zig-zagging through several exhibits before finding the way out.

"Sir! Sir, we're closed!" said a woman's voice behind him.

"Sorry—came up the wrong way," said Donohue. "Can you let me out the front?"

The woman let out a heavy sigh. "All right. Just let me turn off the burglar alarms first."

Donohue fidgeted while she bent over an electronic panel. Finally the sliding glass entrance doors opened.

Without thanking her, he dashed out the entranceway and slid on the newly-waxed floor, almost colliding with a sign in front that said 'Welcome to the John Waters Folk Art Exhibit - This Week: the Plastercasters.'

He was about to start trying to run and balance the container too when he saw an empty press shop to the left with the front grating pulled halfway down. He quickly slid the container inside, ducked below the grating. He hoisted the container again and slipped into the back room.

A newspaper vendor was loading unsold newspapers into a rental truck. "Hey pal, we're closed—can't you read?"

Donohue nodded impatiently, "Yeah, yeah, I know—listen, I need a lift real bad—My UPS truck just broke down, and I got a rush delivery here," he tapped the package.

The vendor looked him over and shrugged. "Sure, why not? Hop aboard. I just got this last stack to load up." He banded the papers and slammed them down, making the truck bounce. He pushed a button, lowering the front grating shut and locked the back door. "Let's hit the road!"

The truck roared off, with Donohue watching out the back, holding on to the loading ties. It was then that it occurred to him: *They can't be FBI—no FBI man would be caught dead wearing Birkenstocks and white socks with suits. So who the hell are they?*

The tallest of the three men emerged from the exhibit. "Jesus! Did you see the *size* of Hendrix's..."

"You dumb-ass!" snapped his colleague, an ill-tempered gnome with no hair. "Forget about that—our quarry's escaped!"

"How? We're surrounded by National Guardsmen..." He looked around and his smile faded. "He's gotta be here somewhere..."

"Oh yeah?" The other folded his arms. "Do *you* see him?"

"Uh..." the tall man looked around uncomfortably, "...nope."

The gnome glared at him. "You know what this means? Donner is gonna fry our asses when he finds out!"

"Don't worry," said the third, who walked in a decidedly Texan manner. "We'll catch up with him eventually." He held up a miniature digital camera and popped open the viewer. " Look, I got a image of his face. We'll put that in the computer system, ID him and nail his ass. After that, Donner will know what to do."

~ ~ ~

Monday, 11:00 pm:

The ringing phone startled Hayte out of a deep sleep. The flu had ruined most of his weekend. Sitting up like he'd been struck by lighting, he cursed when his head slammed the edge of his cedar headboard, and he knocked over the wireless phone as he groped around for the light. "*Do you know what time it is?*" he snarled into the receiver.

The voice on the other end sounded agitated. "It's me, Scotty Bunch—remember me?"

Hayte did. *That sad sack geneticist from GeniTech.* He exhaled slowly. "Yeah, Scotty. You're the world-famous inventor of our most famous street drug..."

"Don't be like that, Lieutenant. My work at GeniTech did some good—my anti-HIV gene mod saved a lot of lives..."

Hayte looked over at his clock and groaned. "Yeah, yeah, I know. Look, it's 2:30 in the morning—what do you want?"

Bunch lowered his voice, "It's about those robbers, the ones called The Phantoms..."

"What?" Hayte sat up in bed. His tone changed markedly, "I'm all ears, Scotty."

"I... think I recognized one of them from the TV pictures..."

Hayte sat up in bed. "*What? How...?*"

"It's a sensitive subject, something from my job..."

Hayte stared at the receiver for a moment. "Well, I'll be damned... Are you saying *GeniTech had something to do with this?*"

"Look, I can't talk, I'm in a bar... I need to meet you somewhere, somewhere nobody will see us."

"OK, can you meet me tomorrow evening at seven o'clock at a place called the Pickled Ape? It's right below the train tracks on 10th Avenue, turn left instead of going over, the number is 356-"

Bunch blurted, "I know the place, my cousin works as a 3D animator, he did the whole Lesbian Wrestling light show there. See you at seven p.m., Lieutenant." The line went dead.

"That's *captain*" said Hayte to the dial tone. He threw the phone aside, ignoring the sounds of bouncing plastic and mini batteries clanging loose on the parquet. He put the ice pack back on his head and closed his eyes.

~ ~ ~

Tuesday, March 1, 9 am:

As he went out of his apartment building, Hayte didn't really notice anything unusual at first. Slowly it began to dawn on him that all the people around him were walking strangely.

Very strangely.

Intrigued, he stopped and watched for a few moments. It was a spastic sort of heavy step, with no rhythm or real direction at all. *Definitely not a dance beat...*

After seeing the tenth person doing the same step, it occurred to Hayte to look down. His face wrinkled in disgust.

The sidewalk under his feet was alive. He bent down for a closer look. The concrete was crawling with newly-pupated flies, not yet able to fly.

And they were everywhere. A few were starting to take off. Hayte immediately started doing the same step, sliding his feet to smush as many as possible under his sneakers.

~ ~ ~

Tuesday, 12 noon:

Putting the UPS cap low over his eyes, Donohue snuck in the freight entrance of the White Elephant and quickly made his way to the NYPD DNA & Forensics lab.

As Perry came through the swinging double doors, Dietrich looked up from reading his newspaper. "Morning, Donohue. Chief Shabazz's been looking for-"

"I know, I know," said Donohue, setting the box down gingerly on the examination table, "but I needed to get this to you first. I need a complete DNA and chemical analysis on this."

Dietrich pushed his battered gold-rimmed spectacles up his pointed nose, "And what's the magic word?"

"Oh, *please*. This is an emergency—aren't you the least bit curious to find out what's inside?"

"Patience is a virtue, Donohue..." Dietrich bent over and examined the Italian customs slip "*Testa*... Why can't they write these damn things out in English? Where'd you get it?"

Perry pointed to the sticker on the side. "Venice."

Dietrich half-smiled. "What, you want me to autopsy anchovies?"

"Very funny. *Not!* Open it up, see for yourself."

"So it's not anchovies. But it had better be, next time..." Dietrich sliced through the thick metal bands with a large pair of sheet metal cutters. "Damn, this thing is cold—look at all the condensation..."

"Careful, it's packed in liquid nitrogen." cautioned Perry.

"Well, better put on those gloves, then." Dietrich handed him a pair, then put on his own.

Donohue put them on, but found the fingers were too small.

Dietrich grinned. "Oops, sorry about that. Those are women's gloves..."

Donohue settled for getting his thumbs and forefingers in halfway.

"Makes your hands look like lobster claws," said Dietrich wryly. He slid the frozen object out of the box and began to examine the covering before carefully unwrapping the black plastic, exposing the nose. "Hey! Looks like a normal everyday, cryogenically-preserved human head!" He slid it out of the plastic and examined it from all angles before placing it on an examining table. "What's the deal?"

Perry peered over his shoulder. "It's a long story. Do you remember the old Interpol exchange program we had?"

Dietrich raised an eyebrow. "Yeah, we still got it—bunch of new ones came in the week before last."

"Really? Well, one of the earlier ones, Inspector Brezzi from Venice, found this little fella floating in one of the local canals."

"Interesting..." Dietrich took the head and placed it in the MRX-AI scanner. He prodded the mouth open and bent forward for a closer look. "Hey, was this lipstick on it when it was in the water? That's impressive— I'll have to tell my wife about it, once I do a brand analysis..."

Donohue shook his head. "Brezzi tells me Interpol added the lipstick."

A look of disbelief crossed Dietrich's face. "Since *when* is Interpol doing makeovers for severed heads?"

"Obviously, they've been infiltrated by some syndicate—no, scratch that—by a bunch of *pranksters*..."

"Hell of a lot of effort to go to for a prank..." muttered Dietrich, now typing in commands at the console. Several head scans popped on the big flat monitor screen on the left.

"Tell me about it," agreed Perry. "Is it possible to get a probably cause of death *and* get a computer likeness up to Missing Persons, see if they can get a positive ID?"

Dietrich turned to him, "And what do *I* get in return?"

Donohue took off the gloves and reached in his borrowed uniform. He produced an envelope. "How does a free round-trip flight and accommodations for two to Venice grab you?"

Dietrich smiled broadly and snatched the tickets. "*Now* you're talking! I haven't had a vacation in *three years!*"

"I know the feeling..." Donohue turned to go. "Thanks, Dietrich."

Dietrich called behind him, "Oh, and one more thing—are free meals included?"

Donohue nodded. "Sure—just as long as you can keep this from Shabazz's attention."

"That's asking a lot." Dietrich ran a hand through his wavy gray hair. "I'll try, but I can't promise anything. Severed heads just naturally attract attention."

"What's that?" Donohue pointed to Dietrich's rolled-up newspaper. "Can I look at that a sec? Is that today's?"

"Yup, I just downloaded it a few minutes ago." Dietrich handed it to him.

Donohue spread the paper flat on the formica counter. The headline grabbed his attention immediately.

NEW YORK CYBERPOST
Television News Reporters Found Dead!

The bodies of three VNN reporters were unearthed yesterday on the grounds of a Weehawken, New Jersey graveyard. The reporters, Bernard Duncan, 37 , Barbara Delacroix, 41, and Zane Lewis, 29, missing since last month, were found in a freshly dug shallow grave in a neglected corner of the local cemetery. According to eyewitnesses, all bodies bore evidence of gunshot wounds, although local police officials refused to comment.

All three were last seen publicly seen broadcasting on-site during the most recent Phantoms robbery at the Chase Bank on Broadway.

"*Hmmm…*"Perry skimmed the rest of the article silently. "Can I get a copy of this?"

"You can take that one." Dietrich looked up and smiled quizzically. "I hope *you* weren't the one who shot them—I heard about your little stunt, shooting out the TV transmitters…"

Surprisingly, Donohue laughed. "No, not me. But I'll let you in on a little secret…"

Dietrich raised an eyebrow, "Do I really want to know?"

"OK, suit yourself, wise guy…" Perry smiled enigmatically, "It's about why Shabazz *can't* can my ass for discharging my gun at the TV staff…"

"Really?" Dietrich looked skeptical.

"*Really.* I think I'll keep it under my hat for now—the fewer people know about it, the better."

"Whatever…" shrugged Dietrich.

Donohue gave Dietrich a short salute. "Catch ya later. Let me know when you get those tests done."

"Okay, will do," said Dietrich, "Can you switch off the lights as you go?"

Donohue nodded, flicking the off switch. He strode out the swinging doors, leaving Dietrich illuminated eerily in the bluish light of the new array of head shots onscreen.

~ ~ ~

Wednesday, March 2:

It was almost sunrise. Dietrich was totally exasperated, and his head throbbed from the lack of sleep. He stared at the computer monitor, completely confounded by the autopsy readings, which made little sense at all.

"Age of subject: late 50s, early 60s. Chronic disruption of Broca's area indicates subject had little or no speech capability at TOD. Analysis of arterial walls indicates considerable cardiac trauma, including several areas with high potential for cerebral edemas. Subject tested positive for Chromosome B-23, indicating a family history of cardiac ailments. High concentrations of caffeine and nicotine residuals in fatty deposits. Strong likelihood that subject had Type A personality tendencies that contributed to fatal illness."

"Fatal *illness?*" Dietrich said under his breath.

He brought up the other screen. The news there was equally unpromising: "No matches in Missing Persons for the last 10 years."

As a last resort, he composed another e-mail and attached files of the front and side views. "Probably just a shot in the dark," he said to the screen as the mail icon blinked off, "But at least I can go home now." The apparatus made a short beep, indicating that the shut-down had been completed.

Dietrich switched off the lights, grabbed his coat and locked the doors.

~ ~ ~

At exactly eight o'clock, Hayte poked his head around Shabazz's door. "You wanted to see me, Chief?"

Chief Shabazz was looking out his office window. He turned and waved to a chair. "Please be seated, Captain."

Hayte sat down hesitantly. From the very first moment, Hayte felt uneasy to be around him. Just from his appearance, it was obvious that Shabazz was Black Muslim to an extreme. Close-cropped black hair with streaks of silver. A wide, flat nose, framed with heavy frown lines. Always, an immaculate jet black dress suit and white starched cuffs. His maroon bow tie was always perfectly in place.

Hayte found it easier to stare at the bow tie than to look into those penetrating, red-rimmed eyes, significantly magnified by frameless eyeglasses.

Shabazz walked over from the window and sat down. That was the first time Hayte noticed the Chief had a limp.

Shabazz folded his arms. "I assume, Captain, that you will want to get to work on the Phantoms case immediately."

Hayte coughed self-consciously. "Uh, Chief, that's what I wanted to talk with you about. I... really don't have time to handle it, sir. I still have the state bar exam to pass..."

Shabazz swiveled round in his chair and stared at his wall calendar. "Bar exams are held four times a year, Captain. I expect you to devote your full attention to this."

Hayte pulled a thick file out of his satchel and tapped it. "With all due respect, sir, I don't think you've given Captain Donohue a fair shake on this case—he got dumped on the robbery scene without *any* briefing beforehand. He was pretty much thrown in the deep end, *and* he still managed to rescue 30 hostages from a very dangerous situation."

"And completely trashed the bank interior in the process" added Shabazz harshly.

A hand reached over Hayte's shoulder and pulled out a sheet. He looked up and saw Shrini's angry face. Nobody had noticed her entering the room, but now she waved the paper in the air and chimed in, "It says here that most of the damage resulted because of the Phantoms *and* the Deto Squad's *questionable* decisions. For example, Nehru set the charges to *make* the safe door roll."

Shabazz glared at her. "Lieutenant Shrini, you're out of ORDER!"

She was unrepentant. "Sir, union rules say that I cannot be saddled with a merry-go-round of partners on a case. Donohue was the *third* one this month! Why do you *think* we can't make any progress? I have to constantly go back and brief every new officer from point zero, instead of trying to do any actual investigating. I say we should try and keep Capt. Donohue and quit hanging ourselves in the foot."

Shabazz shook his head. "That's *shooting* ourselves in the foot, Lieutenant. And Captain Donohue is unacceptable. It's a classic case of an officer self-destructing. An assignment he can't come to grips with..."

"Which *nobody* has come to grips with" said Shrini sharply.

Shabazz said dismissively, "As I was saying, the evidence is clear. First he loses his cool and discharges his weapon at unarmed civilians at the scene of a robbery..."

"Those TV reporters were blocking the way of the Deto Squad to the crime scene!" Shrini angrily retorted. "One more minute and you would have had 30 dead bank hostages on your hands. Think about that!"

Now, Shabazz glared at her. "It's the responsibility of the officer in charge to secure the crime scene."

Shrini folded her arms. "Not when we were outnumbered five to one by the press! Read my report—you'll see!"

"And if I read the report correctly, the press was already at the crime scene by the time Capt. Donohue was given command of the case" said Hayte evenly.

"That doesn't excuse the fact that he fired on *civilians*," Shabazz jabbed his index finger on the desk.

Hayte shook his head. "It so happens, Capt. Donohue stopped using real bullets about two and a half years ago—at the time, he went on record with the union leadership as saying the risks outweighed the benefits. Since then, he's been using the rubber riot pellets exclusively." "You can look at his ammo requisitions log yourself online."

Shabazz quickly downloaded the file and scanned it, mouthing the text soundlessly. He drummed his fingers and frowned. "Lieutenant Shrini, could you leave us for a moment? I have to discuss something with Capt.

Hayte *alone*."

Her face angry, she stalked out of the office without comment.

Shabazz said quietly, "So does this mean you're *refusing* to follow my orders to take over the Phantoms case, Captain Hayte?"

"Sir, I follow orders when they are reasonable *and* follow the guidelines established in the 2032 court settlement between the New York City government and the police union. If you want to give me a three-week transition period to fulfil my existing commitments, *as* the rules *specify*, then, sir, I will be happy to take over the case. Otherwise, sir, it might be more prudent to give Capt. Donohue another chance."

Shabazz looked him silently over for a moment. He exhaled noisily. "Okay, Captain. You seem to have all the answers. So tell me, where *is* Capt. Donohue? I'd sure like to talk with him."

"I'm working on that, Chief" answered Hayte, hesitantly. "I *think* he's back in town, but I'm not sure..."

"That isn't good enough, Captain—and you know it!" said Shabazz flatly. "I want him *here*, in *my* office by this time tomorrow." He threw up his hands. "It frankly amazes me that Donohue has gotten this far in the force. First he took unauthorized leave to fly to Europe..."

"Sir, union rules say every officer is *entitled* to paid holiday leave—and that was the first leave he had taken in over four years," said Hayte evenly. "As I understand it, he *did* give notice."

"And what about *now*? He was due back yesterday." Shabazz raised his eyebrows. "Have you got an answer for that?"

"Sir, he worked for years without any absenteeism. There *has* to be a good reason for this."

"Well, he can lie low all he wants—*without* pay. But, if he cares to *defend* himself, first he'll have to see me *tomorrow*, *then* come to the disciplinary hearing."

"Listen Chief..." Hayte chose his words carefully. "Keep him on the case. Give him 48 hours to report in. You really don't want to suspend Capt. Donohue..."

"Oh yeah? Try me!" A solitary bead of sweat rolled down Shabazz's cheek. "Donohue's a chronic hothead with a real talent for stirring up a hornet's nest!"

Hayte folded his arms. "Honestly, Perry Donohue's the only person that can crack the Phantoms case. Besides, nobody wants it. Everybody else knows it's a career-breaker."

"Including *you*?"

Hayte nodded. "Including *me*."

Shabazz let out an exasperated sigh. "*If* he surfaces within the next... alright, I'll make it *two* days... and provides a satisfactory explanation for his behavior." He turned away for a moment, then looked Hayte coldly in the eyes. "You really trust that *Cracker* so much?" The word almost seemed to echo in the room.

Hayte was shocked. "Are you still hung up by that color thing? Man, you Black Muslims ain't learned noth..."

"For your information, Captain, *no*, I don't trust those white devils!" Shabazz lowered his voice, "I can't *afford* to, not in *my* position. And we prefer the term 'Muslim', not *Black* Muslim."

"I'm sure Capt. Donohue prefers the term 'Caucasian'. Or even 'WASP', said Hayte.

"Captain, I don't care if he wants to be called green, black and blue, as long as he shows up within the next 48 hours. Is that clear, Captain?"

"Thank you, Chief." Hayte got up to leave.

As he walked out, Shabazz said, "Captain, if he doesn't show..."

"Yes, Chief?"

"If he doesn't show, consider your three-week 'transition' notice to be in effect—is that clear?"

Hayte nodded curtly and walked out.

~ ~ ~

Hayte peered over Shrini's cubicle. She was obviously still fuming as she jabbed at the touch-sensitive keypad.

She looked up "So?"

"We gotta find Perry in two days, otherwise the whole mess is in my lap." said Hayte.

"*Our* laps, you mean," said Shrini grimly. "So what are you planning to do now? All my traces on Perry's whereabouts are still ongoing."

"Nothing we can do, except call Perry's home phone, leave messages, or send e-mail and wait... but first, I got to go meet Scotty Bunch. He might have a lead on this Phantoms mess. Wish me luck."

"*Him?* You're going to need more than luck with that sleazebag. I still remember arresting him for soliciting. Wonder what kind of mess he's gotten into now?"

"Dunno. Probably something *unreal*..." Hayte rolled his eyes. "I'll let you know if it's anything useful."

~ ~ ~

The Wednesday night match was in full swing as Hayte entered the back room at the Pickled Ape, ducking just in time to avoid banging his head on the top of the entranceway.

Bunch was already seated at the back far corner, eyes fixed to the monitor bank. He waved at Hayte.

Hayte slid into the booth. "What do you got, Scott?"

Bunch's round face was perspiring. He downed a shot of Jägermeister and took a swig of beer as a chaser. He exhaled noisily. "I... I think one of our classified company projects is linked to your Phantoms problem..."

"What do you mean?" Hayte turned around and ordered a pia colada.

Bunch wiped the beer foam off his upper lip. "A U.S. government cloning program produced five distinct clone series several years ago. I *think* one of the series matches the face on the wanted bulletin your department sent out after the last robbery. I only caught a glimpse on TV, but I'm pretty sure."

A skeptical look crossed Hayte's face. "What do you mean, *series?*"

"I mean *exactly* that—production series of human clones." Bunch said flatly. "We got the Government commission to produce artificial zygotes a decade ago, but until 2039, we weren't able to get the test cultures to survive beyond the second month. Then me and a colleague, Dr. Caramond made a breakthrough about two years ago. We made amazing progress after that. We came up with five different lines of clones with potential lifespans that rival our own—unfortunately, that was a bit *too* much longevity…"

"What do you mean?"

"There are two lines that had to be quarantined because of severe psychotic tendencies. They both were tagged as only for certain applications—nobody I know has any idea what for—but they were in no way intended to interact with the population at large. That directive came from the very top."

Rich raised his eyebrows. "So they *aren't* quarantined any more?"

"As far as I know, the one line still is. But, one or more of the 'Johnny B' line is loose."

"How do you know?"

"The Phantoms robberies. One of the suspect's faces in the video broadcast I saw is a Johnny B."

Hayte looked at him penetratingly. "Are you *sure?*"

Bunch fidgeted in his seat. "*Pretty* sure. If the TV images weren't manipulated…"

"Which station was it?"

"Dunno. VNN, I think…"

"Ho-boy…" Hayte put both elbows on the table and leaned forward. "Do you have *proof*, Scotty?"

Bunch looked nervously over his shoulder. "Yes. I've got extensive files and intra-firm communiqués on my home computer."

"Did you bring any of that?"

Bunch shook his head. "I came here straight from work. I haven't had the time to put them all on XD-ROM yet, anyway. The files are way too big, so I'll have to quadruple-compress them and do cross-indexing to direct you to the relevant stuff."

"How long will that take?"

"I don't want to arouse suspicion. Give me two or three weeks."

"Scotty, I need it much sooner. If you want me to do anything on this, you had better get it to me, pronto. Like tomorrow morning—I'll be at my desk at 9…"

Bunch looked like a deer caught in the headlights. "I *can't* come to the station, Lieuten..."

Hayte was in no mood for a flaky witness. "It's *Captain*, Scotty. And yes you *can*—we got a discrete back entrance through the City parking garage on the street behind the station. Just tap in my extension number in the keypad next to the big steel door."

Bunch flinched visibly and started looking round again. "I... I..."

Hayte tapped him on the wrist. "Look. If you're so goddamned nervous about this, Scotty, why not pull an all-nighter and get this hot potato off your hands?"

Bunch gripped his beer glass so tightly, Hayte expected it to shatter at any moment. Scotty sat silently chewing his lip. Finally he looked around and said, "Okay. I'll do it. I know I won't get any sleep tonight anyway."

Hayte took another sip. "Man, clones... people been talking about that shit for as long as I can remember, but hell, that was banned years ago..."

"Not really." Bunch seemed relieved at the change of subject. "The Bush Administration—the second one—banned human cloning as soon as the first successful trials leaked out to the press. But GeniTech never stopped working on their projects—I found a cached file of all these internal company communiqués from the first years of the ban. The DOD merely diverted the funding through other channels, like 'Combat Research'..."

Hayte paused in mid-swig. "Wait a second—so GeniTech *is* government funded?"

"Yes, but only for sur... certain projects." Bunch laughed a bit too loudly. "That particular Presidential Administration was *notorious* for its in-fighting—outside of fighting terrorists, anyway... My dad used to work in the State Department—he used to tell 'war' stories at cocktail parties about it all. The Attorney General was a Fundamentalist fruitcake, and the VeePee was a real shark who could've cared less about religious or moral scruples. And then there was that new group they formed as part of the Anti-Terrorist Bill—or Patriot Act—my dad used to rant and rave about that bunch..."

"Homeland Security?"

"No."

A puzzled frown crept across Hayte's face. "Office for Domestic Security?"

"No—another one they never made public. A covert operations group."

Hayte tilted his head skeptically. "C'mon, Scotty. This all sounds like some Cold War bullshit."

"No! I'm telling the truth—I still think they're the ones responsible for Dad's disappearance from the retirement home. *I'm* really afraid of them too." Bunch started watching the array of security monitors intently again. "According to what Dad told me, their main job is to erase all the mistakes other government agencies make—especially the covert stuff. They operate in the same way as the Death Squads in Chile during the Pinochet regime ..."

Rich looked even more skeptical. "You been reading too many spy novels, Scotty?"

Bunch's voice took on an even more imploring tone. "Look, I know it all sounds crazy—but take a look at the stuff I have before you write me off." He finished his beer in a long gulp, then laughed nervously. "You'll probably think I'm really bonkers when I tell you how to recognize their operatives..."

Hayte toyed with another pia colada. "Uh-huh..."

Bunch laughed again, a kind of yelp. "They... would you believe it—all wear...ha! Birkenstocks and white socks!"

Hayte choked on a mouthful of the sweet concoction. He finally gasped out, "*Those* guys?"

Bunch's eyes widened. "You *know* them?"

"Yeah..." Hayte momentarily looked scared too. He glanced at the monitors involuntarily, then recovered his composure. "But that's not important, Scotty. I *need* those files. ASAP."

Beads of sweat rolled down Bunch's chubby face. "I *can't* go to the station. They'll nail me for sure!"

Hayte sighed impatiently. "Scotty, I'll do you a *big* favor. I can see you before I go to work." He pulled out a paper scrap and a pen. "Normally, I don't give out my home address—but I'll do it this one time only on the condition that you *be* there at 7 am.—with the files."

Bunch nodded gratefully. "I'll be there, Lieu..."

"That's *Captain*. And Scott, please destroy that note after you memorize it."

"Okay, okay." Bunch's hands shook as tore it up. He downed another shot of Jägermeister and took a last swig of beer. Then he left a $50 bill on the table. "See you tomorrow, Lieutenant."

Hayte sat and watched him go, shoulders hunched and head bowed as always. He eyed the fifty dollars and deliberated paying for his drinks himself. Finally, he downed the dregs of his pina colada and said to himself, "Fuck it."

He got up and walked out, only just remembering to duck down again through the doorway.

~ ~ ~

Thursday, March 3, 3 am:
Hayte awoke to the sound of dull thumping. He half-smiled, expecting it to be more of Stanley's adult soundtrack mixing. He sat up and listened intently for the tell-tale sounds of sampled moans and sleazy jazz music.

Then he realized the noises weren't samples. They were coming from *his* apartment. Not just thumping, also intermittent buzzing.

He got up and tip-toed into his living room. Another thump. He watched the front door intently. Someone was pushing against it. A short buzz. He looked around, still sleepy and confused.

Suddenly he recognized what was happening. *Some bastard's trying to bypass the electronic lock.*

He dashed back and got his gun. He raced back silently on his bare feet. The thumps continued, slow and methodical. He took a deep breath, then pressed the 'door open' button on his remote. "FREEZE!" he bellowed, gun drawn.

Clearly startled, the hooded figure jumped back and ran down the hall before Hayte could fire. Hayte dashed after him.

The would-be intruder dashed in an open janitor's closet and slammed the door shut before Hayte could wedge his foot in the door.

Hayte was about to try and kick the door down when he remembered he was barefoot. He cursed, then began to smile.

He's trapped. No thief's gonna get out of there…

He leaned against the opposite wall, gun at the ready. His pulse slowed down. Minutes dragged by. He stifled a yawn.

His feet began to get very cold. With a start, he realized there was a breeze, coming out from under the closet door.

He suddenly remembered the short crowbar he kept in his old riot gear stash. He padded noiselessly down the hall, through his open door and to his living room closet. He fished around in the darkness.

There, in the canvas bag next to his face shield. He grabbed the bag off the top shelf and rummaged in it until he found the crowbar. He raced back down the hall.

Two tries with the crowbar and the door popped open in a shower of splintering wood. He cursed again, aloud this time. *Empty.*

The tiny vent window at the top of the back wall was open. He switched on the light. *Nothing but goddamn cleaning supplies.*

He got on a foot stool and tried to look out the window, but his head was too big for the opening. By now, he was totally perplexed. *Could anyone human fit through an opening that size?*

He shut the closet as best he could and went back to his front door. He saw the scrape marks around the electronic key slot. He went inside, found his digital camera and took photos of the slot.

After searching fruitlessly for further clues, he shut the front door, rolled the sofa against it, and went back to bed. It would be an uneasy rest of the night.

~ ~ ~

Brooklyn, 3:30 am:

Donohue got up and was momentarily spooked by a multitude of reddish points of bright light in the darkness. He froze in mid-step and tried to focus.

One cluster looked like a series of numbers, but the figures refused to make sense. He rubbed his eyes.

Slowly it hit him that his framed pictures were reflecting the displays of his answering machine, rotary light timer, computer on standby and satellite-controlled digital luminous clock.

He exhaled slowly and rubbed his eyes again. "Jee-sus. I *am* working too hard..." he said to the darkness. "This can't go on like this... *can it?*"

Chapter 9

NEW YORK CYBERPOST
'Giftwrapping' to Solve
Noise Day Plague?

*Today, Mayor Clinton announced that the Norton-Humes building complex
would be covered in a thin transparent shroud designed to prevent Noise Days
from ever happening again. The Mayor's Office was forced to declare Noise Days
almost immediately after the buildings were unveiled, as the space-age architecture
and its unique window installations produced a now-notorious piercing whistle
plaguing Manhattan on windy days. Local residents have been forced to wear
OSHA-approved ear protection to endure the sound, a whistling so intense that it
was unbearable to the human ear. Repeated attempts to solve the problem using
conventional solutions have all failed.*

"Don't call it a condom!" the mayor snapped angrily at one reporter.

~ ~ ~

Thursday, 7:45 am:

It was a meeting Donohue was not looking forward to. He went to the
men's room several times. Each time he came out, he darted a tense glance
upstairs to see if the lights in the Chief's office were on. They were still out.
He walked over to the water cooler and back.

Finally the lights went on. He quickly climbed the stairs and poked his
head in the door. "You wanted to see me, Ch..."

"No," laughed the cleaning lady, "Never seen anything like it—all these
fellas wantin' to see da Chief." She shook her head and emptied the
wastebaskets. "Ah thinks he's a-comin' in later dis mornin', but Ah dunno
for sure."

"Uh-huh. Thanks." Donohue shoved his hands in his pockets and went back downstairs.

"Might as well work on the Phantoms stuff," he muttered under his breath. He switched on the monitor, logged in and made the necessary file requisitions.

One by one, the 24 faces came onscreen, each with "No previous record" written below. He started reviewing his list of leads to follow up. He pondered swallowing his pride and contacting the FBI about putting them all on the Most Wanted list. As he stared at the images, he started making copious notes, losing all track of time in the process. Finally, he stopped and rubbed his eyes.

"Glad to see you at work again, Captain..." said a voice behind him.

Startled, Donohue swiveled around. "Hello, Chief. The cleaning lady said you'd be in late."

"She was right. It *is* ten o'clock, you know."

Donohue looked at his watch. "Oh."

Shabazz bent over to look at the displays. "Those the Phantoms?"

Perry nodded, "Yessir. Absolutely no priors on any of them. No 'finds' with the Facial Recognition Software, *nothing*. I was thinking of trying to get the FBI to put 'em on the Most Wanted..."

"Gotta set a bigger reward first," said Shabazz. "$10,000 is chicken feed to the Feds. In your absence, I've petitioned New York State to up the finder's fee, but they're still saying it's a local problem, and that's probably what the FBI's gonna say too."

Donohue leaned his head on his elbows. "Which means they're afraid of getting the blame if this doesn't get solved."

"Which is why *you* gotta solve it. I suggest you try the National District Attorneys Association—they got links to State Police agencies all over New England." Shabazz moved a stack of printouts off a neighboring chair and sat down. "Captain, I'll cut to the chase. You show me significant progress on this case and I'll take you off the Disciplinary Hearing list. And, I want a progress report every 48 hours. Is that clear?"

Perry nodded, his throat dry. He coughed and took another sip of water. "Can we make it a weekly report—give me more time to do follow-up, instead of report writing when there's more field work to be done..."

Shabazz was silent for a few moments. "All right," he finally said, "Weekly. Make it the first thing every Monday." He reached in his wallet and pulled out a business card. He stuck it in Donohue's shirt pocket. "Use this Intranet address. It's encrypted." He walked out without waiting for a reply.

Donohue closed his eyes and exhaled very slowly. Then he slowly began making a list of things to do.

He pulled out the card. It was for a local mosque in Harlem.

~ ~ ~

Hayte got up at six-thirty, feeling somewhat the worse for wear. The morning sky was a deep, beautiful blue.

Seven o'clock came and went, but no Scotty Bunch. Hayte impatiently channel-surfed through the insipid morning shows but gave up after finding more commercials than he could bear. He started pacing around, wanting to go outside. He looked at the wall clock, with its twin silvery dots pulsing with the passing seconds. He debated whether to file a report on the attempted break-in. Finally he said "Fuck it" and reached for his coat.

The door chimes sounded. Hayte raced to the door and opened it.

Seeing Hayte's expression, Stanley Bialystok looked insulted. "What? You were expecting the fucking Avon lady? Or are you waiting for Tupperware?"

Rich laughed in spite of himself, "Sorry, Stan. I was really expecting a witness for the Phantoms Case."

"Oh *yeah!* The Phantoms, I heard about those guys! Makin' the NYPD look pretty second-hand, aren't they? Oops—sorry, didn't mean to say that..."

"Come in, Stan," shrugged Hayte. "I won't take it personally—it's not my case, not really. I'm only doing part-time duty now, anyway."

Stanley stepped inside. "Only part-time? Great—got any free time this afternoon?"

Rich hesitated. "Well... I'm only putting in four hours today—but then I got to come back and cram for the bar exam."

Bialystok's eyes widened. "Bar exam? Ain't that for lawyers?"

"Yup. That's my next career move—do a couple years in the D.A.'s office as rep for the NYPD, then maybe try for a local circuit court."

Stan let out a low whistle. "Hoo. That's heavy stuff. Say, listen—can't the cramming wait till tomorrow? I mean, you can stick your nose in the books if you really want, but you're gonna miss some fun stuff..."

"What kind of 'fun stuff'?"

Stanley clapped Hayte on the shoulder. "Man, you're gonna love it! We got a location shot in the Boroughs, and I figured you'd like to come and watch—see how the pros work!" Seeing Rich's expression, Bialystok pressed further, "Come *on*, you can hit the books later—nobody's gonna know! Come on, you won't regret it—*trust me!* What time you get off from work?"

Hayte deliberated for a few moments. Finally he shrugged. "OK, I get off at one."

"Great!" Stanley slapped him on the shoulder. "I'll pick you up at the Dunkin' Donuts across the street from the White Elephant."

Seeing Hayte's look of surprise, Bialystok grinned, "Yeah, I *know* where you go to lunch, my man! My cousin's the landlord, rents the shop space to a Pakistani family. See ya at 1 pee-emm, sharp!"

~ ~ ~

Hayte made sure they got a dozen maple-frosted doughnuts before going on their way. Stanley stared at him enviously. "Man, I sure wish I could munch down a whole fucking dozen frosted donuts like that... How do you do it without blowing up to the size of a blimp?"

"My metabolism is just that way," said Hayte in between bites. "I'm hypoglycemic, so I got to keep eating to stay alert."

"Sounds like my appetite for pussy," grinned Stanley.

"Uh-huh..." said Hayte dubiously. He pulled out his cell phone and took out the batteries. Stanley looked at him, "Why'd you do that?"

"I want to make damn sure nobody can summon me on duty. No way do I want to have to explain where I am," he gave Stanley a look, "or what I'm doing there..."

Stanley laughed, "Quit worrying! You're gonna be in for a treat!" He guided the van over to an empty space on the curb. "What luck! I can actually leave this thing here without having to feed the parking meters every goddamned half-hour! Anyway, here we are."

The 'film studio' was a large top-story loft in the Bronx. "This is it? You got a porn studio in *the Bronx?*" said Hayte, opening the door.

Stanley laid a hand on his shoulder and hissed, "*Shh!* Not so goddamned *loud!* I don't want a pack of spectators gawking around!"

Hayte put his hand to his mouth. "Sorry."

They got out and entered through a heavily-insulated door, which made a 'whooshing' sound as it closed behind them. They got in a freight elevator, which clanked the whole way to the top. Stanley swung open the ancient iron grating and popped the steel door open to reveal a tiny carpeted hallway with a high-tech metal door. Stanley tapped in a five-digit code and the door opened noiselessly. They stepped inside. The door made a 'whoosh' and shut firmly behind them. Hayte was baffled. "Is this all you got?" he said, pointed to the three tiny laptops on a small desk in the corner.

"That's it!" Stanley said with a wave of his chubby hand, "Ain't hi-tech fabulous? Three computers are all we need to synchronize an entire film!"

"Really?" queried Hayte, munching on the last doughnut in the box. "So what kind of sound effect samples you got?"

Stanley popped up the screen and clicked on a menu. "You name it, we got it, moans, groans, vaginal burps..." He hit the sample.

Rich wrinkled his nose. "*What?*"

Stanley clicked on the sample again and grinned, "Hey, we're talking realism here—this is a discriminating audience, they want the real thing," he gestured with his hands, "...you know, the sound of *insertion*, that 'slurrrp...'"

"OK, okay, I get the picture, Stan." Hayte rolled his eyes. He pointed to the next room. "What's in here?"

"That's what we're here for! That's the 'recreation room'—today, we got it set up like a Turkish bordello! C'mon, let me introduce you to our actors!" Stanley opened the door with a flourish. "After you, sir!"

Hayte ducked his head to clear the top of the door frame. The room was filled with curvaceous women. An exotic brown-skinned woman in a bathrobe came up and looked Hayte over admiringly. "All right, Stan-lee! Blaxploitation! We're gonna re-make *Shaft*?"

Stan shook his head, "Sorry, Verona—he's just a guest. Meet Captain Richard Hayte of the NYPD."

"Too bad." She smiled and fingered his lapels. "Any time you want to *participate*, Captain, let me know... I'm sure I can find a *place* for you..." She looked at him over her shoulder as she walked gracefully to a gel-bed and sat down. "Oh well, back to 'bidness'." She unscrewed the cap of a liter of mineral water and winked at him. "Bottom's up..."

Hayte nodded self-consciously. "Uh, thanks."

Stanley looked around. "Where's Marilyn?"

"We're waiting for her—as *usual*!" said a big-chested brunette.

Stanley grabbed his cell phone. "God damn it! She's always late! I'm gonna..."

"Oh no you're not!" said a voice behind them. "I'm here! I'm here. Enough already!" In a blur of blonde hair, she bent over and squeezed Stanley's love handles. "I got up early, just for you, Stanley Bialystok, and all you do is bitch, bitch, bitch!"

"What you consider *early*, Marilyn, most people..."

She opened her compact and applied lipstick. "Man, get off my back." she whined. "C'mon, let's just go. I wanna get this scene done—is everybody ready?"

"Ready as we'll ever be" said Verona, rolling her eyes. "I'll go wake up our 'leading man,' I think he's asleep in the next room..."

Stanley wasn't through with Marilyn. "You see? Harry fell asleep—waiting for *you*..."

Marilyn snapped in his face, "*Don't* bug me, I did what you wanted—my bladder's so full, it's gonna *burst*!" She twisted her legs in pain.

Hayte looked mystified. "Doesn't this place have a toilet?"

She looked at him like he was a complete idiot. "Who is this guy?" she demanded. She turned and looked at Hayte suspiciously, "What? Were you born yesterday? Of *course* it fucking has a toilet!"

Stanley tapped Hayte on the shoulder and whispered, "Listen. I'll explain it to you. Let's take a walk to the control room..."

"Just a sec." Hayte poured himself a coffee and asked Marilyn, "So there *is* a toilet. Well, why don't you go and use it?"

She snapped, "That would ruin *everything*! Then we'd have to wait for another hour to be full again!"

Hayte stirred his coffee. "Let me get this straight. You *want* to have a full bladder?"

"YES! YES! OF COURSE!!" She tried to storm off, then winced at her full bladder pangs set in.

Stanley whispered in Hayte's ear. "Otherwise we have to re-do the whole fucking scene *again!* We'd have to wait around here all day to get ready to set it up!"

Hayte looked amazed. "What scene is *that*, Stanley?" He took a sip of coffee

Stanley said between clenched teeth, "The god*damn* choreographed golden shower scene."

Hayte almost choked on his coffee. "The choreographed *what?!*"

"Get in here!" Stanley yanked him back into the control room and shut the door. He sat Rich down and waved his arms. "Do you *know* how difficult it is to choreograph a golden shower scene? God forbid that we should screw up and have to shoot again—after mopping it all up and getting all the actors to tank up again and then wait..."

Hayte looked mortified. "Stanley, please promise me one thing..."

"You name it, Captain."

"Please tell me you didn't bring me to do the clean up work..."

Chapter 10
THE NEW YORK CYBERPOST
CAUSE OF AIRPORT BAT PLAGUE FOUND!

Today US and European scientists have published a controversial report that attributes recent bat plagues at international airports to—of all things—vaporized waste water dumped out of passenger planes after they land. "It seems not all the uric acid being dumped in the air is properly stored and treated before it's released into the environment," said EPA scientist Dr. Cyrus Pauling. "Some of it has been seeping into underground caverns, especially those located in Europe. [The uric acid] arouses the bats' reproductive urges to the point of hyperactivity"

The result is a mating frenzy that continues into the early morning hours, centered mainly around the airports with the worst contaminations and highest local bat populations. "You can't even think of landing planes in [expletive deleted] conditions like this" said one veteran airline pilot.

Monday March 7, 2 am:

It was almost deserted at the White Elephant. All the custodians had gone home and all the night duty patrolmen were out doing routine patrols. Inside, it was eerily quiet, save for the beeps from the security and fire detection systems overhead. Dietrich's face was only illuminated by his monitor screen, which was displaying cranial scans of several victims with fatal head wounds. The only other light was from the various dials and lighted displays on the other side of the lab.

Dietrich was not, however watching the screen, which began bouncing a large cartoon cannonball between the skull scans after the screen saver kicked in.

Instead he was focusing most of his attention on his pastrami on rye sandwich, which was hemorrhaging seriously from both sides, leaking out gobs of Dijon mustard with every bite he took. Over the noise of his own chewing and the 'plops' of mustard hitting the waxed paper, he heard a familiar sampled ding, meaning a new e-mail was demanding his attention.

It took several undersized paper napkins to clean up the mess on his hands enough before he could retrieve the cordless mouse and open the message. The mail was marked 'confidential - for your eyes only' and therefore unable to be opened by voice command—even if his mouth weren't full. After several attempts, the file popped open.

He read the first sentence and almost choked on the rest of his sandwich. He immediately clicked the 'call Donohue' icon.

No answer. He checked his watch.

He wiped off his fingers and the mouse. As he did, a thought occurred to him. He clicked on another directory and found Donohue's cell phone number. He clicked on it

A tired voice answered immediately, "Donohue here. What you need?"

"It's Dietrich—where are you, anyway?"

"In the goddamned White Elephant, at my desk, working late. What's up?"

"Ha! The last place I expected to find you. I'm here too, over in the lab. Listen, we gotta talk. I got the test results on your uh, parcel."

"Parcel?" Perry sounded a bit confused. "What do you mean?"

"The package from overseas. The head's a hot potato. I got a 40-page document attachment you've *got* to see."

"Can't you e-mail..."

"Nope. Too sensitive by far. Can you look at it now?"

"Not right now, Paul." Donohue stifled a yawn. "I'll come over and take a gander when I have time, but I'm up to my ass with bank surveillance camera footage at the moment. I'm working my butt off trying to get *somewhere* on this goddamn Phantoms case."

"Listen Perry, I think we could use some extra help on all of this—the head, the Phantoms—everything. Believe me, the extra brainpower might come in handy."

Dietrich could hear Donohue drumming his fingers on something. Finally, Perry said "All right. I'll see what I can do. Maybe I can bring Rich and Shrini with me. When should we meet?"

"It's got to be a late lunch. I got night shift all this month, and it's dead certain that nobody's gonna want to be awake when I get off at 4 am. You'll want to be wide awake for this, believe me."

"Well, I won't be, but Rich and Shrini could take up the slack. I'll leave them messages at their desks."

"All right...", Dietrich hung up the phone, muttering, "but you were the one so hot to find something on this head thing." He shrugged and started printing out a copy of the report. Just on a whim, he brought up the file on the severed head and stared at the 3-D image for several seconds. He hit his favorite key, the 'squiggle', which made the image shake violently, as if invisible hands were roughing it up. "What the hell were you doing in Venice, anyway?" he muttered to it, halfway expecting it to answer. Its jaw flapped open and shut, but no sounds came out.

~ ~ ~

Tuesday morning, March 8:

It was past sunrise and the sky was a dirty gray.

"Hey STAN!" Hayte's voice boomed down the hallway. "I was hoping to run into you!"

Stanley was on all fours, feeling around with his hands. Startled, he looked over his shoulder as he retrieved his key chip from the floor. "Oh! hiya, Rich…" he said doubtfully.

Hayte produced a brown manila envelope from his brown leather satchel. "This showed up in my mailbox yesterday. I opened it up by mistake…"

Stanley's eyes widened in panic. He started sweating profusely. "I, ah…ah…"

Richard saw his expression and started laughing. "Don't worry, Stan…" He pulled the magazine out, "Dog & Pony magazine. Hee-eeh-eh…" He handed it to the terrified Stanley, "I don't normally approve of stuff like this—but *this* is great!" He patted Stan on the shoulder and walked away, his laugh booming through the hall, until the door closed.

Then it was back to the books.

He brewed his second cup of coffee of the day, going back and forth to the computer as he memorized a list of possible test answers and compared it with a stack of open law books.

After an hour, he closed the laptop and rubbed his eyes. He looked at the clock. *Jeez, eight o'clock in the morning, and already I'm sick of this stuff…*

He decided to put in a few hours at the precinct. He got out of his pyjamas and into his warm-up suit. He threw the rest of his things into his satchel and headed out.

He opened the front door and was almost physically thrown backwards by a painful wave of sound attacking his eardrums. *Another Noise Day.*

In agony, he fumbled for his earplugs, dropping everything else in the process. He stuffed the earplugs in and pushed with his fingers until the plugs expanded enough to stop the pain. His vision un-blurred gradually.

He retrieved his key card and umbrella off the sidewalk and began the long trek uptown to his parking space across Canal Street.

He could still hear the shrieking blasts rise in pitch with every gust. His Lakers cap blew off. Everywhere along the way, people were holding their fingers in their ears. Richard had trouble getting past them all. He saw infants in strollers, their beet-red faces contorting horribly as they screamed inaudibly. He handed out what spare earplugs he had and moved on.

When he got to Canal Street, traffic was at a total standstill. He was just about to try a mad dash to the center line when he saw a NYPD

Mercedes stranded in the midst. He ran toward it, hoping to flag it down.

As he got closer, his eyes widened. He recognized Donohue behind the wheel.

Knowing Donohue would react badly if he came up and tapped on the window, Hayte decided on another tack. He fished out his cell phone and hit one of the programmed keys. Five cars ahead, he saw Perry look around. Hayte trotted up along the driver side window and waved his phone.

Startled, Donohue rolled down his window and immediately regretted it. He winced and grabbed his ears. Hayte reached inside, opened the rear door and quickly got in. He reached over the driver seat and pressed the window button until it closed. He took out one of his ear plugs and put it in his pocket. "Hi Perry, long time, no see. Forget your earplugs?"

"Thank Elvis you did that, Rich. I've been stuck in this mess for almost an hour—the Noise must've started after I left the White Elephant."

Hayte looked at the dark circles of Donohue's eyes. "So *that's* where you've been holed up—pulling all-nighters?"

Perry yawned and rubbed his eyes. "Yup. Dunno how I got off the suspended list, but I've got to solve this Phantoms thing or Shabazz will can my ass. And I need to talk to you, Rich, I got a lot of stuff to fill you in on..."

"I think we all should all get together—you, me, Shrini..."

"And Dietrich too," added Donohue.

"Okay. Say 12 noon at our favorite daytime place?"

Donohue nodded, "Yeah. That's way too early for the Pickled Ape, anyway."

Hayte pointed to the other side of the street as traffic began to inch forward. "Can you drop me off at the next intersection? My car's parked a block away."

"All right, but you'd better make it quick," said Donohue. "When traffic gets unsnarled, it's like a demolition derby. And give me a second or two warning before you open the door—that last blast of noise made my vision blur..."

Hayte saw a gap between the stranded trucks. He reinserted his ear plug and tapped Perry on the shoulder. "*Now!*"

Donohue stuck his fingers in his ears.

In one fluid motion, Hayte opened the door, leaped out, slammed it shut and raced across the street, oblivious to the inaudible honks and curses as he jumped across the hoods and trunk lids of the cars in the oncoming lanes. Donohue sipped coffee as he watched Hayte snake around a final truck and disappear down a side street. His lane started moving, so he put his coffee back in the holder and took his foot off the brake.

~ ~ ~

Tuesday, 12:15 pm:

The Dunkin' Donuts was almost empty, as the last dregs of the lunch crowd filtered out. Hayte took a swig of instant coffee, grimaced and dunked a donut in it instead.

"Don't look at *me*..." said Donohue, half-smiling. "We could've gone to Starbucks."

"We didn't all come here for coffee." Shrini fiddled with her teabag. "So, guys, what's the news? You got us all here for *something*..."

"Well, Rich and Dietrich both asked me to set up this meeting," said Donohue.

"Speaking of, where is Dietrich?" said Hayte, looking around.

"Probably still sleeping. He was pulling an all-nighter, last time I saw him." said Donohue.

Shrini pulled out her mobile and speed-dialed. She shook her head, "His cell phone's disconnected, so I bet he's not coming." She looked at Donohue. "Since you're the one making all the waves with Chief Shabazz, why not start the meeting, Perry?"

"Well, I don't know if it's *good* news, but I'm back and working on the Phantoms case, for what it's worth..." Donohue scratched his head. "But, there's one thing I can't figure out—how is it I was threatened with suspension from the Force *and* then reinstated in the space of 48 hours without so much as getting a hearing or getting chewed out by Shabazz? I didn't expect him, of all people, to be so reasonable..."

Shrini and Hayte exchanged knowing glances.

Perry noticed. "Aha, so you interceded on my behalf."

Hayte nodded.

Shrini added, "I almost had to kick the chief's balls to get him to listen to me." As she spoke, a stray strand of black hair kept clinging to the corner of her mouth. She tried repeatedly to brush it away. "Gaah! I'm sick of getting nowhere on this case, Perry. I argued that if anyone should've gotten the blame for the robbers escaping, it should have been the media—they obstructed the Deto Squad getting in. And this is a favor I can hold you to."

Donohue raised his glass. "So which one do I have to thank first?"

Richard said. "You can thank both of us. It wasn't fun, believe me."

Donohue grinned ruefully, "Do you want *one* apology, or a whole six-pack?"

Hayte waved him off. "No apology necessary." A grin snaked across his face. "Because I don't want the Phantoms case. I got the bar exam to pass."

Shrini folded her arms, "And I need someone to do the legwork while I do all these data scans on the video footage we got from the crime scene." She tilted her head slightly. "But why did you bugger off to Europe in the first place, Perry?"

Donohue smiled enigmatically. "I think you'll be quite intrigued. You remember our Interpol Exchange Program? Well one of our alumni from

Venice found a severed head in one of his canals..."

~ ~ ~

When he finished telling them, Shrini commented, "Venice must be a really quiet place. So much excitement over one head."

"Oh yeah," said Donohue, "It's really different over there. Small town murders make the headlines in national newspapers over there. House fires too."

"Guess those are not an everyday thing over there..." said Hayte. He absently started tapping his spoon on the plastic dish.

"Will you *stop* that?" snapped Donohue.

"Jesus, you're *jumpy*, Perry." Hayte set the spoon down. "Speaking of the Phantoms, Perry, I got someone who may know something—Scotty Bunch. He was supposed to come by with some interesting documents that could shed some light on one of the gunmen."

"Really? What kind of documents?" asked Perry.

"Company documents about some kind of GeniTech cloning program."

"Oh lord, GeniTech again." Donohue shook his head. "I *think* I'd like to see the stuff you got—but then again..."

Hayte frowned. "Could be trouble. Scotty never showed up this morning. I'll try and get in touch with him again tonight, see if he just flaked out on me. He seemed real nervous."

Donohue kept glancing over his shoulder.

Shrini looked at him. "What's wrong, Perry? You look like you expect trouble."

Perry turned to look at her. "Alright, I do."

"Why?"

"All right, I'll tell you. I had a problem coming back from Venice. Because of my 'unusual' carry-on, I decided to fly in to Baltimore instead of the local airports here—I wanted to be inconspicuous, and I knew a back way to get past customs. But someone obviously knew I was coming in, because I had a 'welcoming committee' waiting."

Hayte raised an eyebrow. "But how? Are you sure?"

"Yes, I'm sure. I don't know how, but there was a squad of Feds, and they chased me through Baltimore airport."

Shrini raised an eyebrow, "Who are *they*? FBI?"

Donohue drummed his fingers on the tabletop. "That's what I need to find out. Something tells me they're not standard issue G-Men. They don't dress quite right..."

Shrini looked skeptical. "What does *that* mean? *Is* there a standard FBI outfit"

"There used to be, at least when I was an undergrad. The threesome that chased me reminded me a lot of the campus recruiters I used to see—except for one thing. Call me a stickler for details, but their choice of footwear just doesn't add up..."

Hayte pulled his Lakers jacket on. "How so?"

"Would you wear a no-frills black suit, white shirt and a skinny tie with... *Birkenstocks?* "

Shrini started to laugh, but the look on Hayte's face stopped her. "You look like you've seen a ghost, Rich."

"You could say that." Hayte pushed away the rest of his coffee. "It's nothing, really. Just too many unanswered questions, that's all."

"Maybe it's just my lack of sleep, but..." said Donohue. "I really feel there is someone watching."

"You're right," said Dietrich, standing behind him.

Donohue almost jumped off his seat. "Dietrich—you bastard! 'Bout time you showed!"

"Sorry. I overslept. Anyway, I'm here, and I got something to add to 'Perry's 'head story'...'"

Hayte turned to him, "What do you mean?"

Instead of answering, Dietrich grabbed a donut, chewed for a while, then washed it down with coffee. Enjoying the suspense, he slowly looked and smiled at everyone. "The Italian inspector was right, the head *is* American."

Perry winced. "Oh *great!* As if we didn't have enough to do already..."

"You'll probably need a little help with this one." Dietrich shook his head. "I know *I* did. It was pure luck that I got anything back at all when I sent the scans to the Feds. Only when a clerk sent the scans to the National Archives by mistake did they find a positive match—and it set off quite a few alarm bells, let me tell you..."

"*Really?* Well, what is it—a celebrity murder case?" asked Shrini.

"You could say that..." Dietrich eyed the three of them. "The vic *was* famous, but he died of natural causes—which explains the signs I saw before, the ones indicating brain death following massive cardiac arrest..."

Donohue looked at Dietrich skeptically. "Wait a sec—how can we have a severed head found floating in a Venice canal if the victim died of a heart attack?"

Dietrich pushed his glasses up his long nose. "You tell me, you're the detectives. Maybe the identity of the victim would be a good place to start..."Dietrich reached into his leather satchel and pulled out a thick sheaf of official-looking printouts.

With his long arms, Hayte snatched the top pages.

"Hey!" complained Shrini, "Ladies first."

"I just want a quick peek," said Hayte. He started reading aloud "...and before that, the head was attached to... oh..." He knocked over his cup of heavily-sugared coffee.

Donohue grabbed the sheet. "Who's Ronald Wilson Chesney?"

Dietrich shushed him, "Jesus! You want everyone to hear?"

"I seriously doubt anyone here," Donohue surveyed the Hindi counter help behind them, "would either know or care. On the other hand, *I* do. So *who* is he?"

"A vice president of the United States," replied Shrini, reading from another page. "He died in office, it says here, after surviving *ten* heart attacks and spending much of his term in office with an IV tube in his arm. He had his body donated to science."

Donohue's mouth dropped open. "*Ten* heart attacks? Wha—why didn't they transplant?"

Dietrich answered, "It says in the dossier that the early ones did too much damage to his circulatory system, especially in the chest cavity."

"Wait a sec," Hayte held up his hand, "Let me get this straight—this particular Vice President had *ten* heart attacks while in office..."

"No." Dietrich tapped the report again for emphasis, "Three happened *before*, when he was a US Representative, one happened just after the election, and the rest while he was VeePee."

Hayte looked at the photo, "So how come I can't recognize the guy, either from his name or his face—which I've seen plenty of, very recently?"

"Because it was over 35 years ago." responded Dietrich, smiling lopsidedly.

"Oh Christ..." Donohue put his head in his hands. "Let me get this straight—a severed head from a 35-year-old corpse gets dumped in a canal in Venice? I basically put my career on the line, investigating a probable Halloween prank, like who went around smashing pumpkins in Rockaway last..."

"Wrong time of the year," said Hayte, "and anyway, why were you chased through Baltimore airport?"

Donohue thought hard for a moment. "I dunno. Maybe I have something else they want..."

Shrini waved another sheet. "It says here he willed his body to a quasi-Federal program called 'Cell Kern research', whatever that means. This makes *no* sense at all..."

"No kidding..." agreed Dietrich, "But it does explain why the head was found *floating* instead of submerged. It was cryogenically frozen, so all the water round it would have instantly frozen too, even though it was salt water. After a few minutes, it must've looked like a chunk off a glacier, until many hours later, when it thawed enough to recognized as a human head."

"Time to call Henri..." said Perry. "This is going to blow his mind."

Hayte frowned. "I got a feeling there's more to this floater, a lot more. Why keep a head cryogenically preserved for over 40 years in the first place? We ought to do some more digging..."

Donohue sighed. "Well, I've heard enough. If you all want to look further, be my guest. I got to concentrate on the Phantoms case—or my ass is headed to the unemployment line ..." He got up to leave, then turned back around. "But before I do get the boot, I'd sure like to get my hands on the fink who keeps informing the press about the Phantoms robberies before we even get to the crime scene…"

~ ~ ~

Tuesday, 5th Ave and 135th St, 6:57 pm:

The heavyset cashier felt cranky all day. Even the store muzak was getting on her nerves. The last thing she felt like doing was putting up with some stupid teenagers like the ones that had just come in. She looked at the three as they slunk past the counter, hoods up and backs turned to her.

She rolled her eyes and fingered the police alert button under the counter. *Shoplifters, most likely.*

She saw one grab something and put it in his pocket. Without thinking twice, she pushed the alarm button under the counter.

One of them knocked over a table of brassieres in the far corner. Then the others started throwing the brassieres and women's underpants about in a frenzy. She bellowed, "You fucking kids either treat the merchandise with respect, or get the fuck out of here!"

They ran off. She yelled a number of insults and waved her fist at them, but it was too late to do anything else. Cops never came quickly to alarms triggered at Goodwills.

She was about to try and bend over to pick up the mess they had left when she saw someone's foot. "Why the fuck are you?" she snapped.

The man was small and wiry, his face was strangely expressionless.

She glared at him, "Hey pal, I'm talking to you—what do you want?"

The man suddenly jumped on her, catching her off-balance and knocking her flat on her back, despite the extreme weight difference.

Suddenly afraid, she began screaming and struggling. Her cell phone slipped out of her coat and hit the floor in slow motion, spewing tiny batteries across the yellowed linoleum.

The small man sprayed something in her face. Her stuggles grew more and more sluggish, then ceased altogether.

He reached around his belt buckle and pulled at something. Both their bodies vanished in a flash of white light.

The store muzak continued to play pleasant easy-listening jazz.

~ ~ ~

About half an hour later, sounds of approaching sirens echoed down the street.

"A possible robbery?" Officer Vaughn was first on the scene. "Why would anybody rob a Goodwill?" he complained to Dispatch.

"Beats me," said the dispatcher. "All we know is that the alert button was triggered and that three suspects were seen fleeing the premises."

"All right, I'll check it out." He stepped out of the car and approached the shop. All the lights were off.

The front door hung open. His shoes crunched on broken glass as he shined his flashlight inside. He took his night stick and hit the light switch. He squinted in the sudden light, almost colliding with an upturned shoe display. Then he noticed the hand. He immediately keyed his headset mike. "Ho-boy, dispatch, Vaughn here—better send the meat wagon and a few homicide detectives. Looks like we got a body here," he looked around, "uh… somewhere."

The dispatcher sounded dubious. "A body *somewhere*? Are you sure?"

"You tell me—there's a severed hand in the corner, with a big burn mark on the carpeting. I can transmit video if you want."

"Uh, better not." came the response. "Remember, the networks all have access to our video and audio channels—wait for homicide to do it, otherwise the prosecutor's office will be all over us for transmitting over open airwaves."

"All right." Vaughn bent down to look at the burn mark and winced. "Jesus…"

"What's that?" said the dispatcher.

Vaughn tried to breathe through his mouth. "Dispatch, you wouldn't believe the smell." Static crackled in his earpiece. "Sorry, didn't catch that—please repeat."

The dispatcher said louder, "Just let Homicide take care of it. Over."

~ ~ ~

Vaughn heard footsteps crunching on broken glass. He poked his head out the employee entrance. "The uh, *hand* is over here!" he called to the grim-faced Asian, "You from Homicide?"

"That's me. Lt. Takuma." The detective pointed to Vaughn's headset, "You transmitted pictures?"

Vaughn shook his head, "No. Didn't know how long it would take you to show, but I got orders to wait for a secure hookup."

"Screw 'em. It's always a good idea to transmit pictures at a crime scene. While you're at it, let's do a video scan of the parameter—first in infrared, then with UV."

Vaughn complied, aiming his headcam around the room, stopping to scan all the upturned racks and half-scorched merchandise "Here, I'll send it to your palmtop. Stop me if you see anything interesting." Vaughn switched to UV mode. He began walking along the far wall.

Takuma held up his hand. "Stop! What are those symbols?"

"Where?" Vaughn squinted. "I don't see any."

"Go back two steps—yeah, there!" Takuma put his hand on the back of Vaughn's head like he was aiming a tripod-mounted SLR. "Now go from bottom to top. Yeah. Okay, that's enough." He held up the palmtop so

Vaughn could see the images as well.

As if by magic, Vaughn saw the unintelligible symbols smeared and glowing on the cinder block wall. "Well, I'll be damned."

"Ego." Takuma almost chuckled. "It never fails—you get killers this methodical, there's almost bound to be some kind of manifesto."

Vaughn peered at the images. Finally he shook his head. "It's all Greek to me. What do you make of it?"

The homicide detective shrugged. "It could be gang-related, but I doubt it." He bent down and put the hand in a plastic evidence bag. "The whole thing's too sophisticated by half. Gangs shoot their victims and drive off. They like to leave a body as proof that you don't wanna fuck with them. Leaving a charred hand and a big burn mark in the carpet just doesn't have the same effect." He walked over to the counter. "Any info on the cashier on duty at the time?"

"Dispatch is checking with Goodwill HQ right now about that," said Vaughn.

"Radio them back now, see if they've gotten anything back." said Takuma. "My headset's busted, I can only receive audio. I'd like to have at least a name and home address to work with."

Vaughn keyed his mike. "Hey dispatch, any luck with the Goodwill people?"

"Yeah. The person on duty was a 45-year-old woman named Wanda Wettington, about 5'7", morbidly obese, some 300 pounds plus. We should have her home address and driver's license photo in about half an hour."

"Thanks, dispatch." Vaughn looked over at Takuma. "Got that?"

Takuma nodded. He crouched next to the burn mark. "Hey-zeus... three hundred pounds and *nothing* left!" He scraped some of the ash into another evidence bag.

"I don't get it," said Vaughn, "the whole place should've been blown apart..."

"Or burned to a crisp," added Takuma. "But the blast wasn't so violent, and the fire apparently contained itself." He scanned the ceiling. "Shit, the place doesn't even have sprinklers installed..."

"No, it doesn't," agreed Vaughn.

Takuma rocked back and forth on the balls of his feet, deep in thought. "This is so neat and tidy, like nothing I've ever seen before..." He got up and studied the wall where the symbols were. "The lab analysis of the hand and ashes will take some time. The best bet would be to do follow-up on the graffiti, if that's what this really is." He took a photograph, then started chipping at the edges of the paint and putting the dust in a plastic bag. "This your normal beat?"

"Yeah," said Vaughn.

"Good. Here's what I need for you to do: I want you to use your hand-cam on the rest of your beat tonight and do a scan of every bit of graffiti you see. We'll get all the beat cops to do the same, then we'll compile the images in a data base—see if we can find a match..."

"It's a good idea," Vaughn looked again at the tiny screen at the UV photo, "but this looks like it's incomplete."

Takuma frowned. "How do you know?"

"I've seen a lot of graffiti before, but almost never *without* lettering—all this spiral stuff looks like the background stuff..."

Takuma waved his hand impatiently. "Look, let us worry about that—just *do* it, OK?"

"OK." Vaughn shrugged. He knew it was time to shut up.

~ ~ ~

Wednesday, March 9, 8:45

Despite feeling like hell, Donohue came in to work early anyway. He decided to spend most of the morning sifting through what available Phantoms data there was and see if he'd been overlooking something.

The file itself seemed annoyingly skimpy. Eight robberies and, in every case, only video images of three robbers per crime scene. No face appeared twice. None of the faces had registered a hit with either the FBI or New York State databases on known criminals. It was tempting to put all the faces together and assume these comprised all or most of the ring, but something nagged at Donohue's consciousness. Still not knowing what it was, he got up to go to the men's room.

As he reached for the roll of toilet paper, he suddenly got an idea. Zipping up his trousers in a hurry, he then washed his hands in a frenzy and ran out without drying them.

He peered over the first cubicle he came to. "Hey, Zakowski! Got any playing cards?"

Zakowski's burr head turned round. "Huh? You mean *real* paper playing cards or the virtual ones?"

"Real ones. You got any?"

"Naw." Zakowski drummed his sausage fingers on his tabletop. "Mmm, try Dietrich. I seen him play solitaire sometimes in the lab when things are slow."

"OK. Thanks." Donohue rushed through several sets of double doors. "Hey, Dietrich!"

Dietrich was kneeling over a very large corpse, holding something red and slimy with his forceps. He turned as the door opened. "Hey Perry! Put a mask on, will you?"

"Sorry..." Donohue complied.

"No harm done," Dietrich shrugged. "This woman's past caring. I just got called in to do this autopsy. She got axed, literally."

"Yee..." Perry briefly peered over Dietrich's shoulder. "Hey, wait a sec. If she got axed, why are you still working on her? "

"Gotta find out why they chopped out her ovaries—could be a ritual murder, something Satanic, or maybe an organ donor racket. Won't know until I do a bunch of tests. "

"I get the picture." Donohue winced and looked away. "Changing the subject, got any real playing cards, like Hoyle?"

"Aha. You *do* have some free time, after all!" Dietrich pointed a bloody finger at his desk. "Top drawer. *Don't* get them dirty."

"I won't. Thanks!" Donohue grabbed the cards and went to a vacant counter. He laid out a king, queen and jack of each suite on the desk. Then he laid out the ace, two and three of each in another row. He studied them intently.

Dietrich finished inserting the liver into a baggie and took it out to Analysis. When he came back, he peered over Perry's shoulder. "Whatcha doing? Figuring out the ultimate three-card stud hand?"

"More like blackjack..." Donohue looked at his watch. "Aw hell, I need to get going. There must be a pattern here, but I'm just not picking it up." He looked at Dietrich. "Paul, can you do me a favor? I gotta go do get talk to some witnesses. Can I leave the cards just as they are on your desk and come back later to get them, maybe this afternoon?"

"Sure," said Dietrich. "I'll be playing around in the Toxicology lab all afternoon. Just put 'em back in the deck when you're done"

~ ~ ~

It was unseasonably cold and gusty outside. The reception Donohue got at VNN was equally chilly. Before Perry could even get to the reception desk, a brown-suited lawyer stopped him. "You'll need more than a District Court subpoena."

Donohue almost screamed, "To get what you broadcast *on the air?*", but he stopped mid-sentence. Instead, he just smiled and mimed pointing his finger like he was firing a gun. "Catch ya later. We'll be seeing a lot of each other, buddy boy."

He turned and left without another word. He walked across the street, turned around and looked at the building. *Someone's got something to hide — and is worried enough to phone ahead...* He bundled up his coat against the bone-chilling gusts. He quickly hurried to the next name on his list.

The afternoon turned out not to be a total waste, as the CyberPost was rather more accommodating. As it turned out, they had recorded 15 separate TV and Internet broadcasts. He asked for and received all 15 on cyberdisk and also left with a stack of CyberPost issues reporting on each Phantoms robbery.

Back at the White Elephant, Perry triumphantly waltzed in to his cubicle and began playing some of the broadcasts. About halfway, he stopped and looked again at the Phantom composites. He thought for a moment, then reached for the phone.

No answer. He touched his mini-pointer on 'home phone' and clicked again. After about seven rings a sleepy voice answered in Italian.

"Henri! Perry Donohue here—did I wake you up?" Donohue smiled wickedly as a torrent of Italian curses resounded in his ear.

Brezzi stopped and chuckled "*Ciao*, Perry—you have your revenge." He struggled to find the right words in English, "Eh... important is... is it..."

"Very important, Henri. First, we now know who the head belongs to."

"*Fantastico!* So, don't keep me in ah, suspense..."

"Are you sitting down?"

"*Si.* I mean, yes."

"His name was Ron Chesney." Perry read out the details.

Brezzi was stunned. "So this was a frozen head of a man who died 40 years ago?"

"That's it," said Donohue. "So there is no murder case."

"Oh, this is unbelievable!" Brezzi let out a sigh of relief, "No murder! This saves my job! How can I ever thank you?"

"Well," said Donohue, "you can help me out with a problem..."

"Name it—I will do it!"

"Great. I got 24 composite sketches of faces of the Phantoms—and no positive IDs in America. Can I send them to you, see if your colleagues at Interpol can get a positive on any of them?"

"With Interpol?" Brezzi let out a yawn. "I don't understand. Can't you do that yourself?"

"C'mon, Henri. I don't know a soul there. No connections, no favors I can pull in—and besides, they're in your time zone."

Brezzi sounded resigned. "All right, I see what I can do."

"By the way, what time is it over there?"

"Three a.m. I think I go to sleep now. Goodnight, Perry, and thanks again." He hung up.

Donohue chuckled to himself, then made a mental note to shut off his phone when he went home in the evening. Uploading the 24 likenesses took about eight seconds, an onscreen message informed him. He clicked on the OK button.

Perry pulled out his deck of cards and laid them in the same order as before. This time, he laid a small photo on each card, until each of the Phantom henchmen were staring back at him in all their computerized 3-D glory.

"What are you trying to tell me?" he muttered to the cards. The king and queen of diamonds seemed to mock his stare.

Suddenly he had an idea. He reached in a desk drawer and pulled out the full-length hard copy Phantoms report. He flipped through and made notes on each robbery. Then he re-shuffled the cards, grouping the faces according to robbery scene.

Without exactly knowing why, he drew four more cards and placed them away from the others. On each, he laid a small blank post-it note.

Then he remembered the passport he'd found. He'd left it in his suitcase, which was still lying on his bed, half-unpacked.

He ran over to Shrini's cubicle. "Hey Shrini, why don't U.S. passports have any kind of fool-proof encryption to prevent forgery—like iris data or something?"

Shrini looked up from her terminal and rolled her eyes. "As a matter of fact, all passports *do* have iris data."

"Yeah, but how come we still have so many problems tracking down illegal aliens in New York City—and most of their passports are forged? And when I went through Frankfurt airport, the scanner failed to read the barcode on my passport—but they just shrugged and waved me through anyway."

"I guarantee that wouldn't happen if you weren't American—and light-skinned..." said Shrini sourly, "But it's not surprising you got through anyway."

Donohue tilted his head. "Really?"

"Really." In her clipped accent, she recited, "Most of the illegal aliens get through because of the high volume of people coming and going—especially the coastline. Iris data checks are supposed to be done on everybody, but the reality is that they are only done sporadically, simply because comparing any one face against 5 billion passport cyberfiles is so time- and computer memory-consuming that most airline passengers get through check-in without being checked. I mean, how many criminals are notorious enough to make airport authorities feel justified in holding up a domestic flight for 45 minutes? Not to mention what it would cost when you do it for international flights..."

"Thanks for the lecture, Shrini."

"Glad to do it, Perry. Maybe someday you can tell me what this is all about..." she said, but he was already dashing back to his cubicle. He grabbed his coat and wool cap and raced out to the parking garage to retrieve his car.

He walked through the front doors and nearly slid down the massive front steps. He looked around in shock and realized everything was coated in half an inch of ice. Traffic was paralyzed in all directions, with cars everywhere, including the sidewalk. He cursed to himself and slid off towards the commuter train station.

~ ~ ~

Wednesday, 7:30 pm:

By the time he left his apartment, Donohue was pleased to find that the streets were mostly cleared of ice and debris. The mysterious passport was now safely in his coat pocket. He decided to come back to the White Elephant to check the passport out and see if any authorities had flagged it as belonging to a felon or as being a forgery.

It was a quarter past ten, and the White Elephant was almost deserted, with only a skeleton night crew on the ground floor. Donohue made his way stealthily to his cubicle and was pleased that he had apparently entered unobserved.

He switched on his terminal, logged in and instantly groaned. His incoming mail box was full of voice and text messages, many from Shabazz. He closed his eyes and massaged his forehead. He took another sip of coffee and scanned the message list.

At the special US State Dept. website for law enforcement personnel, he scanned in the data from the mysterious passport and hit enter.

"Aha, I thought so!" The passport was flagged as stolen, and the photo did not match the one on the State Dept. data bank. Perry sat and drummed his fingers. That doesn't necessarily mean the stolen passport is linked to the Phantoms, but that's a distinct possibility. In any case, the train was a drop site for something illegal.

Could be they're using night trains all over Europe as passport drops—trains are ideal places to swap identities, ever since border checks were stopped within the European Union.

Just as he was about to log off, Perry saw another mysterious message in his in-box. Against his better judgment, he clicked on it and was instantly blinded by a flash of nasty white light. When he managed to open his eyes again, he started to sweat. Written in red, the message read:

"Captain P. Donohue, YOU have been charged with handling stolen US Government property!
We WILL be in touch, like it or NOT. "Heads up!"
Sincerely, Your Friends at The NPDi."

Perry shut off the computer immediately without seeing the message from Brezzi and hastily departed.

He decided to pack up his suitcase again and head home. Then he could make discrete inquiries and hit the road again.

Traffic was heavy, so it took the better part of 90 minutes before he got across the bridge and managed to locate a parking space. Fortunately, the floodwaters had receded enough to find one around the block from his apartment.

As he was walking up the stairs, Donohue mistakenly hit the 'scan' button on his apartment's all-purpose remote instead of the 'unlock front door' button. He almost fell down the stairs when the device started shrieking and flashing red. Shaken, he picked it up and read the display: Apartment security seriously compromised.

He ran back down the stairs, picked up his suitcase and went back outside. He waved down a passing cab and got in. The cabbie asked, "Where to, pal?"

"Uh..." Perry's mind raced. Having no better idea, he blurted "Grand Central Station." He leaned forward, "There's an extra 20 bucks if you can get me there in ten minutes..." The cab left tire marks on the sidewalk as it raced toward the Manhattan Bridge. Perry watched out the back window as the cab set off. He had no doubt someone was watching, but with the subway still out of commission, his options were extremely limited.

~ ~ ~

Thursday, March 10

They sat in the lobby of empty concert hall in a semicircle around Brezzi's chair. "Well, Signore Brezzi, what have you to tell us?" said Bresco, his arms folded.

He stood up and switched on a nearby beamer. "I have news about the severed head, good news."

"You solved the murder?" Signore Rossi of Hotel dei Dogi.

"No," said Brezzi smugly. "There was no murder!"

"No murder? How can that be? We saw the knife cuts!"

"Surgical knife cuts—made on an already dead body," said Brezzi. "He died of natural causes. A heart attack, to be precise."

An angry murmur started among the hotel proprietors. "How can this be?" Rossi waved his arms.

"Because, the man in question donated his body to science, some 40 years ago. His name was Ronald Chesney, he was the Vice-President of the United States in the years 20..."

"This is utter nonsense!" shouted Bresco. "I don't believe you!"

"*Sta Zito!*" muttered Brezzi under his breath. "I will prove it to you," he said to the group. He turned the beamer on and pointed to the photo. "This is the severed head, the death mask. Take a good look at the features, memorize them if you can." He went to the next image, a photo of the then-Vice-President sitting beside his boss, his legs twisted strangely as if the sides of his feet itched. "See?" Brezzi folded his arms. "Any questions?"

Bresco remained defiant, "Photos, they can be manipulated! Who can guarantee that this is true?"

Brezzi let out an exasperated sigh. "The New York Police Department, that's who. They even did DNA tests and a Carbon-14 analysis to verify the year of death. There is no question that the head once belonged to Ron Chesney and that he died over 40 years ago. The head was cryogenically preserved and was in transit to a private exhibition in Switzerland. So there was *no* murder. Repeat, *no* murder!"

"But, the head, how did it end up in the Rio Orsolo?"

Brezzi shrugged "Who knows? Why would anybody steal a severed head? Probably a stupid college prank. It's not a major crime, people throw worse things in our canals." He shut the beamer off. "So now you can go home and make your precious money, secure in the knowledge that the tourists will flock to you just as always. Good night!"

With that, he took the beamer under his arm and walked out a side door.

Murano followed him. "That was quite a performance. You shut them up completely."

Brezzi shrugged. "Maybe. Now they can go back to counting their money." He climbed aboard the small speedboat. "Franco, you know what bugs me the most?"

"No." Murano cupped his hands to light a cigarillo. "What?"

Brezzi gestured with his hand. "We live in beautiful, historic city, a monument to its own grand history." He made a face. "But underneath, there is nothing but rot. And it's *spreading*."

~ ~ ~

Manhattan, 10 am:

Hayte was sitting at his console when a flashing red icon flashed on his computer screen. Puzzled, he tapped in Shrini's intercom number, but she wasn't at her desk.

He clicked on the icon. A red box opened: Security Violation!

He saw his home address below it. Stifling a curse, he jumped up, snatched his keys off the desk and started out of the building.

Shrini was coming back from the rest room. "Hey, Tree-Top, I got to..."

"No time!" yelled Hayte over his shoulder. "Someone's breaking in to my apartment!"

"I'll send a patrol car!" she yelled behind him.

He ran out into the street, desperately trying to flag down a cab. They whizzed past, paying no attention. Dodging a large Pepsi truck and several cars, he ran back to the curb. Something silver caught his eye. *There.* A Merc patrol car.

He ran toward it, fishing out his badge in the process. A grey, dreadlocked man poked his head out the window. "Wot you need, mon?"

Hayte reached instinctively for his holster. "Are *you* a cop?"

" 'Corse Ah'm a police-mon!" barked the Jamaican, pointing to his badge. "Officer Hudgins, mon. Wot you need?"

Hayte opened the back door and slammed it shut. "Attempted break-in, Greenwich..."

Hudgins looked dubious. "Not me district, mon..."

"It's *my* apartment, Goddamn it!"

"Okay, okay, we gonna go!" Hudgins pulled out and floored the accelerator, snapping Hayte's head back as they screeched off into heavy traffic.

Cars scattered to each side, and Hudgins went onto the sidewalk to get around the others. A riot shield flew sideways, catching Richard in the face, and the rest of Hudgins' riot gear started rolling around on the floor. Then they got stuck in a traffic jam at Canal Street.

The wait seemed like eternity to Hayte. He tapped Hudgins on the shoulder, "Can't you run the light?"

"Sorry mon, wit all dem trucks, we got no chance. Better to go wit da light." The light changed and they went through the intersection at a crawl, then Hudgins floored the accelerator again.

Finally, they pulled up in a cloud of tire smoke at Hayte's apartment building. As Hayte extracted himself from the back seat, Hudgins was already halfway up the front walkway, dreadlocks swinging. Richard ran up and tapped in his entry code. The front door popped open on his first try, surprising him. Hudgins raced to the elevator, which opened, a second surprise. The doors started to close before Hayte could make it to the lift.

Too late, the elevator doors closed on Hayte's fingertips, leaving him cursing in the entrance hall. The indicator showed elevator going up. He started up the steps, taking them three at a time.

When he got to his floor, he was very out of breath and had to lean against the wall. He opened the fire door and found Hudgins with another uniformed cop, a short, stubby man in his late 40s.

The uniformed cop said, "Captain, I'm Officer Vaughn." He pointed to Hayte's door. "Looks like an attempted break-in."

Hayte took another deep breath. "*Attempted?*"

Hudgins nodded, "Yah, mon." He looked at Vaughn "Ah 'tink we scared da bugger off."

Hayte peered down the hall. "Did you see him?"

Vaughn nodded. "Only for a moment. Small, dark, wiry, with curly black hair cut real short. Didn't get a good look at his face, though." He pulled out a note pad and made a crude sketch. "Like this."

Hayte looked at the drawing. "Hmm. Which way did he go?"

Vaughn pointed. "The far stairway. After that, I don't know. I chased him, but he was goin' way too fast, like some kind of monkey. Never saw *anyone* take stairs that fast—without falling, anyway..."

Hayte peered at his front door. "What is all this shit?"

Vaughn pointed at the carving. "Looks like perp couldn't get past your electrolocks, so he vandalized your door instead." He ran his finger over the images. "Can't make heads nor tails of all these symbols. And the way the rows are spaced is really odd."

"Looks like some kinda weird religion, mon," said Hudgins. "Maybe voodoo, maybe not, but de mon wanna put some kinda hex on ya. Dat's wot Ah gonna put in mah report, anyway..." He took out his cell phone camera and shined the pin-light over the symbols as he pressed the 'record' button. "Ah'm a gonna call New Orleans, see if dey got any shit like dis in der data base." He tuned back to Hayte. "You say dis not da first time?"

"No, mon." Hayte caught himself mimicking the Jamaican. "I was woken up in the middle of the night last week, but I opened the front door and scared him off.

"Ah, you saw him?"

"He had a hood on, so I didn't get a real good look at his face..." Hayte squinted at the sketch again, "but I think that's him. Real short and wiry."

"Ja mon," said Hudgins, shaking his head. "He run real fast, like some kinda primate..." He furrowed his forehead. "One t'ing bugs me, mon. Dis guy is real persistent and... real obvious he wants *somethin'*."

"Persistent is right," Hayte turned and looked again at the symbols. "This makes twice—if it's the same guy."

"But why?" persisted Hudgins. "Ain't normal for burglar to try and knock over a police-mon pad, especially you, bein' on television and magazines..."

Hayte leaned against the opposite wall. "Well, I'm stumped, at least right now. Hell, I've only been here a few weeks, ain't even had time to unpack everything." He shrugged. "I don't have all that much stuff anyway, so it can't be that I'm a prime target for burglary." He looked at Vaughn, "So all we got is that sketch of yours to go on."

Vaughn's face brightened, "Not only that. Didn't you share that *Newsweek* cover with Captain, uh, what's the name?"

"Donohue, Perry Donohue. And it was *Time*, not *Newsweek*," corrected Hayte.

"Well, have you asked Capt. Donohue if he's had similar problems?"

Hayte shook his head.

Vaughn tapped his palmtop screen. "Maybe we should show him and see if it's a celebrity stalking case."

Hayte nodded. "It's worth a shot..." He fished out his cell phone and hit one of the automatic dial buttons. He put the earpiece to his ear and counted the rings. "No answer."

"Have him call me, OK?" said Vaughn. "The sooner we get to the bottom of this, the better. I'd hate to think somebody's going after cops."

Hudgins nodded emphatically. "Ja, mon. I seen it happen. Much better to be da hunter than da hunted."

Chapter 11

Hudgins poured himself another cup of Hayte's coffee. "Da best t'ing Ah kin do for ya is a patrol, meebee every 30 minutes. Dat might scare da leddle bugger off."

Vaughn frowned, "Question is, do we *want* to scare him off? Seems to me, we should set a trap for him."

"I don't know…" said Hayte, scowling into his coffee mug. He started to pace the living room. "I'd *like* to trap him, but he's got a real knack for slipping the noose. I still don't know how he squirmed out that closet window."

"Well, wot we gotta do, mon? We gotta do somethin'…" Hudgins turned to Vaughn, who was busy rubbing a spot on his uniform. "Hey, mon—we got any gizmos dat trigger an alarm at HQ?"

"Yeah, we do, we could hook it up to your office computer, Captain…" Vaughn paused and shook his head, "But it won't do much good—not with a perp that quick. A better thing would be to set up a neighborhood watch on your floor. Captain, do you know any of your neighbors yet?"

"Ooh." Hayte sat back down. "Only one—and I don't know if he's the right person for the job. Stanley Bialystok. He's an adult film producer. He keeps real odd hours."

"Hey, don't laugh," said Vaughn, "he may turn out to be perfect. He have a lot of visitors?"

"Oh *yeah*…" nodded Hayte. "Like a revolving door sometimes."

"Perfect. You get along with the guy?"

"He's all right in small doses. Got some nice lady friends, though. He once invited me to a film shoot."

Vaughn said with a laugh, "I almost envy you, Captain, but I suggest you do some more hanging out with Mister Stanley. The less you're actually here, the better. Meanwhile, we can stick GPS micro-transmitters on your valuables. So, if this little creep's a burglar, we'll nail his ass when he tries to pawn the stuff off or sell through a fence."

"I don't know about this hanging out with Stanley stuff. I may just move out temporarily to a motel. I need my peace and quiet so I can pass my bar exam. I don't have much time—it's coming up next Friday."

"Well, maybe we can nail dis creep before then," said Hudgins.

Vaughn sat up. "Oh, by the way, have you spoken with Capt. Donohue yet?"

Hayte shook his head. "Perry's getting real hard to get in touch with. I'd say he's obsessed with keeping his job at the moment."

~ ~ ~

Donohue paced the dingy hotel room. After deliberating for almost an hour, he decided it was worth the risk. He picked up his cell phone and dialed Dietrich's extension.

"Yo, Dietrich here."

"Paul, Donohue here. Got an idea—can you e-mail the mug shots of the Phantoms to your friends in DC?"

"Wish I could, Perry, but I ran into a little complication today."

"What kind of complication?" A gust of wind made Donohue shiver some more. He moved away from the leaky window.

Dietrich sounded agitated. "My e-mail account's been cut off, no explanation why. I spent all morning trying to get authorization, but no luck. First, I tried talking with the Chief, then the mayor's office, then I found out the city government has no jurisdiction, so I spent the rest of the time trying state and federal agencies."

Donohue lay back and closed his eyes. "What the hell's going on?"

"I said the head's a hot potato, but I didn't know how hot. When I got back from talking to the chief, I discovered that somebody's been through my desk and took all the hard copies I'd printed of the report."

"*Great*. We *are* in deep shit…" Donohue hung up and folded up the phone. He started pacing again. The pinched nerve in his right leg hurt worse. He stretched the leg out on the flimsy couch, but gave up after a little while and peered out the dirty window. Small clusters of people struggled on the street below as nasty gusts tore at their coats and hats. The neon Chelsea Hotel sign next to his window began to swing wildly as it flickered, then an especially violent gust tore it from its moorings. It hit the ground in a shower of sparks and shattered into four large pieces. The wind continued to whistle between the gaps in the window.

Perry retreated to the bed and tried to bundle up as best as he could against the cold. He dropped into an uneasy sleep.

~ ~ ~

Friday, March 11:

The tiny alarm beeped at 4 a.m. Donohue awoke with a start and quickly changed back into the same clothes he came with. *Save the outfit change for when I really need it…*

He shaved with soap, splashed water in his face. He thought about a quick shower, then rejected the idea. Too little time. He stuffed his few belongings back in the suitcase and locked the door behind him.

He slid the key into the automated night deposit slot, got his receipt and stepped out into the night. The stars were out, but Perry didn't look up. He hit the 'go' button on his suitcase and chased it down the bumpy street, round the corner where he had the rental car parked. He didn't see anyone watching him.

~ ~ ~

The rain was hard and cold as Donohue pulled off the Jersey Turnpike. The town of Elizabeth still had its streetlights on at 8 am. He wanted to drive on past this dismal area, but nature's call had to be answered. Frantically he searched for a filling station or restaurant that was open, but all he saw were boarded-up houses and abandoned shopping malls. Finally at the outskirts, he found a sprawling truckstop.

He had to bully the cashier into handing over the men's room key. He rushed off in a crab-like walk as his bowels threatened to explode with every step. He fumbled with the key, yanked open the door and slammed it shut.

He sat down and immediately made a face. *Gawd, I hate it when the toilet seat is still warm from somebody else's ass...*

When he was finished, he heard the deep throb as a semi rolled past, blotting out everything else. He zipped up and cursed the lack of soap or paper towels. His cold, dripping hands had trouble gripping the doorknob. He finally shoved the door open with a hearty kick with the side of his foot.

There was a quick motion on the left. The muzzle of Donner's gun jammed him right in the nose. Perry sneezed convulsively, slamming his head against the wall. Then Donner slugged him, making him fall down on his knees in a puddle. Rough hands grabbed his legs and arms, quickly stuffing him in the waiting black van with blacked-out windows. Immediately the van started rolling as he was sat on and bound with duct tape.

A cherubic-faced man with a thick shock of black hair smiled at Donohue. He had a strange, high-pitched voice that sounded halfway between a man and a boy. "Hello Captain. I'm delighted to finally make your acquaintance. The name's Donner." He held up a syringe. Donohue twisted savagely.

"Now, now. It's no use struggling." Donner drove the needle home.

~ ~ ~

Saturday, March 12, 9 am:
"No answer," sighed Shrini, pressing the disconnect icon for the

umpteenth time. "It isn't like Perry to not return calls."

Dietrich fiddled with a mechanical pencil. "Did anybody notice which way he was headed after he left the donut shop?"

"Looked like he was headed home to Brooklyn," said Hayte sourly.

At her monitor, Shrini gnawed on a cuticle. "But he never made it back to his apartment. The security log would've registered his entry time. The last record was when he left for work Wednesday."

"I think I'd better talk to the Chief again," said Hayte wearily. He started up the stairs.

Hayte saw that Shabazz's door was open. He poked his head around the doorway.

Shabazz looked up briefly. "Yes, Captain?"

"I heard there was bad news, sir."

"Concerning Captain Donohue?"

Hayte nodded.

"Sit down, Captain." Shabazz shook his head. "Why am I not surprised?" He opened up a packet of Alka-Seltzer and dropped them in a very dirty glass.

"Perry's disappeared, sir. I checked his desk and his apartment. The security people in his building say he hasn't been home for 72 hours."

"Probably buggered off again to Europe—or somewhere else exotic. I've seen this sort of behavior before, Captain. I think Donohue's coming unhinged—a mid-life crisis, or something similar."

"It's not like Perry to do that, sir, not without notice. You said yourself that he left word about going to Italy..."

Shabazz leaned forward. "Did he also tell *you* that he was skipping his psychoanalysis sessions?"

"What?" Hayte's eyes widened. "No, he never said anything about that."

"He's been skipping sessions for the past six months, Captain. I got the report last week. This alone is serious enough to get him suspended, even if I *don't* factor in his recent erratic behavior."

"Sir, can we put out a missing persons bulletin first?"

"Normally, his family has to do that, Captain."

"Can't we make an exception for an on-duty policeman? I've worked alongside him for years, and there *has* to be something serious going on—for something like this to happen, believe me."

"Captain, is he really worth all this effort you're making to defend him? Anyone else would've given up on the man by now."

"Sir, I just talked with Dietrich in Toxicology, and he says Perry was working his tail off on the Phantoms case, even pulling some all-nighters at his desk, trying to get a breakthrough on it." He got up and stood behind his chair. "You don't just up and disappear after all that hard work—for not good reason at all."

Shabazz let out a heavy sigh. "All right. You win—but *only* this time.

There will be no second—no, *third* chance. He's already blown his second chance."

Hayte nodded, "I understand what's at stake, sir." He turned to go.

"I'm not too sure about that..." said Shabazz behind him "Good luck with the bar exam, Captain."

~ ~ ~

Monday evening March 14, 11:15 pm:

Murdoch vs. the State of New York was a tedious, though important case, dealing exclusively with the right of a state agency to prosecute U.S. Government agencies for high crimes and major procedural violations. Hayte rubbed his eyes and closed the thick volume after finding that he had been reading the same page repeatedly without noticing it. He glanced at his watch and discovered that the Metropolitan library was about to close in fifteen minutes.

He stood up, stretched and yawned. He looked around and saw the place was virtually empty, except for the staff and a few janitors making the rounds. He wrote down the name of the volume and page number in his notes, then returned the heavy book to its shelf. *Good thing I don't have to read this stuff electronically...*

He tucked the notebook back in his satchel and turned to go. As he passed by, the desk clerk asked to look in his satchel.

Hayte flashed his badge and grumbled, "You'd think the City Library would learn to trust policemen by now."

"Not likely..." retorted the acetic-faced clerk. "Cops, firemen and the mayor's staff are the worst offenders."

Hayte stuffed his papers back in the satchel and left without another word. A cool breeze met him as he took the stairs, two at a time, down to the street.

The subways were still *hors de combat*, so he briefly looked around for a cab, then gave up. He started hoofing it back to his apartment. A spring rainstorm had come through while he'd been inside, and the street lights reflected on the wet asphalt. Steam clouds issued from the manholes, a few cars drifted by. The late bus passed him by, too far between stops for him to catch a ride. As the skyscrapers drifted into view, he avoided the temptation of looking up like a tourist. The trek seemed endless.

When he finally rounded the corner to his street, one light above him did catch his eye. *My apartment.*

In his haste, it took him three tries to get the key card successfully in the front door slot, and he almost bent the card in the process.

The door to the building popped open with a hiss. The elevator was broken again, so he raced up the stairs.

Badly out of breath, he stopped to clear the spots before his eyes. He yanked open the fire exit and was halfway down the hall before he noticed the splashing.

He looked down. *Water.*

More splashing noises. Stanley came waddling up. "Hey Rich! What the hell's going on? First I hear a big pop! and the power goes off for thirty minutes. I ran down to find you, but all I heard was the sprinkler system going off inside your..."

"Inside *my* place?" Hayte winced.

"Fraid so, pal."

Hayte pushed on his door, which opened to the touch. Water seeped past his feet and out into the hallway.

He took one look inside, cursed loudly and then called 911 on his headset.

~ ~ ~

A quarter past midnight, Tuesday morning:

Hudgins and Vaughn came in and surveyed the damage. "Man, I just don't get it..." said Hayte exasperatedly. "I live my whole damned life in Harlem and never *once* get burglarized. I move down to Manhattan for six weeks and get hit *three* motherfucking times!" He splashed through his living room. "There's gotta be at least an inch of water here."

Stanley said, "Yeah, I had to block off my door with towels, otherwise my video mixing console would've shorted out."

"Did anyone see anything?" said Vaughn, as he slowly aimed a digital camera at all the damage in the room.

Stanley shook his head. "No. I didn't see anything. Like I told Rich, I heard a big bang, then all the power went off for half an hour. I came by and knocked, but nobody answered."

'What was plugged in here? "Vaughn frowned at a blackened wall socket, "An entertainment console?"

"Nope, my computer." Hayte bent down to look. "Shit, the plug's still in the socket!" He pointed to the frayed wires sticking out of the plug and the scorch marks around it.

"No wonder the sprinklers went off," said Stanley.

"I can't believe this shit." Hayte looked around sourly. "Most burglars have enough brains to unplug the damned computer before taking it."

"Fucking crackheads don't have many brain cells..." muttered Stanley.

"Yeah, but this guy got past the front door locks to both the building and my apartment" Hayte started wringing out a sofa cushion.

"Maybe this fellow has something else in mind..." said Vaughn, surveying the damage. "Does anyone have it in for you, Captain? Somebody seeking revenge? Maybe I'm being premature, but this sure looks like some kind of revenge stunt."

"Not that I know of," said Hayte. "Hell, I've been spending all my time cramming for the New York State bar exam." They splashed into the kitchen. "Luckily the building has a sprinkler system, otherwise the whole building would've gone up…"

Vaughn said briskly, "That's been in the Manhattan building code regs for years, ever since 2001. All commercial and residential buildings must have them—or the place gets condemned."

"And what about the elevator? It's always out of order."

"Not part of the fire code regs—you know that, Captain. In the event of a fire…"

"…don't use the elevator. Yeah, yeah, I remember that from grade school." Hayte started opening all the kitchen cupboards.

Vaughn persisted, "Are you *sure* nothing else got taken? Have you checked all your police gear?"

Hayte looked in his closets. "Yup, I checked it. They didn't take anything else. It's all there, my riot gear that hasn't been used in 15 years, my guns, everything."

"Forgive me for asking, Captain, but is there anything on that computer that might attract any nutcases?"

Hayte shook his head. "Man, I been spending the bulk of my days in the library, cramming for my bar exam. I'm only working part-time at the White Elephant, and I been spending most of that time in Chief Shabazz's office, bailing out colleagues of mine, so go figure."

Vaughn handed him a business card. "Well, Captain, if you think of anything—and I do mean *anything*, no matter how trivial, don't hesitate to call or e-mail me. Attacking the home of a NYPD man is serious business— and this is one case I want to solve." He glanced briefly at the torched bed. "Bad timing, too. I'd offer you the spare bed we got, but the missus has got the in-laws over…"

"That's OK," said Hayte, shoveling a few essentials into his satchel. "New York has tons of hotels. I'm sure I'll find something."

Hudgins looked at his watch dubiously. "Not at dis time-a night, mon…"

~ ~ ~

Hayte spent the rest of that night in his car. The night watchman at the White Elephant parking garage was sympathetic. "Sorry to hear about the burglary. Hope the perp doesn't start hitting places in Copland…"

Hayte winced at hearing that name. The idea of spending the foreseeable future in a Jersey suburb filled with beat cops seemed just about as appetizing as living in his car. Especially in a police car, as the front seats did not recline. He folded his large frame into a fetal position in the back seat and tried to doze off.

It seemed like he had barely closed his eyes when he was woken by the morning shift patrol cars roaring by, on their way to patrolling lower Manhattan. He sighed deeply, rubbed all the dried mucous out of his eyes and sat up. He had a horrible taste in his mouth, and the chill in the car made his back hurt. He decided to get a drive-thru breakfast and start searching immediately for a hotel on the BigAppleNet.

~ ~ ~

It was now noon, and Hayte was getting desperate. He had tried booking a room online, but every affordable motel and hotel in Manhattan had a flashing 'no vacancy' graphic. The same was true for Brooklyn, Queens, Harlem, Jersey and even New Bombay. Hayte muttered to himself, "I ain't fucking trying the Bronx..."

Then he remembered a dubious establishment frequented by drifters back in the days when he was still a rookie walking his beat. He sighed and reached for the phone.

~ ~ ~

After double-parking next to a newspaper van, Hayte winced when he walked to the front door. *Jeez, still as seedy as ever...* He slung his satchel strap over his shoulder and walked inside.

He booked that night and the following three at the Chelsea. Seeing his skeptical look, the young desk clerk nodded sympathetically. "I can see you ain't wild about staying here."

"Well... I *was* hoping for something a little more... upscale, but I don't have the time. Besides, every other place I tried was booked solid."

"Can't blame you for trying," said the desk clerk, "but everything's been booked up for weeks."

"Why? What's up?" said Hayte.

"National Proctologists Association is having their 200th Anniversary convention. You wouldn't believe how many hotel rooms they booked all over—even in the boroughs." The clerk shook his head. "I never saw anything like it."

Hayte raised an eyebrow. "What's the deal? I never thought proctology was such a big thing."

The clerk made a face. "Do yourself a favor, Captain—*don't* ask. I *did*, and got an hour-long lecture on what junk food does to your colon. I never thought fiber would be so friggin' important. That's why I mostly eat nothing but this," he pulled out a bag of brown rice. "I'm thinking macrobiotics are the way to go. Anyway, here's your key, hope you enjoy your stay."

"Mmph... thanks." Hayte took the key and started for the stairs, when instinct made him turn around. "Hey, didn't you just call me 'Captain'?"

The clerk nodded, "Yup. Sorry 'bout that, it just slipped out. I remember seein' you on the cover of some magazine, something about that drug Smash. Didn't it end up getting legalized because of you?"

Hayte nodded. "That was me, yes. I'm surprised people remember."

"I *knew* it was you! Well, it sure cleaned up the clientele around here, lemmie tell ya." The clerk frowned momentarily. "Oh yeah, now I know why I recognized you—that *other* fella on the cover with you..."

Hayte's eyes widened. "Perry Donohue? Short and wiry, medium-blonde hair?"

"That's him. He stayed here the other night—acted like he didn't wanna talk. He seemed kinda nervous. He checked out in a real hurry."

"When was that?"

"Well, let's see..." The clerk flipped through a coffee-stained ledger. "It was Wednesday this week, two days ago."

Hayte quickly wrote that down in his Palmtop. "Thanks for telling me that." Without waiting for a response, he turned and went to the stairs.

When he got to his room, its seediness barely registered. He set down his bag and opened his cell phone. He dialed Shrini's number. "Hi, Shrini, it's me. We need to talk—yeah, it's about Perry. Right now, I'm at the Chelsea..."

"The Chelsea?! What for?"

"I'll tell you later. Listen, we got to meet. I just spoke with someone who saw Perry two nights ago."

"How about lunch? I haven't eaten all day. Know any place good?"

Hayte thought for a moment. "Yeah—Harpo's cafeteria. It's all you can eat and one of the few places in Manhattan that won't run you out after you finish eating. It's just down the street from me."

~ ~ ~

The cafeteria was packed. Hayte and Shrini were just able to squeeze into a booth before a new gaggle of medical men descended and took all the remaining seats.

They both were famished. They got halfway through the meal before they started noticing the conversations around them.

The table behind them was particularly hard to ignore. A fat doctor came back from the serving table with a mound of food on his tiny plate. "I just *love* these all-you-can-eat buffets!" he exclaimed to his colleagues.

"Me too" said a second doctor. "Loads of good roughage!"

"You know it!" The first man began shoveling in food without stopping talking. "Man, I need to start eating more healthy stuff. You wouldn't believe all the new cases of rectal dysfunction I'm seeing. My test case has new symptoms—his anal aneurysm actually *exploded*—you've never seen *anything* like it!"

"Oh, is that Patient Wilbur?", said another doctor, turning around and grinning.

"That's him! Thank God I'm in the same HMO as he is! Got all that good health insurance money to run *all kinds* of tests—Carte Blanche! This time, I used local anesthetic and sewed his anus shut..."

"*I* prefer the anal tampons, myself," said the second doctor, a portly proctologist from Maine.

The first doctor nodded emphatically, "Oh yes, I got a new batch in, laced with methadone. I'm gonna start using those next week. And I can't wait to do the follow-up. You wouldn't *believe* the anal abscesses he's got this time!" He waved a fork animatedly. "Pustules the size of half-dollar coins—remember them? I used to collect 'em when I was a kid. Wish I still had 'em, be worth some money today. Anyway, where was I? Oh yeah, back to those abscesses—it's unbelievable! You *can't* teach these people about *proper* anal care..."

Shrini turned around and bellowed, "WILL YOU *PLEASE* TALK ABOUT SOMETHING—*ANYTHING* ELSE?"

There was an uncomfortable silence. Finally the fat doctor from Maine said, "Uh, Bernie... so, how's the golf game coming along?"

Shrini turned back around and looked at Richard. "So what's this about Perry?"

Hayte blew on his hot coffee. "The desk clerk at the Chelsea says Perry stayed there two nights ago and left in a real hurry. I think he's in real trouble."

"Perry stayed at the Chelsea? Why?"

"I think he's on the run."

"From who? Those guys with the sandals?"

Hayte nodded. "I think so."

She looked at him skeptically. "Perry Donohue's never been afraid of *anybody*. Why should he..." She broke off in mid-sentence when she noticed his expression. "Why are *you* afraid of them, Tree-Top?"

Hayte pushed his plate away, "Man, my vomit-pump is acting up again..."

Shrini looked at the greasy deep-fried hush puppies on his plate. "No surprise, seeing what you regularly put down it..." She stopped and looked at him inquiringly. "Don't try to change the subject—what's the deal with you and those guys? Something to do with your past?"

Hayte fiddled with his fork. Finally, he looked at her and said. "...Yeah. Alright. It was back when Mayor Juilliani was shot... Those guys are *bad* news."

Shrini looked confused. "I thought Rudy Guiliani died a natural death."

"*Juilliani*, not Giuliani," corrected Hayte, "Everybody calls our precinct HQ the Guiliani Building, but that's wrong. You pronounce the name as 'Hoo-lee-an-ee'. Do you remember him at all? He was our only Cuban-born mayor—but he only made it a year in office before he got shot. That was about 12 years ago."

"Twelve years ago?" Shrini sat back. "I wasn't even *in* America back then. But assassinations are big news—how come nobody ever talks about it?"

Hayte drummed his fingers. "Actually, there *wasn't* much news—it all got hushed up, big time. And we never found out who or why—because the NYPD wasn't ever officially *allowed* to investigate. That's also why we don't have a police commissioner any more, only a police chief. I was only a rookie cop when it happened, but everybody knew not to ask any more questions after those guys became involved..." Hayte cut himself short. "Listen, you don't want to know, believe me. They're a real spooky bunch. I know enough about them to avoid them—I don't want my mind jammed by experts."

She folded her arms. "So you're not going to tell me anything more?"

"Shrini, it's for your own good. I don't want you involved."

"Tree-top, if you don't go to the Chief about this, I will." She looked him in the eyes. "Now, what's it going to be?"

"Shrini, I need some time to think about this."

She frowned. "You got the rest of today. Period. But if Perry ends up dead because of this..."

"He won't end up dead," said Hayte quietly. They finished eating in silence, then she got up and left him alone. As she walked out the front, Hayte muttered to himself, "He won't be dead... But he won't be the same old Perry..."

Chapter 12
THE NEW YORK CYBERPOST
FLOODWATERS RECEDE!
Subways to Re-open

Finally! The New York Metropolitan Transit Authority announced yesterday that floodwater levels "dropped significantly" over the past week and that subways could re-open "in the near future". At a press conference yesterday, MTA head Constance White said "every effort will be made to clear out underground tunnels" and that "work will begin immediately." Huge thermal driers on loan from NASA will be used in the coming week. Added White, "while it is impossible to predict when all lines will be operational, it will be soon."

Thursday, March 17, 8:00 am:

He was in total darkness, and the cell was too small to stand fully erect. Perry couldn't lie down either, not even diagonally—he had to fold his knees. After a while, his legs cramped painfully.

There was not even cracks of light from a doorway. Perry hoped there *was* a door. It felt like he was deep underground, like in some sort of modern tomb.

He didn't know how long he had been lying there. He was starving and his head throbbed. When he'd come to, he tried to stand up and had bashed his head on the ceiling in the darkness.

Why am I here? He needed answers, anything to focus his attention and keep him from panicking. He fought the urge to scream and thrash against the hard concrete.

Now he could feel the calm returning. His breathing steadied. But still, the images of the past 24 hours remained etched in his mind, tormenting him.

~ ~ ~

When Perry first stirred, he saw his clothes were gone, replaced by an

145

ill-fitting uniform. *The bastards are trying to take away my identity. The uniform probably has a number stenciled on it.*

He almost chuckled. *The idiots haven't figured out this won't work on a cop...* Then he stopped laughing.

Am I still a cop?

The cell door opened. Donohue lay still. He opened his eyes a little and saw three sets of Birkenstocks and white socks. The socks of the middle man were bloodstained.

Rough hands grabbed him by the shoulders and dragged him to a holding pen that looked and smelled like it had housed a few animals. Harsh white lights mounted outside the pen cast all sorts of strange shadows. Perry could see the images through his eyelids. It felt like he was hallucinating.

Donner walked into the holding pen like he owned it and Donohue too. He was a wide-faced man with a square jaw gone flabby. It was the first time Perry had gotten a good look at him, albeit clandestinely.

"Get up, prisoner!" said Donner, prodding him with a white night stick. "Time for your first seminar!" Donohue acted like he was still groggy, only raising his head a fraction and mumbling incoherently.

Donner grabbed Perry by the neck and pulled him to his feet.

Donohue tried to punch him in the mouth. But Donner was surprisingly fast for a man his bulk. He dodged nimbly aside and nailed Donohue full in the crotch with his Birkenstock.

Donohue folded up like a portable card table, spewing all over his shirt. Donner hit him again and Perry hit the wall of the cage with a thud and slid down gasping.

Donner grabbed him by the hair and got in his face. "Don't you ever hit me in the head again, you little shit!"

As soon as the nausea subsided, Perry tried to surreptitiously nail Donner's exposed toes, which were inches away from his face, but Donner executed a neat Tai Kwan Do move, squeezing Perry's head in a lock between his knees. "*Obey*, you little shit!"

"Why don't you stuff your ass with broken glass and circumcise your daddy... uh!" Donohue gasped as Donner grabbed him by the hair and yanked his head back.

"Just remember this, Donohue, if you cause me enough trouble, my boys will make your face look like red... *raw*... hamburger." He spaced out the words as if enjoying the sound. "I... *love*... hamburger."

Perry spit at Donner's feet. "What do you want from me, Donner?"

"For starters, I want the head back."

"What head?"

Donner grabbed Perry's hair again and yanked his head back. "The one you brought through Baltimore Airport, you little shit! The one you *stole!*"

"I didn't steal your precious head. It was given to me by..." Donohue cut himself short.

"Who?" Donner's eyes lit up. "*Who* gave it to you?"

Donohue started silently at the floor. *If these goons really do have international clout, I don't want to drag Henri into this…*

Donner yanked his head back again. "Who? *Who* gave it to you?"

"Interpol. While I was in Europe, they wanted me to help ID it."

Donner released his hold on Perry's head. "Bullshit. You cops are always piss-poor liars. That's one reason you're so useful—once we're done training you, you won't ever be able to pull one over on us."

"Training?! What the hell for?"

Donner said quietly, "Do you want to get out of here?"

"And leave these quaint surroundings?"

"Smart-ass." Donner shoved a grey hand-held device in Perry's face.

Donohue looked at it blankly. "What's that?"

"It's for you to sign, dumb-ass."

Perry got to his feet slowly and dusted himself off. "What's it for?"

"You're in no position to ask. Now *sign*."

Donohue folded his arms. "I could be signing my own death warrant."

"Nope. You're far to useful to us—unless you don't sign, of course, in which case you would be indefinitely incarcerated in random locations until a military tribunal gets around to your case—if your fellow inmates don't tear you apart first…"

"And why would they do that?"

"Because." An ugly grin spread across Donner's round features. "The majority are Islamic extremists. We're part of Homeland Security—or weren't you aware of that?"

"What?" Donohue was stunned.

"Ignorant bastard—no wonder you didn't answer our e-mail. You could've saved yourself a lot of trouble by turning yourself in and giving us our property back. But fortunately for you, you still have a chance to redeem yourself. Sign here. Once you get done with your training, you'll be free to go."

Perry played with the pointer. "What am I signing?"

"All right, I'll tell you. A Promissory Agreement granting the NPDi full rights to put you on active duty when needed, after we train you as we see fit. It's just like the Army Reserve."

"You expect me to allow you to conscript me whenever you *feel like it*? You're fuckin' nuts!"

"No, *you're* nuts if you don't sign, because then you won't see the light of day ever again, Donohue." He stared holes all the way into the back of Perry's head. "I'll make *sure* of that."

Perry looked away. He took the tiny pointer and scribbled a signature.

"Good! Now your training can begin!" Two henchmen grabbed Perry and dragged him down a hall to another cell. He was strapped to a chair. Rough hands held his head still. "Got a real treat for you!" said an unfamiliar voice.

A virtual beamer was strapped to his head.

The video started. It was a history of the NPDi.

After the brief intro credits, Perry felt himself swallowed up by the images as they suddenly went 3D. It was suddenly 2036, a sunny September morning. He had never seen the buildings in person, but he knew instantly what they were—and that he was inside, on an upper floor of the hospital. He wasn't sure which floor, all he knew was that he had to start running now. He could hear the roar and feel the rumble of the jet engines of the oncoming jumbo jet.

He felt the plane hit with sickening certainty. The floor buckled under his feet and the air around him filled with flames and smoke. He imagined himself running to the stairs, but the door was blocked. He felt panic rising all around him.

~ ~ ~

Friday, March 18:

When Hayte came in to work, the red message light on his desk phone was on. He picked up the receiver. "Chief wants to see you, Captain," said the crisp recorded voice.

Hayte grimly got to his feet and walked to the staircase leading to the Chief's office. *Seems like all I'm doing lately is climbing stairs...* He knocked on the Chief's door.

Shabazz looked up from his paperwork. "Morning, Captain. I understand you're having problems with break-ins."

"Not just break-ins, sir. My apartment's totally ruined—the perpetrator somehow set off an electrical fire, which then triggered the sprinkler system. It'll take at least a week to dry the place out."

Shabazz frowned sympathetically. "Well, that certain explains why you've been so hard to contact lately."

"I'm sorry about that, sir, " said Hayte grimly. "I'm at the Chelsea Hotel, sir, room 100."

Shabazz looked shocked. "The Chelsea? Surely Captain, you can afford something better on your salary?"

"Everything else is all booked up, sir. The International Proctology Convention took everything in Manhattan from what I hear. Hell, I didn't even know there were so many proctologists on this green Earth..."

"Oh yes," nodded Shabazz. "You know why? People don't eat enough fiber. Have *you* ever thought about that, Captain? Your eating habits are not the best." He leaned forward with a conspiratorial tone, "Do you know what the secret is? *Macrobiotics!*"

Hayte coughed politely. "Sir, you wanted to speak to me about something?"

"Oh yes." Shabazz's tone became businesslike again. "I have some potentially damning news about Captain Donohue. We have reason to suspect that he's somehow mixed up in that murder of three VNN reporters. The top brass at VNN—or their lawyers, to be precise—are alleging exactly that."

Hayte looked at Shabazz incredulously. "That's crazy! What possible connection is there between Perry and those reporters?"

Shabazz looked grim. "The reporters' bodies were found in Jersey, in the back of an abandoned graveyard. A rental car checked out in Donohue's name was found not far from the murder scene." He read from a printout, "One point oh five miles away, to be exact." He handed the printout and accompanying photos to Hayte. "The ballistics tests indicated that the same kind of gun as Donohue's was used."

"But what about the ballistics fingerprint?" said Hayte. "All NYPD-issue guns have them."

"No ballistics fingerprint was found," Shabazz eyed him coldly. "So it has to be a civilian-issue gun. I seriously doubt Donohue would have used his police-issue magnum—that would've been suicidal. But he might have used something similar—we do know a large number of confiscated guns have disappeared from the Central Evidence room over the years, including a few magnums of that caliber."

Hayte scanned the photos and leafed through the report.. He set the photos down. "This doesn't look good, sir, but I am sure they're wrong. I can vouch that Perry had nothing to do with those reporters being murdered..."

Shabazz interrupted, "But VNN and the rest of the press won't see it like that."

Hayte looked at him skeptically. "But to accuse a police detective of murder? That makes no real sense. Are there any other connections between Capt. Donohue and VNN? He normally has nothing to do with reporters."

"From what I've gathered, it all stems from that confrontation during the last Phantoms robbery. VNN also has eyewitness are saying Capt. Donohue recently visited VNN to obtain video of the last Phantoms robbery. They suspect he wanted the reporters' names and faces."

Hayte began jotting down notes. "Did he *get* the footage?"

Shabazz shook his head. "No. They said they needed a court order first."

"Sir, do you *really* think there's any connection between Perry and those dead reporters?"

"Word has it that he was seen talking to all three—within 48 hours of their disappearance."

"And what about Perry's disappearance?" said Hayte.

Shabazz looked at him. "You really think he's disappeared? From all appearances, it looks more like he's on the run."

"Maybe he is, but from what?"

Shabazz sat back. "You tell me. Or better yet, find him, so he can testify at his disciplinary hearing. That's the only way he can clear himself."

"I just hope he's still alive." Hayte got up to leave. "A dead cop can't defend himself."

~ ~ ~

Now Perry found himself running through the atrium at the ground floor lobby. He saw strange shadows all around, so he looked up. Suspended from branches, he saw human torsos hanging from safety belts. Other body parts were scattered on the glass panes above.

He kept running. A terrified-looking uniformed cop urged him to keep going, and he was rushed out onto the street. The scene suddenly faded.

A voice-over started: "Never again shall we allow our brave law enforcement officials to be slaughtered by murderers masquerading as terrorists. Homeland Security is our MISSION. We are the NPDi."

~ ~ ~

Hayte poked his head into Shrini's cubicle. "Hey—we got more trouble. Perry's rental car was found abandoned near those dead VNN reporters."

Startled, she looked up, then frowned. "What's that mean?"

"It means Perry's now a suspect in the murders."

Shrini scowled. "That's bullshit!"

Rich nodded, "Yeah, but we have to prove that it is."

Her eyes widened. "Wait a minute—when was the car rented?"

"Three or four days ago, according to Shabazz's data."

"Well..." She typed in some parameters for a data search. "Aha—found it! It says here that those reporters were found dead some time last week—and that's when Perry was still in Italy."

Hayte looked over her shoulder at the monitor. "Yeah, you're right! I should've remembered that." He shook his head. "Man, this lack of sleep's getting to me."

She looked him over. "You *do* look tired. Ready to move out of the Chelsea?"

"More than ready. That sagging bed is killing me. I wanna go back home. The repairmen should be done by tomorrow." He rubbed his eyes and yawned. "But, you know we'd better get the exact dates of Perry's trip to Italy, just to make sure—I need a printout to show Shabazz."

"Give me a few minutes, Tree-top." She started typing rapidly.

"OK, I'll grab a few candy bars from the machine."

When he came back, she waved him over. She swiveled around in her chair with an air of triumph. "There! I've got Perry's personal calendar onscreen."

Hayte peered over her shoulder. "What's it got?"

"The travel dates clear him—but that's not all." She pointed to the tiny script at the bottom. "See? Last modified April 11."

"Roughly 48 hours before we put out the missing persons bulletin on him. Give me a printout of that, and I'll take it to Shabazz right away."

"Right." She scrolled back several weeks. "And here's something also very interesting, especially for Chief Shabazz."

"Huh?" Hayte leaned forward and squinted at the display.

"See? Appointments with a Dr. Max Jacobson IV."

Hayte was still puzzled. "So Perry had a medical condition?"

"No. See here..." she clicked on Max Jacobson IV's name, bringing up the Manhattan telephone listing. "Doctor of Psychology."

Hayte's eyebrows arched in surprise. "Well, what do you know? Perry was going to brain drain sessions after all. But why doesn't Chief Shabazz know about this?"

Shrini tapped the monitor display with her fingernail. "Probably because this particular doctor is not one of the NYPD in-house psychoanalysts. Our ones don't have listings in the phone book."

"This is getting curiouser and curiouser..." said Hayte, "Guess we have to pay Dr. Max Jacobson IV a visit."

"Don't expect much. Remember, they have a doctor-patient confidentiality agreement."

"I know all about that, Shrini—I study law, remember? But we can at least get Dr. J. to clear Perry of that charge of ducking his 'brain drains.'"

~ ~ ~

"Dance, bear, dance!" It was Donner's shrill voice.

With a start, Donohue suddenly realized he was awake and standing. On all fours. He felt heavy and slow. And he was wearing something thick over his whole body.

"Dancing bear, you will obey! *Now!*"

A bear suit?!

Donner jabbed him with large rapier-like apparatus that glowed blue with electric current.

Perry let out a yelp. The pain was white hot.

Somehow the costume was not a costume at all—his skin was bearskin. Perry was startled by his own voice—he tried to yell insults but it only came out like a wounded roar. He tried again and it sounded more pitiful, like a bawling sound.

Donner jabbed him again, making Perry bellow deeper and louder.

"Stand on your head! On the stool!" barked Donner.

Perry found himself going to the stool, but his head was too big and clumsy, knocking the stool over.

"*Bad* bear!!" Another jab of high voltage. Perry let out another bellow.

Then he heard the laughter. He swung his massive head around and saw them in the bleachers.

I'm in the goddamn circus!

"Dancing bear—go swim in the pool!"

On the edge of the stage there was a huge glass tank. Perry got on his hind legs and roared in protest.

Someone else went behind him and shot a pure white voltage stream up Perry's ass, sending him lumbering up the steps to the diving platform. The platform was narrow and slippery, making it impossible for him to turn back around.

He took one look at the water, at least 15 feet deep, and shrunk back.

Another flash of voltage, and his fur caught fire. Panic-stricken, he plunged into the water with a huge splash.

He trashed about hopelessly in the water as he sunk to the bottom. He could see the children's maliciously smiling faces pressed against the tank.

In total panic, he started to ram his head into the glass between him and the air outside.

Then he blacked out.

~ ~ ~

Armed with the printout of Donohue's flight itinerary, Hayte went back upstairs. He was just about to knock on Shabazz's open door when he heard the Chief yell "I ain't *believing* this shit!"

Too late, Hayte saw the Chief looking at him. "Uh, I guess this is a bad time..."

"What is it, Captain?" said Shabazz harshly.

"Sir I..." Hayte took a moment to compose himself. He waved the printout. "I got some evidence concerning Captain Donohue."

Shabazz quickly scanned the printout and lowered his voice. "I'm sorry, Captain..." He looked decidedly unsettled. "So do I—but I'd rather not discuss it here." He reached in his desk and pulled out a scrap of paper, then scribbled on it and handed it to Hayte. He waved at Hayte to leave.

Hayte nodded silently, took the paper and put it in his pocket. He walked back down the stairs before he fished it back out. It was a business card for a Brooklyn mosque. On the back was scribbled "Can you meet me here Saturday morning at 8?"

An address near Central Park was scribbled below.

~ ~ ~

Saturday, March 19, 6 am:

Perry had now gone 34 hours without any normal kind of sleep. He noticed he was no longer wearing bearskin but was strapped to a chair bolted to the floor—and the floor and the ceiling had been inverted. Water and glucose were being fed through an IV in his leg. A suction tube was clasped to his penis.

He'd had this experience once before, at the NASA Space Flight Simulator in Huntsville, but only for a few minutes. And not in total darkness like this.

He was fighting it for all he was worth, but his morale was flagging. Every time he started to drift off to sleep, the chamber began to spin, but he wasn't sure if it was really rotating or all in his head.

His temples throbbed horribly. He was wearing the virtual beamer again, and it was strapped on too tight. He started to hope the visuals would start again. At least those would keep his mind off his misery.

~ ~ ~

Saturday, 7:45 am:

Stepping out of the Chelsea, Hayte saw a tiny glimmer from his car headlights and his heart sank. *Why didn't the car tell me I'd left the lights on?*

He briefly considered kicking the headlights in, then realized he was already wasting time. He looked at his watch and realized he would be late for his meeting with Shabazz if he didn't hurry. He ran up and down 23rd Avenue, looking for a cab.

To his great surprise, one stopped half a block away. A short, stubby man with bad teeth poked his head out the window. "You need a cab?"

"Yeah!" Hayte ran up and got in quickly. "Thanks—I wasn't expecting you to stop, especially in front of the Chelsea."

"I wouldn't normally," said the driver, who had oily black hairs running down the back of his neck, "But you're so friggin' tall, I figger' you ain't no robber, so I said 'what da hell?' Where ya headed?"

"I ain't no robber, that's for sure…" grinned Hayte, flashing his badge. "I need you to go to Central Park and West—*real* quick."

In the rear-view mirror, the cabby's eyes widened. "Youze a cop? What da hell you doin' at a flophouse like da Chelsea?" He steered the cab out into traffic.

Hayte said sardonically. "Man, the International Proctology Convention got all of Manhattan booked up solid. I had no idea there were so many of them."

"Oh *yeah*—Dem butt doctors are doing *big* business—but me, I do my best to avoid 'em. Otherwise you'd better pony up for a cloned colon—and dat takes *years!*" He leaned over and said conspiratorially and winked, "Know what? I got a diet secret… *macrobiotics*—it's da best thing in da world!"

"Yeah, macrobiotics…" Hayte looked away, slightly embarrassed. Suddenly he noticed they were almost past Central Park. "Hey! There's my stop!"

The cab slid to a stop and Hayte handed out a ten and ran off, leaving the cabby to grumble "fucking cheapskate cops!"

Hayte made his way to a stately 40-floor townhouse at the park's edge.

He checked the scrap of paper to make sure he had the right address. It was.

He pressed the talk button at the gate.

~ ~ ~

8:35 am:

Shabazz's apartment was a prize one, a three-story penthouse condo with a brilliant view of the Manhattan skyline. As always, the Chief was dressed immaculately, this time in a light brown suit and starched white shirt. His bow tie was red.

"Why did you want to speak with me, Chief?" asked Hayte quietly, as he settled his long limbs into an easy chair.

"Quintessential Captain Hayte..." Shabazz half-smiled, "No 'nice place you got here, Chief,' just straight to business."

Hayte looked around at the exotic décor. "The thought did cross my mind, but I thought it might sound like criticism." He uncrossed his legs. "Besides, it's obvious anyway. But this isn't a social call, right?"

"Right. I can only offer you coffee or soft drinks, Captain."

Hayte shook his head, "Maybe later."

"All right, let's get down to it." Shabazz fingered his empty coffee cup. "One question, Captain. How is it you and Lieutenant Shrini have been so willing to go to bat for Captain Donohue? There must be something about him I'm not getting."

Hayte looked at the Chief's eyes and saw they were bloodshot. "It's because we're a team. The three of us cracked the Smash case, and Perry's saved my ass more than a few times." He stopped when he realized his slip.

Shabazz folded his arms. "That's all right, Captain, please continue."

Hayte leaned back. "I can't speak for Shrini, but I think Donohue is also braver than any other cop I've ever seen—I've watched him single-handedly defuse a riot in Harrods on the Bowery, we've crawled through sewers in Harlem—we really do our best work together. Does that answer your question, sir?"

"Somewhat." Shabazz walked over to the large bay window and stared at the clouds rolling in. "At any rate, thanks to Captain Donohue, I've got a whole new situation to deal with."

Hayte looked at Shabazz's silhouette in the windows. "Is that why I'm here?"

"Yes." Shabazz turned back around. "I've been on this job for almost three months and the grey in my hair has doubled..." He rubbed his eyes. "I'll get to the point, Captain. Yesterday morning, I got an urgent message from the NPDi. Do you know who they are?"

Startled, Hayte avoided the Chief's gaze. "I... uh..."

Shabazz raised his eyebrows. "Aha, I see you *do*. Much as I'd like to know what you know about them, I have other priorities to deal with first."

Hayte raised his eyes again. "Do they have Perry?"

"Yes, I'm afraid they do." Shabazz stepped closer. "Have *you* ever worked for them, Captain?"

"No." said Hayte quietly. "*Never.*"

"Interesting, most interesting…" Shabazz folded his arms.

"So that message told you they had him?"

"Yes. I had just received it when you came by yesterday morning. They said Capt. Donohue has signed with them, despite his existing contract with the NYPD, and it's all legal—nothing we can do about it. I can't believe the *nerve* of those people—they sweep right in and co-opt a New York City Police officer like it's their *birthright* to do so!"

"Did the message say anything else?"

"Oh yes, that he would be away for training for 'an unspecified period of time' but will continue to work on his existing cases—as time allows. How in hell's name that's supposed to work, I do *not* know… *And* it goes on to say that NPDi conscripts like Donohue 'may periodically have more training seminars *when the need arises.*" He shook his head. "In the meantime, I am specifically prohibited from withholding his salary *and* from any disciplinary action. I am to sit tight and wait for Donohue or the NPDi to contact *me.*" He closed his eyes and rubbed them.

Hayte looked the chief point blank in the eye. "Sir, I'd like to try and find him, get him out of their clutches."

Shabazz met his look. "Do you really think it's possible?"

"Yes." said Hayte quietly. "I *am* studying law, remember? Signing something while under duress carries no validity and can be successfully challenged in court.."

Shabazz paused a few seconds. "Let me think about that over the rest of the weekend. I'll let you know." He shifted awkwardly and cleared his throat. "But there is another thing I do want to say, Captain." He stood up and walked over to the window overlooking Manhattan. "I want to apologize for calling Donohue a 'Cracker' the other day... it was wrong of me. He was my best hope of getting the Phantoms case solved. Sometimes it's hard to keep your mouth shut when you're angry, especially when you're under pressure."

Slowly, Hayte nodded almost imperceptibly.

"You don't need to say anything, Captain. Right now, the Department is under a lot of pressure. We—or, more exactly, *I* need this Phantoms case solved. And it seems like we're getting nowhere on it." He turned and looked Hayte in the eye. "I may not be Chief of Police too much longer. City Hall is talking about bringing back the Police Commissioner's position."

Hayte raised an eyebrow. "You don't want to run?"

"Captain, how much of a chance do you think an African-American Muslim would have in a city election? Even with Farrakhan dead and

155

buried, we're not exactly universally loved around here."

Hayte fingered his chin. "Maybe things'll change. When will you find out for sure?"

"I don't know," said Shabazz, "But nailing this Phantoms thing shut for once and all would sure help my bargaining position."

"If I could find Perry," said Hayte, "it would sure help *both* of us. *Especially* with the Phantoms."

"I'll assign Lieutenant Shrinithan to help you look for him."

"Thanks, Chief. Oh, one more thing..."

Shabazz sighed and rolled his eyes. "*Yes*, Captain?"

"Can you spare Lieutenant Pierce, too?"

Shabazz pursed his lips skeptically. "You really think the Gay Squad can help with this?"

"They hear about everything, sooner or later. That's why none of the city's religious leaders has ever managed to get City Hall to eliminate them, *ever*. Ask the Mayor's Office, they'll tell you."

"That's an idea, Captain, that is an idea..." Shabazz drummed his fingers and leaned back. "OK, you got him too."

"Thanks Chief," said Hayte, glancing at his watch, "I need to go. I got to round up everyone for a meeting tonight to discuss strategy."

Shabazz raised an eyebrow. "Big plans already? So you expected me to say yes, didn't you?" He waved Hayte away. "Don't worry about it. Just be sure and let me know when you find out something."

Hayte turned and went to the door. "I'll do that."

"Oh, one more thing I wanted to ask you," said Shabazz suddenly. "I realize Lt. Shrinithan was defending Capt. Donohue, but there was something about her manner that disturbed me. Why was she so aggressive? Does she have something against me, or the fact that I'm Muslim?"

Hayte chewed his lower lip. "I don't think it's *that*..."

"She was born in India, right?"

Rich nodded. "Correct. In Bombay, I believe..."

"Well, Hindus from there do have a thing against Moslems."

"But she was born Moslem," said Hayte.

"But she isn't Moslem *now*—it's obvious. A woman of faith would *never* act like that to *me*."

"Uh..." Hayte chose his words carefully, "When she was a girl in India, Shrini was told in advance by one of her sisters—about the ritual female circumcision. Shortly before it was to done to her, she sought refuge in a foreign embassy—the American one. The US media got wind of the story— and that's why she's a US citizen now." He glanced carefully at Shabazz, who was standing totally motionless.

"I appreciate your telling me that." The Chief let out a deep breath. "All right. Good luck, Captain."

~ ~ ~

9:55 p.m:

> *"My country 'tis of thee,*
> *Sweet Homeland Security—*
> *Obey our laws!*
> *We'll crack foreign access codes,*
> *Flush out terrorist abodes!*
> *We won't stop 'till we're in full control*
> **So watch your ass!"**

"I still don't like the last line," said Cheshire, frowning.

Donner turned on him like a Doberman. "WHAT'S WRONG WITH IT?"

Browning spoke up, "It's too trite. It doesn't sound anthem-like..."

"Never mind." Donner whipped around and grabbed Donohue by the hair. "I didn't hear *you* singing, prisoner!"

His hands cuffed behind his back, Perry could only struggle by trying to kick. "Kiss my a—OUCH!"

Donner slammed Donohue to the floor and planted a Birkenstock between his shoulder blades. Despite his pain, Perry could still smell the distinct odor of dog shit.

Donner barked, "Agent Cheshire, administer discipline."

Cheshire's face lit up, "The coat hangar?" He fished out the wire hanger, which had been unwound into a thin, flexible spoke that could be whipped back and forth at great speed.

"Yes." Donner nodded with a smile that quickly disappeared as Cheshire drew back to start flailing. He grabbed Cheshire's arm, "No, you IDIOT! Not in the FACE! On the *back of the knees*—where it's TENDER!"

Cheshire looked petulant. "Why *can't* I whip him in the face?"

"*Bonehead!* You wanna know why there aren't any agents or undercover cops called 'Scarface'? Facial scars are *visible!* You're only allowed to do that to terrorists—NOT our police recruits!" Donner leaned closer to Cheshire's ear and lowered his voice, "The *only* scars we want are *emotional.* We don't want any legal trouble..."

Browning rolled Donohue onto his stomach. Donner sat on Perry's feet. "Ready for administering."

The first blow made Perry bite into the yellow-brown linoleum.

After ten minutes, the pain was so intense, he blacked out.

~ ~ ~

Sunday, March 20, 8 am.

Hayte wasn't able to round up everyone on Saturday night, so that left Sunday morning. The upstairs meeting room at the White Elephant was not ideal for a group of participants in various states of hangover, but it was the only place available at short notice. The room was littered with the remains of the last seminar, with multi-language booklets scattered on all the tables, as the room was still being used for the Interpol Exchange Program lectures.

When he first walked into the room, he smelled burning dust. He looked around and realized that someone had left the beamer on. He quickly switched it off. Everyone came in and sat down.

Almost all the attendees were present and accounted for.

Hayte cleared his throat. "Thanks everyone for coming at this ungodly hour."

"You'd better be..." grumbled Dietrich, yawning conspicuously.

Shrini opened one of the booklets and wrinkled her nose. "Why did they include a condom inside?"

"Because syphilis is making a big comeback," said Dietrich. "The reported cases in Queens alone tripled last year."

"Can I get everyone's attention?" said Hayte, rapping on the podium. "OK, here's the situation. We got a runaway series of robberies we've got to solve. It's still Perry's case, but he's been co-opted by a Federal agency called the NPDi..."

"What's the deal with Perry? And who exactly are the NPDi?" said Dietrich.

"They're a government agency that handles homeland security" said Hayte. "They draft in state and local police personnel as they need them, to combat terrorism and other threats to public safety."

Dietrich said, "All I know is they've got clout. They impounded all the files I'd accumulated on the severed head..."

Shrini interrupted. "Where is the head, by the way?"

"I got it stashed in a secret location..." Dietrich took off his glasses and chewed on the earpiece absent-mindedly. "They want the head, right? Why not give them a trade—the head for Perry?"

Hayte shook his head. "Won't work—those bastards don't trade, they only *take*. And anyway, I'd sure like to find out more about why Mr. Chesney's head is floating around in the first place."

"Can't we issue a court order demanding Perry's whereabouts?" asked Shrini. "He's still on active duty—we have a right to know where he is."

Hayte made a face and sat down. "No way. They're a part of Homeland Security. The Chief gave me a few documents on them." He pulled out one and read aloud, "Under the Homeland Security Act, it says detainees can be quarantined indefinitely without any kind of protection under Miranda—no attorney, no contact with family or friends—and he could be transported between any number of secret locations without even the courts being notified."

Shrini grimaced. "Meaning, if the NPDi really do have him, chances of finding Perry are slim to none."

"So what does NPDi stand for, exactly?" pressed Dietrich. "I'd like to at least know who we're up against."

"The National Protection Directive," said Shrini, reading from her files, "It says here that they started as part of a working group designed to interface between the FBI, CIA, and local and state law enforcement—but they rapidly outgrew their original purpose. Nobody I know is really sure what they do now..." she turned to Hayte, "Can you tell us anything, Treetop?"

Hayte looked uneasy. "They're spooky, real spooky... from what I've seen, they're a clean-up squad. But you could almost call them a cult..."

"What's all this 'cult' nonsense?" said a melodic voice behind them.

Everyone turned around to see Lieutenant Pierce entering the room. Pierce, head of the NYPD Gay Squad, was dressed spectacularly for the occasion, with purple and pink ostrich feather boas and lavender stack-heel hiking boots that looked especially rugged.

Hayte raised an eyebrow at the garb. "New boots, Miss Clint?"

"Ooh yesss." purred Pierce, better known as Miss Clint. He thrust a lavender boot in Hayte's lap. "They're the latest Justin Timbernooks. Aren't they just *precious?* And they also come in turquoise, puce and lime green! I want to order the whole set!"

Hayte discretely but firmly shoved Pierce's foot off his leg. "I think we should talk about what might've happened to Perry."

"Oh, we'll get to that—but first, the fun stuff!" said Miss Clint. He held out a printout. "Look, everyone! Hot off the press—what everybody's going to be talking about tomorrow!"

"Gimme that!" said Shrini, grabbing the paper. She put it on the beamer.

THE NEW YORK CYBERPOST
'Nude' Olympics: The Naked Truth

Is nothing sacred? The IOC is reportedly considering returning the Olympic Games to its naked roots, according to reports yesterday.

In an effort to stem the disastrous tide of declining television ratings, the Olympic Committee is seriously considering making selected athletic events for the 2046 Winter and 2048 Summer Olypics nude, much as in the original games held in Ancient Greece.

Under the proposed system, events and athletes would be arbitrarily segregated into two categories: clad and au natural, with the au natural events only being televised on late night pay-per-view TV in most countries.

The proposed move is widely seen as a last-ditch effort to rescue the Games from obscurity, following almost a half-century of genetic manipulation, doping and bribery scandals.

"Only athletes participating in the Summer Games would actually be in fact nude" said a source, who refused to be named. "The Winter contestants would

wear a transparent unisex garment make of XlieX-D, the new clear synthetic material developed by a joint venture between NASA and DuPont. "It was a huge challenge to find a material that wouldn't cloud over when competitors sweated" said the source.

"Au natural events would of course be selected based on their artistic merit, exclusively" huffed another source, when grilled on the proposal. "Of course, swim events won't need clothing at all, but others like the pole vault would be all but impossible without some kind of athletic supporter."

A further controversy has erupted over events dominated by competitors under 18, considered by most countries to be when a person is considered adult. In response, the IOC has proposed a new, non-nude so-called Junior Olympic Games for all under 18 competitors, thereby eliminating the long-controversial prepubescent advantages in some disciplines, primarily high diving and gymnastics.

"Can you believe this?" said Shrini, taking the printout off. "*Nude* Olympics? What is this world coming to?"

Miss Clint smirked, "*I'm* looking forward to it! I just love the idea of watching all those perfect cocks swinging in unison."

Hayte grimaced. "*Man*, can you talk about something *else?*"

Shrini put her hands on her hips, "See? How do you think we women feel about men and their 'shop talk' about bouncing boobs?"

Miss Clint gave her a look. "I guarantee my 'shop talk' has nothing to do with 'bouncing boobs,' unless we're talking about what's on Perry Donohue's *mind…*" Pierce suddenly went pale. "Holy Elvis! I just though of something *horrible!* What about those high hurdles! Gawd, it makes me feel *faint* just thinking about it! What would happen if one runner didn't jump high enough? You know how testicles sometimes hang low without you knowing it…"

"Let's get back to finding Perry," snapped Hayte, "or solving the Phantoms case!"

"All right, alright, don't get your panties in a wad!" Pierce glared at him, "I'll make inquiries, ditty—just don't expect results overnight. I've got to keep up appearances…"

"I'll do what I can," added Shrini. "But I have to be really careful about finding Perry's trail because of the risk of back-tracing. It sounds like these NPDi types like to stick their tentacles everywhere—and I don't want to get snared." She looked again at Rich. "Which reminds me, you never explained *your* involvement with them. Or how you got out of it."

Hayte grimaced. "It wouldn't help, the case is history—and a little knowledge might be real dangerous." He changed the subject by pulling out a deck of cards. "Let's get back to the Phantoms." He began laying cards out on a nearby table.

"What's with the cards?" said Dietrich "You and Donohue both have developed a fondness for them. He borrowed my deck and hasn't brought them back."

Hayte nodded. "That's what I've heard. Do you know why he wanted them in the first place?"

"He said it was something to do with the Phantoms—and why there haven't been any repeat offenders."

Shrini walked over to them. "What do you mean, no repeat offenders?"

Hayte explained. "The robbers are never the same. They use different people each time."

"Must be a huge gang." said Dietrich.

"Maybe, maybe not…" Shrini walked over to the beamer and switched it back on. "Let me get all the crime scene stills up." She began typing in commands.

After a few seconds, everybody sat looking at the security camera stills of the Phantoms.

Shrini frowned. "If only we could find someone who could give us a positive ID of even one of them…"

It was at that moment Hayte remembered Scotty Bunch. "Oh shit—I gotta go. Bye!" He rushed out the door, leaving the others to stare blankly.

~ ~ ~

Sunday, 11:30 am:

Hayte rushed back to his apartment. He remembered he had Bunch's address written down in his case notes from the Smash case.

As always, the elevator was broken, so he took the stairs. As he reached the top floor he ran into Stanley walking up and down the hall, looking totally distraught.

Momentarily forgetting his haste, Rich looked at him. "What's wrong, Stan?"

"A catastrophe, a goddamn fucking catastrophe!" Bialystok was waving his arms dramatically. "It's a goddamned stake through my heart!—the *worst* of all possible disasters!"

Hayte was alarmed. "Really? Did somebody die?"

"Almost. I feel like dying, I tell ya." Stanley sighed.

"Well, what *is* it?"

"We had to cancel shooting for the next goddamn three weeks—we got a bad batch of bottled water and the whole fucking cast came down with bladder infections!"

Richard fought the impulse to laugh hysterically. He patted Stanley on the back. "Stan—cheer up. It'll be OK—I tell you what, we'll go out and have a drink to forget about all the bad stuff. I just gotta go and check up on a friend of mine, then I'll call you tonight."

Still upset, Stan nodded weakly. "OK, see ya."

Hayte closed the door and went back to the pile of debris on his desk.

~ ~ ~

1 p.m:

After interminable hours in total darkness, suddenly Perry was blinded by the light of the next presentation inside his virtual beamer. He found himself back at Ground Zero Dallas, staring into the blackened holes in the ground that once were the buildings of Parkland Medical Center. To his horror, Perry discovered that closing his eyes only intensified the images to a white flash.

The smooth-voiced voice-over announced, "You can PURGE the hurt, the pain, the negative energy of those tragic events—and all those that followed."

The louder words echoed between his ears as the text pulsed.

"In the AFTERMATH of those tragic events, we as a nation became STRONGER.

WHY?

Because something GOOD came out of it.

How did we do this?

By FOCUSING our ENERGY.

We now have a mental capacity to FOCUS on the NECESSARY. CLARITY is KEY.

This is now YOUR goal TOO.

YOU are a part of a GREATER whole. That greater whole is AMERICA.

After the tragedy of September 11, 2001 and the further tragedies last decade in DALLAS, our nation's purpose was redefined into ONE word: SURVIVAL."

The word pulsed as the letters changed from black to red and then to blue. It moved to the side and became the subject of the sentence:

SURVIVAL is the ONLY goal.

The voice-over started again. "We must THINK LIKE OUR ENEMIES. There is a single source of all PSYCHOTIC behavior, all compulsive REPRESSION, all... ENVY.

Our enemies want what they CANNOT have.

Our WEALTH.

Our POWER.

Our GLORY.

They will do ANYTHING to BRING US DOWN."

How do we DEFEAT these ENEMIES?

By SCIENCE—MENTAL science.

What is 'Mental Science'?

It is:

    * The UNDERSTANDING of your INNER self.

    * ALL the POSITIVE and NEGETIVE energies flowing through our bodies.

    * And especially it means CONQUERING THOSE ENERGIES which seek to DESTROY us, both OUTISDE and INSIDE.

    * Psychosomatic illnesses are EIGHTY percent of ALL illnesses.

* By learning to CONQUER YOUR NEGATIVE ENERGY, YOU will LEARN TO DESTROY THEIRS TOO.

YOU will learn how MS works and what it can do for YOU.

~ ~ ~

Sunday, 7:30 p.m:

It took all day for Hayte to locate Bunch's address. Now he stood at the apartment building, a big gentrified brownstone in the Bowery.

He pressed the apartment bell repeatedly. He spoke into the tiny speaker in the wall. "Scotty? Hey Bunch, you there?"

Finally growing frustrated and more than a little uneasy, he reached in his coat pocket and took out a blank chip card. He slid it in the keycard reader. It popped back out 'rejected,' and he stuck it immediately in his hand-held card reader.

The signal was weak but readable. He hit the 'new card' button, waited a second, then popped the newly-programmed card back in the keycard reader.

The front door of the brownstone popped open with a pneumatic hiss.

Hayte found the hall lights weren't working. He fumbled for his penlight. He stepped cautiously inside and went down the corridor. He shined the light over the door numbers.

There.

To his surprise, Bunch's door was unlocked. He put on his gloves and pushed it open. He tried the light switch. No power.

His eyes adjusted to the dim light filtering in from the windows.

Suddenly the objects on the floor came into focus. Bits of furniture were strewn all over, sofas overturned, wood splinters everywhere.

On the far wall, there was a bed, with the mattress blown out in the middle. He stepped gingerly over the debris, but couldn't avoid scattering some of it. He looked over the bed. The odor was revolting, a mix of chemicals and charred flesh.

He reached in his kit bag for his regulation flashlight. The unusually large bed frame looked like it was either antique or, he thought more likely, second-hand, made from brass. The outer form of the top mattress was still intact, but all the inside padding was gone, except for the charred bits clinging to the sides. He could see clear through to the box springs, which glittered in his torchlight. The ones in the center had obviously been melted by the heat.

He shined the light over the rest of the bed. Bits of blanket and sheeting were wadded up between the wall and the bed.

On a hunch, he slid the bed frame away from the wall. Something hit the floor behind the bed with a muffled thud.

He reached down and felt something creepy. He pulled it out. A human hand and half a wrist, attached to a set of charred handcuffs. It was obviously a man's hand, from the size and shape, despite all the scorching.

He shined his torch over the floor around the bed. The carpet was scorched, silhouetting the form of the bed.

But what about the wall? Why didn't it ignite?

The wallpaper was scorched, but that was all.

Hayte was no expert on explosives, but something here was wrong, very wrong. He decided to check the rest of the room. A fridge on the other side of the room was still intact, amazingly. He opened it and saw it was full of soggy Mexican food. There was s six-pack of Cerveza gold on the bottom shelf and some rotting apples in the crisper. *Hell, the shelves inside weren't even dislodged…What is going on here?*

He shined the flashlight over the windows. The inner glass was only cracked and charred up to halfway.

The whole thing puzzled him no end. *I gotta get help on this…* He fished out his dial-a-pad and activated his headset.

A sleepy voice answered, "NYPD Forensics, Dietrich here."

"Dietrich—it's Hayte. Listen, I got a probable murder scene." He read out the address. "I can't say for sure, but the victim's name is probably Scott Bunch"

"Ouch!" Dietrich snapped awake. "Shit! Sorry 'bout that—I just spilled my coffee. Did you say Scott Bunch—wasn't that the possible Phantoms robbery witness you mentioned at the meeting?

"That's him." replied Hayte, his voice grim. "It's his apartment, and he lived alone, from the looks of it. Looks like he was blown to bits—there's only…" he looked down, "a human hand left."

"Aw jeez…" More yawns on the other end. "Sorry bout that. So no need for rush ambulance service…" Dietrich paused, "Do I even *need* to send the meat wagon if there's only a hand left?"

"Go ahead and send it. Trust me, defense attorneys just love deviations from standard police procedure."

"If you really think we'll get that far… Finding a perp won't exactly be easy." Dietrich paused for a moment. "Have you got a camera handy?"

"Yeah, I do," said Hayte. "I'll see what I can get."

"OK, just three or four wide-angle digital shots that we can analyze later. Have you got 3-D capability?"

"No, not enough light. The electricity is off in Bunch's apartment, and I tried the hall lights, but either they're out or the bulbs have been taken out."

"Means the neighbors won't be getting curious yet." Dietrich paused. "Just get me what you can, before the boys from Homicide come tramping in and wipe out half the evidence."

"I gotcha. Call you later." Hayte took the headset, folded it in his pocket. He fished out his palmtop computer and activated the camera function. There was just enough juice in the battery for a few quick shots.

Behind him, he heard a noise. He quickly whirled around, his revolver out.

A small child was peering in the doorway.

Hayte yelled, "HEY KID! GET AWAY FROM HERE!!!"

The kid ran away.

Hayte immediately regretted chasing the kid off. He looked out. The hall was empty. He didn't even know which direction the kid ran. That was one possible witness, gone.

He sighed and put the gun back in his holster. He needed to hurry with lining up potential shots. First priority was a picture of the hand and the bed, next would be the charred outline of the blast-

Without warning, the sound system in the corner switched on and began blaring a song at full volume. Hayte recoiled and almost dropped his palmtop.

The holographic display on the portable home entertainment complex sent colored flashes of light around the room like an old-fashioned mirror ball. The music was strangely familiar.

An old Beatles tune?

The light flashes rotated, blinding him in perfect 5-second intervals. He stared at the portable, mystified as to why it had switched on.

He recognized the chorus: *"Baby, It's You"*—he remembered it from a shoe commercial that was currently running on all the Moviscript billboards around the city.

As the 'sha-la-la's' of the background vocals swirled round the room, a sudden thought flashed through his head. *How would I know if it is Scotty?* He pondered the question, and decided to photograph the hand from both sides. He did so, then he moved back to take a wide-angle shot from the far corner of the main room.

He switched on the infrared sensor and looked around. *Footprints in the carpet?*

He zoomed in, but the image lost its contours, so he went back to wide-angle mode. *No, it's more like trampling, some kind of struggle around the radiator…*He snapped the image.

The next song, *"Do You Want to Know a Secret?"* came on the stereo. He blanched when he recognized that that one came from a deodorant commercial.

He looked through the infrared sensor at the refrigerator. Nothing new came up. He looked through the viewer at the rest of the room. Nothing.

On a whim, he opened the apartment door to look for prints with the infrared. It was then that he saw something written on the door's front. Through the viewer, strange helixes appeared, adorned with symbols. He snapped several photo of the symbols, trying to get the helix swirls in as much detail as possible.

Then he went back inside, to the opposite side of the room, stepping delicately around edges of the char marks in the carpet. The next song started on the portable. This one he didn't recognize—somehow, he found that reassuring. *But why did the thing switch on?*

Shaking his head, he took a last shot, of the sound system.

He took out his pocket-vac and ran it along the carpet along the imprints next to the bed and went out and did the same below the hieroglyphics outside the door. He didn't really expect to find any foreign hair samples, but he figured it was worth a shot. He went back inside. Another song started.

Just as he was about to leave, a thought occurred to him. He scribbled the song order on his palmtop before he set it on standby. He walked outside.

A few minutes later, Dietrich showed up with the County Coroner's van. Hayte came out just as Dietrich walked up, still working on another box of Chinese take-out. "Hi Rich. So it's a weird one."

"Real strange" said Hayte. "I took as many photos as I could and vacuumed for DNA samples but I don't think there's much to go on." He kicked viciously at a whisky bottle lying nearby. It shattered against a curb.

Dietrich looked him over. "Rich, what's wrong?"

Hayte let out his breath slowly. "I should've checked up on Scott earlier."

"You couldn't have known..."

"Yes, I could've. He was so jumpy that night." Hayte wadded up his coffee cup. "I should've checked on him the next day, when he didn't show."

Dietrich had no reply to that.

Hayte nodded wryly. "I'll take your silence as agreement."

"Well..." Dietrich looked away. He pointed to the blackened window. "What's with the windows? Normally an explosion would've..."

"...blown them out. In a huge fireball, which should've had the Fire Department and the Deto Squad swarming all over the place within minutes. No, this looks a whole lot more sophisticated. I haven't done any questioning of the neighbors yet..."

"Homicide will take care of that."

"Yup, but I'd be willing to bet nobody saw or heard anything. Nobody called 911—and there weren't any rubberneckers until you showed up a few moments ago."

"Did you put the hand in an evidence bag?"

"No.. Every time I get close to it, I feel like puking from the smell. There's something about charred flesh..." Hayte took a deep breath. "...it just *got* to me."

Hayte suddenly remembered something. He turned and looked at Dietrich. "You remember that exhibition from Germany, *Körperwelten*, I think it was called?"

Dietrich nodded. "Those human corpses dissected and stretched out to make 'art'? And then laminated under clear acrylic? Yeah, I remember going to that when I was a kid. Had to go up to Canada to see it."

"My family went too," Hayte scratched absently at his neat goatee. "I thought it was all so cool, and my parents were horrified. It wasn't until I saw the one with the little bit of skin on the arm, and I looked closer and saw that there was part of a tattoo… Then it hit me that this was once a human being, and I vomited all over the display!"

"Aha! So that was *you!*" smiled Dietrich, pushing his glasses back up his long nose. "That's where they must've gotten the idea to hand out barf bags at the entranceway, with the 'Bodily Universes' logo printed on it." He ran a hand through his wavy gray hair. "… I *think* I still got mine, stashed away at my mother's place somewhere…"

Hayte looked around and saw that Homicide was cordoning off the block. A puffy-faced detective with a pony tail came up to him. "You Captain Hayte?" He pronounced Captain as "Cap'n".

Hayte nodded. "That's me."

"I'm Lt. Briley, Forensics. You get any samples from the crime scene?"

"Hair samples and a lot of dust." Hayte unhooked the mini-vac from his belt and handed it to Briley. "I need this back when you're done."

"Is that all you got?" Briley held out his hands for more.

"No, I got infrared and UV scans to download. I'll burn you a disk when I'm done…"

"Can't you give them to me now?"

"Not yet. I got some specific leads to check up on. You see, I know the victim."

"C'mon, can't you…" Briley was interrupted by a sudden screech of tires and blaring horns. Hayte looked over and saw a string of media vans approaching. He left Briley standing and went over to Dietrich, who was trying to block their entry.

"Looks like we got company," said Hayte in Dietrich's ear.

"At least they showed up after *we did," said Dietrich, surveying the throng of reporters.*

"I know what you mean…" said Hayte. "They usually beat *us* to the crime scene. I'd sure like to know where they're getting their info."

"So would I," said Dietrich. "I'm surprised Internal Affairs isn't swarming all over us."

Chapter 13

Monday March 21, 10 am:

The memorial ceremony started on time. Surprisingly, the church was half-full. Hayte quietly slipped into a pew in the back. It was no surprise to Hayte that Bunch's casket was closed for the funeral.

As he looked at the back of the mourners' heads, Hayte realized just how little he knew about Scott Bunch. *Are these friends? Colleagues? Relatives? I don't even have a list.*

He was hoping to find a few colleagues ready to talk about particular projects Bunch had been working on at GeniTech, specifically the ones involving cloning. The task was proving more difficult that he expected.

A search of Bunch's apartment had turned up no address books or list of associates, and GeniTech had been unsurprisingly uncooperative about providing any information at all about Bunch and his work. Hayte had briefly even considered interviewing hookers in Harlem, knowing that Bunch had been a regular customer. But finding a hooker who remembers names? Not likely.

No, the people who would know anything would likely be here. But would any of them be willing to talk? It looked like it would be a long morning. He tried to sit up straight in the hard wooden pew.

He looked intently at the other mourners, then he suddenly realized they were looking at *him*. Not all at once, but he could see heads turning in his direction as word spread. It was then that he realized he was the only African-American there.

He decided to take advantage of that, but he waited until the service concluded before approaching anyone. He was really hoping to find Bunch's personal secretary in the crowd, but that was a remote possibility at best: he didn't know a name or have a description.

Could the secretary be male? He rejected the thought immediately because men usually make lousy secretaries—too disorganized, lousy phone etiquette, too much ego... No, the men here were more likely to be colleagues. He decided to try and talk with one of them, mainly because there were too many women present to just select a couple at random.

The service came to an end, and people started getting up and leaving.

Hayte knew he had to act quickly. He selected a tall, balding man with aristocratic features.

"Excuse me—did you happen to work with Sc—Doctor Bunch?"

The man turned around. "Yes, I did. Who are you, if I might ask?"

Hayte produced his badge. "Capt. Richard Hayte, NYPD Plainclothes. I'm investigating his death."

Ah yes, Captain." The man studied him intently. "What can I do for you? I'm Dr. Caramond, by the way."

"Doctor, I need more information about Scott's job, his work habits, how long he worked every day, things like that."

The man looked around nervously. "Not here. Can we meet somewhere? Some place my colleagues don't frequent?"

"I know a place off of 125th Street," said Hayte. "Sylvia's Restaurant."

"125th Street?" Caramond looked alarmed. "That's Harlem... I don't think they like white folks there."

"Naw, 125th's like Times Square now—Disney owns it all. They bought up everything two years ago." said Hayte. "You don't have to worry—it's full of tourists and small children."

"All right." Caramond waved to a passing cab.

~ ~ ~

They sat in the back booth. "How did you know I worked with him?" said Caramond tensely.

"I didn't. You just look like a scientist," admitted Hayte. "And you weren't behaving like one of the bereaved—no sudden weeping, that sort of thing."

"I see." Caramond paused awkwardly. "I don't know what to say about that."

"You don't have to," said Hayte, leaning forward. "Could you tell me what you know about the deceased?"

Caramond fiddled with a slice of lemon and painstakingly extracted the seeds before squeezing it into his water. "I know his personal life was a bit... out of control, but that was his own affair." he said finally. "I mourn his loss professionally, though." He sipped his mineral water thoughtfully. "Sometimes I know he seemed like an idiot savant, but he wasn't really. Dr. Bunch was brilliant in his element—the laboratory."

"How's that?"

Caramond started to loosen up a bit, "Genetic modification is the hardest of all disciplines to learn—to do it manually, as with cloning, it takes a special eye-to-hand coordination you must be born with. I've seen people just about work themselves to death trying to master it, but if you don't have the knack, you'll *never* make it. I thought I was really good until I met him."

He shook his head sadly. "Scotty Bunch was the best I've ever seen—

no matter in what shape he was in. His personal life was a bit of a mess, I'm afraid, we all knew that. I know he drank a lot, but his hands never trembled, *ever*. He could do gene splices that even computer-guided micro-robotic installations *couldn't*. When he did cloning, his fertilized eggs made it to the blastocyst stage *sixty* percent of the time—the best I could ever do was *eighteen* percent. Made me really jealous, sometimes… but truth is, I was glad to have him on our team. We *all* were. Without him, we would never have developed the anti-HIV gene mod vaccine—*he* was the one who managed to successfully graft it onto a retrovirus—to this day, I have no idea how he did it—all I know is that it *works*. He was absolutely irreplaceable… " His voice trailed off.

"So what cloning projects did you work on together?"

Caramond took off his glasses. "I'm sorry, Captain. I signed a confidentiality agreement. General questions about the profession are OK—that one is *not*, I'm afraid…"

"It just means you'll have to answer the same questions later, at a Grand Jury hearing."

"That would be a different matter," Caramond fiddled some more with his glasses. "I suppose then I would have no choice. That would not be a violation on my part."

Hayte decided to try another tack. "Would you be prepared to *deny* you worked on human cloning experiments with Dr. Bunch at GeniTech?"

Caramond smiled and folded his hands.

"Your non-response has been noted," said Hayte. "Now, would you *deny* those experiments violated the ban on human embryo cloning?"

Caramond smiled again and sipped his water.

"Would you deny this work possibly led to Dr. Bunch's death?"

The Doctor frowned and drummed his fingers. "Captain, that I cannot say. I really don't know, to be honest."

"No further questions. Doctor, thank you for your time. This gives me something to work on." Hayte flagged down a waiter. "*I'll* pay."

~ ~ ~

Monday, 11:15 a.m:

Perry writhed and tried to lash out, but it was no use. His head was now clamped firmly between Donner's legs.

It was then that he saw Donner's socks, which were again bloodstained. "Hey Donner—don't you *ever* change your socks?"

"Got news for you—those *are* clean." He placed a Birkenstock on Donohue's head, "Donohue, I want you to *understand* something. This war is *primal*, just like the rival races of apes battling nature and each other in a war of survival years ago, to find out who would be Mister Neanderthal's successor. What? You thought natural selection was *divinely* ordained? Uh-uh, it's always been hand to hand combat. You got to rip out those mutant

171

strains *by the gonads*! You defend your country from extremists by *being* extreme!"

~ ~ ~

It was on the ride back that it suddenly occurred to Hayte. Traffic had stopped moving, and he started reflecting on all the intricate whorls of the helixes on his front door—something about it was familiar. Ahead in traffic, he saw a pimp's car, with all the loud purple and gold trim. And the translucent hologram in the rear window gleamed its message: It's the DNA, baby. A light went on in his head.

The spirals scratched on my front door on the metal anti-burglary plate matches the ones painted on the wall at the Bunch murder scene.

Hayte rifled through his wallet until he found Vaughn's business card. He switched his police headset on and keyed in the number.

Two rings. "Sgt. Vaughn here."

"This is Capt. Hayte." He spoke rapidly, "Didn't you say you were at the murder scene in Queens—the one where that woman got blown up?"

"Yeah, I was the one who found her, or what was left of her, if you know what I mean."

"Were there any strange messages or symbols left at the scene—painted or carved?"

"Yup, sure was. Weird stuff—hieroglyphics. I took some photos."

Hayte felt his stomach sink. "Can you get me any prints of those? I think they may be the link to another murder."

"I can get you copies by Friday, Captain."

"That may be too late. Remember the vandalism at my apartment? If those symbols are the same ones that were carved on my door, it might be my ass in danger."

Vaughn let out a low whistle. "Woah! I'll see what I can do. I think me and Hudgins ought to come out and see you, Captain, maybe ASAP."

"Agreed. Name a time—and a place. I ain't going home tonight." He looked at the stack of books next to him in the passenger seat, "I got plenty to keep myself occupied."

Chapter 14
THE NEW YORK CYBERPOST
"BODILY UNIVERSES"
EXHIBIT TRASHED

Yesterday, an unnamed assailant attacked several plasticised bodies in the long-controversial "Bodily Universes" exhibit in the NY Metropolitan Museum of Modern Art, destroying several exhibits. The exhibit organizers issued a joint statement with the New York Mayor's Office deploring the "wanton destruction of irreplaceable pieces of art."

The exhibition, which debuted fifty years ago in Germany, features plastic-sealed dead human bodies surgically dissected and opened to reveal the inner organs. Bodily Universes was originally barred from entering the USA in the early 21st Century on religious grounds.

Yesterday's incident was only the latest in a series of violent public reactions and calamities that have dogged the exhibits since the very beginning. Years ago, right wing protesters in Marseilles disrupted the event by releasing hordes of wild rats into the gallery during a bank holiday weekend. Other problems included exhibits being infested during transit by a new species of fly larva that was able to eat through plastic coatings with enzymes secreted in its mouth organs.

~ ~ ~

Tuesday March 22, 5 p.m:
　　When Brezzi came in the front door of the building he and his wife owned on Fondamenta di Borgo, he noticed the odor of wine, and it vaguely disturbed him. He didn't know why. He sniffed around the hallway, then realized his olfactory capability was already impaired. For some reason. But he could still *taste* something in the air...
　　He stepped back outside and decided to walk along the Ponte Longo for a while. The light began to bathe the Canale della Giudecca in a dirty

orange glow, silhouetting the oil refineries in the distance. He turned back when the setting sun started hurting his eyes.

When he opened the front door again, he knew instantly what was wrong. *The smell was a mixture of red and white wines!*

Horrified, he rushed to the door in the back of the hall, the one that led to his wine room. Throwing it open, he recoiled. He gagged from the odor and took a few staggering steps back, in total shock.

After a few minutes, he recovered enough to reach in and switch the light on, revealing the worst—his vast, carefully constructed series of wall-mounted wine racks had toppled. The floor was a sea of broken glass and wood peeking out of a sickly orange mess. He wanted to cry.

Cazzo! Maledizione! How could this happen? Fully loaded, the wine rack had to weigh half a metric ton. It simply made no sense at all.

He opened his flat and looked back in his living room, but everything else was as it should be. No earthquake, no tidal wave, no explanation at all.

No, the reason would have to be found. But the first step would be the worst: the clean up. He dug around his hall closet for his gas mask, which he had gotten when he was a cadet at the Police Academy. He hoped it still worked.

~ ~ ~

Harlem, 12pm local time:

Hayte sat in Jimmy's Uptown with Vaughn and Hudgins. "*Why* are they after me?" said Hayte, clearly agitated. "What do they think I know? I don't have anything—no tangible proof whatsoever. Bunch gave me an earful of wild tales, but I got no way to prove anything..."

"Who's 'they?'" said Vaughn.

"GeniTech." He shoveled another spoonful of blackeyed peas into his mouth.

Hudgins shook his head. "How can you know dat, mon? Is just a company."

"Because they have a long history of protecting their investments." Hayte tapped the table for emphasis. "There are too many of these to be coincidences. We got an off-the-record confession that they 'helped' Chief Hershey commit suicide three years ago. And Scott Bunch was blown to bits after telling me about a clone of theirs that's running amok."

"But dere's no proof," said Hudgins stubbornly. "Sooner or later, we gotta have de proof. Otherwise it makes you sound like a conspiracy freak, mon."

Vaughn looked puzzled. "Why the hell can't we go after GeniTech and put an end to all this shit? If we get the proof."

Hayte shook his head. "We tried—many times. You need a Grand Jury indictment. Apparently GeniTech can buy off grand juries anywhere in a matter of hours. I suppose we could try someplace remote, say Barrow, Alaska…"

Vaughn played with the sugar dispenser. "If we can capture this Johnny B, that would be proof enough—particularly if we caught it doing something illegal." He looked at Hayte intently, weighing his reaction.

Hayte didn't like that look. "What do you want me to do, *let* it kill me?".

"No, no, no," Vaughn held up his hand. "You'd just have to capture it during a B and E—that would be enough. After that, all we would need to do is prove it's a clone and trace it to GeniTech. The last part's probably gonna be the hardest one."

"I beg to differ," said Hayte. "If I'm right about it blowing up Bunch, it doesn't take a genius to figure out what the next one's gonna do to *me*."

"Look, we can help—if you let us—but don't you think you'd better tell the Chief—otherwise he's gonna wonder what's going on with you. Your work hours haven't exactly been regular lately."

"Shabazz already knows about the break-ins. But no way am I gonna tell him about this," said Hayte, folding his arms. "I may be going crazy, but I ain't stupid."

"What do you mean, you can't tell the Chief?" said Vaughn. "Now *you're* the one being illogical."

"No, I'm not!" snapped Hayte. "Look at the facts. Officially, we got two separate murder cases with no direct link—the woman at the thrift store at 135th Street and the Bunch murder. If I go walking in to him and say that a) I think the perp is a clone that Scott Bunch worked on at GeniTech, he's gonna think I'm nuts. If I tell him b) that same model of clone also was possibly one of the Phantoms who did the Chase Bank robbery, he's gonna think I'm even more nuts. And, c) if I tell him another one is after *me*, he'll have me carted off to the funny farm in no time flat. Goodbye law school, goodbye Bar Exam, goodbye NYPD career…" Hayte took a big gulp of coffee. "To top it all, I have a new apartment with a binding long-term lease and a mountain of moving debts. I don't wanna live under an underpass, know what I mean? What the hell am I gonna do?"

"Set up da 'lectronic surveillance, mon," said Hudgins, who had been sitting silently in the corner, playing with a stray dreadlock. "Dat's de only way you gonna save your ass from being blown to bits."

"All right." Hayte sat back wearily. "Either of you got any ideas?"

"Yup," said Vaughn. "I got a guy I can bring in from Jersey who can set you up an entire surveillance system in about six hours. Just name a day, and he'll be there. Oh, and be sure and bring your neighbor—whatshisname—the porno guy. You're gonna need his help, too."

~ ~ ~

Venice, 8 p.m. local time:
Brezzi and his wife Sophia sat glumly on his workbench. The stinking

mass of glass and shattered wood had been pushed into a corner, and the floor had been mopped up enough to reveal the cause. He pointed helplessly at the stone wall, which bulged markedly, much like Brezzi's own beltline. Until now, he had considered the bulge to be benign. "I called my cousin the stonemason, he say the wall, she is collapsing slowly. He wants to look at it himself, but he's not optimistic. He says it would cost much more than a policeman's salary if it is as bad as he thinks. So we must move out."

"Oh no!" Sophia looked at him pleadingly. "Are you sure, Henri? But I love this place! The courtyard and the garden, they're so beautiful! We can't just let the building crumble down! And why is this happening? The sea wall is supposed to protect us."

Brezzi shrugged, "My cousin, he say the sea water stopped rising, but the damage was done probably 20 years ago, before they put up the tidal barriers. Now we pay for it."

She shook her head. "*Merde*. Well, if there's nothing we can do, let's at least go and have a good meal and some wine."

"Why not?" He shrugged again. "But it's late, which means only the Taverna will be open."

"OK, we go to the Taverna." She stood up. "*Vieni qui tesoro.*"

~ ~ ~

Brezzi was in the middle of some veal scaloppini and spaghetti on the side when his mobile rang. He reached in his coat. "Ciao, Brezzi..."

The ringing continued. He stared blankly at the phone. "What?! *Testa di Caz-*"

"Henri, don't ruin the evening!" snapped Sophia, "It's your *other* phone."

"Oh!" Brezzi reached inside his satchel, producing a miniature police mobile. "I forgot about this one... Ciao, Brezzi."

"Ciao, Henri, it's Franco Murano..." Murano's voice faded in static.

"Franco, I can't hear you."

"Sorry—I will step out of the terminal... there. Can you hear me now?"

"Yes, *Franco*. Since when do you have a first name? OK, I'll be serious—why are you at the airport?"

Murano sounded excited. "I got some good news. We caught another Russian"

Brezzi was confused. "What do you mean, *another* Russian?"

"Oh yes, I forgot to tell you. Do you remember that man you shot and wounded in the ass last month?"

Henri sat up. "*Si*. Do you know who he is?"

"*Si*. His name is Ganaddy Zrinenko. He's a small-time bank robber from the Ukraine with a long history of prior arrests in the former Soviet republics. Your friend in New York will be *very* happy."

"Perry Donohue? Why?"

"Because Zrinenko's face also appears in that list that your friend sent, those robberies in New York, what was their name..."

Sophia tapped Brezzi on the shoulder. "Henri, darling, what is wrong? You just dropped your spaghetti spoon."

"'Scuse, Franco..." Brezzi looked down and realized his lap was covered with pasta and tomato sauce. "I call you back, OK?" He nodded and switched off the phone. "Sorry, my love. I must call New York..." He grabbed a napkin and started cleaning his lap.

She looked annoyed. "Right *now?* We were having such a lovely evening."

"*Si*. Right now. I must see if there's any reward money for the criminal I shot at the airport last month. Americans always have big reward money!"

Her dark eyes widened. "You think?"

"Yes, I think." He started fishing around frantically in his satchel for his black book.

~ ~ ~

Manhattan, 4:14 p.m:

Dietrich was just walking past Donohue's vacant cubicle when he noticed the flashing red message light. On a whim he decided to pick up the phone, so he set his bag of Chinese take-out food on Donohue's desk and sat down. "Lt. Dietrich here, subbing for Capt. Donohue—you got a message for him?"

"Yeah," said a woman with a thick Bronx accent, "It was a real bad connection—somebody calling from a cell phone, can't tell if he was a Latino, Italian or some kind of Albanian, but he's called Capt. Donohue's number five times so far this afternoon. He left a long-ass phone number to call back..."

"OK" said Dietrich, grabbing a pen, "give it to me."

She read out the number. When she finished, Dietrich thanked her and got up to find Shrini. Her cubicle was also empty.

He located her just as she was leaving the ladies' room. She eyed him suspiciously. "Don't tell me you were just coming in."

"Hey, don't look at me like that," said Dietrich, "you're still safer than an altar boy at communion..." Before she could reply, he waved the note at her. "Perry got a bunch of phone messages from somebody Hispanic or Italian, something about a..." he squinted at his own writing, "Fantom-eh."

"Gimme that!" She grabbed the note, "Is that the phone number?"

Dietrich nodded. "Looks foreign."

"Let's find out." She marched to her cubicle and tapped in the number on her keyboard. "Directory assistant says... country code Italy!" She clicked on the 'dial' icon and put on her headset.

~ ~ ~

The ringing jarred Brezzi from his wine-induced slumber. Momentarily disoriented, he groped about vainly for his mobile. "Sophia! What's my mobile doing in my shoe?"

She opened a bleary eye and sat up. "You *put* it there. I watched you do it."

"Never mind." He fumbled with the folded-up phone, trying to open it. "Ciao, Brezzi…"

"Chow-what?" said an unfamiliar woman's voice, "Do you speak English?"

"*Si*… eh, yes" Brezzi blinked and tried rouse himself.

"This is Lt. Shrinithan of the New York City Police. You were trying to contact a Capt. Perry Donohue, is that correct?"

"*Si*, can I speak to him?"

"He's unfortunately unavailable at the moment. Who exactly am I speaking to?"

"This is *Inspectore* Henri Brezzi of the *Polizia Metropole* in Venezia… eh, Venice."

"Ah! Perry visited you last month! What is you want to tell Capt. Donohue?"

"It's a long story… I captured a Russian a month ago in our airport. I just saw his photo as part of eh, these gang you call the Phantoms…" He related the details of the capture to her.

When Brezzi finished, Shrini said "Thank you, Inspectore. That's very good news indeed—I will be sure to relay that information to Capt. Donohue. I'll also check and see about that reward—I'm sure it's pretty substantial. Goodbye."

Dietrich watched her take off the headset. "And?"

She swiveled round, her cherubic face beaming. "I think we finally got a break in the Phantoms case!"

Dietrich looked skeptical. "From *Italy?*"

"*Si*," she mimicked, "From Venice. Perry's trip there uncovered an unexpected clue. I can hardly wait to see the look on Shabazz's face when I tell him!"

Dietrich threw the remains of his Chinese takeout in the garbage. "I'd like to see the look on Perry's face as well. Too bad we don't know where he is…"

~ ~ ~

Wednesday March 23, 8 am:

Donner and Agent Cheshire stood outside Donohue's cell. "Why are we training this guy? He's a runt."

Donner looked pityingly at Cheshire. "Agent Cheshire, have we taught you nothing? It so happens Donohue is small, quick and wiry—just like our quarry."

Cheshire said stubbornly, "But that doesn't mean he'll succeed in catching all those Johnny Bs alive."

"And how many agents has our department lost so far? And do you want to be next?" Donner shook his head. "Police are expendable—we are not. I'm running this department on 60% of necessary manpower, and I'm sick of attending funerals. Anything else you'd like to argue with me about?"

Agent Browning walked up. Cheshire persisted, "Why do we need live Johnny Bs anyway?"

"The more live ones we catch, the easier it is to prove to the Justice Department that they are a menace to society. Right now, our hands are tied—killing humans, even artificial ones, is against the law. Do you want our existence to face public exposure?"

"No, of course not!" they said in unison.

"Well then." Donner folded his arms. "Once we get the laws changed, we can do what we want. If we have to kill 'em, we kill 'em. If we capture them alive, we can use them for other purposes..."

"What other purposes?" said Cheshire.

Donner gave that smug smile. "When the need to know arises, I shall tell you. Not before." He peered inside. "Ah, our subject has finally collapsed. Now we can really work on his head."

Browning looked at a list. "It's also time to take him off the IV feeds and put him back on solid food."

"Yup," said Donner, "he's gonna need all his strength for this. But first..." He unlocked the cell and motioned for Browning and Cheshire to go in.

~ ~ ~

6:30 p.m:

The horse-faced technician with the pony tail pointed to Hayte's palmtop screen. "All it takes to activate the security system is for you to touch that icon—all the pyroelectric sensors and relays will be activated."

Hayte fiddled with the pointer. "So I'll be able to tell exactly where an intruder is trying to break in?"

"Exactly, and if you are away, it'll notify your designated neighbor."

"That's me," said Stanley, who looked a little tipsy. "Then all I do is dial 9-11."

Hayte glanced around. "So the system is activated now?"

"Not yet." The technician hurriedly scribbled some notes. "First I have to activate your account. We aren't allowed to do it via remote—I gotta do it manually."

"How long will that take?" said Hayte.

"Maybe an hour," shrugged the technician, "depends on traffic. Would've been a lot quicker, but the subway's still closed." He packed the rest of his equipment into his tiny case and made ready to leave. "Should be up in about 90 minutes at the latest—you'll hear a beep and all the sensors will flash green." He shut the front door behind him.

Stanley turned and clapped Hayte on the back. "You hungry? Me and the girls are gonna go to Hudson's deli."

"Not me, thanks," said Hayte, "I just ate."

"Suit yourself. Me, I'm starved. Something about catastrophe that brings on my appetite…" As Bialystok walked out, he said over his shoulder, "You gonna be OK? I should be back in about an hour, Hudson's don't like folks hanging round none…"

"I'll be fine, Stan." Hayte watched the door close. As he did, he noticed all the sensors flash red onscreen for an instant. He put his gun in his holster and went from room to room.

Nothing.

He sighed and went back to his books.

~ ~ ~

Wednesday, 11:59 p.m:

Perry woke up in darkness. The beamer was no longer strapped to his head—but he could tell it had been recently. His throbbing eyes and temples told him that much.

In fact, his whole body hurt. He felt something pulling at his arm hair. He ran his hand over his upper arm and found another small bandage on his upper arm. They must be shooting me up with all sorts of strange drugs…

~ ~ ~

Thursday morning, 1:33 a.m:

Hayte looked at his watch. "One more question to go…" He took another swig of coffee and resumed reading.

Question 69 was particularly vexing—it involved an extortionist named Goon who one night blew up the kiosk of a local businessman who had refused to pay up, after the kiosk had closed for the night. The kiosk exploded just as a cleaning lady was getting off a city bus, and she was killed immediately when a self-sharpening Ginzu knife in the unoccupied kiosk was sent flying at a fearsome velocity by the blast, decapitating her instantly and sending her head rolling down the aisle of the bus, severely traumatising the driver and remaining passengers.

Later the same night, Goon was stopped on the sidewalk and questioned in the town's red-light district by a rookie vice squad cop investigating prostitution rings. During the conversation, Goon inadvertently dropped a brown paper bag he was carrying, and the cop picked it up and found it contained child pornography. The rookie cop then busted the perpetrator, took him to the city jail and booked him on the kiddie porn charges.

Another detective named Bogie had earlier been trying to locate Goon for questioning about the kiosk explosion/arson. Bogie learned of the arrest and raced down to the jail to question Goon before Goon was formally charged with possession of kiddie porn. During the interrogation about the kiosk crime, Goon was read his Miranda rights and told he had the right to a lawyer. Despite understanding this, Goon indicated he was willing to cut a deal to avoid a Capital Murder charge; he subsequently made and signed a written confession about blowing up the kiosk but said he had no intention of hurting or killing anyone.

The core question was: Are the physical child porn evidence and the written confession admissible in court?

The answer was *no*, because Goon dropped the bag but did not abandon it or give up ownership, so his Fourth and Fourteenth Amendment rights to privacy were violated by the vice squad cop. The initial arrest was therefore illegal.

The answer to the second part was more complex, because a lawyer was not present when Goon made his confession. However, because the confession concerned a crime unrelated to the initial charges, it was admissible because it had no correlation with the illegal arrest.

Hayte closed the thick legal tome and rubbed his eyes. *Hell, I should know all that stuff by now...Time to schedule the bar exam. Maybe next week...*

He didn't know where Stanley had disappeared to. He started getting a craving for a late-night cheeseburger. The only place open at this hour was the White Castle on the corner. *No, wait—Louie's also serves them...* And he could also get a drink or two. He quickly put on his coat and stepped out.

Half an hour later, after a burger washed down with a couple of beers, he headed back.

He got halfway up the stairs before he remembered he hadn't re-activated the alarm system.

Shit—I'll have to write myself a note.

He walked down the hall to his door and stopped. On a hunch, he pushed on it with the side of his foot.

The door opened a couple of inches.

He reached instinctively for his gun, but his holster was empty. He felt around for his headset, but he didn't have that on, either. He pulled the door shut without letting the latch catch.

Cursing silently, he tip-toed to Stanley's door and pressed the buzzer. No answer.

That meant if he wanted to catch the bastard red-handed, he'd have to do it himself.

Catching a burglar was one thing. But capturing a suspected suicide bomber was quite another.

Especially when you're the desired target and you've got no weapons to speak of...

His guns were in the bedroom closet. Or..." He thought carefully. He suddenly remembered the big self-sharpening Ginzu knife in the kitchen. He went quickly back to his door.

He pushed it open very slowly and looked around.

The living room was empty.

He peered into the kitchen. Empty too.

He grabbed the knife off the magnetic mount on the side of the fridge. As he did, he heard a noise in the living room. He looked around the edge of the doorway and his pulse started racing.

The same fucking intruder.

The small man saw him and froze. He started grabbing for something on his belt. Without thinking, Hayte charged at him, hoping to stop the bastard from pulling the pin.

Being so tall, he unfortunately forgot to duck for the kitchen doorway and his forehead slammed into the door frame. The knife went flying and clanged against something.

Hayte fell down with a howl of rage, then got up and charged again. He pinned the intruder on his stomach and grabbed frantically for his arms. Hayte was stronger, but the little man twisted like a snake and kicked him in the face.

Spitting blood, Hayte nailed him in the nuts and the intruder collapsed in a ball and lay gasping in the corner. Richard stood over him, waiting for the little bastard to try and slip past to either side.

He was caught totally off guard when the man suddenly jumped at him, the Ginzu knife outstretched.

The blade sliced him low. He stared in horror at the hilt protruding out of his groin, then passed out in shock.

The intruder curled himself around Hayte's torso and pulled the pin on his belt.

Nothing happened. A minute passed.

He stared at the broken pin in disbelief, then inspected the belt.

The tiny detonator chip on the underside was crushed.

Enraged, he took the belt off and threw it against the wall, knocking down a framed photo in the process. Then he froze.

A noise.

He grabbed the belt and quickly put it back on.

Footsteps sounded down the hall.

He grabbed Hayte's prone form by standing behind him and reaching around under his armpits like firemen would do. He locked this hands around Hayte's chest and dragged his inert form into the bathroom.

There was a knock on the front door.

It opened.

Stanley peered around the doorway, "Hey Richard, where the hell are you?"

No answer. Something metal clanged on the floor in another room.

Perplexed, Stanley walked around the living room. "What the fuck is goin' on here?"

He heard the window in the bathroom open and shut. He yelled out, "Rich! Are you OK?"

No answer. The marks on the dark red carpet looked suspicious.

He walked to the bathroom door and rapped on it. "Rich, are you there? What's with you, are you sitting on the crapper?"

The door opened to his touch. He pushed it open and his mouth dropped open.

"OH MY GOD!" He waved his hands helplessly at all the blood, then ran out in the hall and gestured frantically to his companion, "Verona, come here—no—*don't* look! Just go to Rich's icebox, yeah—get me all the ice you can..." He grabbed the ice tray and turned her around, slapping his cell phone in her hand. "*Now*—dial 911! Jesus, he's cut real bad..." He began frantically grabbing handfuls of ice and packing it around Hayte's wound.

~ ~ ~

The ambulance crew came in with a gurney. One of the wheels stuck, leaving skid marks down the hall. They burst through the front door.

"Over here!" yelled Stanley, "I got him in the bathroom!"

A bearded attendant with an Afro peered in. "Oh SHIT!" He tried to get the gurney in the bathroom door but it got stuck in the doorway.

"Man, he's too tall!" said the other attendant. He looked at Bialystok, "Yo man, can you hold that ice bag on his groin while I lift him—yeah, like that." He yelled to the other attendant, "Come on, Clarence, quit puking and help!"

Clarence came back in and grabbed Hayte's ankles to hoist him on the collapsible gurney. "Benny, how are we going to fit him in the ambulance? Those long legs ain't gonna fit..."

"Bend his knees up, make him cradle the ice in his groin. Yeah, like that."

Hayte groaned. Benny unwrapped the IV bag and yelled, "Clarence, hit him with 50 cc of sedative—he's gonna start thrashing otherwise."

Clarence found a vein, then stuck the hypo under Hayte's left ear. Rich's eyes fluttered briefly, then shut.

~ ~ ~

When Hayte awoke, a man with a mask was staring down at him. Reacting instantly, he went for the man's eyes, sending the blood IV bag flying.

"Nurse! RESTRAIN HIM! More sedative!" A mask was clamped over Hayte's face, and the room went dark.

~ ~ ~

Thursday March 24, 7:30 p.m:

Hayte opened his eyes, crusted round the edges. At first he only saw blurry shapes. "How ya doing, guy?" *Dietrich's voice.*

Slowly, Dietrich and Shrini's faces came into focus, hovering above him like specters.

"Didn't your mother tell you that Ginzu knives were dangerous?" said Dietrich. "You had us worried, pal. What the hell happened?"

Shrini put her hand on Hayte's forehead. "Paul, be quiet—he's been through a lot."

Hayte weakly raised his head and looked under the sheet at all the bandages covering his groin. A look of intense panic crossed his face. "Shit—is my-?"

Dietrich said, "Easy, Rich. Your family jewels are still there—the doc says the surgery to reattach it was 100% successful. You should regain feeling in a few months. You did lose a lot of blood 'coz the blade nailed a major artery in your left leg...Your neighbor, what's his name, the fat guy, found you unconscious."

Hayte started shivering uncontrollably.

"Rich, are you OK?" Shrini reached for the nurse summons button.

Hayte slowly steadied his breathing. "I... I think I'm OK now." He exhaled slowly. "Who found me again?"

Shrini set the buzzer down. "Your neighbor, the porno guy, the one you told us about. And he took your, uh... severed parts and kept them on ice..."

"Stanley Bialystok..." Hayte nodded weakly, "I owe him one for that."

"I'll say," said Dietrich. "I can't imagine a having a career in the NYPD without a penis..."

Shrini gave him a fierce look. "You might not have *yours* for much longer..."

"Sorry." Dietrich buried his face in his notes.

"We've been keeping the press at bay so far," said Shrini. "We got a guard at the door round the clock, and apart from the surgical team, only five others know the nature of your wounds."

"Thank you," said Hayte. "That would be *all* I need—seeing my stitched-up you-know-what on the front page of the CyberPost..."

"We've been real lucky," Dietrich glanced back at the door. "The floods and Noise Days are getting most of the attention at the moment."

"Which means we don't have much time to waste." Shrini leaned closer. "The assailant must've been small and light enough to slide in and out of that narrow side window you got in the bathroom. And I have no idea how he got down from five stories high. Do you remember at all what he looked like?"

"I'll never forget that face," said Hayte, shuddering. One of his oxygen tubes detached itself from his nose.

"Your attacker?" Shrini reached over and put the oxygen tube back.

"Yes. I don't remember anything else—like how I wound up here in the hospital, but every time I close my eyes, I see that fucker's face."

"Well, let's not waste any more time, then." Dietrich opened his palmtop. "Let's go ahead and get a composite image, so we can check for matches on the law enforcement network."

"Here's the basic description," said Hayte. "Small, wiry build, short curly black hair, buzz-cut on the sides, longer and parted in the middle. Thin face, medium-large aquiline nose, average mouth size with an overbite, small teeth. Receding chin."

"Like this?" Dietrich held up the computer-aided sketch.

"Almost. Make the eyes closer together."

Shrini broke in. "Any trace of foreign accent?"

"Dunno…" Hayte sank back into the pillow. "He didn't talk."

Shrini looked at the image. "He looks kind of familiar. But I can't place the face…"

"You've seen him before, trust me." Hayte's voice sounded very weak. "His name is Johnny B."

"Who?" Shrini looked puzzled. Is this somebody you've busted before?"

"No." Hayte closed his eyes and lay back. "Johnny B, one of the clones Scott Bunch was working on at GeniTech."

"Uh, Rich…" Embarrassed, Dietrich fiddled with the pointer. "You were attacked by a clone?"

Richard looked at him earnestly. "I know it sounds crazy. And there's nothing in the legal system about this…"

"I'll say…" Shrini frowned, "especially if it wasn't a one-off clone. Imagine what it would be like trying to get an arrest warrant…"

Dietrich chimed in, "…to arrest a whole clone line for the crimes of one? Or, if you don't go that route, what would you do? Blood samples and DNA tests would be totally irrelevant. How can we prove the exact identity of the one that did attack you…"

"…I know. It's about as crazy as proving the identity of the one that blew up Scott Bunch or the one who joined the Phantoms," added Hayte, rolling his eyes.

"What?" said Dietrich and Shrini in unison. "Joined the *Phantoms*?!"

"That's what Scott Bunch told me the night I met with him."

Shrini scowled at him. "Richard Hayte, if you weren't already hurt, I'd slap you! Why didn't you tell us that?"

Hayte sank back into the pillow. "I thought it was nonsense from the mouth of a drunken paranoid." He looked up at Shrini, "Hell, it still sounds like nonsense. But Bunch got himself blown to bits, just like that woman at Goodwill—and there was similar graffiti at both crime scenes—and the same graffiti at my apartment. And I actually saw Johnny."

Shrini looked at Dietrich and made a face. "Wonderful, this means there are cloned suicide bombers running loose in Manhattan. I'm sure glad the press doesn't know about this…" She sighed and turned back to Richard. "Can you pick out the clone from the Phantoms stills?"

"If Bunch is right, then yes. I must be getting close to the truth—too close." His eyelids began to flutter. He struggled to keep his eyes open. "Guys, can you do some legwork for me?"

"I'll try," Dietrich opened his palmtop calendar, " but I got my hands full at the moment—the Phantoms case is stalled, but we also got those murdered VNN reporters they found in Jersey, and I'm still working on that severed head case…"

Hayte yawned and said, "Well, come back tomorrow, both of you." His eyes closed.

"I'll bring the Phantoms stills," said Shrini, making a note.

The head nurse's voice came over the intercom. "Visiting hours end in five minutes."

Shrini gently prodded Dietrich. "Let's go. He needs to rest."

Chapter 15
THE NEW YORK CYBERPOST
Star Cop Hospitalized

Captain Richard Hayte was hospitalized late Wednesday evening, after being attacked by a knife-wielding assailant at his home. The assailant escaped after the attack. Police are currently searching for the suspect, a mixed-race male in his mid-20s, about 5' 3" and 135 lbs, with a wiry build and dark hair.

Hayte is listed as being in "serious but stable condition" according to a NYPD spokesperson and is expected to make "a full recovery." When queried about the nature of Capt. Hayte's injuries, the spokesperson said the wounds were "in the abdominal region."

Hayte became nationally famous as part of a team that broke the Smash case four years ago.

Sunday March 27, 3:30 p.m:
The cell door opened again. Donohue shielded his eyes.

"Congratulations!" Donner's voice boomed and reverberated through the cell. "You made it through basic training. Now, we just need to balance your consciousness and start you back on case work."

"What basic training?" grumbled Donohue. He held out his arm and pointed to all the red spots. "Training me to be a lab rat? I counted nine needle tracks on my right arm."

"All right, Mister Inquisitive, I'll tell you. We've been training your R-Complex to deal with your intended quarry."

"My what?"

"Your R-Complex. Bet you didn't even know you had one," smirked Donner. He slapped a membrane monitor on the cell wall, then activated the screen. A diagram of the brain came up. "Let me educate you. The human brain is a triune model. The outer layer is your cerebral cortex, or grey matter, where your consciousness or sense of self resides. It's too slow for our purposes, though."

Perry squinted at the display, "So you're just practicing psychoanalysis, in other words..."

"No, we're not!" snapped Donner. "We don't believe in that crap—all psychiatry is nonsense. Its fundamental flaw is to focus on the grey matter. *We* focus on the basic building blocks of the mind."

"Uh-huh..." Perry got slowly to his feet.

Donner moved the pointer. "The layer below the cortex that is what you have in common with dogs and horses. It reacts much faster, but not fast enough, and it's way too emotional."

"So the layer below that is the R-Complex?"

"You catch on fast, bright boy." Donner let out a high-pitched giggle, "The reptilian complex is like a rattlesnake's brain—it's your survival instinct. Remember that first visual presentation we gave you? Survival is your priority. We just gave you better tools to do that."

Perry scowled at him. "How do you know they're better?"

"You proved that yourself." Donner grinned unpleasantly, "Heh-heh-heh, you did great in the shark tank—scored 9.5 out of ten..."

"*What?*" Donohue started inspecting himself for bites.

"Later, Donohue." said Donner dismissively. "Someday, I'll have to show you the footage , but right now, I want you to start with your re-acclimatization. You will resume your police casework from here, starting tomorrow..." He handed Donohue a thick file.

Perry pushed them away. "Wait a sec—I got another question."

Donner folded his arms. "All right. Ask and you *might* receive."

"How come I got all this sick Hawaiian music running through my head? Have you brainwashed me to a soundtrack?"

"Hah!" That sickly giggle again. "I'll show you just before you go back. Here's all the things you had on you." He handed Donohue his jacket, belt, and holster.

Perry took the holster and looked at him expectantly.

"Oh, *sure!*" Donner looked at him like he was nuts. "Your gun will be waiting for you when you go back to your precinct—*not* before! Oh, and I almost forgot," He handed over a deck of cards. "Nice to know someone else uses real ones. By the way, you will be allowed to make a few calls out. Today's Sunday, so you'll have to wait until tomorrow. See ya!" The cell door closed behind him before Perry could open his mouth.

~ ~ ~

Sunday, 5:30 p.m:

Hayte was sitting up in bed when Dietrich leaned in the doorway and waved. "Howya doing, Rich?"

"Could be better..."

"I'll bet," Dietrich smiled lopsidedly. "When do you get to leave this wonderful place?"

"Dunno..." He pulled the covers aside and slowly moved his legs over the edge of the bed. "I can't seem to get any direct answers."

Dietrich fished around in his satchel, "Got a question, Rich."

"Shoot."

"Are you sure it was a clone that... nailed you?" Dietrich tried not to morbidly stare at Hayte's exposed legs.

Hayte nodded, "Yeah, I'm sure. There were too many alien... aspects about the guy."

"What do you mean, 'alien'?" Dietrich arched an eyebrow, "Physical characteristics?"

"No, behavioral. Think about it—if you look at our society, one of the few hard, fast rules we do have is a kind of unwritten code among men about the genital region. Wait, hear me out first—I've had a lot of time to think about this. People in most civilized countries, especially men, have a code—you do not shoot somebody in the nuts, and you sure as hell don't knife another guy in the groin. Only a certain Ms. Bobbitt violated that code—and that was a *very* long time ago, and she paid dearly for breaking it. But a clone wouldn't know about that—especially a clone that's only been trained to kill."

Dietrich started to open his mouth, then stopped. He walked over to the window and looked out for several seconds.

Hayte looked at him. "Do you think I'm full of shit?"

"No, I don't." Dietrich turned around, his hands folded behind his back, "I'm just not sure, that's all. Just let me mull it over for a while. It explain some of the results that I got..."

"Whaddya got?"

"Homicide gave me some feedback from the Bunch case."

"Oh yeah?" Richard reached for his trousers and began pulling them on very carefully.

"Yup." Dietrich opened his handheld and started reading from his notes. "First of all, you were right, none of Bunch's neighbors heard or saw anything. One said he heard a muffled 'pop' that night, but other than that, 'nobody saw nothing', like they always say."

"Figures..." Hayte shifted uncomfortably, "Ow!" He struggled to get the zipper shut. "Anything else?"

"Uh-huh, here's the weird stuff. The lab analyses on your vacuum samples tested positive for explosives, but not any kind that we know of. All we know is that it must be quiet, it has to burn fast—and it's self-extinguishing. No fire afterward." Dietrich played with the pointer on his hand-held. "Guy in Homicide has a bad feeling about all this. He says only the Pentagon would have the bucks to pay for developing something that is so tricky."

Hayte raised an eyebrow. "*Only* the Pentagon?"

"No, not only them..." Dietrich thought for a moment, "Maybe a company *associated* with Defense."

Hayte got up gingerly. "I wish somebody could catch the perp who nailed me. That would sure help answer a lot of questions." He took a few halting steps.

"Would've been nice," agreed Dietrich, "but we looked at the bathroom window and that tiny vent in the cleaning closet. Neither had any signs of climbing gear…no hooks, no ropes, no nothing. Our boy's a real climber. I doubt we could've caught him without setting a trap…"

Hayte flashed him a dark look, "Yeah, why didn't we, instead of the alarm system—which didn't work at all?"

"I talked with Vaughn and Hudgins, and we all agree that we weren't prepared enough," admitted Dietrich. "This guy climbs like a monkey— an urban monkey. We would have needed nets and tranquilizer guns."

"That'd be the way to nail him next time," said Hayte.

Dietrich shook his head. "Even that might not be enough. Our boy seems to be an expert escape artist." He took off his glasses and thought. "If the GeniTech - clone story of Bunch's *is* true, that would explain how our boy got out of quarantine in the first place."

Hayte sat down on the edge of the bed and thought intently. "What about the helix stuff? Did Vaughn give you the files on that?"

"The 'invisible' graffiti? Yeah, Shrini did the computer analysis on them. The patterns are similar—but not identical. I talked it over with Shrini, she thinks it might be some secret form of communication…"

"That's it!" Hayte snapped his fingers, "I bet I know what that is!"

"What?"

"They're marking the victims! That would make perfect sense…" Hayte paced gingerly. "It would also mean that there's some sort of teamwork— one goes and does the reconnaissance work, then another comes, reads the message and…pow!"

"That would explain it," Dietrich paused. "…I *think.*"

Hayte stopped and shook his head. "But that doesn't explain everything. There's no link between me and the other victims. I never knew the Goodwill woman, and Scotty was barely an acquaintance. I mean, he called me out of the blue after three years."

Dietrich folded his arms. "But you met with Bunch, right?"

Hayte got back into the bed. "Yeah, *once.* At the Pickled Ape, after he phoned me up the night before."

"That may have been enough. Did you check to see if you were being followed?"

There was a long silence. Finally, Richard shook his head, "No, I didn't. And I remember Scotty was awful jumpy."

Dietrich pushed his glasses back. "Did he furnish any proof about the Johnny B program?"

"Nope, he was supposed to hand over a bunch of computer files to me on Thursday, I think it was March 5th, but he never showed up."

"Because he was blown to bits," said Dietrich grimly. "He probably was attacked the same night you met with him."

"And then I found him—what was left…" Rich lay back down. "I know who I'd like to question about that, but I don't dare."

Dietrich raised an eyebrow. "The NPDi?"

"No, not them. GeniTech." Hayte leaned back on his pillow and closed his eyes. "Man, I'm sleepy…"

Dietrich watched him drift off. As Hayte started snoring lightly, he shut off the palmtop and got ready to leave.

There was a knock. Shrini peered round the doorway. "Hi Rich, sorry I'm so late. I got that stuff…"

Dietrich held a finger to his lips. She came over and handed him the Phantoms stills.

Dietrich mouthed the word, "thanks."

Shrini turned to leave. "Oh—I forgot something!" she whispered. She pulled out a tiny cartridge and waved it at Dietrich, "What should I do with all these microfiles I got from Brezzi?"

Dietrich looked at her. "What are they?"

"They were for Perry. They contain details that Inspectore Brezzi got on that Albanian he busted at Venice airport… Something about checking the FBI's Most Wanted List…"

"I'll take 'em." Dietrich took out his palmtop again, "I'll check the list tomorrow. I'll put them here, so I don't forget." He took the tiny cartridges and put them in a plastic sleeve, which he slipped in the palmtop's case.

"Thanks, Dietrich. And I forgive you for that crack about dicks in the NYPD." She vanished before he could reply.

~ ~ ~

Monday March 28, 9:30 am:

The lights came on in his cell with blinding intensity, startling Perry, who hadn't realized he had fallen asleep. His mouth tasted like decay and his teeth hurt. He picked his head up off the cold concrete and looked around. Slowly his eyes began to focus and he could open them without pain.

Next to the door there was a bowl. He slowly crawled over to look at it.

Cornflakes. There was a small carton of milk and a plastic spoon next to it. He fumbled to get the thing open.

After eating every last morsel, he put the bowl down. He rubbed the stubble on his face. What to do, what to do…

He needed *something* to pass the time before those assholes came back.

For lack of anything better, he started doing a rundown of everything he know about the Phantoms. He found the notepaper that had been left in his cell from yesterday and started making an itemized list. Oh, and the cards were still where he'd left them in the corner.

He started laying out the cards again.

No two robberies with the same robbers…

A light went on in his mind.

It's simple…too simple.

"That's it!" he said, staring at the playing cards. "That's why there aren't any repeat offenders in the Phantoms!"

They're running a temp agency! They recruit the workers from outside the country—probably either in Central America or Eastern Europe, where the central records systems don't exist… The ringleaders get the 'temps' to do all the legwork…

Perry stopped writing and rubbed his forehead. "But what's to keep the 'workers' from taking the money and running?"

No one answered him. He got up and resumed pacing. *How do they escape, anyway? They can't be carrying huge bags of money…*

A system of decoys—somebody else to carry the cash?

He stopped pacing. *They aren't carrying any cash! There is no cash. Much simpler that way. The 'transaction' must happen later.*

He scribbled down more notes. *Next question: No cash stolen, no robbers seen escaping—are the banks faking the robberies?*

He immediately rejected the idea. *Gut feeling says no. Why call attention to the thefts—much easier to embezzle when nobody is looking.*

A sudden thought occurred to him. *We've never gotten a look at the bank logs. Time to change that!*

He absently chewed on the end of the pen. *Insurance fraud?* Again, he immediately rejected the idea. *All the major banks are owned by insurance companies or vice-versa. Besides, all those priceless museum pieces were destroyed…*

He frowned intently. "So who is doing this?" he said aloud. *Disgruntled employees? No—too much trouble, much easier to embezzle and cook the books. Former employees? Possible—but still easier to embezzle. Making high-profile robberies is not what present or former bank employees would do—doesn't fit the 'number-cruncher' personality. Not to mention the vandalism and the stunt with the raw sodium.*

No. Somebody outside the biz is running this ring. Someone who is a banking expert or has access to a lot of information, unlimited access to hazardous materials, and… a nasty sense of humor.

He started frantically scribbling more notes.

The cell door opened and Donner came in. He smiled when he noticed Perry's notes. "Good to see you're still acting like a detective."

"You said I would go back to the NYPD, and I intend to hold you to that." said Donohue, looking up.

"Bold talk for a prisoner…" grinned Donner. "C'mon, let's go to my office."

"So I *am* a prisoner?" said Perry. "What am I charged with?"

"You ain't charged with nothing." said Donner evenly. "Because you're co-operating. Follow me."

They walked down a concrete corridor that changed directions every

20 yards, their footsteps echoing.

"Listen, Donner, I don't know where the head is."

"You're a detective. I have every expectation you will find it," said Donner, refusing to be perturbed, "And when you hand it over, you will be rewarded. Simple as that."

Perry looked around and saw no guards or surveillance cameras. "Where are your other friends?"

"You mean Agents Cheshire and Browning? That's none of your concern, Donohue."

Donohue's eyes narrowed, "Oh yeah? What's to stop me from attacking you and trying to escape?"

"Hah! You'll figure it out eventually..." smirked Donner. "Of course, your every move is monitored. He stopped in mid-hall "We're here."

"Where" All Perry say was a blank expanse of concrete wall.

"My office." Donner pressed some invisible button and a previously unseen door opened in front of Perry.

"We believe in the system of rewards." Donner pointed to an old rotary phone on the desk. "And here's proof. See what a generous guy I am? It's time to call your buddies. *Go ahead*, it's on me."

"*What?*" Donohue looked mistrustful.

"Go ahead—call your precious NYPD and report in—don't look at me like that—just do it!" He winked as he closed the cell door behind him, "But I wouldn't try to mention anything that compromises our operation here..." He pressed another button and another door opened. "Catch ya later..." he grinned. The door slid shut.

Donohue tried Hayte's number first, but Rich's voice mail was on. He tried Shrini next.

"New York Police Dept. Lt. Shrinithan here."

"Shrini—it's me, Perry!"

"Perry! How are you? I was just writing a 200-page report on the latest Phantoms robbery..."

"I'm fine. Another Phantoms robbery? What bank did they hit this time?"

"The Bank of New York, at 48 Wall St." Puzzled, she paused for a second. "Why didn't you hear about that? Where *are* you, anyway?"

Donohue lowered his voice. "I'm being held captive by the NPDi in a cell somewhere..."

Shrini sounded annoyed. "I don't care about the weather, Perry. *Where are* you?"

Donohue looked at the phone for a moment. "I just *told* you—I'm *being held captive* by these NPDi assholes—they're part of Homeland Security..."

Shrini's tone grew more irritable. "Perry, is this some kind of joke? Or a code? I could care less about the New York Yankees."

Now Perry was totally confused. "*What?*"

"The *Yankees*. I don't even *like* baseball—I don't understand the game at all. Now, cricket, that's another story. India has a test match against Britain this week, I can hardly wait..."

Donohue stared at the phone like it would bite him. "Wait a second—I didn't say anything about baseball..."

"Yes you did! You just told me you were mad the Yankees had lost their doubleheader against the Diamondbacks. What is a doubleheader, anyway?"

Perry paused for a moment. Finally he said, "It's two games played against the same team, on consecutive days."

"Oh, that's good to know. Maybe the Phantoms will do a doubleheader too, that way we might catch up with them. Your friend Brezzi called some days ago, gave us a good lead to follow up on. Dietrich will give them to Rich—you did hear about..."

Donohue closed his eyes, "Whew! I thought I was going crazy for a moment there. I said nothing about baseball or the weather, and then you go on and on like I did..."

Shrini said sharply, "Perry—wait a sec. You say you mentioned nothing about either baseball or weather? Just say yes or no."

"Yes, that's right."

She started laughing nervously. "Ah… I bet I know what's happening. Perry, you're being filtered—this must be the new Censorship software! If you say something you're not supposed to, it blocks it out and changes the subject to something safe—and it uses your own voice without you knowing it!"

Donohue was incredulous. "*Censorship software?* So I can't tell you where..."

"There it goes again!" she said in triumph, "Now you said something about the Stanley Cup!"

"So what *can* we talk about?" said Donohue exasperatedly.

She drummed her fingers, "Let's try the Phantoms again. Brezzi called, said he's identified one of the robbers, a Russian he wounded last month in Venice airport. You got that?"

"Yes, got it all," said Donohue, "Go on."

"Brezzi's got the man in custody and will extradite him once the Justice Department files extradition papers with the Italian government."

"Great! If we can interrogate the guy, it might confirm my theory..."

"Ah-hah!" Her voice got excited, "So we *can* discuss this subject. OK, what is it?"

Donohue glanced at his cards. "I *think* I got it figured out. I've had a lot of time to work out theories… The ringleaders of the Phantoms bring the actual bank robbers from outside, provide them with fake passports and fly or ship them in to the U.S. of A. That train I rode down to Venice on, the 'Bordello Express'..."

"The *what?*"

"Never mind. What's important is that I found their drop point for passports—or at least one of them. Henri's arrest confirms that part. Anyway, the imported robbers do the dogwork, the ringleaders just supply them with weapons and pay them off when they've finished the job."

"Why don't the robbers just run off with the cash? That's what a New Yorker would do..." said Shrini.

"They *can't*. Because if I'm right, there *is* no paper money involved," said Donohue. "The robbers only have to catch the employees off-guard after they've already logged into their bank's computers. They herd the employees into the bank safe, lock them up *and then* go and plant deep viruses in the bank's central computers—everybody's already logged in, so the firewall and password protection is totally compromised."

"What do you mean 'deep viruses,' Perry?"

"Alright, that's my term for them—I just made it up to illustrate a point. Probably, they're not viruses at all, just regular transactions that fall due on a certain pre-determined day during peak hours. The cash gets transferred later by the deep viruses, say a couple hundred times through some Cayman Island accounts, so no one can trace it. You get all that?"

"Got it, Perry. Yes, that would make sense..." Shrini paused, "Let me ask you something—did you get help figuring this out?"

"Not really," said Donohue guardedly. "I *did* get access to all the case files I had before, but I really have had time to think about the particulars. Oh, I also got access to all the banks' insurance claims, so I have a real good idea of what actually was stolen. The figures were so high that the robbers couldn't physically have carried it all out—not at the robbery you and I witnessed."

She sounded skeptical, "But what if the banks are lying and artificially inflating the claims?"

"They couldn't, for two reasons: first, all the best private investigators I know of work for the big insurance firms—they get routinely cherry-picked from the IRS with double the government salary."

"And the second reason?"

"The banking industry is way too cutthroat. Sooner or later a competitor will hear rumors of fraud—it always comes out, sooner or later—then, the Justice Department investigates. The bank either goes under or gets swallowed up in a takeover. No, what they've lost in these robberies is just a drop in the bucket compared to the risk of getting nailed in an insurance fraud case."

Shrini tapped furiously at her keyboard, "There—got it all. Should I pass all this on to the Chief, show him you're making progress?"

Donohue said, "Already done—should be in his e-mailbox by now." He shifted the phone to his other ear. "But there's still one important thing I'm missing."

Shrini took a sip of tea, "How do they escape?"

"Exactly." Donohue caught a glimpse of Donner re-entering the office, "Look, I'm about to get cut off—I'll talk to you later, OK? Bye."

~ ~ ~

Shrini clicked the 'hang up' icon onscreen. She felt relieved to have heard from Donohue, but still she sat back and shuddered. Though she was loathe to admit it, her first experience with the Censorship software had shaken her badly.

When she had first heard about it, about six months ago, she found the rumors very hard to take seriously. The algorithms of the actual software had seemed impossible to her because of the infinite number of unpredictable variables to factor in.

But no more. Censorship voice control software was reality. *And it works.*

She stared blankly at her monitor, but her mind was racing.

How did the thing know when a person was going to say something it wanted to censor and react so precisely—with a synthesized voice that sounded so real?

She began to wonder if television newscasts could be manipulated with it.

She made a mental note to ask Richard if there was any legal means to stop the government from using it further.

The minutes passed. The more she thought about it, the more anxious she became..

Now she really felt creepy.

Where is Perry?

Chapter 16

Wednesday March 30:

The buzzer came on, waking Hayte from his slumber. He picked up his watch and saw it was 7 a.m. "What the hell?" he grumbled.

The floor receptionist's voice came on the loudspeaker. "Visitor for you."

"Oh… thanks," Richard yawned and stretched. He gingerly sat up.

Dietrich came in with a handful of printouts. "Morning, Rich. Got some more stuff for you to see."

"Morning, Dietrich." Hayte got up when he saw the printouts. "Good news?"

"That depends. Both good and bad news, I think."

"What do you mean? Did you get a match on the perpetrator.?"

"Oh, yes…" Dietrich made a face. "We got matches." He held up a composite likeness, "Recognize him?"

Hayte nodded, "That's my attacker." He looked closer at the likeness, "but that's not the same sketch I did, right? Doesn't look like my style, but I'd recognize that face, those beady eyes and the nose anywhere."

"Oh yeah? Meet the latest Phantom." Dietrich pulled out another composite. "And this one?"

Rich turned the image around and scrutinized it. "It's the same guy, right?"

"*Maybe.* Wanted for a series of rapes in New Jersey over the past seven weeks." Dietrich pulled out another sketch. "How about this one?"

Hayte laid the three side by side on his bed. "Same guy again. Or is it?"

"My gut feeling says no." Dietrich pointed to the third composite, "*This* one is wanted in connection with the rape of a 9-year-old girl in Jamaica-Queens. It happened the same week you were attacked, possibly within the same 48 hour period."

"Uh-oh…" The frown lines on Hayte's face deepened. He pointed to the rest of Dietrich's stack, "Are all those printouts like these three?"

"I'm afraid so, Rich," Dietrich set the rest of the stack down. "You should look through them all, but I think you're right—it's a clone problem."

Hayte let out a deep sigh and sat down on the bed, "Wonderful. Why haven't these composites triggered any alarm bells before?"

Dietrich made a face, "Maybe they *did* trigger an alarm *somewhere*... but I didn't get these through standard police channels—I didn't get any matches *at all* when I tried. Something told me the searches weren't getting through somehow, so I sent the comp to regional newspapers in all 50 states, via snail mail. *That's* when I started getting results."

Hayte's eyes widened, "Are you saying this information's being suppressed on an official level?"

Dietrich nodded, "Nationwide. Every time I tried to do a search of local, state or national mug shot archives—even at the FBI level, the search terminated abnormally, no explanation given. I know that the big Internet backbone providers are all bankrupt or are in shutdown mode, but the emergency networks should still be functional." He shook his head in bewilderment, "Something's happening, and I don't know what..."

"If this is what I'm beginning to think it is, all the standard law enforcement networking resources might be totally useless." Hayte sank back into his pillow. "This could be the ultimate legal nightmare. God, I don't have the energy to think about it..."

"Get your rest, Rich. I'll go now," Dietrich collected all the printouts and put them back in the binder.

"Thanks, Dietrich for bringing those by." Hayte closed his eyes, "I'm gonna need to sleep on this ..."

~ ~ ~

Wednesday, 11:30 am:
Shrini went upstairs again. Still no sign of the chief. It was starting to piss her off. She wanted to confront Shabazz with the different mug shots of Johnny B and find out why the NYPD and State databases hadn't found any matches.

But without Shabazz's clout, there was little chance Internal Affairs would take her allegations seriously. Shrini scowled to herself. *Because I'm a woman...*

She looked around the office. It always looked as if nobody ever worked there—everything was like it was last week after the cleaning service had come in.

She glanced in his trash. Nothing.

She noticed the post-it note she had stuck to his computer screen a week ago was still there. *Oh, great... that's all we need, another missing chief. Hope Shabazz hasn't gone and gotten himself killed like Chief Hershey did...*

But, no piled up messages either. That means he must be running things somehow, maybe via his cell phone. But from where?

She briefly considered hacking into his planner online to see if he could be located. *No, not yet...*

She was just about to walk out when the phone rang. She grabbed it on impulse, picking up before the automatic call-rerouting kicked in. "Hello, New York Police Department, Chief Shabazz's office."

"Hello," said a gruff male voice, "who is this?"

She forced herself to respond politely, "This is Lt. Shrinithan speaking. How may I help you?"

The man sounded really irritable, "I *want* to speak to your chief. I've been trying all damned week."

"I'm sorry about that sir. Can I get your name and number..."

"Oh hell... Alright, I'm sick of talking to that damned voice mail system. My name is Carrouthers."

Shrini grabbed a pen. "And the first name?"

There was an awkward pause. "I can't give you that. Or my number, either."

Her patience started to evaporate. "Well, what *can* you tell me, sir?"

His tone remained stubborn. "Well, I really need to speak to your chief, miss."

Shrini was starting to become really annoyed. She was just about to hang up on the guy when she looked at the phone display. Her eyes widened when she saw it was totally blank. *Only Level 5 callers can do that.* She hurriedly said "Can you hold on a minute?"

"Yeah, OK..."

She walked to the door and looked nervously in both directions to make sure she wasn't being watched. She went back inside the office and closed the door. "Sir, what is this about? If I have something important to pass on to Chief Shabazz, it'll get a *lot* quicker response..."

"All right. My uh, granddaughter was murdered."

"Murdered? Why?"

"That's what I'm calling to find out. They found her body in a shallow grave in New Jersey someplace, along with a couple of other bodies."

"A light went on in Shrini's head. "Ah—was she a television reporter?"

"Yeah, that's right. She worked for VNN—she was covering this... what do you call 'em, Phantoms case. To make a long story short, I saw the mug shots online, and I recognize one of the robbers..."

"You do?" Shrini's mind raced. "Which one? Sir, can you come in to give evidence?"

Carrouthers paused. "It's... not that simple. I gotta get off the line—I'm in the Federal Witness Protection Program, and I'm not supposed to call longer than five minutes..."

That explains the Level 5 clearance. Shrini decided to chance it. "Sir, can you call me at home? I've got a secure line. Nobody will trace you there. *If* this is *really* important..."

Another pause. Finally, he answered "Oh hell. Sure—can you give me the number?"

~ ~ ~

Shrini stayed late at her desk, pausing only to get some take-out food. She halfway hoped Perry would call again, but she also knew there was no guarantee that the censorship software would allow any meaningful discussion. Besides, she wasn't sure she had anything new to tell him anyway. Carrouthers hadn't actually given her anything concrete, only a tantalizing possibility of leads on the Phantoms and the three murdered reporters.

She opened the data file on the three reporters. She quickly saw it was so slim that there was no point in studying it at all. No clues, just three corpses all murdered with a .22 bullet to the back of the head. Nobody saw anything until the freshly-dug graves were discovered by a cemetery gardener in Jersey. *No fabric samples, no foreign DNA, nada...*

She mulled over what Perry had told her about the Phantoms. His reasoning seemed to make sense: a changing cast of robbers imported from outside... *But who does the recruiting? Who orchestrates the robberies so perfectly so that nobody is ever nabbed?*

She sat frowning, deep in thought. The Phantoms must be phoning up the press networks right before they strike. Otherwise, how could they know about the robberies before we do?

She wished she knew someone at the networks—that would be the only way to find out who the Phantoms were calling. *But would there be a contact person at every single network, all 300-plus of them?*

No. *They all spy on each other, big time... All it would take is a few calls, then the word would spread.*

She rubbed her eyes. *But how do I find those contacts? The press must employ about a million people in the Big Apple alone...* She suddenly felt very tired.

Hell, I sure hope Carrouthers has some useful information...

Carrouthers... She suddenly realized it was getting very late and she was expecting him to call her at home. "Shit!" She grabbed her stuff from her cubicle and dashed for the side door.

She dashed to Grand Central, almost falling a couple times on the newly-waxed floor. She caught the last commuter train north just as the doors were closing, almost losing her handbag in the process. It took her several stops to catch her breath. *Thank heavens I can wear jogging shoes to work...*

It was 10:30 by the time she walked in her front door. She immediately checked her voice mail. No encrypted calls. *Whew! Only some telemarketers.*

She decided to watch TV, but there was nothing on, so she stared at the murals on her wall and tried not to doze off.

She waited until midnight for Carrouthers to call. Finally, her eyes closed and she drifted off without knowing it.

She awoke to the phone's shrill ringing. She looked at the wall clock and groaned. She let the phone ring for a moment as her eyes focused on the readout: encrypted.

She grabbed her headset and picked up immediately, "Shrinithan here."

"Carrouthers. Sorry about the time, but this is the only chance for me call for any length without being traced."

She stifled a yawn, "How do you know that?"

"Trust me, I *know*. My security clearance has never been revoked. I still have a few friends in Homeland Security who keep me up to date."

"So what do you need from us? You said your granddaughter was one of the murdered reporters..." Shrini walked into the kitchen and put a tea bag in a cup of water.

"Yes. Her name is—was Zane..."

"...Lewis. She worked for VNN." said Shrini, "I know the case. We're working with the police in New Jersey."

"Have they found out anything substantial?"

"Not yet. The DNA tests didn't turn up anything we can work with. Let me check the file." She sat down at her terminal and typed in some commands. "Here—I got the file up now. Did you say you had official clearance? I need some kind of proof of that before I can say anything more."

"Yes, I can get it sent to you within 24 hours."

"Okay, do that." Shrini switched ears. "Another question—when did you last have contact with her?"

"Back in February. She phoned me, she was all excited about being assigned to cover the Phantoms robberies. I understand that case is still open as well."

"Um, I'm not allowed to com..."

"That's OK, I know it still is."

"Did your granddaughter give you any information on the Phantoms?"

"Yeah—well, not directly..." Carrouthers coughed. "The funny thing is that she sent me the mug shots on them—and I recognized one of the faces from a project I was working on at GeniTech. I was gonna tell her, but I never could get in touch with her again."

"Why are you in the Witness Protection program? Is it because of your work at GeniTech?"

"Partly," admitted Carrouthers, "but there are other reasons as well. You could say the Justice Department is protecting me against their own wishes..." He started to chuckle, then broke off. "But I'm not calling about that—I want to nail whoever killed my granddaughter."

"What did you do next, sir, after you couldn't reach her? Did you file a missing persons report?"

"No, I couldn't..." Carrouthers paused awkwardly. "Actually, she's not exactly my granddaughter..."

"What do you mean by that, sir?" Shrini put the tea in the microwave.

"Listen, I can't answer that now—my time window is too short." The microwave beeped. "Hey, what's that?"

"It's only the microwave. I'm making tea." She took a sip and let the silence drag out. "Sir, do you have anything else you can tell me?"

"Yes. Lots. But I can't do it over the phone. I have to do it in person, but I can't come to you—I'm out of your area, and Witness Protection won't allow me to travel. I need you to come and record my testimony."

"Testimony? There has to be a Grand Jury investigation first..."

"It's within my rights as a witness to give a sworn deposition in a murder case. As far as a Grand Jury investigation, believe me, there will be one, soon enough. I am pretty damned sure I know who murdered my granddaughter. And that's just the tip of the iceberg."

Shrini frowned. "That won't be so easy. I have to see about getting authorization."

"Don't worry about that—I can help with that."

"Why do you need me? Can't your friends in Homeland Security help?"

"Not at this level. There's not a direct terrorist threat involved. Anyway I want to make a recorded disposition—and if you can bring another witness you trust, that would be even better."

"Hmm... I'll have to see." Shrini sipped the last of her tea. "How can I reach you? Can you send e-mail?"

"No. Not secure enough. I'll put the address on my voice mail system and give you the number and PIN to access it."

"I can do that. But why can't you go to a prosecutor yourself and give a sworn deposition?"

Carrouthers' voice sounded strained. "No, that won't work, not at my level of clearance. Here, just write the number down, then call at about the same time tomorrow night. Believe me, this is very important—it concerns mismanagement at the very highest levels."

She grabbed a pen and started writing.

Chapter 17

Friday, April 1:

They had him handcuffed and blindfolded before he had woken up. They stuffed the semi-conscious Donohue in a van and started off. "Hey! I gotta piss!" he yelled, as he realized what was happening.

After half an hour, they dragged him out and let him urinate against a tree. Then they dragged him back into the van by his handcuffs and took off again.

A couple more hours, and the van stopped. Perry heard Donner say, "Time to set the little bird free." He was pulled back out and forced to stand still at gunpoint.

The blindfold came off, as did the handcuffs. The van drove off, leaving Donohue and Donner standing under an awning. Perry tried to rub some feeling back into his wrists. His legs still felt numb from the ride, and the parole box strap chafed against his ankle.

It was still dark. There were only a few other people standing around, reading newspapers under the streetlamps. Donohue looked around the dilapidated station and decided they must be somewhere in Connecticut. "Why the train?" he grumbled to Donner. "I *hate* riding on trains."

"Bad day to drive," said Donner. "They're putting the big condom on the Norton-Humes building today. The streets will be filled with rubberneckers and film crews—everybody wants a piece of the action."

"So why do we have to go today?" Donohue tried surreptitiously tapping his ankle against a bench support.

"You can't break it that way, son..." Donner looked at him in amusement. "We're going today because today is special. I'm gonna present you to your new controller. Whenever we need you, he'll be in touch. Then we're going to meet with your chief. From here on out, it's gonna be *smooth sailing*..." He grinned smugly and handed Perry a roll of coins. "Here's some dollar coins for the pay phones. Trust me, you'll need 'em. We don't want you contacting us through insecure lines."

"Pay phones?" Donohue looked at him incredulously, "There *aren't* any pay phones any more."

"Oh yeah? You just walked past one," smirked Donner, pointing toward the station entranceway, "Open your eyes, Donohue, you're *supposed* to be a detective. All the train stations have 'em, it's required by law."

The ancient commuter train clattered to a halt, its brakes protesting noisily. Donner waited for the wave of departing passengers to go by before he boarded the train.

Donohue followed suit. There was no other option. If he tried to break away or jump out right as the doors shut, the parole box would emit a piercing shriek and release a powerful tranquilizer that would knock him out cold.

The train started its lumbering progress down the tracks, past the still-uncompleted skeleton of the monorail rusting in the first glimmers of morning light.

Perry avoided looking at Donner as much as possible. Instead, he studied the other passengers intently, as if searching for a familiar face. Nobody glanced up from their newspapers.

The train plunged into a tunnel and came shooting out moments later, causing Perry to wince as the rising sun's rays hit him full in the face. He sat crossways to ward off the glare, sneaking a glance and seeing with some satisfaction that Donner was having to shield his eyes as well.

Suddenly, the brakes slammed on, and Perry was dumped off his seat and slid down the aisle on his side. The wagon tipped over and shot up at a crazy angle, then righted itself.

A large woman landed on top of him, knocking the wind out of him. "Sorry, honey," she said in a husky voice. She tried to move but couldn't.

He tried to wiggle out of the folds of flesh, but the weight was too great.

It was strangely silent. Minutes passed. It felt like eternity. Starved for air, he began to panic.

The woman finally managed to roll off of him. The other passengers began disentangling themselves slowly. Perry laid there, catching his breath. His vision swam and then came into focus. Seats were scattered everywhere, but the wagon was upright. Sort of.

His nose felt like it was broken. He tasted blood running down, but at least his eyes weren't swelled shut—yet. *Nothing else seemed broken... no other bleeding...*

Hey! He felt a tingling sensation around his foot. He reached down and felt around both ankles.

No transmitter—only bare skin. He looked around and saw the carbon-fiber band had broken and that the transmitter was lying in pieces. *And Donner was nowhere to be seen...*

"Ain't you gonna fucking *look* at me? I *said* I was sorry!" snarled the woman, glaring at him.

Without a word, Donohue got to his feet and started making his way through the wreckage.

The woman yelled, "*Hey!* I'm *talking* to you..."

Another man collided with her with an loud grunt, and they went down in a heap over the back of one of the uprooted bench seats.

Perry was able to get a side window open and slither out. It was about a five-foot drop to the ground. He landed with a thud and looked around.

The tunnel was blocked. Perry saw train cars lined up like an accordion behind him. He turned and ran to the front—and headlong into a gaggle of well-dressed people brawling with each other and with the few uniformed policemen who had made it down the ravine.

He recognized some of the austere faces, but in his haste, he couldn't place them.

It was only later that he realized they were all well-known in New York.

On the tracks ahead, he saw a man's body. He came closer and saw it wasn't a body at all—rather, an overlarge paper mâche effigy of the President, tied symbolically to the tracks.

Electric fences blocked him in on both sides of the rails. He quickly decided there was only one way to escape.

After a few stumbles, he started running toward the effigy, prompting several screams. "HEY! HE'S GONNA STEP ON THE SCULPTURE!! *STOP HIM!!!*"

Donohue sprung into the air. There was an audible gasp as Perry's feet just missed grazing the head.

He slipped down the gravel incline on the other side of the tracks and looked around desperately.

Nearby, he saw a service ladder mounted to the side of the culvert. He raced toward it. He saw that it led to a pedestrian crossing above. Donohue scrambled up the ladder, missing several rungs as his feet fought for grip. At the top, he barely made it over the edge, badly winded. He dashed across the pedestrian bridge and took off down a side street, running until his legs started to buckle.

As he leaned against a brick wall, gasping for breath, he looked hurriedly around and saw no one was pursuing. Sweat stung his eyes. He wiped off his brow and decided to keep moving.

He stumbled out into a main street. A crowd of dark-skinned faces swallowed him up, brushing past like he wasn't there. Brightly-colored turbans and shawls paraded past, along with a red fez or two, emblazoned with strange symbols.

He struggled to orient himself. The place looked totally unfamiliar. *Westchester? Couldn't be...* it bore no resemblance to the place he remembered from ten years ago.

The street signs were totally alien, written in a script he didn't recognize. *Swahili? Pakistani?* Definitely not Asian or Arabic. The air was filled with strange musky smells, exotic incense, curry and ginger.

Perry walked in and out of shops to ask for directions, but nobody spoke English.

The only thing he could say for sure was that many different languages were being spoken—or screamed, depending on where he looked.

The streets were choked with beat up cars, some with plastic garbage bags duct-taped where windows and doors should have been. The sound of car horns was everywhere. Even more puzzling, he looked down and noticed cow patties on the sidewalks and streets. *At least they smelled like cow patties...* But there was no farm in sight.

He clambered on top of a dumpster to get a better view of the chaos. It was then that he saw the steady stream of albino hunchbacked cattle wandering aimlessly in the street. Somehow the masses of cars miraculously missed colliding with them.

One especially large bull ahead loped along the middle of the street, and cars scattered like flies to avoid the beast. Perry got off the dumpster and ducked into an alley.

He noticed a sign lying face down. He flipped it over. *New Rochelle city limits?!*

He looked around, mystified. *So what is this place called now?*

He walked out the other end of the alleyway and saw a newer sign written in several languages, mounted on a cable between buildings. At the very bottom, written in English, it said New Bombay, pop. 401,000.

~ ~ ~

"I'm fine, *just* fine," said Donner between gritted teeth. He sat leaning against an overturned rail car, holding a bloody bandage to his temple.

An ambulance attendant applied tape to the bandage. "Sir, you require treatment—you cannot go out on the street in that condition."

Though badly shaken, Donner still had his wits about him. "I see you're from Bronx-Lebanon hospital—that's not in my HMO." His voice became steadier. "Unless I am attended to by a member hospital, they will not pay for either the ambulance or the treatment."

"I can't just leave you here," said the attendant firmly. "Your eye requires immediate treatment, or you might lose it. And your foot looks broken too."

"If you could give me another bandage for the eye, I could focus enough..." He fished out his tiny mobile, "to call my HMO, and they will..." he winced as a sharp pain shot through his head, "...send one of their ambulances."

"OK, suit yourself." The attendant finished bandaging him and went to the next injured person.

Donner was surprised to see that the mobile was still working. He dialed a short emergency number. "Yeah, it's me—what? Yeah, I was... *we* were on the train. There was a wreck. In Westchester, I think... What? Yeah, the whole train's kaput. No, I haven't located Donohue—I want you to check all local hospitals. Zap him with the parole box if you come up empty-handed—no, forget that—check all emergency rooms first—I don't want him dying on us..." Suddenly he noticed people were staring. "Look—I gotta go—I'm out in the open and I got a head wound. Bye."

He folded up the phone and tried to stand. *So far, so good, but still wobbly. No broken bones, except maybe my head...* He winced as another stab of pain crossed his temples. He started walking, hoping to find a place where he could telephone discreetly. He stopped and shook the gravel out of his Birkenstocks.

~ ~ ~

By late afternoon, Perry was penniless. He found himself sitting exhaustedly in a street café, looking gloomily at the last of his pocket change. He ate a little more of his tandoori chicken, which made his mouth burn and his eyes tear up.

He desperately wanted to call somebody—anybody—he knew, but there wasn't a phone box anywhere to be seen. Donner had of course confiscated his cell phone. His head throbbed. He felt around the inside of his mouth with his tongue. *No broken teeth, thank god...*

A loud screeching of brakes made him turn his head. A few yards away, a startled white cow loped down the sidewalk, overturning carts of vegetables in its wake. Perry got up and moved to the side moments before the beast trampled through and sent chairs and tables flying.

Donohue ran the other way, feeling worse than a shoplifter for not paying the bill. He saw a flash of silver in the street ahead of him, and his heart went in his mouth—it was a Mercedes with NYPD-issue spotlights on its outside mirrors. He ran toward it, not caring if it was coming to arrest him or not.

A familiar face poked out the driver's side window. It was Shrini, waving frantically, "Perry! We've been looking for you everywhere!"

Donohue ran over, got in and slammed the door. "Thank Elvis—or hare krishna or whatever—you wouldn't believe all the shit I've been through!" He got in the back and collapsed onto the seat.

"I can not only believe it—I can *smell* it" laughed Shrini. "Those fooking sacred cows crap everywhere—and the wild dogs too!" She steered expertly through the streams of people, pushcarts and animals crisscrossing the street.

They came to a stoplight and she looked him over in the rearview mirror. "You look like a wreck, Perry."

"Train wreck, to be precise..." said Donohue. He held up his bloody hands. "I'll tell you all about it, but I think I need some first aid..." he sniffed his shirt, "and a bath too."

"We're almost there, Perry," said Shrini, pulling out across traffic into a side street.

"Where? The White Elephant?"

"You must be joking—that's way down in Manhattan," said Shrini. She drove up to what appeared to be two enormous bamboo doors. She hit a button on the steering wheel, and the whole façade flipped up, revealing a small but modern parking garage. She drove in, and the door flipped back into place. Fluorescent lights came on.

Donohue stepped out and looked around. "What is this—the local police precinct?"

"Nope," said Shrini, "my apartment building."

~ ~ ~

The pain in Donner's temples was getting worse. He was standing outside the Hillside Hospital emergency room, shouting into his cell phone, oblivious to the stares of all the smokers standing in front of the double glass doors. "*Jesus!* Even a donkey's doormat would know more than you do! What do you mean, his parole box ain't responding? Shit! *Yes*, I need you to come pick me up—what, did you think I could *walk* all the way to HQ *on a broken foot*?" He hung up in disgust, muttering to himself.

~ ~ ~

It was now early evening. Donohue was showered, bandaged and somewhat recovered. He glanced in the mirror in the bathroom. His black eyes were puffy but not swollen shut like he had feared. His nose still throbbed, and there was no way to breathe through it, but at least he could still swallow a bit. He wandered into the living room in one of Shrini's silk bathrobes.

"Nice choice, Perry" grinned Shrini, "pink really is your color."

"Yeah, *right*," said Donohue. "Hell, I'm just glad to be clean. I thought I'd never get all that filth scrubbed out."

She nodded, laughing. "You did look something like a coal miner, come to think of it…"

Perry looked at all the hologramic computer-generated 3-D images on the walls. Images of the Mayan pyramids faded, replaced by a mural of the Great Wall. "I didn't know you'd moved, Shrini. Shows how out of touch I've been."

"That's an understatement," she said in her clipped accent. She pointed a remote control at the huge TV on the wall and clicked on the 'news' icon. A menu popped up. She chose the train wreck headline. A few more clicks and the images of a train wreck filled the flat screen. "This the train you were talking about?"

Donohue nodded. He pointed to the last car, which was bent in the middle. "Can you zoom on in that wagon?" He walked up to the screen and peered closely.

Shrini pointed to the middle of the room, "Stand back here, Perry. You'll see better."

Donohue complied. "There! That's me—the guy running," He pointed to the image that was frozen in mid-leap.

"You mean stumbling," commented Shrini. "What's that crowd of rioters the police are fighting—Greenpeace?"

"No. Art collectors."

"What?!" Shrini looked at him like he was nuts.

"*Art* collectors," repeated Donohue. "Look to the lower left-hand side—there!"

"The body on the tracks?" Shrini squinted.

"That's no body—look at the size! It's a paper mâche effigy of our dear President of the United States. And those people there are gallery owners who are fighting to the death over who gets to cart it away and auction it off. Same thing's been going on in Europe for years now. Sounds like you're the one out of touch, Shrini..."

"PAH!" Shrini rolled her eyes. "*One* trip to Europe and you think you're a man of the world!" She let out a big laugh. "Well, Perry, one trek into New Bombay burst *that* little balloon!"

He ignored her gibe, "Must be the cheaper rent that brought you here, right?" he said, peering out the window to the street below.

"True. I *own* this apartment, Perry." said Shrini, "In fact, the whole building is mine. No way could I do that, even in Jamaica-Queens. And here I can speak my mother tongue. I'd almost forgotten *how*." She hit another button on her remote, and the computer-generated wallpaper switched to scenes from India. She walked to a wicker chair suspended by chains to the ceiling and sat down. The image of the Taj Mahal flashed up behind her. "So tell me, Perry—how *did* you end up in New Bombay in the first place? And why did you drop out of sight?"

"It's a long story. It started with the severed head. Seems the current 'owners' (whoever the hell they are) were a little pissed off at having lost it... To make a long story short, the NPDi kidnapped me..."

"Kidnapped you? Let's go after them!"

"We can't" said Donohue, resignedly, "They co-opt people from State and Local law enforcement, legally. You don't have a choice..."

"Why not?" said Shrini.

"They mostly use blackmail. In my case, they filed stolen property charges."

She looked at him incredulously. "For Chesney's head?"

"Exactly—the NPDi claims it belongs to them, so they 'charged' me with transporting stolen property, went after me and drafted me into their program."

"What? How can they do that?"

"Easy. Blackmail *works*. In my case, the accusation *wasn't* true, but that was all it took—my job was hanging from a thread anyway. The other cops

I saw later, they got co-opted for taking bribes, doing drugs, anything that could've gotten them thrown off the force. The NPDi had us all locked up underground and isolated—it had to be somewhere around D.C., I think. They wore us down through sleep deprivation, put us through all sorts of indoctrination and brainwashing, then sent us back to our jobs with parole boxes strapped to our ankles."

"Parole boxes?" She looked down at his feet. "Where's *your* box, Perry?"

"Came off in the train wreck. That's why I'm here—and on the run. Donner was personally bringing me into Manhattan to introduce me to my NPDi controller. I must be one of the first NYPD recruits. He was real pleased with himself when he got me, that much I can remember."

She looked him over. "So *are* you brainwashed, Perry?"

Donohue chewed his lip. "I'm not sure. I know I've been programmed to do stuff, because my dreams are so weird, but..."

"But what?"

"Well, for instance, normally I used to like to drink a few before turning in."

"There's some vodka in the fridge if you want some."

"No thanks." Seeing her look, Perry added, "See? That's what I mean— I automatically said no without thinking. Hell, I don't even *want* to drink. I don't like to admit it, but their training *has* changed me."

"So what were they training you for?"

"Well, one task was to capture some illegal clones that are running loose at the moment—they're called Johnny B..."

"Oh God!" Shrini's mouth dropped open. "Like the one that attacked Rich?"

"What? Rich was attacked? Was he hurt?"

"Yes, he was hurt. He got stabbed in the wanger," Shrini said matter-of-factly.

"Oh Elvis..." Perry cringed and drew up his limbs in a fetal position. "Does Rich know if everything will function? You know what I mean..."

"He'll be alright," continued Shrini, "The doctors sewed it back on in time. The urologist predicts a full recovery eventually, but Rich is still worried."

"I would be, too. What does 'eventual recovery' mean?" Donohue shuddered. "I wish I could go see him."

Shrini shook her head, "But you can't..."

"No, I can't," Donohue took the glass of water she offered, "So how did Rich get attacked in the first place? I thought he was going to law school." He took a deep swallow.

Shrini watched Perry's reaction, "He was the last person to meet with Scott Bunch before he was blown to bits."

The water went down Perry's windpipe. After the fit of coughing, he gasped, "Scott Bunch of GeniTech? Holy shit!"

"Rich thinks Bunch was probably killed by a suicide bomber," said

Shrini.

"A *what?*"

"A suicide bomber. Rich was probably target number three."

"Number *three?* There's Rich, Scott Bunch—so who was the other one?"

"Dietrich tells me it was a woman who worked in a Goodwill."

"Huh?" Donohue set the empty glass down. "So who are these suicide bombers? Is this some kind of weird religious cult?"

"No. According to Rich, these are all clones that Bunch was working on—the so-called Johnny B—exactly like the one that went after Rich."

"Is there any link between either Bunch or Rich and that woman?"

"We've got no idea about the Goodwill woman. All we know is that Rich probably got attacked because he met with Bunch."

"So why did Bunch meet with Rich? It's not like they were old pals..."

"Bunch was in a panic after seeing a Johnny B in one of the mug shots we circulated from the Phantoms robbery on Broadway. And he told Rich some details about GeniTech's running a human cloning program, despite the human clone ban in the U.S."

"Oh great, GeniTech again." Donohue let out a huge sigh. "Is there such a thing as justifiable arson? I'd love to torch those fuckers." He sat back and stared at the ceiling. "Now, it all begins to make sense..." Donohue shook his head wearily. "I feel like I went through shock treatment—I only remember fragments."

"Like what?"

"OK," Donohue sat on the couch. "I'll start at the beginning, that much I recall pretty clearly. They grabbed me off a crapper in New Jersey and stuffed me in a van."

He described waking up in the cell, the ritual humiliation and sleep deprivation. "And then they started with all this pseudo-religious gobbledegook..."

~ ~ ~

"The Spirit Emasculation is the most ESSENTIAL step in YOUR transformation..."

The music faded out and the virtual screen went blank, then dark.

Slowly the walls of the cell became visible again. Donohue wasn't much aware of anything at this point. His mouth was dry and his eyes could not focus at all. His head lolled about helplessly.

After a few minutes, he found he could rub his eyes by sticking his fingers under the viewer. It was then that he noticed he could see normally, even with the virtual headset in place. Still, it was uncomfortable and strapped on way too tight. He tried to take it off, but it wouldn't budge. After a few futile attempts, he gave up. To his surprise, he discovered he wasn't strapped to his seat. He got to his feet and looked around.

The cell door opened and Donner walked in. "Hope you liked our presentation," he said with a grin. "Now you're ready for the next stage."

"Next stage to *brainwashing*, you mean! Don't you ever feel bad about corrupting people's minds, Donner?"

In reaction, Donner leaned forward and stared into Donohue's eyes. "Oh, don't give me *that* crap! Hidden agendas make the world turn round! Let me give you an example: Did you know all the James Bond books that guy Fleming wrote had a hidden agenda?"

Donohue cocked his head slightly. "Huh?"

"Hah! You need to brush up on your conspiracy theories," He poured himself another coffee. "All those detailed bits about weapons, especially the guns, were intended as secret communicaes to the IRA— recommendations of what guns to buy with the donations they got Stateside."

"You're bullshitting me!"

"Not at all. It was 100% effective." Donner grinned wickedly, "And that's not all. Many of the things you always take for granted now had other, more... sinister uses. You know how the microwave oven was invented, don't you?"

Donohue looked even more skeptical. "No..."

"It was a Defence Department project originally. They were developing a system to literally roast enemy soldiers inside their own bunkers—any water-carrying object would literally explode under the bombardment of intense microwaves which could penetrate any shielding materials used for bunkers by the Soviet forces. Turns out one of the Joint Chiefs of Staff was a gourmet. He started asking if they could make a smaller version, so they could cook stuff quickly during their marathon planning sessions. Everybody looked at him like he was crazy, but in testing it worked fabulously! Later, he retired and founded the company that brought it to the consumer market." Donner spread his hands. "So you see, a lot of good technology comes out of ideas on how to kill people." He pointed a fat finger at Perry, "But you needn't worry your lowbrow cop mind about all that—you have other tasks. Your P-meter readings absolutely *suck*! You need to work on your attitude!"

Perry looked him over again, trying to figure him out. "I don't get it. What's all this shit about P-Meters and this Contact-Reprogram-Instinct-Purge-Enforce pentangle?"

"Basic principles of Violentology," said Donner evenly.

"What?!" Donohue's mouth dropped open. "You mean the NPDi is connected to Violentology?"

"Well, *duh*!" laughed Donner, "You cops—either you're all body and dead from the neck up, or the other way round..."

Donohue ignored the insult, "But how does your precious Ashcroft Doctrine allow an entire Bureau to be run by Violentologists?"

"Right you are, we all are believers in the power of Venometics..." Donner feinted with his left.

Donohue countered with his left, but Donner nailed him in the nose with a super-fast right jab. "Give up—you'll never win! I'm a DDT VIII—that's the level you will never achieve."

"What the hell does that mean?" Perry pinched his nostrils to stop the bleeding.

"It means I can anticipate your every move. That's what Expanded Venometics does for me—it gives me a blueprint on people's characters, *and* with only a minimum of effort—the No Sweat principle, you can..."

Donohue wiped the blood off his face with his sleeve. "But that doesn't answer my question, Donner. How is it a right-wing fundamentalist government like the present Administration tolerates a bunch of heretics like you?"

"We're not *heretics*," hissed Donner in a sudden rage, "We're an *officially recognized* institution, just like any other *legitimate* church! We may have different rituals and terminology, but we're all working towards the same end! Because we *get the job done.*" Donner did an Ali-style jab and dance on his feet. "Don't you see? Religion is the opiate of the people—an *essential* opiate! Religions and governments function best when they work *together!* And it's not exactly unusual for *different* religions to form *alliances...*" He began goose-stepping around the cell like a demented robot, "What about the U.S. and Israel? Close as can be—blood brothers, even! We Violentologists work hand in glove with the White House in both the NPDi *and* the FBI. And we're not the only ones—the Mormons have the CIA and the IRS!"

Donohue sat back down, stunned. "But *why?*"

"Because it *gets the job done.* Neither we nor our Mormon brothers have any motivational problems, drug habits—heck, *they* don't even drink *coffee.* Why has the government tapped certain religious groups to run their Anti-Terrorist Program? Simple! *Symbiosis* in the best sense of the word—we now have *legitimacy* in the eyes of the Government, they get our *efficiency.*" He turned and gave Donohue a look of mock pity, "Aw, jus' look at the poor boy—so dejected. *Cheer up!* You may not like us now—*but you will!*"

He turned to go. "In time, you'll love working for us—just like I do! And, best of all, you'll be *substance-free!* No expensive rehab with us—we'll eradicate your foul *blockage*—your harmful mental energy picture. You'll be *free!* There's nothing more *intoxicating* than the taste of *Freedom!*"

Perry looked at him like he was insane. "And how will *you* know?"

"Our V-Meters are *very* advanced" grinned Donner smugly. "Trust me on that! Right, break time is over!" He turned and walked out. The door closed behind him with a dull thud.

~ ~ ~

"I don't know what was worse, when that cell door opened or when it closed again..." Perry shook his head. He related how he woke up with needle marks on his arm, and what Donner had told him about training him in a tank full of sharks. "But some of that stuff, I'm not sure I dreamed it or if it really happened. One time, I thought I was a bear in a goddamn circus..."

Shrini looked shaken. "I really thought Rich was joking about those Birkenstock creeps. *Unbelievable.*"

"And worse yet, the whole thing *is* supposedly legit," said Donohue sourly. "Which means we can't go to Shabazz or the Mayor's Office and expect any help. The only alternative would be to go to the press, but that's out, because we have absolutely *no* tangible proof..."

"*And* because you shot out a bunch of their transmitters during the Broadway Phantoms robbery..." said Shrini. She switched on her monitor and waited for the system to boot, "We have to figure out what to do next. You can't got back to work."

"That's for sure. Sorry to be such trouble. I feel like a big black cloud's been following me ever since I got back."

"It's not all bad news, Perry. You're safe," said Shrini, looking up from her monitor, "And we cleared you of murdering those three VNN reporters,"

Perry's head snapped around. "What? *I* was a suspect?"

"Yes..." She typed in some more commands, then closed the program and looked up. "Shabazz thought you might be—your car was found abandoned not far from the bodies. And you did shoot at those television reporters during that Phantoms robbery."

"With rubber bullets," Perry shook his head, "but of course they'd dispute that." He got up and started pacing. "Do we have any leads at all on who killed them?"

"Not really, other than the fact they were all shot in the back of the head with a .22 caliber," said Shrini frowning.

"Wish I could work on that case," said Donohue. "First thing I'd do would've been to interview the families of the three victims—chances are they'd know of any feuds, or power struggles going on within the network."

"Ah! That reminds me—there's someone we need to talk to," Shrini's eyes lit up.

"Who?"

"A guy named Carrouthers. Only one problem—he's on a ranch somewhere out west."

"Who is he?"

"One of the good guys—if you could call anyone who worked for GeniTech a 'good guy'. One of the victims is his granddaughter. He's now in hiding under of the Federal Witness Protection program."

"Will he agree to talk with us?"

"From what I hear, he'd be glad to have anyone listen—seems nobody has taken his accusations seriously, up to now." said Shrini.

"How did you hook up with *him*?"

"He was trying to call Shabazz, but I picked up the phone. Shabazz was gone for some reason that day."

A police siren sounded in the distance. Donohue went to the window and looked out, "I hope that isn't coming for me..."

"If the NPDi is after you, Perry, we need to get out of here quick," said Shrini. "Your parole box may be gone, but they probably have access to all the wireless security cameras in the area. I can't keep you here indefinitely."

"I know," said Donohue, "I planned on running off to Baltimore and lying low until I figured out what to do next."

"I have a better idea," said Shrini, "a long road trip."

"What would that accomplish?" Donohue paced around, "I have my job and my open cases to consider. At least in Baltimore I could keep in touch with voice mail and get some work done, using someone else's user space or something."

"Well, I sure could use you as a witness when he gives his deposition. And we could share the driving."

"Without me, you could fly," said Donohue.

"A plane ticket can be traced, even if you pay cash," replied Shrini evenly. "The NPDi is looking for you, but it's only a question of time before my name pops up as one of your known associates. Besides, I don't want to handle this alone, and Rich is out of commission."

"Out west, huh?" Perry looked skeptical. "That's a long way to go for a deposition—I sure hope his information's useful."

"Oh, I'm sure it'll pan out," Shrini smiled and waved a thick manila envelope. "His security clearance alone should guarantee that."

Donohue shrugged. "All right, you won me over. But, I need some new clothes first. A pink bathrobe is not my idea of outdoor wear, and going around in my bloodstained clothes will get us nabbed for sure."

Shrini pointed to the bedroom. "Go look in my closet. Lucky for you, I got some men's clothes—some dress shirts and jeans. I think they might even be around your size."

"Great," said Perry, fishing them out. He looked at the tags. "They're a bit large, but I can live with them for a while. Now all I need is clean underwear..."

"Look in the dresser, there should be some boxer shorts—and some black socks."

When he was finished, Donohue came out of the bedroom and stuffed his dirty clothes in a garbage bag. "Ready when you are."

They stepped out in the hall. Shrini locked up the apartment with her remote. The double fusion locks buzzed shut with a bright blue glow around the door's outline.

They walked downstairs to the garage. Shrini closed the access door and activated her security system. "We'll have to take my patrol car, my other one's in the repair shop. Besides, it's safer, we won't get stopped." She slid behind the wheel.

"Yeah, until we get outside New York," said Donohue, getting in reluctantly. "After that, we'll stick out big-time."

"Beggars can't be choosers, Perry." She handed Donohue a tiny device. "Here, look at this, do a quick scan when I drive out and see if we're being watched. She opened the garage door and pulled out slowly.

"Nope, nothing at all," he reported.

"Good. Let's roll! Keep down, will you?"

"All right." Perry folded up his legs and crouched down in the footwell. "We better do *all* our traveling at night. Our biggest enemies will be highway patrol cars and especially truckers. Do you know any hotels that will let us check in at dawn?"

Shrini nodded. "No problem." Suddenly she slammed on the brakes.

Donohue poked his head up. "What the hell?" He heard something bellow in the darkness. A pale, almost spectral shape loomed in the road ahead.

"Fooking sacred cow—it's in the way!" Shrini leaned on the horn. "*Always* in the way! MOVE IT!"

The beast panicked, and started lumbering down the middle of the street between all the parked cars. Donohue winced. "Jesus, Shrini—*don't* use the horn—it's way past midnight!"

"And we're stuck behind this... overglorified piece of moo meat!" She pounded the steering wheel. "Get out of the road, you fat bugger!"

Lights started coming on in the buildings lining the street.

The cow bellowed in terror and kept right on loping down the middle of the road.

She crept the police cruiser forward, "I'm going to *ram* your bovine butt!"

The cow kept galloping in the middle of the street, too spooked to move to the side. Shrini yelled out the window, "Fooking ignorant beast!"

Terrified, the cow bellowed again in protest.

"This outta work..." Teeth gritted, she turned on the siren menu and selected 'staccato honk'. Ear-splitting guttural blasts echoed between the buildings. Donohue put his hands over his ears. To his horror, he looked up and saw more lights coming on in people's windows. "You're gonna get us busted!" he yelled at Shrini.

"No, I'm not!" She found a no parking zone to the left. She floored the accelerator, knocking the cow over as she cut back in front of it.

Aghast, Perry stared out the back at the shaken beast on its side. "What the hell was that for?" he snapped, "That's a *sacred animal!*"

"That was *fun!*" Shrini started sniggering. "You really believe that shit, Perry? Nothing is that sacred."

She hit the gas hard again, slamming Perry's face into the seat cushion. "Damnit, Shrini—slow *down!*"

She let out a guffaw, "Ha! For once, I get to scare *you* with *my* driving, instead of the other way around! Don't worry, I'll slow down before we get to the bridge."

The dash clock showed midnight as they crossed the George Washington Bridge over to Jersey. Donohue poked his head up, "Once we get to Newark, I'd sure feel safer if we could stop and rent a car."

"That's exactly what I planned, Perry. We're going to the airport to pick it up."

"What?" Donohue gave her a look, "At *this* hour?"

Shrini laughed, "What century are you in? It's all automated. I made the reservation while you were talking about the NPDi. Didn't you see me typing?"

"Ah, so that's what you were doing... But isn't the Internet kaput?"

"I haven't used it in two years—I always use the Krishna Portal. You wouldn't know of it because you don't understand Hindi."

"Huh?" He shook his head. "You made car reservations in Hindi? What kind of company would do that?"

"You'll see..." She pulled off at the first exit to the airport and took the access road. "You can sit up now, Perry."

They pulled up to an unfamiliar lot. Donohue stared at the sign. "Guru Nanak Car Rental?! What the hell kind of cars do these guys rent?"

"Same as everyone else, Perry. Chryslers, Mercedes, Ford, Chevrolet..." She reached handed over her wallet to him. "Perry, can you pull out the greenish-black credit card for me?"

"Sure," Perry pulled the card out and turned it over in his hand. "Never heard of it."

"It's the biggest credit card in India," said Shrini. "Almost 800 million people use it worldwide."

"Really? And you can rent cars with this thing?"

"Not only cars, also trucks, motorcycles, computers—you name it. But not anything at Wal-Mart. I think because they tried and failed to launch some stores in New Delhi." She drove over to what looked like a cash dispenser and rolled down the window. She reached out and typed in a confirmation number. The machine screen flashed different colors, then a small compartment opened. She grabbed the chip key and turned to Perry. "Here, park the cruiser—I'll find the rental car." She turned to get out, then grabbed his arm, "Oh, and don't forget to memorize the space number where you park. I want to call Dietrich later so he can come and drive it back to the White Elephant. Leave the parking ticket stub in the glove box."

"OK." Perry slid behind the wheel.

~ ~ ~

Saturday, April 2:

It was now 2:15 am, but all the lights were still on in NPDi headquarters. "There's no way Donohue could be outside the Greater New York City area!" snapped Donner. He stared at the map and fumed, "Damnit! He was in the same fucking train wreck I was!" He picked up his crutches and hobbled over to where Cheshire was working the control center. Cheshire looked doubtful. "Honest, sir, we've tried every single surveillance camera, even in the new boroughs, and there's no sign of him at all."

"He's got to be holed up somewhere," Donner said flatly, "probably in that god-awful New Bombay area—he has to be as banged up as I was."

Browning perched on the edge of Donner's desk, scratching his foot with a pencil. "You didn't give Donohue his police mobile comm unit back, did you?"

"No and hell no!" Donner shook his head, then winced as the pain shot through his temples. "I only handed him a roll of—Shit!"

"Dollar coins?" Browning raised an eyebrow.

"Yup." Donner slapped his thigh in disgust.

"That's all he would need," agreed Browning, "He must've phoned one of his pals in the force. How many close associates does he have?"

Cheshire looked at a list. "He has ten on his rosters of subords..."

Donner interrupted him, "No, forget that. NYPD dicks don't fraternize with underlings. We need a list of all his pals, lovers and drinking buddies..."

"That's profiling!" protested Cheshire, "Any decent cop'll tell you profiling is next to useless to capture criminals."

"We're not chasing a criminal here," snapped Donner, "And it works just fine in finding cops—they're creatures of habit 'coz their job forces them to be. Let's get his dossier together and make a list, from the most to the least trustworthy. Then we'll start making house calls..."

They nodded in unison, "Yes, sir."

Donner got up wearily, "I'm gonna go get some beauty sleep." He looked at them sharply, "And quit staring at my black eyes! You just concentrate on getting that list together and..." he glanced at his watch, "Remember, we start interrogations at the Rudi Juillani Precinct at a quarter to eleven Monday! We're gonna ruin lunch hour for a few folks... In the meantime, FIND DONOHUE!!" He limped out the door.

~ ~ ~

When Perry walked out of the parking garage, Shrini flashed her headlights from way across the access road beyond f the parking lots. Donohue took off towards her at a trot.

He was a bit winded when he made it all the way to where she was parked. He got in the passenger side, huffing and puffing. "Why the hell didn't you park any closer?"

She held up a tiny device. "The whole area's loaded with surveillance cameras. Look here—it says code red, which means over 20 cameras in the area."

"Which means you should've parked the cruiser, the NPDi is looking for me," retorted Donohue.

"It wouldn't have worked, Perry." She shook her head. "You don't read Hindi. I couldn't risk having you waste hours looking for the rental car. We got to get to the hotel by sunrise."

"Speaking of, where the hell can we stay? You need a normal credit card to make a reservation..."

"Not at the places we're going to, Perry," grinned Shrini. "We expat Indians got a whole network of roadside motels—we get discount prices and eat for free!" She started the engine.

Donohue's jaw dropped. "No shit?"

"No shit." Shrini looked over. "For god's sake, Perry, get down. We've got to take the toll roads until we're past Patterson, New Jersey. You'd better stay down until we get past Philadelphia."

"OK." Donohue crouched down in the footwell and took the blanket she handed him. "Let me know when we're clear."

~ ~ ~

After they crossed into Pennsylvania, Shrini pulled into a 24-hour gas station to fill up. "Hope you don't need to pee, Perry," she whispered after she got back in, "This place has tons of cameras."

"I can hold it a while," said Donohue, shifting slightly. "Just stop off down the road and let me piss in the woods sometime soon."

"All right, just five more minutes..." She pulled out onto the divided highway and went looking for a suitable spot.

She let Donohue out at one of the ghost subdivisions between towns. Moments later, he came dashing back to the car, white-faced. "Jesus! Why the hell did you pick here?"

"Because it looks like nobody lives here. We're on the run, Perry, we can't afford to use public restrooms. You said yourself that the NPDi caught you in one."

"And what about you—where are you going to go?"

"I already did, right next to the car."

"Oh thanks a lot, you leave me to run through a rat's nest!"

"That bad?"

"Yes!" Donohue shuddered, "You wouldn't believe—there I was, whizzing away, and I felt all these tiny creatures around my ankles. I turned on my flashlight—and I saw nothing but pink little eyes—everywhere!" He quickly got in and disappeared under the blanket.

~ ~ ~

Donohue poked his head up. "Are we past Philly?"

Shrini looked at him and grinned, "Just got past I-180. You can sit up now."

He clambered back into the passenger's seat and looked, "Fair amount of traffic for 5 am." he remarked.

She nodded. "We're getting close to Pittsburgh. People get up early there."

Perry looked over the interior admiringly. "You picked a nice car, Shrini. I bet this thing flies—can I have a spell behind the wheel?"

"The car's rented in my name, Perry. When I need you to drive, I'll tell you."

Donohue looked miffed. "C'mon Shrini—I promise I won't speed."

She shook her head. "No. Not yet."

"What is it about you—afraid I'm gonna wreck?"

She let out a sigh, "What is it about men? They always want to drive, and much too fast..."

"Hey, you're the one who burned rubber in New Bombay!" protested Perry.

She rolled her eyes. "Look, you're the one they're hunting. I suggest you curl up in the back until we get into Ohio. All we need is for you to get caught speeding and then have some highway patrolman ID you."

"All right, all right..." Donohue reclined his seat and clambered over with a sigh.

They crossed over into Ohio at 7 am and on down through Akron. Donohue poked his head up. "We out of danger?"

"Yeah, I think it's safe." Shrini kicked in the cruise control and looked over. "You still want to talk?"

"Me? Naw, nothing much to talk about."

"Are you sure?" She looked over. "The more you talk about a bad experience, the better you can cope with it."

He drummed his fingers for a while. "That's the problem. I should just talk about everything, but there's so much I don't recall. Too many goddamn gaps..."

"That doesn't make much sense. You know it was traumatic, but you don't remember?"

"Not much—only bits and pieces—the sleep deprivation really did a number on me. And some of it is so weird, I'm not completely sure it happened or if I just *imagined* it did..." His voice trailed off. "Let's just get to the hotel. I'm bushed. We need to be off the streets pretty soon anyway."

"Don't worry. We've only got about half an hour to go. The place is nice and secluded. Nobody will find us. We can rest up a few days before we have to go on."

~ ~ ~

Monday April 4, 11 am:

Just as Donner pulled up in front with a van full of NPDi special interrogators, Cheshire came running out of the White Elephant, breathless and banged on the driver's side window. "Wait, wait, boss! Before we go in, I think I got a hot lead!"

"Alright, what is it?" demanded Donner, rolling down his window. "This had better be good."

Cheshire paused to catch his breath, "I think we should wait to interrogate the cops here—I just talked to a night duty janitor I've installed there to keep tabs on things." He says last week he saw a woman officer walk into Shabazz's office and answer the phone, " said Cheshire. "That's highly irregular. We went back and got the phone records—but the caller number was untraceable..."

"What do you mean, untraceable?" snapped Donner, "All calls are traceable!"

"The call code indicates it came from a protected source—from a secret US Government location."

"From Washington? Naw, that's impossible. I would've known about that." Donner picked up his crutches, then tossed them aside, "Fuck these things—I'm sick of 'em. Did you find out anything else?"

"Yes—I think we should hold off on the interrogations, boss. From the list I got, Captain Hayte is in hospital in serious but stable condition after being stabbed last week, there's a Lt. Pierce on holiday leave, a uniformed cop named Melchers—a subord, he won't know much. There's also a lab tech named Dietrich who works on the night shift, and a woman lieutenant whose name I can't pronounce—I think it's the one who took the phone call in Shabazz's office."

"OK—let's follow up on the phone call." Donner hobbled back and forth, thinking aloud, "You said the caller's from a secret location?"

Cheshire nodded, "That's what the phone logs say, not local, or state..."

"Hmm, interesting... It wouldn't be that they don't have the kind of clout to instigate that level of security..." He stopped and drummed his fingers on the back of a folding chair. "Oh! We need to jump on this now! Get me the name of that woman officer—her name, rank and home address!"

~ ~ ~

New Bombay, 2 p.m:

"God, I loathe this place," grumbled Donner. The van with the chromed one-way windows sat mired in the maze of traffic. "Next time one of those fucking cows tries to shit on the side of the van, ram it!"

"Sir, I can't *do* that!" said Cheshire, fidgeting behind the wheel, "They're *sacred*..."

Donner bellowed "Bullshit—*Nothing* is 'sacred!!' And furthermore, icons do NOT shit on the sides of vans! You think Jesus dropped his drawers and took a dump wherever HE felt like it?"

Cheshire stared straight ahead. "I wouldn't know sir, I wasn't there."

"Never mind." Donner turned to Browning, "How much farther,

dammit?"

Browning scrolled down the navigator screen. "We're two streets away, sir."

"Cheshire! Turn on the hazard lights! We're hoofing it!"

Agent Cheshire's head whipped around. "Sir—we can't just leave the van sitting here!"

"Oh yes we can!" barked Donner, "Just ring up Sattler at HQ and have him send a replacement driver on moped to come and baby sit this thing while we go kick some policewoman's ass. With any luck, maybe Donohue's ass too..."

"Yessir" Cheshire swallowed heavily and began dialing.

~ ~ ~

Akron, Ohio:

It was late afternoon before Donohue woke up. Shrini was typing commands into her laptop. She looked up. "Good afternoon, Perry. Breakfast is over there on the dresser."

Donohue looked. "I only see pizza boxes."

"Right, that's breakfast. Yours is the one with extra pepperoni."

"Pizza for breakfast? Are you kidding?"

"You're the one who complains about Indian food being too spicy. It's 5:30 in the afternoon, do you really think you can get pancakes now?"

Donohue opened the box and took a slice. "Mmm... delicious," he said dubiously. He put it in his mouth anyway.

"I also bought bananas and oranges, if you want some variety." She resumed typing.

Perry set the crust down and was about to pick up another piece. "Hey, can I look at the news?"

"You can't. It's in Hindi." said Shrini, not looking up.

Donohue looked annoyed, "Well, isn't there a website in English?"

"The Internet's still down, Perry. I just read that the Pentagon is demanding $ 45 billion in emergency funding from Congress, otherwise the whole thing is set to collapse."

"Oh great! How the hell can I get some news?"

She looked at her watch, "Well, you can turn on the TV, but it only gets local stations..."

"What the hell kind of hotel is this?" demanded Donohue, "No cable, no satellite TV..."

"It's part of the Nagrati network," said Shrini patiently, "It's the biggest network run by expatriate Indians over here—I told you before, if this NPDi is really part of Homeland Security, the minute we go to a normal hotel chain, they'll swoop right in and capture us while we sleep. Do you really wanna wake up with a gun in your face?"

"No thanks, I've done *that* already..." Donohue waved a hand in resignation. "So is there any source of news here?"

Shrini pointed to the table next to the bathroom, "Try the radio over there."

Perry looked at it dubiously. "This has to be a hundred years old, from the looks of it." To his surprise it came on when he turned the knob. "Hey, it works!" He started fiddling with the tuner until he found a talk radio station.

The voice of a right-wing talk-show host blared out of the small speaker. "Ladies and gentlemen, I can honestly say these Nude Olympics are the DEATH OF DECENCY..." Perry quickly shut it off.

"Why'd you do that?" asked Shrini, "It might be amusing!"

"Sorry..." Perry sat down on the bed. "that just reminded me of something I ran across while I was in captivity."

"What?" Shrini stopped typing and looked up.

"The NPDi is suppressing a huge scandal that happened during the Olympic trials."

Shrini looked up, "Really? Miss Clint would love to hear about it..."

"I'll bet—I ran across the story by accident during one of my 'free study' periods in their underground library, I was looking for details about the Phantoms. I forgot the Internet was down, so I did a search but I ended up being re-routed to their internal archives. Next thing I knew, some goon was holding me a foot off the ground and accusing me of surfing porno sites..."

~ ~ ~

It took Donohue a while to find the CyberPost archives. He opened the site. The first headline made Perry's eyes bug out.

Suddenly rough hands grabbed him by the back of his coveralls.

"What the hell do you think you're doing?" demanded the goon, putting Donohue in a headlock.

Donner burst into the room. "What rule did he violate, Agent Beria?"

"He was surfing porn sites."

"I was NOT!" Donohue struggled to free his head, to no avail. "It's the Cyberpost site, goddamnit!"

"We'll see about that!" Donner clicked off the screensaver and put the site on the beamer.

THE NEW YORK CYBERPOST
Athletes Banned for Indecent Display

Three American Olympic hopefuls, a sprinter and two pole vaulters, were all given lifetime bans yesterday because all three publicly masturbated during the U.S. national anthem played during their victory ceremonies, the New York Cyberpost has learned, despite an attempted media blackout of the incident.

Vaulter Benny Rodman was quoted immediately after his ceremony as saying, "It was so stimulating [to win], I just had to do it." Onlookers report however, that the Women's 10,000 meter race, a nude event, was being run at the time, and that is more likely to have stimulated Rodman and his cohorts.

The display was cheered lustily by many in the small audience, almost drowning out the music in the process.

"He [Rodman] gets high marks from me for displaying such a modest appendage without any trace of embarrassment," said one Olympic official, who later was forced to resign after the comment.

The situation caps several days of controversy after the surprise announcement that all swimming and selected track & field events would be contested nude. The move, which is widely seen as a desperation measure to counter falling TV ratings

"Oh, that..." Donner chuckled in spite of himself, "The CyberPost..."

Donohue was visibly annoyed, "See?" I wanted to search the New York CyberPost archives..."

Donner tapped the screen, "Oh, it's the CyberPost, all right... but that story ain't on their official site, even if the Internet were up and working again."

Perry looked at him unbelievingly. "What do you mean? I found it with an Internet search!"

"You typed in the search parameters correctly," said Donner, "but you accessed one of *our* servers—it's full of files that we confiscated from the CyberPost offices. We managed to get this story suppressed just the other week, as a matter of fact—but it was a real close thing. If we had gotten the court order five minutes later, this is what you would've seen in the headlines the next morning. It would've been a real catastrophe for the IOC, because it happened only one week after they announced the Olympics are going nude..."

Donohue looked shocked, "The Olympics? Going *nude?* You've gotta be kidding!"

"Don't look at me like that. It's true." Donner held a hand on his chest, "Cross my heart."

Perry let out a low whistle, "Holy Elvis, I never heard diddly-squat about this! I remember all that controversy about cheating with genetically-engineered athletes, but that's all."

"Yeah, 'coz the US is the only country that still bans human cloning." Donner reached over and brought up another file detailing the original Nude Olympics story. "See? We let 'em print this story. They really are going nude. It's a desperate ploy to get back television ratings—but then the masturbation incident happened during the trials in Oregon. If word of that ever leaks out, it could mean the end of the Olympic Games and the loss of millions of jobs worldwide. We were brought in to suppress any leaks, the orders came directly from the White House."

"The President *allowed* you to suppress a story?"

Donner tried to suppress a smile, "Hell we do that all the time." He tapped a forefinger on the screen, "As you see, the article never got finished. We literally confiscated it directly off the reporter's computer, in broad daylight, right under the chief editor's nose. It made for a nice little scene—you should've been there. But you, sir, have more training to get done..."

Perry looked at Donner in exasperation. "Hey, that's not fair! You said I would be able to work on my NYPD cases..."

"All right, alright! Ask and ye shall receive," said Donner magnanimously. "The only problem you'll have is sorting through the wealth of data at our Control Central. Follow me."

He led Perry through a long network of corridors. At the end of one, a pair of stainless steel doors slid open. Donner spread his arms. "Behold!"

A vast array of giant plasma computer screens returned Donohue's gaze—with images of his own face, shot from many angles.

Perry turned around and said to Donner, "Very impressive. Now, will you turn this ego trip off?"

"Ask and ye shall receive," repeated Donner. The monitors went blank.

"I need images of the latest bank robbery the Phantoms did." said Donohue.

"In New York City, right?" said Donner. "When was it, approximately?"

"Within the last four days." Donohue turned back to the monitors and his mouth dropped open at the hundreds of different images. *"Holy Elvis! How many different images can you get?"*

"As many as you like," said Donner smugly, "We have access to every videocam on the continent—and maybe the world—if we can ever get our mitts on what Langley's got access to. As long as something transmits a signal in the Continental 48 States, we can intercept it."

Perry began to feel his flesh crawling, "Is all this legal?"

Donner looked even more smug, "According to the Ashcroft Doctrine, it is..."

Donohue laughed in spite of himself, "Wait a sec—if your intelligence is this good, how come I was able to slip through Baltimore airport with Mr. Chesney's head?"

"Human error." The smile remained fixed on Donner's features, "We weren't fast enough, that's all. You have to know *where* and *when* to look. In your case, you didn't come in on the flight you were supposed to. So we had to cover all the incoming flights from Europe that particular week. Quite a task, if I don't say so myself. However, there's another factor, too." Donner looked Donohue up and down, "Most perpetrators—you included—look just like average Joes until they actually *do* something that categorizes them as criminal." He shrugged, "If you're not looking at the right monitor at the right time, you won't see anything wrong. Oh sure, we've tried software to track 'unusual' human behavior. We had it installed in quite a few places a few years ago, but after Logan airport got evacuated last year we stopped."

"Yeah, I heard about that," said Donohue. "What happened?"

Donner let out a sigh, "Lawdy, you do sure like to ask questions... All right, I'll tell you. The software misinterpreted a particular movement in the men's room, thought it was a terrorist reaching in his pants for a gun right before a flight, instead of what it really *was*—some priest diddling a choirboy. What made it worse is the software malfunctioned *again* immediately after and set off the water sprinkler system. At that point, we realized we had to be more *discreet*."

"Wow..." Perry shook his head in amazement, "Are there any more of these incidents you guys covered up?"

"I've told you more than enough already," Donner pointed back to the display, "Captain, you now have at your fingertips the entire NPDi visual virtual library of any and all attempted bank heists for the entire greater New York region for the past 12 months. If you narrow your search parameters correctly, as I'm sure you will, you will no doubt be illuminated. Take as many notes as you need—and happy hunting!" He turned on his heels and walked out. The doors closed behind him with a long pneumatic hiss.

~ ~ ~

"Happy hunting..." muttered Donohue, shaking his head. "I never could figure Donner out—one time it would be the carrot, and then he'd turn right around and beat the crap out of me—or his goons would, anyway. It really doesn't make sense to me, him letting me access their archives like that."

"Did you find anything interesting?" said Shrini.

Donohue looked at her, "Yes and no. They did have tons of stuff in the archives—even had forecasts on when particular liquor stores would be held up."

"Did they have anything on the Phantoms?"

"They had everything we had," Perry closed his eyes and concentrated. "... but they didn't have anything more substantial, just a lot more camera angles. The rotating roster of robbers obviously had stymied them, too. Or maybe they just don't give a shit about bank robbers..."

"One thing that has always bugged me," Shrini toyed with the monitor display, "How is it all the robberies have been credited only to the Phantoms?"

"Well," Donohue rubbed the bruises on his face gingerly, "the MO is always the same, or nearly the same. As is the escape…" His voice trailed off. "We'd better think about *our* situation first… wonder how long it will take Donner and his crew to come after us?" He picked up another slice of pizza.

Shrini smiled wanly, "If they do trace you to my apartment, it'll take them quite a while to break in… if they manage it at all."

"But break in, they will. They're unstoppable," said Donohue, setting the last pizza crust down. He looked up at her face silhouetted in the monitor's light, "You know what was the worst part about the whole experience?"

"What?"

"The time Donner came marching in the cell, catching me on the crapper in the corner. That's when I really felt like I had been violated."

~ ~ ~

New Bombay, 6:30 p.m:

They burst into Shrini's apartment by sawing through the hinge mounts. Browning and Cheshire rushed in, guns drawn. "It's empty, boss," called Cheshire.

Donner limped inside, cursing at the door, "Goddamn fusion locks, should've been banned years ago!" He looked around the front room, "What weird-ass décor… Now where is she—and was *he* here?"

Cheshire went into the bedroom, "Looks like she left in a hurry, all the drawers are opened and the usual toiletries are gone."

"Usual toiletries?" Browning frowned, "What do you mean?"

"Women always have 500 different kinds of skin cream lying around— here, come look at the bathroom counter, you can see the outlines in the residue and mildew."

Browning went instead to the second bedroom, "Looks like the guest bed's been slept in, I see some bloodstains and…" He rifled through the trash bin, "Somebody's hurt—there's a lot of bloody bandages!"

"Lemmie see that!" Donner hobbled over, "Gauze, bloodstained first-aid tape—YES! Donohue's been here—I *knew* it!"

"So where are they?" Cheshire ran a comb through his buzz-cut.

"Seize the hard drive on that computer!" said Donner, "that might have something useful." He looked around at the exotic furniture and wall hangings, "Too bad I'm hurt… I would really *enjoy* trashing this place." He fingered the hanging wicker chairs.

Browning put his gun back in his holster, "Let's go and see if her cop car is gone."

"Yeah…" Donner limped to back to the front room. "If it isn't gone, it means they're renting and we can probably trace them that way. He tugged futilely at the front door, which somehow had closed again, "Here, come help me get this fucking door out of the way. Goddamn fusion locks…"

Browning pulled the on heavy door. He turned to Cheshire, "Can you help me with this?"

Cheshire obliged. The door refused to budge. "What the hell?"

Donner was enraged, "Are we locked in?"

Browning grabbed the handle and pulled again, "We *can't* be—we sawed through the hinge mounts!!"

Cheshire kicked it, forgetting his toes were exposed, "Oww!"

"Jesus Christ on A Pony!" Donner fumbled in his pockets for his mobile.

Chapter 18

THE NEW YORK CYBER*POST*
GIANT CONDOM BLOWS OFF!
Lands on Morristown, NJ Home

The latest lame-brained solution from the Mayor's Office for the Noise Day problem came to a predictable end Tuesday as the gigantic prophylactic covering for the much-maligned Norton-Humes Building came off in high winds and landed miles away, in Morristown, NJ.

Rainer Lachs, 76, a retired tiles specialist from Leverkusen, Germany, received the shock of his life when he came home from vacation later the same day and found his home cloaked with the enormous white sheath. "He was at a complete loss for words," said a health official from Morristown Baptist Hospital, where Mr. Lachs was hospitalized for shock.

~ ~ ~

Shrini came out of the bathroom and saw Perry was at her palmtop. She got up and tip-toed over to see what he was doing.

He was accessing the HindiNet, she was startled to see. She took a look onscreen and blurted out, "Dog & Pony magazine?! *Perry*! That's immoral!"

Startled, Donohue almost dropped the palmtop. He recovered quickly. "It's *not* illegal any more—the Supreme Court said so last month."

"But… but that's *sick*!"

Perry said defensively, "Hey, I don't normally like that kind of stuff—but *this* is great!"

Shrini caught a glimpse of the screen display, "Is that—*omigawd*—I *know* that face!" She started giggling in spite of herself.

"See?" Perry started grinning, "It's better than Raw Comix!"

~ ~ ~

On the ride back to Headquarters, Donner sat silently in the back of the paneled van.

"What's wrong, boss?" said Browning. "Still mad about the door?"

"Shut up!" said Donner irritably, "Let me think…" He fiddled absently with his crutches, "We need to draft a few more conscripts from the NYPD…"

"Don't worry about that, boss. We are about to bag a nice one," gloated Browning. "We'll be getting him into training next week."

"Oh yeah?" Donner raised an eyebrow. "That's good to know… Why wasn't I informed about this?"

"When's the last time you checked your mail?" shrugged Browning, "I only checked mine this morning—had over 600 messages in my in-box. Too much stuff going on."

"Maybe so," Donner peered out the back for a moment, then turned around, deep furrows on his brow. "Things are about to get real busy. We need to go on high-alert mode. We can use the existing security cam network to hunt for Donohue and that Indian bitch *inside* the city, but I'm beginning to suspect they're not here at all. Agent Cheshire, a question."

The light ahead turned red and Cheshire braked to a stop. He turned around, "Yeah, boss?"

Donner leaned forward, "That business about that phone call to the police chief bugs me. Normally, *every* phone call five seconds or longer should be traceable." The light changed and Cheshire leaned on the horn.

Browning piped up, "*Except* ones from people in the Federal Witness Protection Program."

Donner grabbed Browning's shoulder, "*What* did you say?"

"Anyone in the Federal Witness Protection Program would have an untraceable number. They are the only ones who are allowed to have the trace-squelching phones."

Donner's mind raced furiously, "*This* changes things…" He looked up at the van's soundproofed ceiling, his mouth moving soundlessly.

Suddenly he sat up triumphantly, "Aha! Wait a second! Could it *be*? Our 'friend' has finally surfaced?" Forgetting his injured foot, he bounced around in his seat like a little boy. "Oh please let it be *him*, please, *please*, *please*…"

Cheshire steered around a double-parked newspaper truck. "What are you talking about, boss?"

"That *rat* who testified in the Senate against us! The guy who tried to get them to snuff us out by crippling our funding!" Donner slammed a fist into the side of the van, startling Cheshire. "We need to turn up the heat NOW! Issue bulletins to all national airports and to highway patrol offices in all neighboring states to follow but *not* apprehend!" An evil grin crept across his face, "If we can latch on to their tail, we might be able to bag *three* little birdies at once…"

~ ~ ~

Wednesday, April 6:

Hayte didn't protest when a wheelchair was offered. The stitches still hurt—the upper layer had been taken out, but it would be another four weeks before his body dissolved the lower layer. He hated the restricted mobility—especially when he got out of bed or sat on the toilet.

He also didn't protest when the doctor recommended he take a cab home. He didn't really want to spend the cash, but the thought of hobbling down the stairs to the subway was daunting enough, and then he would have to get past the turnstiles without being nailed in the groin…

He got in the first cab in line and gave directions. He leaned back and closed his eyes.

The only good thing was that he had all the time in the world to cram for the bar exam. The state exam board had granted him an extension and a special exam date. He intended to take full advantage of that.

Still, it was aggravating that he couldn't go after his assailant. Hudgins and Vaughn had called him with updates on the investigation, but there had been little news of late.

The cab let him out in front of his apartment building. He paid with his chip card and walked gingerly up the front steps.

To his surprise, the elevator was working. The doors shut laboriously, and the thing clanked upward. He just hoped it wouldn't jam between floors—there was no way he would be able to extricate himself through the emergency door in the ceiling. It was bad enough standing in the elevator, waiting. He had to bow his head to keep from hitting the ceiling.

The elevator finally rumbled to a stop. The doors opened to reveal Stanley and Verona holding bottles of champagne, "Welcome Back!!!"

~ ~ ~

In the darkness, Perry continued taking U.S. Highway 224 through Fort Wayne. The dashboard clock showed 9 p.m. Traffic was light, even for Sunday night.

Shrini dialed Dietrich's extension. "NYPD Forensics. Dietrich."

"It's me, Shrini…"

"Ho! Wrong number—sorry!" She heard him hang up.

Shrini turned to Donohue, "Dietrich hung up on me!"

Perry looked at the phone display. "Was it the right number?"

"Of course—I pre-programmed it myself—and *he* answered!"

Donohue looked out the window, "I bet something's going down. Maybe he's in trouble."

Shrini shrugged, "Well, if he is, we got no way of knowing."

"We do, if I know Dietrich. He'll be in touch some way. Put the phone on the dash, so we both can see it."

She nodded and clipped it to the dash.

"Shit—I just thought of something," said Donohue. "Cell phones are easy to trace."

"Relax, Perry. It's not my phone, it's Todd's. He has mine."

"Who's Todd?"

"A friend. He doesn't like his boss tracing him via cellphone, so I take his and he takes mine. We swap phone bills too. Works out fine."

"Oh." Perry couldn't think of anything more to say.

The lights of Fort Wayne faded in the distance.

About twenty minutes later, a small slip of paper came out of the phone. Shrini motioned to Perry, "Can you get that for me?"

Donohue tore the slip off, "It says 'call me at 11 tonite.' There's a cell phone number."

~ ~ ~

It was 10 p.m. in the NPDi New York bureau and most of the personnel had gone home for the night. Trash bags were piled outside of each office, waiting for the cleaning crew to pick up in the morning.

Browning peered through the glass door. Donner had both feet on his desk and his eyes were closed. An empty pizza box lay next to his chair. Cheshire said, "Shouldn't we come back later?"

Browning put a finger to his lips and motioned for Cheshire to follow him. He opened the door slowly and pulled out a paper bag. Cheshire bit his lip. Browning blew it up and snuck up gently behind Donner's chair. Cheshire made tiny snorting sounds as he tried to suppress a giggling fit.

Browning put the bag next to Donner's head and drew his right hand back. He smacked his hand hard into the paper bag.

In response, Donner suddenly rolled his chair over Browning's exposed toes. Browning let out a strangled yelp and fell to the floor in agony.

Donner kept the roller firmly on Browning's toes. "That'll teach you to knock before you come in!" He stared piercingly at Cheshire, "What do you want?"

White faced, Cheshire stammered, "Uh we-we g-got a lead on Donohue, boss."

"Why didn't you say so in the first place?" Donner stood up, releasing Browning's foot. Browning sat holding his foot, gasping in pain.

Cheshire stepped back timidly. "H-we got some security cam footage of him running through the airport parking lot at Newark at night..."

"Running, huh? How old is the footage?" Donner reached in a drawer and pulled out an apple.

"About 36 hours old," said Cheshire, recovering his composure.

"Not good." Donner took a bite. "Do we know what kind of vehicle they're driving?"

"Nope," said Cheshire grimly. "The boys at HQ traced Lt. Shrinithan's cruiser back to the Juilliani precinct parking garage. The airport searches turned up zilch, the car rental agencies had no clients fitting their descriptions. We got no idea where they're heading or what to look for. All we can hope for is that the highway patrol or the trucker's network make a random sighting."

"Great..." Donner devoured the rest of the apple. His mouth full, he continued, "And neither that sonofabitch Donohue or that Indian bitch has a private car?"

"She does, but it's in the shop," said Browning, still holding his foot. "The NYPD allows all cops above the rank of sergeant to use their squad cars for personal use. Hardly anyone at the Juilliani precinct *has* a private car."

"We're beaming their pictures to every state highway patrol and teamster's union," said Cheshire.

Donner tossed the apple core at the wastebasket and missed. "We better damn well get some results," he snarled, looking at Browning, "or toes won't be the only things I'll be stepping on."

~ ~ ~

Donohue was into his fifth hour behind the wheel when they rejoined the Interstate system at the Hammond, Illinois onramp. He just made it up to speed before a convoy of trucks came by.

Shrini's portable alarm sounded. She yawned, pulled the seat back up and fished around for her mobile.

It took 15 rings before Dietrich picked up. "Hello? Hello?"

"It's me—Shrini. Tell me this isn't a wrong number."

"Sorry about that. Shabazz is on the warpath, big time. He was already livid when Perry didn't show up a couple of days ago. Now you've disappeared, and he's gone ballistic..."

Shrini turned to Perry, "You were supposed to meet Shabazz at the White Elephant? He's pissed as hell that you missed the appointment."

Donohue nodded. "Yeah, I was supposed to meet my 'contact person' with the NPDi. I guess Shabazz doesn't consider a train wreck to be a good enough excuse."

Shrini connected the mobile with her headset, "Dietrich, did you hear about the train wreck Perry was in?"

Dietrich's voice crackled in her ears. "I heard about the wreck, but I didn't know Perry was in it—is he OK?"

"He'll live. He got pretty beat up, but nothing broken—he's here with me."

"Good! Tell him I said 'hi.' You can tell him it looks like the wreck was the work of some gang calling themselves the PMT..."

"The PMT—what's that?"

"The Paper Mâche Terrorists. The MTA is up in arms because we've given the case a low priority."

Shrini said, "Why aren't we trying harder to bust them?"

"Lack of evidence, basically—we have no leads on the perps, other than the name, which surfaced on a manifesto written in French on the Village Voice website. They claim hackers must've put it there. Plus, the gallery owner who grabbed the statue won't let the police anywhere near his precious sculpture before he auctions off the piece—and we have no way of knowing who the potential buyers are, because the auction is secret." Dietrich's voice faded out briefly as they went under a bridge. "But what about you? I hope you got a good reason to give to Shabazz for being gone..."

"Don't worry, I do." Shrini scribbled a note to email the chief while Perry steered around a convoy of trucks and barely made the turnoff to Interstate 80. She continued, "We're going to interview a potential witness about the three dead TV reporters dug up in New Jersey."

"That'll be interesting. Let me know about it—but don't call me at work. Call me at this number, and *only* after 10 p.m."

"Is this your new cell phone number?"

"It's not mine..." Dietrich's voice crackled briefly. "It belonged to a corpse that just arrived in the morgue, we ID'ed her as a Miss Noelle Bu..." A burst of static drowned out his voice. "The phone's still a bit waterlogged, we fished it and her out of the Hudson. She was in two pieces, but her cell phone was intact."

"Huh? A homeless person with a cell phone?"

"It's not that uncommon nowadays—there's a United Way campaign that's been doing that for the past three months. Listen, there's something else I should mention."

"What's that?"

Dietrich tone turned grim, "Shabazz had a visitor today. One of your friends with the Birkenstocks. I was at the water cooler when he came marching in..."

"The NPDi? Must be Perry's contact. He was supposed to meet the guy the morning of his train wreck."

"Maybe so. But the guy went up to the Chief's office—he acted like he owns the place, just marched right on up. It must've been a long conversation, 'coz I didn't see him leave. Listen, I gotta go—call me tomorrow, same time." The line went dead.

Shrini took off the headset. "Dietrich doesn't want us calling him at work. He's using the cell phone from a homeless woman. I didn't know homeless people had mobiles."

Donohue shrugged. "As I understand it, there's a whole homeless cellular network—a kind of long-distance self help therapy. I heard you mention the NPDi, they must be swarming all over the White Elephant."

"Not yet." Shrini stifled a yawn. "Dietrich said only one has come by so far, he walked right into the Chief's office like he owned it."

"That's the way they all are. They really do believe they own everything. More are on the way, I guarantee ... "

~ ~ ~

Browning and Cheshire sat transfixed, watching the monitors. Onscreen they could hear Donner start humming a Cole Porter tune. After the sound of a few bones snapping, Donner started singing the words. "I get no kicks from Cham..." He pinched the prisoner's nostrils. *"pain..."*

The thin, swarthy-complexioned man started twitching in panic. The duct tape over his mouth bulged visibly with every muffled scream.

Donner softly sang, "I get a kick..." and released his grip, "...outta youse."

With a pair of steel pincers, he held the man's terrified eyes open and poured lime into them.

The duct tape over the man's mouth sucked in and bulged out in rapid rhythm. His screams became loud enough to hear over Donner's singing.

"Damn, you asshole, you made me forget the words!" Donner stopped singing and beamed happily up at the camera, "Jeez, I *love* my job!" He took off a Birkenstock and luxuriously scratched between his toes of his bloodstained sock. He looked up again at the camera, "You'd think by now idiots like this guy would realize nobody's afraid any more of a goddamned towelhead waving box cutters on a jet..." He took the latex gloves off and cracked his knuckles. "Well, enough R&R. We got fugitives to find."

~ ~ ~

Thursday, April 7:

The doorbell chimed. Cursing silently, Hayte hobbled to the door, very hungover. He stubbed a toe on an empty champagne bottle. *What a rotten way to start the day...*

He couldn't even focus enough to look through the peephole.

He opened the door and found himself face to face with a tall woman. "Are you Captain Richard Hayte?"

Hayte went rigid, "Who wants to know?"

"I do," The woman took off her coat, revealing a statuesque figure in a nurse's uniform. "I'm Nurse Wynnfrey, from Beth Israel, I've been assigned to do your physical therapy. If you are Captain Hayte, that is."

"That's me." Hayte blinked in surprise, "I didn't know I was supposed to get therapy."

"Well, you are, otherwise you won't get your normal functions back," she said crisply.

"Oh..." He shifted awkwardly and looked down.

She shook out her hair, then fastened it back. "Can I come in?"

"Yeah, sure," said Hayte, feeling a bit self-conscious in his bathrobe. He ushered her in, then closed the door. "I... I wasn't really expecting a house call."

"Don't worry about your attire, it's fine." Her tone was very businesslike. "Actually, rehabilitative therapy *is* required by law with injuries to the genital region. If you look in your police union contract, it's specified under Paragraph 2d."

"Oh," Hayte let his arms fall to his sides. "Um..."

She held out a printout. "Just sign here, and we can get working on you immediately."

He scanned at it dubiously. "What's this about me indemnifying you against City Statutes 7, 11 and 14f?"

"Genital injuries are a sensitive issue. If you have certain religious convictions that preclude physiotherapy in that region, then I suggest that you not sign."

"Oh, I got no problem with that." He took the proffered pen and studied her out of the corner of his eye. He scribbled his signature. "So why didn't they send a male nurse?"

"Sir, you're not registered in the Department as homo- or bisexual." She took the contract and put it in her satchel.

Hayte decided she had a very nice smile. "Ah, I see. That's good to know... What should I do now?"

"I suggest you make yourself comfortable—sit in that recliner." Her voice changed dramatically, dropping almost to a whisper.

"OK..." Hayte complied. He leaned back and closed his eyes.

She started to undo his robe, "Can I have a look?"

He started to resist, then caught himself, "Uh... sure."

She spread his robe apart very slowly. "Mmm, red underwear..." She ran her hands gently over his thighs and stomach.

Hayte flinched. "I didn't think about that. Red like... like *blood*."

"Relax, Captain." She looked him over carefully. "You're not very comfortable with this, are you?"

He drew up his robe. "Well... it's kinda sudden. I mean, I wasn't expecting..."

She laughed. "Okay. Let's try something. Can I call you Richard?"

Caught by surprise, he laughed. "Sure, and what's your first name?"

"You can call me Condelee, all my friends do." She opened his robe and pulled his underwear down gently. "Now, don't be afraid."

"Ah—I'm not, it's just real tender. My battle scars."

She kissed the tip and flicked her tongue over her lips. "Doesn't look so bad to me..."

Hayte said, "I know, the scars don't look that big, but believe me, the wounds were. They sewed me up with elastic thread to minimize the scar tissue."

"They did good work..." She ran a finger over the scars and looked up. "I got an idea. Why don't you go to your bed, so you can really stretch out."

"Uh, okay..." He pulled his underwear back up and walked over to the bed. He sat on the edge.

She put her hands on her hips. "Lay down, please. I can't work with you sitting up like that."

"Oh, yeah." He gingerly reclined his torso. "Sorry about that."

"That's all right." Her tone got businesslike again. "So a major artery was hit, too?"

"Oh yeah, and they tell me my, uh... member was hanging on a small flap of skin."

She winced involuntarily.

Rich looked at her. "Sorry, I didn't mean to go in that much detail."

She rubbed his forehead and stroked his chest hair. "It's OK. I *did* ask. Now just *relax*." She lay her head down on his chest. "You're still tense."

"I'm sorry. I'll try and relax."

"I'll be gentle. I promise..." She pulled down his underwear again and reached inside with tantalizing slowness.

He flinched again but didn't resist.

She pulled the underwear off, "Ooh, I *see*. Ooh, poor baby..."

He raised his head and tapped the area gently. "I'm sure glad those stitches are gone."

She ran her tongue suggestively along her lips. "Is the *feeling* all there?" She gave the head a little tweak.

He sat up and started to pull his underwear back up, "I'm not sure, really. I've been afraid to..."

"You can't stay scared forever," She took his hand away and gently pushed him back down. Let's give it a little try..." She bent down and began stroking again.

He looked at her dubiously, "Uh, I don't know about this..."

"What's the matter, Richard? Does it hurt?"

"No-no. It's not that."

She looked at him with those big brown eyes. "Then, *what?*"

"Well..." Hayte shifted uncomfortably on the couch, "it's just that this feels like, well, *prostitution* to me."

She gave him a look. "Do you *want* to get better?"

"I *do*, but..." He looked down helplessly, "this still feels like... like, you know..."

She sighed and stroked his chin, "Alright. Listen, honey, I'll say it. It *is*." Her lovely eyes bored into his. "But it's *still legal*." She jabbed her finger on his chest for emphasis. "*And* there's no way it'll ever be outlawed again, now that the health care industry has found out how much profit there is to be made."

He flinched. "Ow—that hurt!"

"I bet it did! Look, I'm AMA certified—I made it all the way through Johns Hopkins Medical School, just like all the other nurses in my class, but I specialized in Genital Trauma." Her eyelashes fluttered as she briefly glanced down, "You'd be surprised at the number of cases that occur each year..."

"No, I wouldn't... I bet half the guys are just faking it..." he blurted.

"And how might *you* go about *faking* it?" She ran a finger over her lips and sucked on it suggestively.

He frowned, "I... Aw hell, I don't know."

"*Exactly*. You *don't* know. I'd be happy to show you a report about all the documented injuries we've treated since the program was started, but let's not spoil the mood now, OK?"

"All right." He sighed and leaned back, knocking some coins off the headboard. "Hey, how much is this going to cost?"

Condelee gave him a withering look, "*Cost?*"

He cleared his throat. "Uh, let me put that another way. Is this all paid for by my health plan, or is there a deductible?"

"No deductible. And *no*, I *don't* accept tips. I'm just like any other nurse, and yes, I *do* get paid enough." She rolled her big brown eyes, "Richard, honey, quit analyzing it to death. Let *go*."

"OK," He reached down and stroked her hair, "I'm sorry."

She smiled and began fondling his tip again, "Alright, *concentrate*. Can you feel my fingers? I think you *can*... you're getting hard." She bent down and took him gently in her mouth.

~ ~ ~

She paused and looked up. "Getting close?"

"I was almost there a couple of times," admitted Hayte.

"I'd say more than a couple." She ran her tongue around the rim of his head. "Look at you! You're stiff as a board!" She squeezed her fingers around the base of his penis, making the head swell dramatically.

His eyes widened in panic. "Ah—don't do that! *Please* don't!"

"What's wrong?" She squeezed even tighter so his erection wouldn't wilt.

"The scars—they might burst open!"

"No they *won't*, don't be silly!" She deep-throated him a couple times. He let out a big gasp.

She smiled sweetly. "See? Nothing wrong with you!" She did it again, then watched his face. "I can tell you like that—you start twitching like a maniac..."

"Uh, not so much from the sensation, yet. But the visuals are *great*!"

"Well, we'll just have to stimulate those nerves into fusing some more, won't we?" She ran his head over her lips like an oversized lipstick tube, then deep-throated him again.

Hayte closed his eyes and his smile grew bigger. "Mmmm..." He started breathing hard once more.

~ ~ ~

Cheshire's eyes widened when he saw what Browning was doing. "Are you CRAZY?" he hissed, "You can't go through the boss's desk like that!"

"Chill out." said Browning, "While the cat's away..." He opened the bottom desk drawer, "The drawer's hardly full, but it weighs a ton—*wonder why?*"

Intrigued, Cheshire peered over his shoulder. "Let me see!"

"Just be patient," said Browning knowingly. He pulled the drawer all the way out, expertly flipped it over and tapped the bottom, "Hear that? It's hollow!"

"You think Donner's got something to hide?"

"*Everybody's* got something to hide..." said Browning, "You just gotta know where to look..." He pushed a hidden lever at the back and a panel popped open. "Pay dirt!" He pulled out a stack of porn magazines. "Ho-ho-ho! What have we *here?*" He pulled one off the stack. "Shit, these are almost as taboo as kiddie porn!"

"Lemmie see!" Cheshire grabbed an issue and read from the cover, "Dog & Pony Magazine—Where Your Favorite Supermodels Have Sex With ANIMALS!" He started giggling uncontrollably.

"*Yeah*... and in *full color* too!" Browning opened another issue and turned to the , "Wow... I never thought a woman's mouth could hold that much!" His smile grew broader. "*This* opens up a *world* of new possibilities..." He tucked an issue under his jacket, "This'll make him freak when he discovers it's missing!"

Cheshire let out a high-pitched giggle and did the same with another issue.

They had just left Donner's office, when the man himself came walking in the front door, talking to someone on his headset.

"...My understanding, Congressman, is that you once appeared in that old TV series, what's it called, *"Jackass'*? Oh yes, we have the most comprehensive archives of anyone in the good ol' US of A... Yes, that's right, Congressman, if we don't get that additional funding that you're voting on next week, we might be forced to sell off those archives... Uh-huh, I see... So we can count on your vote? Good! Thank you, sir, it's always a pleasure to do 'bizness' with you..." He hung up with a big smile.

Browning raised an eyebrow, "*Another* congressman that was on 'Jackass'? How many does that make?"

"If you include the ones from the movie, over half..." said Donner contentedly. "Now, I can start working on the Senate!" His smile started to fade. He looked at them and put his feet on the desk, "OK, what do you got for me?"

Some of the blood on Donner's socks was still wet. Cheshire looked away. Browning fought to keep a straight face. "Uh…"

~ ~ ~

Friday, April 8, 9 am:

When Hayte went to buy groceries, he immediately began to regret wearing jockey shorts. He had to resist the urge to open his fly and rearrange everything down there. It was still quite painful to walk, and it forced him to take very short steps.

He decided to have the groceries delivered. He wished he could still order food over the Internet.

He was hobbling quite badly by the time he got back to his apartment building. He was grateful the front door to the lobby was open for maintenance, which meant he could wait until later to fumble for his key card. Wonder of wonders, the elevator was working. He got in and leaned against the back wall with obvious relief as it started up. Only a few more steps to go, then I can sit down…

The elevator slid open and he went slowly to his door. Fumbling for the key chip, he bumped clumsily into his door.

It opened wide.

His pulse jumped into his throat.

He reached for the gun in his jacket. Two sets of hands grabbed him and threw him on the floor face-down, sending the gun flying across the floor.

Two hoods as wide as houses sat on him, knocking the wind out of his lungs. One of them stuck the barrel of his own gun at him. "Hello Haytie-boy! Perhaps you can tell us where your pal Donny-poo is."

"Who?"

A fist slammed into the side of his face. "Captain Donohue, you fuckface!"

"Perry?" grunted Hayte, "Haven't seen him in a month."

"Wrong answer!" The other goon punched him in the kidney.

Richard gasped and spat out, "You… fucking… assho…"

"Wrong answer." Another blow, to the other kidney.

Hayte bit into the carpet, choking on the pile of drool spreading under his head.

The first goon grabbed him by the hair and pulled his head up. "You gonna tell us? And where's that Indian bitch?"

Rich spat out blood. "Go ahead, kill me. It's a mandatory death sentence for cop killers—even for NPDi. That's who you are, right?"

The first thug slammed Hayte's face back into the carpet while the second goon took aim at the side of Rich's head and drew his boot back to strike.

The doorbell rang.

"Who the fuck's that?"

Hayte tasted bile. "Might... be... Perry..."

The doorbell rang again.

The first heavy got off Richard and went to the door, while the second one planted a knee on Hayte's head and watched.

Thug number one yanked open the door. "WHADDYA WANT?"

The boy's face was almost hidden by the cardboard box. "Hey mister, here's your grocer..."

The goon slammed the boy in the solar plexus, sending the box and bags flying. Cans rolled all over the floor.

Hayte took the opportunity to slam both his fists into the second goon's groin, making the man double up. "Cocksucker!" grunted the thug. Richard grabbed frantically around on the ground for a weapon.

The first goon grabbed Hayte by the hair and yanked his head back.

Rich bashed him in the face with a half-pound can of cling peaches. He slammed the can again and again against the goon's head, denting it progressively.

Out of the corner of his eye, he saw the second goon roll over and reach for the gun on the floor.

Holding the can like an oversized softball, Hayte side-armed it into the man's head, making him drop the gun. The can rebounded and Rich caught it on the bounce. Without thinking, he stepped back and hurled it into the first goon's head again.

The man yelped like a wounded dog and stumbled out into the hall, bleeding profusely.

The other goon panicked. He stepped on the delivery boy's prone body and hobbled crab-like after his compatriot.

By the time Rich located his gun, which had landed under an end table, they both were gone. Hayte turned and looked at the boy. "You all right?"

The delivery boy was still on the floor in a fetal position, "I think... my... balls... are... crushed."

"Boy, do I know that feeling," said Richard. He reached for the phone.

~ ~ ~

Friday, 9:59am:

Dietrich was just about to clock out when the NPDi came marching in. Up the stairs they went to Shabazz's office. He heard Shabazz yell, "Hey— you fucks can't just..."

"Oh yes we can!" came the rejoinder. The door to Shabazz's office slammed shut. Dietrich quickly made his way to the men's room. He quickly walked to an empty stall, closed it and pulled out his palmtop. He sat on the lid and tried to log in to the system, but could not. His mind raced. *What to do, what to do?*

He quickly decided it was too late to do anything about moving the severed head. *No, better to wait a while until the ruckus dies down before I take it over there.* He smiled to himself faintly. *Besides, they won't find it here…* He just hoped they weren't about to drag him in for questioning. That would be awkward. He ransacked his brain for a better place to hide, but could only think of the morgue. He didn't feel he would make a very convincing corpse. *I could try the bold approach and walk right into the Chief's office…* He immediately rejected that idea. *No, I must go about my normal duties and try to act like nothing's wrong. Not an easy thing to do with the whole place swarming with Birkenstocks…*

He tried to leave the bathroom unobtrusively. He was immediately cornered by a goon big enough to block out the sun. "Hey! Who are you?" demanded the thug, jabbing him in the chest with a huge finger.

"The name's Dietrich, Lieutenant Paul Dietrich. I'm assigned to the Westchester County Coroner's Office."

"And what are you doing here? This ain't the morgue."

"I, ah, was just going to give a progress report to Chief Shabazz, but I see he's busy at the moment."

The goon's eyes narrowed. "Wait here."

He went, Dietrich assumed, to speak with a superior Birkenstock. Dietrich let out his breath slowly. He resisted the urge to bolt. He repeated his mantra. *Give them absolutely no reason to suspect anything…*

Five minutes became ten, which dragged on to twenty. Dietrich started getting hungry.

Finally he decided boldness was better than waiting forever. He found the goon on the other side of the detectives' room, towering over the cubicles. He went up and tapped the man on the shoulder, secretly surprised he could reach that high. "Excuse me—can I go back to work?"

"What?" The goon eyed him with fresh suspicion. "Why?"

Without thinking, Dietrich blurted, "I have a fresh corpse on the examining table. Not frozen, *fresh.* Or it *was* fresh, but now it's been half an hour—do you have any idea how much evidence could be lost because I'm not there to do the testing? Look, I'm talking *bodily decomposition*—every minute means cellular deformation gets more and more pronounced, making it *less and less* possible to do an exact time of death analysis…"

"Hey!" the goon jabbed Dietrich again with his finger. "You said you were gonna talk with Shabazz, not…"

"Which I could've done in ten minutes," said Dietrich with as icy a tone as possible. "I could've been back to work a quarter of an hour ago!"

Dietrich heard a voice in the cubicle. The goon turned and listened, then waved at Dietrich, "OK, you can go."

"Thank you." Dietrich spun on his heel and walked as fast as his wobbly legs would manage. He resisted the urge to see if his pants had a wet spot.

~ ~ ~

Friday, 8:55p.m:

Cheshire looked over at Browning, who was still putting ice on his wounded appendage, "Your foot OK?"

Browning grimaced, "That asshole! My big toe's twice its normal size!" He took his sandal off to show Cheshire. "See?"

"Yup," said Cheshire. "Ever since Donner was appointed chief, he's been a real asshole."

"Yeah, that's for sure. I've been looking for ways to get back at that dickhead for a long time."

"You know what bugs me?" Cheshire lowered his voice. "It's those damned white socks of his—every goddamned day, there's blood on his socks. What does he do, torture Arab terrorists for breakfast?"

"Nope!" Browning started grinning wolfishly. He whispered, "You're gonna *love* this..." He turned the computer display around and clicked on a folder. "I got curious about that, too. But you know his doctrine about making invisible scars, so you can never prove it in court? Well, I must've scanned every last fucking byte of him interrogating anyone, and he never, *never* breaks the skin, not with the unwound hanger, not with the needles in the eyes, nowhere."

"So what is it, then?" hissed Cheshire, "Is he bleeding around the ankles or something?"

"Hee-hee-hee!" Browning winked, "You're closer than you think..." He opened the video file, "Behold!"

"What's that?" Cheshire frowned at the screen. "Looks like an ordinary house..."

"It *is* a house, you idiot! *His* house!"

"I'm not an idiot," said Cheshire defensively. His eyes widened, "You mean Donner *has a house?*"

"Of course he has a house, Mister Not-an-Idiot! Just *watch!*"

Onscreen, the front door opened, and Donner stepped outside.

Cheshire squinted and fiddled with his glasses. "What's he pulling on? *Holy Elvis!*"

"Don't say that around here!" Browning looked furtively around, "Don't *ever* say tha..."

"He's walking the frigging dog! Look!" Cheshire pointed at the miniature Jack Russell terrier that was biting on Donner's ankles onscreen, "Hee-hee-hee!"

"Wait, it gets better!"

The dog sunk its teeth into Donner's heel. Donner let out a silent yell and swung his foot violently into the dog, sending its small body violently against the side of the house.

The dog crumpled in a heap. Donner hopped around on one foot, clutching his wounded ankle.

Browning's chest heaved. "Isn't that priceless? It took me *weeks* to find that!"

Cheshire wiped tears away. He pointed to the image date, "But that was weeks ago—you got anything more recent?"

"Oh yeah..." Browning let out another snort, "Check this one out..."

The camera angle was a little different but it was clearly the same house. Donner's front door opened and again he yanked furiously on the leash.

The now-three-legged dog attacked Donner's ankles with fresh vigor.

"Aaaaah!" Cheshire collapsed in a giggling fit.

"Look!" Browning pointed at the screen, "The damn dog's *faster* on *three* legs!" Donner kicked and missed the dog, which immediately lunged towards the other ankle.

Browning recovered enough to zoom in. "Look—you can see the bloodstains spreading!"

"But..." A puzzled looked crossed Cheshire's moon face, "How come his socks don't have holes when he comes into work?"

Browning gave him an exasperated look. "Obviously, he changes his socks before he goes to work!" A sudden idea occurred to him, "Hey! Wanna watch him step in his mutt's dogshit? That happens almost every time, too!"

Chapter 19

Saturday, April 10:

THE NEW YORK CYBERPOST

BUMBLEFLIES ATTACK MANHATTAN!

A new, very undesirable species of housefly has descended on New York. Dubbed "Bumble-Flies" by local residents, the new mutant is larger than a horsefly and collides with everything in its path.

"Easy as hell to swat" said Craig Schmaus, a retired construction foreman in the East Village, "but the mess left behind is lethal—the guts are like an oil slick."

Particularly affected are cars, trucks and buses, because the flies clog radiators, air intakes and fuel lines—and commercial airlines, because turbine blades become coated with fly entrails when taking off and landing, leading to severe malfunctions.

With Memorial Day weekend coming up, New York City mayor Chelsea Clinton issued a travel advisory cautioning Manhattan residents to stay home. "We cannot guarantee the safety of air travelers because of the severity of the fly plague, and car travel is also ill-advised at the moment," said a spokesperson for the mayor, who herself is currently stranded in Martha's Vineyard.

State health officials were baffled by the size of the individual flies. "It's a miracle they can fly at all with those ridiculous tiny wings." said one scientist. The largest adults measured 1.3 inches in length and up to an inch wide. "Fat f**kers," said one Brooklyn resident, "Fly swatters just don't cut it—you better use a sledge hammer."

New York City health officials had noticed an unusual number of flies hatching

245

in early spring but recognized the threat too late. "We thought they were ordinary houseflies" *said an unnamed health official.* "We had no reason to expect them to grow [so large]."

The same official added, "Unfortunately, the freezing rain we had last month didn't kill them in significant amounts. Most were able to survive by going underground, in the flooded sewers and the subway tunnels."

~ ~ ~

Shrini and Perry pulled into the rental lot in Des Moines minutes before closing time. It was pouring down rain.

Shrini got out and ran into the tiny trailer that housed the rental agency's offices. She came out five minutes later and banged on the driver's side window. "It's all set!" she yelled, "Go ahead and park it!"

"Where?" Donohue unrolled the window a tiny bit and still got wet. "I don't want to walk far in this downpour."

"It's in the back lot!" She got in and slammed the door. "We're getting a truck!"

Perry started the car and pulled into the next lot. "I can't get used to these new streamlined trucks. They all look like gigantic dildoes, especially when they're going down the road." He peered through the windshield. "I don't see any trucks here."

"We're not renting a tractor-trailer rig, Perry, just a small moving truck," said Shrini.

He found an empty space and parked. "Now where is this 'moving truck'?" said Donohue.

"It says on the key chain that it's white, with Utah plates," Shrini peered through the windscreen. "There it is!"

"Huh? That's not a moving truck—it's just a plain old white van!"

"Look, Perry, I promised Carrouthers we'd be there by Sunday. Either we take this, or we go back to the car. I think it's better to swap—or do you really want to go back to the underground cell with Donner?"

"All right, all right!" said Donohue in exasperation. "Let's just do it and keep moving." Shrini opened the doors with a tiny remote on the key chain. They got out, grabbed their things and threw them in the back of the paneled van. By the time they were done, they were soaked to the skin.

"I'll drive," said Donohue, grabbing the keys from her and sliding behind the wheel before she could object. He was just about to start the engine when a though suddenly occurred to him. "Hey, do we even know exactly where to go?"

Shrini fastened her safety belts and pulled wet strands of hair from her mouth. "What do you mean?"

"I mean, you never have told me exactly where this Carrouthers guy is."

"That's because I don't know exactly." She fumbled for her mobile phone. "I think he's in Wyoming."

"You don't know?" Donohue threw up his hands, "We drive all the way to Des Moines, and you don't even know where we're going?"

"Relax, Perry. He said he would leave his address in his voice mail account—I'll get it now." She punched in the access code and listened intently. She folded up the phone.

Perry sat twirling the ignition key round his finger. "Well?"

"Actually, it's not Wyoming where Carrouthers lives—but I was close" said Shrini.

Donohue started the engine and gave her a look. "Meaning what?"

"He's in Colorado—but right on the border. I'll tell you when we have to turn off the Interstate."

~ ~ ~

The afternoon sun took on a dirty orange hue through the filthy windows in the Chelsea Hotel. Hudgins sat on the edge of the bed, shaking his head. "Was two men? *Not* de Johnny B?"

"Nope," said Hayte, shifting painfully in the threadbare chair. "Both goons were as big as trucks. And that's why I'm back here."

Hudgins looked around the room. "Is sure a dump, mon."

"Listen, man. My apartment may be the sweetest bachelor pad in the whole goddamned Village, but one more break-in or attack, and I'm gonna have to kill somebody. That place is a fucking jinx to me! As soon as I'm healthy again—provided I live long enough—I'm moving back to Harlem. I never thought a white neighborhood would be so goddamn dangerous..."

Hudgins' dreadlocks bobbed like wires. "So who were duh goons, you bust a big mafia don or somethin?"

Hayte shook his head slowly and painfully. "Naw, man. They were from the NPDi, I assume, because they wanted to know where Perry is."

Hudgins' eyes widened, "Oh mon! Dey bad news, dey been interrogatin' my partner Vaughn since nine o'clock dis morning! Are dey US Army or something?"

"Uh-uh. Homeland Security."

"Dat explain' dat—dey come in my precinct dis morning like day got carte blanche, mon! And dey's after your partner?"

"Yes. I thought they had Perry captured, but obviously he's escaped." Richard's face was swollen and grim. "Shrini must be in danger too. I tried calling her, but all I get is voice mail. I hope they're together—otherwise... if the NPDi gets ahold of her, they might use her to force Perry to give himself up."

"They may use you too, mon."

"First they got to find me," said Richard grimly. "And I made a deal with the desk clerk here, so I'll be warned about any unwanted visitors. I won't be going out much anyway. I have to get this bar exam behind me, so I can get my law license and really go after these NPDi fuckers."

"If Johnny B don't get ya first…" said Hudgins. He tapped his shoes against the bowling case he'd brought with him.

"They got old-fashioned dead bolts here," said Hayte. "The only things that can get past doors this heavy are the right keys, a big-ass drill or explosives. The last two will set off all the alarms."

"Not right, mon! Not if Johnny use dat quiet explosive…"

"OK, you're right. But first he has to know where to find me. Plus, I carry my gun with me at all times. The minute I lay eyes on Johnny, I'll blow his head off."

Hudgins shook his head, sending dreadlocks flying. "How would ya know, mon? If dey all identical, how ya gonna know if ya shoots da right one?"

Hayte sat silently and fidgeted. Finally he looked at Hudgins and shrugged, "I don't know. But by the time I find out, it might be too late…"

He looked out the window and saw something strange. Small shadowy dots clustering everywhere… "What the hell is that?" He tugged at the window.

Hudgins's eyes widened in alarm. "NO MON—*DON'T OPEN DAT!!*"

~ ~ ~

Sunday, 5 p.m:
"Agent Cheshire!" barked Donner, "We got anything from the airports?"

"Nothing, boss. And nothing from the car rental agencies. No records at all of credit card use."

"You people," Donner rolled his eyes, "know less than a donkey's doormat!"

"We *got* the airports covered," protested Browning. "Each and every one that handles commercial or government airplanes. What more do you want?"

Donner waved his hands in exasperation, "I want Donohue!!!" He began pacing. "We'd better forget the airports anyway. No way is he flying—firstly, he has to be pretty beat up—possibly with head injuries, which rules out airplanes—and secondly, it's Patriot Day weekend. You'd have to pay through the nose to book a last-minute seat to get wherever they're going…" Donner broke off and drummed his fists on the desk, "You know what? We're not doing everything we can! Agent Cheshire!"

Cheshire snapped to attention, "Yes sir?"

"Go and see about getting the credit card records of all of New York City."

Cheshire's face blanched, "Sir, that's a *huge* undertaking! We don't have the software to sort through all the…"

"Well, *call* Washington and *get them working on it*," said Donner. "Without it, I doubt we'll ever find those two. Wait—let's make things simpler—we'll only need records from the day Donohue escaped from the train wreck."

"Yes, sir," said Cheshire, shoulders slumped.

"Cheer up!" Donner started snickering, "you can always flag all the people who bought porn merchandise and sell their names to the Christian Coalition like you did last year over Christmas."

Cheshire's mouth dropped open. "Sir, ah... I didn't... I, uh, how..."

"*Don't* deny it, Cheshire—you think I don't know everything that goes on around here?" He started to laugh, then cut himself short, "Well, guess again! Hell, I would've done the same thing... But *your* priority is to find Donohue—*and* that Indian bitch!! Go to it!"

Browning held up his hand, "Sir, I got a question about the dispatch to all the state highway patrols."

"Well, what *is it*?" Donner said impatiently.

Browning fumbled with the printout, "It's going to be a real problem if we have to alert the ones west of the Mississippi..."

"How's that?" snapped Donner.

Browning pointed to the map on the wall, "Sir, there are not enough troopers and not enough cars. And too many Interstates to search."

"Put out the alert *anyway*," Donner's voice was tense.

"I just thought of something, Chief," said Cheshire, "What if they're using motorbikes—they'll be unidentifiable."

"How's that?" Donner glared at him, "Would that make them magically *invisible*?"

"In a way, yes..." Scowl lines appeared across Cheshire's moon face, "A full-face helmet..."

"Put in a directive for all State Highway Patrol cars to pull over any and all motorcycles, regardless of reason."

"Can't do that, sir." Browning shook his head, "You said yourself that it's Patriot Day weekend. Every two-bit motorcycle club is probably on the road by now..."

Donner turned and punched the file cabinet, which then fell over, scattering files everywhere. "*YOU* FUCKING FIND HIM—I *DON'T* CARE *HOW!!!*"

Chapter 20

The bug bomb had done its work perfectly, but the entire hotel room was littered with dead bumbleflies.

Hudgins continued vacuuming until the machine made grinding noises. He wiped the sweat off his forehead and reached down to change cleaner bags yet again. "We gonna run out of vacuum cleaner bags real soon, mon…"

"Man, I'm sick of this shit!" Hayte threw another gunk encrusted sponge in the trash. "And this smell makes me wanna puke!"

"Told ya not ta open dat window." Hudgins snapped the vacuum cleaner shut, "Ah hope Ah got all dem buggers out of my dreadlocks. Can ya check for me?" He bent his head forward.

"Sure." Hayte pulled out each lock and inspected it, "Yup, you got 'em all."

"Good, mon. Ah hates da idea dat somethin' live is crawling round up dere," Hudgins shuddered. "Fact is, you're lucky the hotel management didn't kick your ass out on the street for lettin' de little buggers in. I had to stop and shake 'em all off my clothes before dey would let me in."

"You could've warned me there was an epidemic," grumbled Hayte, "I got no TV here, no radio, nothing."

"Sorry, mon. I thought ya knew," Hudgins fired up the vacuum again.

Hayte motioned for him to stop, "Hey, wait a second! How come your hair wasn't covered with bumbleflies when you first came in?"

Hudgins reached for the bowling ball carrier and opened it triumphantly, "Ah gots da ultimate in protection, mon! A beekeeper got murdered in the Bronx a couple a months ago!" He held up the mask.

"There wouldn't be another of those lying around, would there?"

"Naw." Hudgins reached in the case again, "But I do got dese," he held up some ancient aviator goggles. "De buggers may get in your hair n' stuff, but least ya can see!"

Hayte took the goggles, "Thanks. Guess I'll tie a bandanna over my face to keep them out of my mouth when I go out."

~ ~ ~

Wednesday, April 13:

Donohue and Shrini were approaching North Platte, Nebraska. Perry tried stretching out in the back, but kept turning over and back again.

Shrini glanced at him in the rearview mirror, "What are you *doing* back there?"

"Trying to get comfortable," Donohue turned around to face the back and started unzipping, "We need to stop somewhere and buy me some proper underwear."

"What's wrong with the ones you got?"

"These boxer shorts you lent me are riding up the crack in my ass." Perry finished rearranging his genitals and pulled his pants up, "Especially *this* pair." He climbed over the passenger seat and sat down exasperatedly.

"I'll be sure and let Todd know," grinned Shrini, "If I ever see the guy again."

Perry raised an eyebrow, "What? Did he disappear?"

"No, no—I don't know if I want to go out with him again. It wasn't really a date anyway, more of a 'let's get together and hump like bunnies' kind of thing..."

Perry gave her a funny look.

"*What?*" she snapped.

"Nothing..." A minute passed. Donohue pointedly avoided looking at her.

She looked at him staring straight ahead, "Like hell it's nothing. Does it bother you that I have casual sex from time to time—is that it?"

"Shrini, I, uh..."

"I was just trying to make conversation, and there you are, sitting there all po-faced. Oh, I see, it's OK for guys to screw around—while you're out being a 'roaming torpedo', we girls are supposed to be sitting at home..."

Donohue shifted uncomfortably in his seat, "Damn, Shrini, your English's gotten a lot better..."

She glared at him, "Don't change the subject!"

Perry let out a deep sigh, "OK, okay. It *does* bother me."

"Why? It's totally unfair."

Perry fiddled with the seat recline button, "It's hard to explain."

"Well, *try*."

"All right," He looked out the window at the bleak scenery bathed in moonlight for a few minutes. "When I think about it, I mean really think about it, we men are brainwashed. We all are supposed to be ultra-competitive studs who can fuck anything." He looked at her profile in the oncoming headlights. "But it still bugs the hell out of me when women tell me about their sex lives."

She looked at him briefly. "Why?"

"Because you're talking about sleeping with *other* guys." He leaned over and tapped the shift lever for emphasis. "Men are *territorial*—just like wolves, I guess. It's this competitive thing we got."

She made a face. "So *that's* it—we women are nothing but *property?*"

Perry threw up his hands, "Now, *you're* the one being unfair. I know for a fact that I'm not alone in this—Rich hates it too when women tell him about being attracted to other guys."

She looked at him skeptically, "Does he really?"

"Yes, he *does*. Look, you can't expect us to be like your girl friends. Men *are* different and you *have* to accept that."

"But why is that? Why can't you see our point of view?"

Donohue opened the cooler and took out another can of Pepsi. "Simple. We're taught not to think like women. Like I said before, we're brainwashed. But women are brainwashed too—you're all crazy about shoes…"

Shrini laughed in spite of herself. "OK, you have a point. We're a bit brainwashed, too…"

"Gawd, I hate that word, brainwashed. Makes me think of Donner," Perry took a long swig.

Shrini glanced at him, "Still don't want to talk about that?"

Perry sat and played with the pop-up tab on the can. He crumpled up the can and started to roll down the window.

"Don't throw that out, Perry. We don't want to get pulled over!"

"All right." Perry fished around for a suitable trash bag. Finally, he found one. He looked over, "All right. Now's as good at time as any. More and more things are coming back to me. Can you hand me the thermos?"

"What—you want *coffee* after drinking a Pepsi?"

"Yeah. I'm gonna need a lot of caffeine to kick start my brain. It's gonna be a long story."

"Suit yourself…" She reached down between her legs and passed the thermos over.

He poured himself a cup, took a sip and grimaced.

Shrini laughed. "You didn't expect it to be *warm*, did you?"

Perry grimaced and swallowed. "No… but I was *hoping*. Anyway, when I first woke up this afternoon, I thought I was back in that underground cell. How long was I missing?"

"Three weeks." Shrini steered past some trucks parked on the shoulder.

"Well, it was the longest three weeks I've ever experienced. Right at the end, I made a chance discovery and found the whole thing—Donner's whole trip—was based on a fucking *lie*. That Donner sure is a weird fuck…"

"What do you mean?"

"He breaks his own rules right and left, when he thinks nobody is looking. I found that out when I finished the 'training'. On our last day of captivity, they actually let us out in a park for a barbeque, of all things…"

~ ~ ~

The cell door opened and Donner poked his head in. Seeing Donohue's look, Donner grinned malevolently, "Always *glad* to see me, huh? Well, time to cheer up! I got a real treat for you." He came into the cell with a huge minder in tow.

"A treat?" snarled Donohue, "Oh, *wonderful*. Another test about Spiritual Purgation?"

"Nope" said Donner cheerfully, "You're going to our company barbeque!"

"What?" Perry was stunned, "You're actually *letting* me go *outside*?"

Donner nodded enthusiastically, "Absolutely—you and all your other classmates!"

"I didn't know I had classmates..."

"Oh-ho! You thought you were *special!*" Donner laughed unpleasantly, "Surprise! There are actually about a hundred others right now getting the same training seminars and indoctrinations—and you'll have the chance to meet each and every one of them today, at..." he whipped out a flyer and stuck it on the cell wall "...the Jeb Butcher Memorial Park today, rain or shine!"

"What—accompanied by machine-gun-toting guards and bloodhounds?" said Perry sourly, looking at the goon at Donner's side. "That'll sure be fun..."

Donner smiled and patted the bodyguard on the shoulder, "Nope! No guards, no dogs, just that electronic parole box strapped to your left ankle!"

Donohue looked down and saw it for the first time. He shook his leg, causing Donner to start laughing again.

"Haw, you can't shake it off! We put it on while you were sleeping like a baby! We could've just implanted a chip under your skin, but we like to make it big enough to remind you who's boss..." He waved impatiently to Donohue, "C'mon—quit staring at it like an idiot and follow me!"

Perry had misgivings about following Donner, but he recognized he had no choice. He didn't want yet another beating.

Donner wrinkled his nose, "First, go get a shower. You're ripe enough to plant." He threw Perry a towel and pointed to where the showers were.

The water was ice-cold. Perry had the feeling he was being watched the whole time. He looked around but failed to find any obvious place for a camera. Still the feeling persisted. As provocation, he decided to soap down the parole box. He halfway expected the goon to come marching in to grab him, but nothing happened. He stuck his leg in the water and watched the soap wash off the box.

Still nothing. He bent down to inspect his leg.

The box didn't even fizz or crackle.

He emerged dripping from the shower and saw a neat stack of fresh towels and clothes next to his shoes.

After he got dressed, he walked out. Donner and the goon were waiting. "All clean and ready to go?"

"As ready as I'll ever be," said Perry.

They set off down another interminable series of corridors.

Several corridors later, they came to a group of elevators. Donner pulled his ID through the card reader and one opened. The goon stood behind them. Perry turned and said, "After you."

The bodyguard didn't move.

Perry shrugged and stepped in. Donner and the bodyguard followed. The doors hissed shut. Sickly background music played softly.

They started down. The muzak started playing the Olympic theme.

Perry turned and looked at Donner, "That reminds me, you didn't answer my questions, Donner. What happened to those cloned athletes after you quashed the Olympic Trials story?"

Donner sighed, "All right. We made a deal with Boner Vista Productions in Hollywierd. They'll be the male leads in some adult features on satellite TV."

"Ha! That fits…" Donohue laughed in spite of himself. "I still can't believe they beat off during the medals ceremony. You'd think they'd have enough sense to wait until after…"

The elevator opened. "You're talking in terms of average people—these are *clones*," said Donner, turning around, "Unfortunately they need genitals too. Without those, the beasts would have no competitive gender. They were bred with one purpose in mind—to swim, run, jump, lift weights or whatever—but *not* to think." They walked through another corridor bathed in halogen light.

Perry studied Donner's face to see if he was pulling his leg. "So this means US Olympic team is using clones too? Even though human cloning is still banned here?"

"Of course," grunted Donner. "They just breed 'em overseas, then smuggle the cultures in while they're still microscopic. Nobody can stop it, not even us. But if we didn't use clones, we'd get our asses kicked from Borneo all the way back to Bugtussle. And nobody wants that to happen— our national pride would take a huge beating." He lowered his voice as the elevator slowed, "And the Olympics would lose the majority of its corporate sponsorship…"

Donohue asked, "Well, can't they breed super-intelligent athletes that are also physically superior?"

"What?! Are you CRAZY?" Donner stopped and waved his hands in exasperation, "They're *our* slaves—not the other way round! You give 'em *brains* and we'll end up becoming extinct before you know it! We don't have the know-how to give them two-year lifespans like that old Phillip K. Dick novel, at least not *yet*."

Perry looked puzzled. "Who's Phillip K. Dick?"

"Oh lawdy…" Donner shook his head sadly. "You really *do* need to learn some of the finer aspects of your own culture."

They came to a stop in front of some massive double doors.

Donner patted Perry on the back. "Too bad the program is about over for you—you need to go through our archives some more, pick up things about what makes our culture tick."

Perry looked at him suspiciously. "Like what?"

"For example, the music!" grinned Donner, looking into the eye scanner. "In addition to our huge data base, we got a multi-media library to kill for! Follow me."

The doors slid open to reveal a large windowless room covered in computer-controlled wallpaper, which lit up in myriad colors when Donner walked in.

The door slid shut behind them. The body guard stood behind Donohue.

Donner pulled out a remote control. An oversize rack popped out of the floor. "This is my personal Tiki collection." He carefully took a slim piece of flat cardboard out of the rack and lovingly pulled out a flat plastic disk. He showed the cover to Perry. "Ever see one of these before?"

"No." Donohue read the liner notes. "Who the hell is Yma Sumac?"

"A musical *goddess*." Donner blew dust off the turntable cover with loving care. He set the vinyl slab down and lowered the tone arm manually. "Listen and hear for yourself!"

As the first discordant strains filled the room, Donohue made a face. "Jesus! What *is* this shit?" Perry could swear that Donner looked hurt.

"You don't like it now, but you *will*." said Donner defiantly. His voice took on an almost dreamlike quality, "Tiki music is one of the only true kinds of white man's music. It's from the golden age, almost a hundred years old, right when stereo was introduced, the Eisenhower era. Everything else, we ripped off from the Africans—or from Krauts like Mozart."

Perry made faces until the song finished.

Donner put on another round slab of vinyl and the strains of "Jambalaya" filled the room. Donohue's face brightened, "Hey, I recognize that tune! It's the theme song for Campbell's Cream of Crayfish soup!"

Donner rolled his eyes. "You *are* a cultural Philistine…" He glanced at his watch. Oh—it's about time for the picnic. Come on, you don't want to be late."

The bodyguard pushed Perry out the door.

Donner and his "friend" led Perry back down another series of corridors to the elevators.

Donner gestured for Perry to stop. "Well son, I'll see you tomorrow. Don't have *too* much fun…" He winked.

The doors opened, revealing a mirrored elevator. He shoved Perry inside, then waved as the doors closed.

When the doors opened again, Donohue found himself looking at a very dark and stately reception area. Out of nowhere, a uniformed butler appeared beside him. "Capt. Donohue, I presume? I'll show you to the shuttle—it's quite hard to find, a bit like a labyrinth around here, I'm afraid…"

As he followed the butler down a long paneled corridor, Donohue gawked at the huge portraits on the walls. "What is this place?"

"It's a country club, sir. Built in the 1840s, I believe. To your left is the official members' dining room. In his later years, *after* the Civil War of course, Robert E. Lee used to dine there. Sometime, Captain, we'd be glad to give you a tour. Now, sir, if you'll follow me..." He led Donohue to a set of massive oak doors, "Your ride will be here shortly." He held the door open for Perry.

Outside, Donohue gawked at the building's elaborate façade.

Behind him, a shuttle bus pulled up. Several other men got in as Perry looked on. The butler peeked out and said, "This is your ride, sir. Enjoy yourself."

Perry got on. He had to take the last available seat, over the back wheelwell.

Nobody talked the whole trip, which lasted half an hour. They came to a large park. The shuttle turned up the driveway, which wound around a good-sized man-made lake. They stopped in front of a small open shelter.

Donohue stepped out of the shuttle last, following the other passengers. He looked around. The park was filled with only men, he noted. He followed the scent of barbeque to a group of wooden tables—and a long line waiting in front of them.

After waiting for what seemed like eternity, he got served. He ate the whole plate in about three seconds flat, then went back to the line for seconds.

It was then that he noticed the beer kegs. In front of them, there was a continuous stream of men filling up their plastic cups. It was obvious from looking at them that they were all cops.

Perry was tempted to go over, but he was still too hungry, so he stayed where he was. He found himself staring at the burly cop in short pants in front of him in line. He tapped the man on the shoulder. "Sorry to bother you, but doesn't it bug you to have that thing on your ankle?"

The cop, a big dark-haired Italian, turned around. "You got one too?"

"Yup" Donohue pulled up his pants leg to show it. He held out his hand, "Capt. Donohue, NYPD."

"Sgt. Graceffo, Montgomery County Police, Maryland. Pleased to meet ya." He pointed to his own parole box, "It bugged me too at first, but hell, I guess we all got the fucking things, so what's the point of bitching? I'm just looking forward to getting outta here and going back to my normal beat."

Perry raised an eyebrow. "They actually *are* gonna let us go back?"

"Yeah, that's what everyone says, as soon as you finish the program— I took my final in Clone Recognition a couple of days ago. I just found out I passed... so I'm home free—or so they say." He filled his plate.

Donohue did the same, getting the last of the barbeque. "Congratulations," he said as they walked to a vacant picnic table nearby

"Thanks." Graceffo took a big bite, but continued talking, "I never thought I'd ever empathize with the crooks I used to bust, but I'm sure glad to be outside, even with this fucking thing on my ankle."

"Yeah, I hear that," Donohue scooped up a forkful of beef. "Those underground chambers were getting to me..." He looked around. "Say, what's the deal with the beer kegs? I thought we were supposed to be kicking alcohol as part of this training..."

"Beats me, but everybody's sure getting shitfaced..." said Graceffo. "Maybe they just wanted everyone sober enough to do the training—and this is the payback for being good."

"Hmm..." Donohue took another bite. He looked around, "Hey! I just noticed something else that's funny!"

"What's that?" Graceffo dumped his paper plate in the bushes.

"No bugs or bees," Perry pointed around them, "Normally we'd be covered with the fuckers, especially with all the barbeque sauce."

"Naw," said Graceffo, scratching his ass, "The laws against insecticides don't apply to the NPDi..." He shook his head, "I got out early and saw a bunch of those boys hosing down the whole park down with foggers this morning. I bet those bastards can break any law they like."

Donohue looked at all the cops getting drunk, "Uh-huh. Even the laws they *make*..."

A few meters away, some heavyset cops started brawling in a pool of spilled beer.

It was beginning to get cold. The sun dipped lower on the horizon, and, as it did, most of the conversations got progressively louder. Empty beer cups were strewn everywhere. A group of middle-aged cops in shorts were trying to throw rocks at the geese in the lake.

On the other side of the water, a few more fist-fights broke out.

He was tempted to go and have a beer. But he still felt like a caged rat, and he knew alcohol would make him feel worse. He looked around at all the brawlers rolling around in the mud nearby. One of the brawlers glanced up and yelled something, so he turned and walked away. *The last thing I wanna do is fight a cop. No way would they fight fair...*

He started to wonder about going back—or finding somewhere to sleep. Just as he was looking for a place to piss, he bumped into Graceffo again, "Did you ride over here in the shuttle?"

"Yeah," Graceffo momentarily stumbled over his own feet, "They said it'd be back around sunset to pick us back up." He let out a loud belch. "Not that I'm *aching* to go back..."

Perry nodded, "Yeah, but did you get a look at that country club?

"Yeah, I saw it. Looked like a haven for rich folks."

"For sure," agreed Donohue." Somebody told me it was built 200 years ago."

"No shit? I didn't know that," said Graceffo. "I only know about those bunkers down below. One of the other guys told me they was built for Congress to go if the Russians ever nuked us. Or the Arabs... 'Scuse me, but I gotta go piss somewheres..." He headed into the bushes.

"Yeah, me too," Perry went off to search for the portable toilets.

The lines for the port-a-potties were too long, so Perry decided to look around for a gas station or a restaurant. He walked over to the nearest road. Strangely, no cars were around anywhere.

He saw a tavern around a bend. His wallet was bereft of cash, so he decided to go inside and ask the waiter if he could use the facilities.

"Sure, pal," The waiter pointed to the back, "Through the double doors, right next to the kitchen."

Perry walked into the rest room and unzipped. His bladder was about to burst, but nothing came out, not even a dribble.

Too damned cold in here. He looked around and found the switch to turn off the exhaust fan above the lone stall.

Suddenly it was very quiet.

He tried again. *Ahh...* He closed his eyes. A long, luxurious sense of relief flooded his senses.

It took several minutes before he noticed the voices.

Loud laughter was coming from somewhere close by. Perry was mystified, as the tavern was empty when he had walked in. He peered out the bathroom door.

Still empty.

He looked around and located a vent above the lone sit-down toilet. More laughter—*and one laugh sounded naggingly familiar...*

Perry got up gingerly on the toilet tank lid and peered through the vent. He saw a back room, with a card game in progress. *Looks like poker.* He almost slid off his perch when he saw that one of the players was Donner.

Another burst of laughter. A man with his back to Donohue said, "You saw how drunk they're all getting? Haw! We ought ta call the local police out to arrest their asses!"

More laughter. Donner anted up a bet. "Not a bad idea, but not this time. But if they start acting up on me later, I might just do that..."

"Ain't you worried about some of them escaping?" said another man in a cowboy hat. He crossed his legs, revealing a Birkenstock sandal. "Not *all* cops have that herd instinct, you know..."

"Worried about escapes? Shee-it!" chortled Donner. He glanced at his open palmtop, which lay open by his stack of poker chips, "Naw, everybody's still within the boundaries. As long as they're within 1.5 miles of this computer, everything's kosher—otherwise the thing would be beeping at me..."

Perry reflexively peered down at the bulge around his ankle. He realized suddenly that it was sheer luck that he'd wandered towards Donner, instead of the other direction.

He looked back through the vent just as Donner said, "They ain't stupid, even if they are cops—they know the parole box will start shrieking if they try anything, and then there's the tranquilizer it shoots into their legs! No,

I ain't the least bit worried. We got Dobermans to go after anyone who figures out how to get the box off their leg or tries anything funny." He poured another shot of bourbon. "But that ain't going to happen. Eugenics never fail. After 30 days without alcohol, all those cops are now out there getting shit-faced on the free beer and pigging out on pork. I flat guarantee all the kegs will be empty by the time they're done."

The cowboy looked at him. "You gave 'em *beer*? But that's against the Spiritual Purgation!"

"Yup! And they all *know* it—and they'll feel guilty every time they fall off the wagon from here on out! They can't help it—the vast majority of cops are genetically fated to behave that way, just as the legendary Jukes descendants were doomed to become criminals, harlots and drunkards. Cops will *always* go astray, and then repent in a cold sweat the next morning. Guilt works like a charm, every time—just ask the Catholic Church! Here's a toast—*to the Catholics*!" He downed the bourbon in one gulp.

The man with his back to Perry said, "And what about *you*, Donner? I see you're not exactly following what you preach…"

"Oh, right, you FBI types are all soooo pure and innocent! I *know* about you Mormons and what goes on when tabernacle doors are closed!" leered Donner sarcastically, "Hey, most of the time, I am *so* good, my halo just *glows*," He downed another shot. "Then I reward myself. With some *controlled* bingeing. But I *always* stay in control. I am *twice* as careful when I drive home."

The cowboy said, "Sounds like half the folks I used to bust when I was stationed in Savanna. Everybody and his dog used to get blitzed and drive— all the big magnolia trees along the streets got scars up and down their trunks…"

"You're a Southern boy? Hell, me too! I went to college, down in Nashville…"

"No shit? Where? I went to Vandy!"

"Me too," Donner shook his head, "That was one wild place — I bet you even been hogging…"

"Yup," said the cowboy, also laughing.

"Hogging? What's that?" said the FBI man with a frown.

Donner's face turned wolfish, "That's a *special* fraternity ritual. You go out in a pack and you draw straws first. The loser has to seek out the ugliest woman in the airport bar, get her stinking drunk and take her to the frat house."

"Ooh, this sounds good…" The FBI man reached for Donner's bourbon. "Can I have some?"

"Oh, it *is*… Yeah, help yourself," Donner took another hit of bourbon and passed the bottle over, "Then he has to get all her clothes off and start fucking her from behind. You have to get her really going almost to the point of cumming…" Donner let out a horrible high-pitched laugh, "And *then*—all your buddies switch on the lights! Too bad I don't have the videos any more—it always was so hilarious! One guy—sometimes it was me — has to wear a rodeo clown costume, and stand between her and her clothes as she panics. All the while, the other guys have to jump on her like a bronco, take her down, tie her up and fuck her in the ass!"

Donohue almost lost his balance. He grabbed hold of the stall and held on for dear life. He felt around in a panic with his left foot, trying to find the toilet lid.

There.

He slowly slid his shoe over and tested it. The plastic toilet tank lid flexed dangerously, but it didn't crack or slide off. He put his right foot down on it, too. The lid held. He let out a deep sigh. He gingerly got off the toilet and tried to steady his nerves.

Luckily, the men's room was still empty. He washed his hands and walked out in a daze.

"Everything come out OK?" said a voice behind him.

Perry's head snapped around, "Huh?"

The waiter looked at him, "What's the matter?"

Perry put on a smile, "Oh, nothing... Yeah, everything came out just fine. Thanks a lot."

"Anytime..."

The tavern was just starting to fill up as he walked out. Perry affected an unsteady step as he walked back towards the park, just in case anyone got curious. He stumbled over to a park bench and waited for the next shuttle to come. He started to shiver. He wasn't quite sure if it was the cold that made him do so.

~ ~ ~

"Did anyone notice you were gone?" said Shrini.

"Nope," said Donohue, "Nobody was there, physically supervising the barbeque—that's why all the other cops could get drunk and fight each other." He shook his head, "I guess it was all part of the plan—I bet this wasn't the first time the NPDi has done this. Only this time, Donner didn't bargain on one cop—me—staying sober and stumbling across his back-room poker game."

"So they bussed all of you back to the underground cells?"

Donohue nodded, "Yup. I got back just in time. About five minutes later, a couple of vanloads of NPDi goons pulled up and started rounding us all back up. They even had wheelbarrows to pick up the ones who were passed out. They were stacking five cops in one wheelbarrow. Talk about no respect..."

"It's that bit about hogging that really gets to me..." said Shrini.

They were now driving past Omaha and plunging into Nebraska proper. "Yeah," said Donohue, "Me, too. After that, I *had* to escape. I just didn't know how at the time."

Shrini shuddered. "Now I'll have nightmares about that guy..." The nighttime traffic started to lighten and stars started appearing in the horizon. "If we don't hit trouble, we can make Cheyenne by sunrise."

"Sounds good to me." Donohue took another swig of coffee. "Why don't we swap at the next gas stop? I'm getting tired of driving."

"I can't believe my ears," said Shrini blithely.

~ ~ ~

They were on a dimly-lit two-lane road going out of North Platte. Shrini hoped it was the one leading to Cheyenne. She allowed herself the luxury of switching on the brights, in the hopes of spotting a road sign confirming their direction. She didn't dare try the GPRS, lest the NPDi was monitoring. She breathed a sigh of relief when a sign appeared in the distance saying Cheyenne was 120 miles away.

Donohue stirred in the back seat and yawned.

Shrini flicked off the brights to accommodate an oncoming truck, "I hope we can make it there by sunrise."

"I hope so, too," Donohue yawned again, "Hey, what time is it?"

She squinted at the dashboard clock. "About 3 a.m. Why?"

"That means it's 6 in New York. Think I'll risk a call to Dietrich."

Suit yourself," She handed the headset to him and hit the dial memory button.

Surprisingly, Dietrich picked up on the first ring. "Yeah?"

"Hey, Paul, it's Perry. Whazzup?"

"Good to hear from you. Well, for starters, I'm in hiding," said Dietrich.

"In hiding? Are you in trouble?"

"You have no idea, Perry. It's like a madhouse over here," said Dietrich, "When I came in to work yesterday, there was a weird vibe, but nothing I could put my finger on. People were walking around real quiet, and there was all this nervous glancing around. It was getting on my nerves after a while, so I decided to find a spare terminal and get all my data files downloaded so I could get the hell out of there. I logged in and found the whole NYPD computer network was paralyzed. I did manage to grab the most sensitive files before I got kicked off." He paused for a second, "Next thing I know, it was total bedlam. Never thought I'd tremble at the sound of Birkenstocks, but they're everywhere. They marched right in, in lockstep—and it really does make your blood freeze."

"Have they questioned you yet?"

"Only briefly, but only because they haven't run across my name on the roster. I was farmed out to the Fleetwood county coroner's office about six months ago, so it'll take them a while to get back to me."

"What'll you do when they catch up with you?"

"Well, I've been covering my tracks, so I think I'll be OK. I made sure the head's somewhere they can't ever touch it."

"So they won't find it?" said Donohue.

"Oh, they'll find it *eventually*," Dietrich started snickering. "But it won't do them any good. You'll just have to trust me on that. Part of the fun will be watching them react when they *do* find it." His tone turned serious, "Catch you later, Perry. I'll let you know what happens."

The connection went dead.

~ ~ ~

Browning dashed in waving a dispatch, "Boss, we intercepted one of Lt. Shrinithan's e-mail messages to Chief Shabazz!"

"Well, what does it say?" demanded Donner, who was fiddling with his sandal.

"You were right, sir. They're going to Carrouthers to tape his testimony, something about his granddaughter being murdered..."

"So *that's* why he's resurfaced!" Donner rubbed his hands eagerly. "We'll just have to drop in as unexpected house guests! Now, all we gotta do is find them..." He stared at the map on his desk.

"Thanks a bunch!" Cheshire hung up his mobile. "Chief! I think the highway patrol in North Platte's got a visual ID on them!"

"Where the hell's North Platte?" Donner dashed over to the control room, hopping on one sandal.

"Nebraska, sir," said Cheshire, pointing to the map, "Right in the middle-south area."

"Well, it's about time local law enforcement picked up their end of the bargain!" Donner fiddled with the broken Birkenstock and muttered, "Have to replace the toe strap again...". He put it back on and looked up, "Did they put a tail on them?"

Cheshire shook his head, "Negative, sir. We'll have to put our men on it."

"Well, why the hell not?" demanded Donner angrily. "That's what they're paid for!"

"The officer in question had just pulled over a speeder and couldn't just rush off without good reason. It says here," Cheshire tapped the report with his yellowed fingernails, "that he only got a fleeting glimpse of the two occupants—a man who might fit Donohue's description—and a woman, maybe mid 30's, with Asian features..."

"Asian features?" Donner rolled his eyes, "I think that State Trooper's been smoking crack." He pulled up Shrini's NYPD file photo, "No doubt in my mind she's from India. No doubt at all."

"Are we sure he's the with same woman?" said Browning.

"Sure I'm sure. Cops always socialize with other cops—he wouldn't be dragging a girlfriend along for a lark. Or conspiring with a terrorist..." Donner's face lit up, "Hey! That gives me an idea! Let's put out an alert saying he's turned! That'll get the FBI added to the manhunt!" He rubbed his hands and looked at the map. "Well, well, well! If this pans out, we might just end up nailing their asses after all... and bag Carrouthers, too!" He stopped. "Hey, who have we got stationed in the Midwest?"

"Um..." Browning made a face, "Nobody, sir."

"*Nobody?*" Donner was incredulous, "How the hell did *that* happen?"

Cheshire tapped a directive, "Your orders, sir. Last month the President wanted full coverage of all coastline areas to intercept all incoming goods from China after they invaded Taiwan."

"Yeah, yeah, yeah—I remember now."

"Well, that meant taking our last operatives out of the farm belt, sir," said Cheshire. "We don't have anyone west of Omaha."

"Well, hell." Donner sighed and put on his jacket, "We'll just have to do it ourselves. Come on, let's go to JFK and commandeer us an airplane."

~ ~ ~

It was still very dark on the two-lane road. Shrini pulled off the highway at a brightly-lit truck stop with an ATM. She came back to the van with a very worried expression: her transaction had been refused. She opened her palmtop and waited for the system to boot up. When it finally did, she logged on to her Bank of India account and found her suspicions were unfortunately confirmed: her assets were frozen. She counted her remaining cash feverishly. There was enough for a couple of more days, but that was all. The likelihood of finding another Hindi-owned motel in this part of the country was remote—there were no listings on any of the Hindu-language sites she checked. She closed the palmtop despondently and decided to keep driving in hopes of making all the way to Carrouthers.

She was dog-tired and she knew it. She almost fell off the road a couple of times. Alarmed, she pulled off on nearest stretch of straight road and nudged Perry in the ribs. "C'mon, wake up! I can't drive any further."

"Lightweight!" said Donohue scornfully. He opened his eyes and looked around, "Where the fuck are we?"

"Miles away from anywhere. It doesn't matter. It's your turn to drive," She opened the door and stumbled over on numbed feet to the other side of the van.

Perry slid over to the driver' seat and yawned, "Oh hell... Not without some coffee and food first. I'm gonna stop at the first truckstop we can find."

Shrini didn't reply. She slammed the passenger door shut and closed her eyes.

Perry eased back onto the road. A few miles later, he saw a garishly-lit structure in the distance. As he got closer, he could see it was a truck stop done up as a huge teepee. He pulled into the gravel parking lot and switched off the ignition.

Shrini opened an eye and looked at him dubiously, "Are you sure you want to stop *here?*"

"What other choice do we have? I gotta get coffee." Donohue opened the door and got out.

She followed hesitantly, "This looks awfully *redneck.*"

Perry looked annoyed, "*Look*, we got no other choices. We have to avoid all metropolitan areas, 'coz the Donner gang will certainly have them staked out, along with any place with surveillance cameras.

She looked at the entrance, "How do you know this place *doesn't?* I better get my camera detector..."

"Trust me. One look inside and you'll know why. We'll be lucky if they got indoor plumbing..." He reached for the front door.

Country music was blaring out of the loudspeakers. "Jesus, It's loud enough to make your balls sweat," muttered Donohue.

All heads turned as they walked in. Shrini clutched Perry's shoulder in a death grip, "Oh my god, they got a stuffed Indian!" She pointed to the nearest booth, where an old chief in full warpaint and regalia stared at them vacantly, with a Blatz beer bottle placed clumsily in his lifeless hand. The skin around the hands was starting to crumble in spots.

"Eeee!" Shrini looked round in horror, "The whole place is filled with stuffed Indians!"

From the looks of the place, at least one whole tribe of Apaches had been sent to the taxidermist—they were now mostly posed in mid-attack, tomahawks, bows and arrows at the ready, encircling the dining area. Others were hanging on ropes from the ceiling in various poses. There was another Indian seated at the nearest booth on the other side.

Shrini judged from the facial expression that he had probably died on the toilet. The sign hung round his neck said, "Ask the Chief about our daily special!"

~ ~ ~

As Donohue struggled to balance the jumbo-size cups of coffee on the bag full of take-out cartons and hot coffee, Shrini dashed to the van and locked it.

"Hey! Let me in!" demanded Donohue. "My hands are burning!"

She glared at him, but unlocked the passenger door. "Make it quick—let's get out of here NOW!" She locked the doors again as soon as he got in.

"Gimme a break," grumbled Donohue, "My doggie bag's leaking and so is my coffee. Why can't you just let me eat it there?" He set the food down and put the cups in the holder.

"You're sick, sick, *sick*, Perry Donohue!" She gunned the motor and drove off in a hail of gravel. The van fishtailed viciously as it hit the road. Ten miles passed before she lifted off the gas pedal.

Perry looked over and studied her profile, "Are we calmed down now?"

"NO!" She still looked terrified, "Got any Valium?"

He looked at her pityingly, "You better let me drive."

Chapter 21

THE NEW YORK CYBERPOST
SECRET US GOVT AGENCY RAIDS NYPD!

Is nothing sacred? At high noon, big black vans descended on the Julliani Memorial Precinct and the Feds marched in, guns at the ready. Forty minutes later they marched out again with Chief Shabazz, confiscating cartloads of paper files and stacks of computer files.

Then they screeched off without comment.

Fact: the NYPD is in deep trouble. But for what?

~ ~ ~

Hayte's alarm beeped, then the radio switched on. He stirred just in time to hear, "Hello, hello, hello, out there in radioland! This is Harry Harnuke—and you're Totally Wired, this Friday morning April 15th on WNEW, New York, New York! And we're taking your calls on today's topic: Those Disgusting Bumbleflies! And now to our first caller—hello, you're talking to Harry Harnuke, what's your BEEF?

"Hi, my name's Janice and , ah… I just can't get over these awful flies, I mean—they're *everywhere*. I can't leave the apartment without them just *swarming* all over me. I guess I should be glad they don't *bite* and stuff, but…"

"Yeah, Janice, so *how* awful are they—come on, be *specific*!"

"Well… I have to wrap myself up like a mummy, with a diving mask, you know, from my high school scuba class 20 years ago—I'm using it now, just so I can see. And the *buzzing* is *horrible*—they fly into *every*thing, especially ears. They're *so* clumsy—it's like they're *totally* blind or

267

something—they fly into walls, trees, *people*, me of course..."

"Oh god, that really drives me nuts."

"Yeah! And it gets worse if they fly into your mouth—they're so BIG! I had one fly down my throat before I even knew it—the whole thing, Harry! It was DISGUSTING..."

Hayte hit the alarm button with expert swiftness. The morning traffic noises started coming through.

He sat up and yawned. He caught himself just before he started to scratch his crotch.

He was just clearing off the remains of breakfast when the doorbell rang. Hayte looked at his watch, then smiled when he realized what time it was.

He walked to the door, opened it with a big smile and stubbed his nose bouncing off a fencing mask, "Ow! What the hell?"

A familiar voice said, "Don't panic! It's just me, Richard—Nurse Condelee."

"Huh?" Dumbfounded, Hayte gawked at the figure in the mask for several moments. "What's with the get-up?" he said finally.

She took off the mask and undid her hair, "Sorry about the mask—it's the best way to fend off those terrible flies. They attack your eyes constantly. Haven't you been out lately?"

"No—but I did open the window once by mistake." He motioned for her to come in, "That's why the room smells like lilac. I hope the bug bomb killed them all."

"I hope so, too." She lifted up the bedspread. "I don't see any bodies..."

"I think I got 'em all. I had to vacuum, then scrub the whole damn carpet out." He shook his head, "Bet it's the first time that carpet's been cleaned in years..."

"I think you're right." She laughed and took off the fencing mask, "When you called, I was a little afraid to come here alone, especially at night. That's another good reason for the fencing mask..."

"So where's your sword?" Hayte smiled, "Seriously, it's OK around here. Nobody bothers you."

"That's good." She winked playfully, "Speaking of swords... ?"

~ ~ ~

All their clothes were scattered across the floor, and the bedspread was wadded up at the top of the bed frame. Both were still breathing hard.

"Oh, that was sooo goood..." Condelee lay with her head on his chest. She wiped the sweat off his brow. "I really shouldn't stay too long..."

"You have to go?" Hayte looked hurt.

She picked up her watch and glanced at it. "Well, I can stay a *little* longer."

He stared at the ceiling for a moment. "Can I ask you something?"

"Shoot." She pointed her index finger like a gun and mimed firing at him.

"What made you decide to specialize in genital trauma?"

"Well," she lay back on the pillow next to him, "the anti-HIV gene mod was a definite factor. What else?" She gnawed absently on a cuticle. "Mainly, I *like* my job. The smiles I get for doing a good day's work are *genuine*. And it's fun to have this much power over men..." She giggled and waggled his penis.

He ran his fingers through her short black hair, "I got another question."

She turned her face, "All right. But it depends what it is—I may not answer."

"Fair enough," said Hayte. He paused.

"Well, what is it?"

"Aw, forget it. It's not important."

"*What?*" She playfully tried to slap him, "*Out* with it! Now!"

He tried to grab her arm and missed, "No—ow! Stop! I'll say it!"

"Well, then say it!" She tweaked him on the ear.

He grinned wickedly and grabbed her wrists, "But *first*, I'm gonna tickle you!"

"Noooo! I'll scream!"

"All right, I'll be serious." He let go of her wrists and propped his head up on one elbow, "I asked you this before, and you said you have documented proof for every case, but do you get guys who, you know, fake an injury?"

She laughed out loud, "You really want to know?"

"Well, yeah, I do."

"I can't believe you!" she snickered, "You're serious?"

"Yeah, I'm serious!" said Hayte, a touch of mock irritation creeping into his tone.

She batted him lightly on the nose.

"Ow! That hurt!"

"You deserve it for asking a question like that!"

"So you're not gonna answer?"

She chewed on her cuticle. After a while, she turned her eyes back to him, "I'll be honest," she said slyly, "I *do* get *some* fakers... We girls swap stories sometimes."

"I knew it!" Hayte let out a laugh, "Like what?"

"I like it when you laugh—your whole chest just heaves," She lay her head on him.

"So what kind of things do they do—to fake an injury, I mean..."

"Oh, little razor cuts, scratches—I remember this one guy got clawed by a cat pretty bad. Another was a masochist performance artist, used to pinch his penis and scrotum with clothespins and twist it into all sorts of..."

He flinched and tried to curl into a fetal position, "Uh, maybe we should change the subject…"

"Now, stop that!" She pulled his legs apart and spread them back out. She ran her finger along the edge of his nose. "I like you, Richard."

Surprised, Hayte looked at her. "I like you too, Condelee."

She met his stare, "But I got to tell you something—you're kinda squeamish for a cop, if you don't mind me saying that."

He lay silently for several seconds. "…yeah, I guess. I wasn't like that when I was younger. But why should you care about a cop being squeamish?"

"You wanna know what *I* did when I was younger?"

"Yeah, sure."

"I worked my way through med school by doing ER at night. You don't know jading until you do ER after dark around here." She raised her head. "*Look* at me, Richard. What I do now is pure pleasure. Both for me and for you. ER detail was *hell*. I'll never forget the lightbulb craze…"

"The lightbulb craze?"

"Yeah. There was one summer where it seemed like every case I had was another busted lightbulb up the rectum—it was a big sex fad for both straights and gays that year. Mostly gays, though. And when the bulb burst…" She shuddered and her voice dropped almost to a whisper, "I had to watch them die, one by one, crying in the arms of lovers, family, fellow clergymen, you name it." She sat up and wiped her eyes. "I really have seen more death than the law should allow."

He reached for her.

She turned away and starting putting her bra back on, "I'm sorry, I shouldn't have talked so much…"

"That's alright, Condelee."

"No, it's *not* all right—you're the one who's supposed to be getting therapy, not me. It's just… Sometimes it just comes all pouring out, I'm sorry."

Hayte stroked her chin, "Do you have a steady partner, Condelee, someone you can talk to?"

She turned away and drew the covers up.

Hayte put his arms around her. "I'm sorry, I shouldn't have asked that."

"The answer is *no*," she said finally, "There's precious little companionship in this profession, Richard. Lots of sex—and the money is good, but there's precious little else."

"Altruism has its price, I guess…"

"You wanna know why? It's because men are too goddamned territorial!" She saw his hurt look. "I'm sorry, I didn't mean *you*, it's just…"

"It's OK," He reached for her hand. "It's OK."

She drew away and looked at him from the corner of her eye. "And what about you?"

"What about me?"

"When the therapy program stops, would you be willing to be just a friend? Can you handle that—or is possession a serious thing for you too?"

Hayte sat silently a few moments. "I *think* I could handle that..."

She buttoned her blouse, "Just remember one thing, Richard Hayte. You can have *me*, but you'll never win my heart. If you try, I'm *gone*. The hooker with the heart of gold is just a fairy tale. Do you understand that?"

"I never believed in fairy tales."

"I would like to believe that, Rich. I really mean that..."

"Condelee, you should think more about the future."

"What do you mean by that?"

"Think about where you'll be in ten, fifteen years' time."

"What are you getting at, exactly?"

"Uh... well, you won't always be *so* beautiful..."

Her look was piercing. She picked up her handbag. "Goodbye."

The door closed.

~ ~ ~

Saturday, April 16:

Hayte was still in a funk the next morning. He sat on the toilet, his hood pulled low over his head, with no motivation to get up. Suddenly, he heard pounding on his door. He grabbed his gun off the top of the toilet tank, yanked his orange sweatpants up and walked slowly on tip-toes to the door. It still hurt to walk, and he winced even more when he felt a warm trickle down his left leg. He resisted the impulse to check and make sure it wasn't blood.

The pounding grew more insistent.

He exhaled, then turned both deadbolts in a flash. He held the gun on his thigh with his right hand and yanked the door open with his left.

"DON'T SHOOT!" yelled Hudgins, holding up his hands frantically.

"Aw fuck, man—don't scare me like that!" Hayte sneezed and bent over double.

"Sorry mon," Hudgins' eyes were bulging, "Da Johhny B..."

"What?" said Hayte sharply.

"He—da Johhny, he struck again!"

"Why didn't you call me? Instead of scaring the shit out of me?"

Hudgins started walking down the hall, "Come wit' me, ya gonna see..."

Hayte sniffed the air, "What's that odor?"

Hudgin's dreadlocks bobbed, "Dat's wot Ah mean, mon. Yo know dis place gotta elevator?"

"What the hell are you talking about? I've never seen any elevators here..."

"Look here!" Hudgins tugged at what looked like the door to a broom closet, revealing a dilapidated service elevator. The odor was intense like charred flesh but also somehow chemical in nature. And *familiar*...

Hayte looked silently at the scorched interior and nodded. *Johnny was here.*

He reached inside and picked up a pair of charred gold-rimmed spectacles that lay in the corner. He turned them over in his hand. The style was unusual. He ran a mental checklist, trying to remember where he had last seen such a pair.

Then it hit him.

"Dr. Caramond..." he said under his breath, "he was here..."

"Is *still* there, mon. Ya can smell da flesh. How do ya know his name, mon?"

"I met him at Scott Bunch's funeral," said Hayte slowly. He let out a sigh and rubbed his eyes. "Caramond was Bunch's colleague at GeniTech."

"What was he doing *here*, mon?"

Richard exhaled slowly, "My mistake. I left this address on his voice mail, just in case he remembered anything useful. I was hoping he could testify against GeniTech about this clone plague."

"He was comin' ta see you?"

"Yes, I think so."

Hudgins looked up at Hayte. "Dat means *you* gotta move! Or da next Johnny 's gonna come a knockin."

"No it doesn't," said Richard irritably. "Caramond was the target, not me."

"Dey gonna put two an' two together, whoever's sending da Johnnys," said Hudgins emphatically. "You really gonna wait 'round to be blown up? Ya almost lost ya dick da first time, what's it gonna take ta convince ya, pardner?"

Hayte winced. "Did you really have to put it like *that*?"

~ ~ ~

Easter Sunday, April 17:

Shrini and Perry pulled up to the end of the long driveway. "We're here!" said Shrini, the exhaustion audible in her triumphant tone.

"About damned time..." grumbled Perry, squinting in the morning sun. He got out and staggered to the door. Shrini climbed out and wobbled in his wake.

Donohue was about to press the doorbell when the door opened.

"Jesus, you two look like a couple of mountain climbers above the Death Zone," said a middle-aged man in a plaid flannel shirt, "Come in, I was expecting you." He closed the door behind them and pointed to some stairs, "Here, you'd better go upstairs and lay down—I got a couple of guest beds."

He showed them their rooms. "The bathroom's over there, you'll have to share it. Now, get some rest—I want you both to be cognizant when you tape my testimony."

Donohue turned to Shrini. "Did we even bring a camcorder?"

Carrouthers interrupted, "Don't worry 'bout that—I got one all set up in the den. Now get some rest."

~ ~ ~

Night had fallen by the time Donohue and Shrini woke up.

Upon seeing Shrini on her way to the bathroom, Carrouthers called out from another room, "If you're hungry, which I assume you are, there's some instant dinner in the cupboard."

They went in the kitchen and rummaged around. Perry added water to some instant meatloaf. They devoured it in no time flat.

Carrouthers was watching the evening news in the living room. He switched off the TV when they came in. "Have a seat. I know you're Lt. Shrinithan, but who's your friend?" He looked inquiringly at Donohue.

"Captain Perry Donohue, NYPD." They shook hands.

He spoke with a soft Texas drawl, "Pleased to meet you, Captain. Looks like your home town's getting..."

"Can we get down to business?" interrupted Donohue, looking at the clock. "We need to get as much testimony as possible and hit the road ASAP."

"Sure," said Carrouthers, unperturbed. "The camcorder is over there. It's an old one, but it's all set up."

"Great." Perry went over and switched it on. As he fiddled with the focus and the lighting, Donohue looked Carrouthers over. At first glance, he looked like an ordinary fifty-year-old. Short, thin grey hair slicked back, heavy five o'clock shadow. About 5' 9", weight about 190, once muscular but becoming flabby around the gut and chin. But somehow, the man seemed different, and he smelled... strange. It was a musky, rather unpleasant odor, even though Carrouthers himself appeared to be quite clean and wore new clothes.

"So let's get started." Perry pushed the record button and turned the camera around. "This is Capt. Perry Donohue and Lt. Shrinithan of the New York Police Department, today is April 17, 2044." He swiveled the camera around again. "And your name, sir?"

"My name is Dr. Douglas C. "Deke" Carrouthers." He read out his driver's license and Social Security numbers. He cleared his throat, "I do hereby swear to give the whole truth, so help me God. I wish to give testimony regarding the disappearance and subsequent murder of my relative Zane Cheswick Lewis. She was a TV reporter at Virtual News Network, and her last known assignment was to cover the Phantoms robberies."

"Please clarify the term 'Phantoms'," said Shrini, off-camera.

"To my knowledge, they are a group of bank robbers currently at large in New York City. Zane was very excited to get the assignment."

Shrini said, "When did you last have contact with her?"

"On Monday, February 23, 2044, at 9:30 pm or so—she phoned me on the way to a meeting, she told me she'd just uncovered a hot lead on the case..."

Donohue broke in, "Did she say what the lead was?"

"Not specifically. She did say it pertained to the way the robbers were eluding capture after doing the heists."

"Really?" Perry shifted in his seat. "Did she mention anything more?"

Carrouthers shook his head, "No, unfortunately not."

"Did she mention who she was going to meet?" said Shrini.

"She did mention a Bernard Duncan of VBS. But she also said some of her bosses would be there as well and that it might lead to a promotion."

Perry glanced at his watch impatiently, "This is all rather vague. Can you give us something more substantial?"

"Yes. As it turns out, I know the identity of one of those Phantoms, I mean one of the robbers at the Chase Bank heist on Broadway."

Donohue raised an eyebrow and leaned forward. "And that individual *is?*"

"It's not an individual, Captain. It is a cloned humanoid."

"Really?" Perry raised his eyebrows.

"Code-named Johnny B, a cloned, single-purpose humanoid created as a joint project between the United States Government and my employer at the time, GeniTech." Upon seeing Perry's expression, he added, "If you want proof of the cloning program, Captain, you should check my testimony for the Senate. I have transcripts you can take with you."

Without waiting for an answer, he went to the bookshelves and pulled out a big binder.

"No, no, that's not necessary!" said Donohue. He let out a long sigh. "I don't think..."

Shrini nudged Perry in the ribs, "We'll take the transcripts anyway—we're going to need all the proof we can get."

Carrouthers handed the binder to her, "Here you go."

Shrini took it. "Thanks, we can definitely use this."

"*Great*, some more stuff to lug around," said Perry. He turned back to Carrouthers, "So you are saying GeniTech is behind the Phantoms and Ms. Lewis's murder?"

"Nope, not at all," Carrouthers calmly shook his head, "I have no idea how this particular Johnny got involved in a bank robbery ring. Johnny B was bred to be a suicide bomber, intended solely for the Middle East and the Indian subcontinent."

"*India?*" Now it was Shrini's turn to gape.

"Yes. He was designed to give terrorists a taste of their own medicine without needlessly sacrificing 'human' lives. I should point out that I was only peripherally involved in the development. Officially we were told that the project was for 'sports research' purposes—I bailed out when I got wind of the *real* aims. That's one of the reasons I'm in the Witness Protection

Program."

"How *did* you find out?" said Shrini.

"Well, to answer your specific question, one of my golfing buddies was an ex-Army Reserves explosives expert, worked in Utah at one of the remote R & D labs up there. He called me out of the blue, one day, very agitated. Seems he was part of a team working on a new quiet explosive. Shortly after they got to the testing phase, he started finding body parts on the testing grounds. Some were human, some were simian. He got real curious about *that*, so he figured out a way to watch the testing one night—he didn't say how. They let out a bunch of lab apes—big ones—in a field. They'd be running round like monkeys do at night, and then these small men came out together. Each of them picked an ape and they all went and chased their ape down and tackled it—this got Marty's attention, because normally monkeys are much stronger than men. Then these little guys would all pull at something on their belts and BOOM! Only there was no boom, just a kind of muffled pop and a flash of light. Hardly any smoke and not much smell either. Means it's probably something pyrophoric as hell."

"Pyro-what?" said Shrini.

"Pyrophoric—it means the chemical ignites or explodes spontaneously when exposed to air. Marty was real spooked by all of this. Really shocked me too, to be honest. A few days after he told me, he brought me back the remnants of a finger as proof, and I recognized my handiwork—a small diamond pattern on the fingernail. Every Johnny B has it."

Shrini scribbled more notes. "Do you still have the finger?"

"Naw, the Senate Committee took it away and never gave it back."

"Did the Senate Committee ever publish its findings?" asked Perry.

"No. I never found out why they didn't, though—I was too busy being relocated."

"What happened to Marty?"

"I lost touch with him when I entered the Witness Program. I sure hope he followed my advice to do the same."

"Can you describe this Johnny B?" said Shrini.

"Small, wiry, about 5'2" or 3". olive-skinned, medium-large nose, kinda aquiline but not prominent, brown eyes, spaced kinda close together, medium-thick lips, making him easy to disguise." Carrouthers took a drink of water, then continued, "According to what I found out later, he was designed to blend in at any street corner, anywhere in the Middle East. Marty told me the bugger could even pass for a woman in a veil, if need be."

At that, Shrini frowned and tapped the pointer on her knee, "Was the suicide bomber program ever implemented?"

"No, it hit a few snags. Mossad got wind of the plan and pressured the White House into dropping it." Carrouthers shook his head admiringly, "Three cheers for Mossad. It took a *lot* of balls to do that."

"Do you know why they were against the plan?" said Shrini.

Perry interrupted, "And how did this lead to a Johnny being in the Phantoms?"

"Something obviously went way wrong, some got loose…" Carrouthers shook his head in wonderment, "It never ceases to amaze me how our worst enemies are the ones we create ourselves. Extremism in the defense of liberty may not be a vice, but it sure ends up costing a lot…"

Shrini tapped Donohue on the shoulder, "Perry, what's that flashing light?"

Donohue got up and inspected the camcorder, "Oh crap—the tape's jammed!"

Carrouthers walked over, "Here, I'll get it." He opened the side and pulled out the cartridge. A long ribbon of tape spooled onto the floor. "Well, so much for that…" he said resignedly. He grabbed a pencil and started winding the capstans to get the tape back in the cartridge.

"How old is that thing?" said Shrini.

"It's ancient," said Carrouthers ruefully, "but it's never failed before." He got the rest of the tape spooled in. "You wanna try it again?"

"No," said Perry, "We'd better take what we've got."

"My palmtop can record video," volunteered Shrini, "We just need to hook it up to the camera on my cell phone." She fiddled with the tiny interface on the side. "What kind of port is this?"

It took 45 minutes of tweaking with incompatible software to get the palmtop to accept the video feed. "There!" said Perry, "We can start again. Where were we?"

"I don't remember. Too bad we didn't attempt to clone females." Carrouthers took a sip of coffee and grimaced. "This artificial coffee makes me wanna puke. I think I'll get something better." He reached for a bottle of scotch, "You want any?"

Donohue held up a hand, "No thanks."

Shrini also shook her head then stopped, "What do you mean, artificial coffee?"

"We ain't had real coffee beans in 20 years," said Carrouthers, "Fucking hole in the ozone wiped out 90 percent of the world's coffee plants about 20 years ago—that, and the big solar flares later, caused all the alkaloids in the plants to break down—you drink a cup of java made from the resulting beans, the hydroxyl ions in them would've reacted with the hydrochloric acid in your stomach, producing potassium chloride, which unfortunately is poison. I've had a lot of time to bone up on my chemistry out here in the middle of nowhere, it's a hobby of mine."

Shrini jotted down notes in her palm top, taking care not to disturb the video optic line, "So, how *did* you get started in all this?"

"Science is in my bloodline," Carrouthers laughed and swirled the ice in his scotch, "My dad helped invent Viagra."

Perry let out a laugh, "Oh *really*."

"*Oh yes*... really. I really used to think it was true, that bit about 'better living through chemistry.' And my dad went to his grave believing it. I can remember when he got home from work, he was still buzzing about the stuff he'd be working on in the research lab. After he'd have a few, I mean drinks, that is, he'd start rambling about this 'fountain of youth drug he'd discovered, how it would make his elderly male lab rats screw like mad—until they dropped dead. He said he didn't *dare* try it on rabbits."

Shrini made a face. "God. That doesn't bear thinking about..."

Carrouthers laughed again, "Would've been like setting off a thermonuclear population explosion, he told me. 'Imagine the streets littered with piles and piles of dead bunnies...' Dad always had a real creepy sense of humor. Anyway, he skipped rabbits and went straight on to monkey trials—but only after giving them all vasectomies. And the human trials came next—there were US Congressmen begging to participate, phoning him up and telling everything about their sex lives... I mean *everything*." He shook his head, "Back when I was young, I thought, now *there's* a line of work for me!" The smile faded off his face. "But my interest in reproductive cycles instead got me sent over to genetic manipulation... and then into cloning. It might've been OK if the Defense Department hadn't gotten interested. I don't like the way we're headed."

Shrini looked at him, "And where are we headed, if I might ask?"

"No telling, now that a few Johnnys have escaped."

"Well, why didn't the FBI or GeniTech just go and hunt them down?" said Donohue. "I know from personal experience that GeniTech is pretty good at exterminating."

"They probably tried," Carrouthers started chuckling, then stopped abruptly. "But *nobody* was expecting Johnny to have the capability *to reproduce*." He let the words sink in, then stared into the camera, "We weren't sure, at first, but then the sightings got way too numerous. There were sightings in Virginia and California on the same *day*, for Christsakes. And, according to everything I've heard, every time the FBI or ATP came in and tried to trap one, little Johnny got away."

"How do you know that?" said Shrini.

"The FBI had to testify in front of the secret Senate Committee hearings as well. I was allowed to watch the hearings on closed circuit TV."

"You were allowed to watch secret Senate testimony?" said Donohue.

"Yes. The head of the committee wanted me to see the full impact of what I had been part and party to. I came into the hearings as just another dumb little scientist and came out a different person altogether. That's really when the true horror of what we'd been doing actually sank in. We ended up creating the human housefly. Nobody knows how the hell the little bastard reproduces—but every time you turn around, another one pops up, like in those mug shots of the Phantoms—which nobody intended or anticipated."

Donohue looked skeptical, "This doesn't make sense. Wasn't human cloning banned years ago?"

"Oh *yeah*," laughed Carrouthers bitterly, "The government banned human—i.e., *homo sapiens* cloning. But the truth is, none of the government-sponsored programs for organ transplants, nerve regeneration, etc. *are homo sapiens*. You just go back—or forward—a few links in the evolutionary chain, and *presto*, no legal restrictions! We had carte blanche to do whatever we wanted. Those fundamentalist bozos are easy to fool if you know how."

Donohue suddenly noticed the time. He pointed anxiously at the wall clock, "Can we wrap this up? It's 3:30 a.m."

Carrouthers looked at him, "Why are in you in such a hurry? If you don't mind me saying this, you'd be a lot better off getting some rest and starting out tomorrow night..."

"No time," said Donohue, shaking his head, "We got the NPDi on our ass, big-time."

"The *NPDi*?" Carrouthers let out a roar, "Boy, I can tell you some tales about them! In this tri-state region, most of us in Witness Protection know each other. We even got a special Intranet file server in the old NORRAD Headquarters in Colorado. Hell, I bet there are 20,000 of us spread over this region, being protected *from* our own government, *by* our government. We trade stories all the time about the NPDi, because they're the ones who'd like to liquidate most of us. I got piles of files I can give you on them, like how they 'disappeared' a British News of the World reporter who found evidence Bin Laden died in dialysis clinic on the Virgin Islands 25 years ago—or how they covered up all the secret oil drilling in the Alaska Wildlife Preserve. Or, if you like dirt on individual politicians, I can give you records on DUI arrests of presidents, senators and congressmen, if you like." He stopped and looked at Perry with curiosity, "And how did *you* attract the NPDi's attentions, if I might ask?"

"It's a long story..." Donohue looked antsy. He got up and went to the window.

"Don't worry, you got time—the alarms would sound if anyone uninvited comes."

Perry turned back to Shrini, "Have we got enough hard drive space for all this?"

"It's OK, Perry. I'll compress everything as we go."

"All right," Donohue started relating the encounter in Baltimore airport. "...and after I escaped from the train wreck, I luckily ran into Shrini and we've been on the run ever since. Thanks to the fact that the NPDi appears to be running the Department of Homeland Security, we got every goddamn law enforcement agency in the country after us. It's a miracle we're here at all to say that."

"What did you say? The NPDi is part of Homeland Security?" Carrouthers looked at Perry like he was nuts, "Who the hell told you that?"

"*They* did—the guy who's running it, a cretin named Donner. They made me sit through countless virtual propaganda films that stressed that point—they even put me through reenactments of the Parkland Memorial and Eiffel Tower attacks."

Carrouthers let out a belly laugh, "Those guys are the most amazing bullshitters..." He walked over the sink and spat. He turned on the spigots to rinse it down the drain. "The NPDi started as a private security company for *us*."

Donohue almost choked on his coffee. "In *GeniTech?!*"

"No, not exactly. They were actually part of another biotech firm called KronJen, but when KronJen merged with Head AG to become Kron-Head AG, which in turn got swallowed up by Dildong-Cling-Peecham, and when *they* merged with Karposi-Hodgkins-USOL, KronJen was spun off and eventually sold to Dohdodyne, which then merged with... you guessed it, GeniTech."

"Then what gives them the authority to forcibly abduct cops?" said Donohue.

"The NPDi got government clearance because *we* had government clearance. But their original job at GeniTech was to eliminate any so-called dirty laundry before it leaked out to the press. They were so good at it Washington got interested."

"Wonderful, just wonderful," said Donohue, "but it still doesn't explain why they got after me for flying back from Europe with H. Ronald Chesney's cryogenically-preserved head. They were on my ass the minute my plane landed in Baltimore..."

"You went through the airport with *that* severed head?!" Carrouthers could barely conceal his glee, "Haw! You couldn't have picked a better way to attract their attention!"

"How's that?"

Carrouthers let out another guffaw that sounded like a death rattle, "Because Chesney *founded* GeniTech!"

"*What?*" said Donohue and Shrini in unison.

"Actually, it was a consortium of lawyers and politicians, but *he* was the head, er, mastermind."

"That explains the interface chip wired to his neck," said Donohue.

"I'm almost 100 percent sure he was uploaded," said Carrouthers, "There were all these rumors at Genitech that he was virtually still in charge and calling all the shots."

"Well, that resolves why they are so intent on getting it back," Donohue made a face, "But we never have figured out how his physical head ended up floating in a side canal in Venice."

"In Venice, *Italy?*"

Perry nodded.

Carrouthers thought for a moment. "Probably someone made off with the head and dumped it when things got too hot. But I can't tell you anything more than that."

"But nobody reported the head as stolen," protested Shrini.

Donohue shook his head. "The theft probably wasn't reported because no policeman in Europe's gonna give a flip about someone pinching the head of a former US VeePee that died 40 years ago."

Carrouthers shrugged, "It doesn't really matter now. I assume the NPDi has gotten their precious head back."

"Nope!" said Shrini.

"Ooh, boy, no wonder they're hot on your ass—you might want to think about cutting your losses and just giving it back. It can't be *that* valuable to you."

"There may be incriminating information in that upload chip in Chesney's neck, for all we know—and they have no way of knowing if we've checked that out," said Donohue gloomily, "And anyway, once you've been charged with receiving stolen goods, you can't expect to get away with just giving them back and saying you're sorry. Besides, they invested so much in my 'training'. The minute they see me, they'll grab my ass and slap another parole box on my ankle, and that will be that."

"Well, what were they training you for?" said Carrouthers.

"To stop drinking, obey orders, follow all those shitty rules of Violentology and feel guilty if I don't."

"I don't mean that—all fundamentalists preach the gospel of guilt. What practical function did they train you for? There had to be some reason why you were useful to them."

"Well, they did want me to capture Johnny Bs for them."

"Ha! So they're training cops to do their dirty work!" Carrouthers laughed until a fit of coughing overcame him. He doubled over and hacked into a handkerchief.

"Are you OK?" said Shrini.

Carrouthers fumbled with an inhaler and took several deep draws. "There, I'm better."

"You sure?" Donohue handed him a glass of water.

"Yeah. Thanks." Carrouthers downed the water in one gulp.

"Hey!" Shrini reached for the palmtop, "I just thought of something! You know a lot about the Johnny B project, right?"

"Well yeah, of course..." Carrouthers took another draw on the inhaler.

"My colleague and friend, Captain Richard Hayte was attacked by a Johnny B. It would sure help if you could try and clear up some strange details about the attack."

"Your friend—is he dead?"

"No, but he was badly hurt."

"I'll *bet*," said Carrouthers, putting the inhaler in his shirt pocket. "He's damned lucky to be alive. So what do you need clarified? I can't promise anything."

"Well, before the attack, his apartment was vandalized twice with some strange kind of graffiti that was also found at two murder sites he was investigating. I have the pictures on file in the palmtop."

"Sure, I'll take a look at 'em," said Carrouthers. "How big are the images?"

"They're super high-res, so we can blow them up really big," replied Shrini.

After some fiddling around with the software, Shrini was able to beam the digital photos on the wall. She pointed to each. "These are the shots we took of the inside of Captain Hayte's apartment after the first and second attempt at vandalism."

Carrouthers squinted at the images. "Yeah, I can explain these, all right. Those are notations of DNA strands, but why are they up on the wall like graffiti?" He paused for a moment. "You know... I think I got a handle on *why* your colleague was attacked. See that symbol over there, above the slashed couch?"

"Uh-huh..." said Shrini.

"Well, that refers to the genetic code, a special part of the Johnny B model. I bet he—or *they* put that up there because they think Captain— whaddya say his name was? They think your Captain is associated with the team of genetic engineers with GeniTech—in other words, *their* creators. That's really the only explanation for those symbols. They're meaningless to anyone else, that's why your colleague didn't know anything about what they meant. The symbols identify the particular DNA strand that we modified to eliminate the technical resemblance to homo sapiens. They're not only tagging him, the message here is also a kind of *taunt*..."

Shrini propped her head on one elbow. "Why do you say 'taunt'?"

"It's psychological, a way of making us the hunted instead of the hunter."

"I don't know," said Donohue, shaking his head, "Johnny can't be *that* intelligent. Intelligent people, or *creatures*, anyway, usually disobey stupid orders. Personally, I can't imagine anything stupider than being ordered to blow yourself up."

Carrouthers folded his hands together against his chin, "But these are robots, just made out of flesh and bone instead of metal. They were trained to blow themselves up and probably instructed to do the graffiti—just to add a dimension of terror before going in for the kill."

Shrini rubbed her eyes. "But that doesn't explain the Johnny you ID'ed as one of the Phantoms."

"You're right..." He drummed his fingers on the table, "But I bet that's one of the ones that escaped! It's probably the ones that *didn't* escape that are blowing themselves up." He poured himself another coffee, "If you want to leave GeniTech, and you know how the company really operates, you either end up like me, hiding out in the Federal Witness Program, in the middle of fucking nowhere..." he emptied a packet of artificial sweetener in the coffee cup, "or killed off like Scotty Bunch."

Shrini looked up, startled, "Wait a sec—you knew about Scott Bunch?"

"I still have sources inside," Carrouthers looked down, "That's all I'm going to say about that."

"Something doesn't add up," said Donohue. "I don't know *my* DNA. How do these Johnnys know theirs?"

"Someone taught 'em," Carrouthers said flatly. "Whoever is sending them out to blow up their quarry is also coaching them to make those helixes."

"Which means there must be a Johnny with *your* name on it," said Shrini, looking directly at Carrouthers.

"Right," Carrouthers made a face. "I probably signed my death warrant for the umpteenth time by talking to you both today. If they ever do catch up with me, it'll either be a Johnny, or the NPDi, 'coz anything else can't touch a Federal Witness."

"So why are you talking with us?" asked Donohue, "...*if* it's not too personal."

"It *is* personal." Carrouthers smiled faintly. "When I went before the Senate, I thought I was doing my country a big favor..." He made a face. "Instead, the senators at the hearing acted like I was some kind of contagious disease. Once the true nature of the project came out, the hearings disbanded, and I was shunted off to Witness Protection without another word."

"Couldn't you have gone to the press?"

"That's what I should've done, back then... but I didn't think of that until I was already out here in the middle of nowhere. And now, indirectly because of my work, poor Zanie gets snuffed." He shook his head. "But there's nothing I can do about that now. Everything's going to hell in a handbasket. I really should be too old to give a shit any more. Look at me. No sex, no booze, I'm on my third set of artificial ears..."

Donohue looked him over, "You don't look so old to me."

Carrouthers met his stare, "I'm one of GeniTech's anti-ageing experiments, that's *why*. You're looking at a 120-year-old man."

Shrini's mouth dropped open, "*What?*"

"You can look up the records yourself." Carrouthers took another swig of coffee, "Listen, I'm *tired* of being old, appearances aside. My skin's been bleached so many times for liver spots, I almost look like an albino when the morning sun catches me outside. There are too many things modern medicine *can't* cure. I've been wearing adult diapers for going on 20 years now. I can't even get into ogling cute nurses anymore." He aimed the reading lamp at his face, making the plastic lenses in his pupils flash red. "I don't get the young nurses any more—my bodily 'accidents' gross 'em out too much. And nobody ever tells you that when you get past one hundred, you begin to *smell* like death. I have to bathe every six hours to get rid of the smell—no deodorant works against it. Plus, my nerves are wearing out, the big ones in my spine. If a leg fell off, I'm not even sure I would feel it."

A look of horror crossed Shrini's face, "But how can you move, how can you walk?"

"*Implants.*" Carrouthers held an arm up to the light, "In every goddamn joint I got, there's a microchip and tiny glass fiber cables that correct my failing muscles and make me move the way I used to. Cartilage injections by the dozens to keep the bones grinding away. But they don't help me piss, shit or come—all that is beyond the reach of 'today's technology'—or so they keep telling me. Only a virtual upload would correct those problems..." he said bitterly, "by eliminating this goddamned body altogether."

"Have you thought about that?" asked Donohue. "Uploading yourself?"

"Ha! Are you kidding? With all the dirt I know? No chance. The only reason I'm still alive is because I'm their human guinea pig for all this cybernetic stuff." He sat down slowly, "But when my brain goes ga-ga, they'll be popping champagne corks in the GeniTech boardroom, and probably in Washington too, because that'll be one less whistleblower to worry about." He looked at his watch, "Well, I just took up another hour of your precious time with all that. You'd better get going."

"We can't just leave you here to be killed," said Shrini.

"Oh, I intend to fight back," said Carrouthers, "It doesn't matter what they send after me. I'll either shoot a few Johnnys down or nail a few of those NPDi fuckheads. *Every*body's armed to the teeth in these parts." He went to the window and looked out, "That your white van?"

"Yup," said Donohue. "We got a long drive ahead of us," he looked furtively at Shrini, "*...if* we can find some way to pay for fuel."

"Naw," said Carrouthers, "You can't go back in that thing—you've been ID'ed by the WHP by now, I guarantee it. The minute you hit the highway, you'll be taken in. Let me make some calls." He disappeared into the kitchen.

Fifteen minutes later, he reappeared, "It's all set—a couple of my buddies can fly you back with the parcels..."

"What kind of parcels?" asked Shrini.

"Postal service stuff," said Carrouthers. "You know, letters, packages, that kind of stuff..."

"All the way to New York?" said Donohue, "I thought the major airlines took over all that, so they could keep from going bankrupt."

"Oh, there's still room for the small entrepreneurs, especially round these parts," grinned Carrouthers wearily, "These boys even turn a profit, or so I'm told. They mostly do oddball stuff, mostly out-sourced. You two will fit right in. Listen up, there's a small airport just the other side of Cheyenne—you can avoid all the main roads and still get there in time to catch their next run if you go now. Just drive up to the main hangar and ask for Doug-Bob or Dilly-Bob..."

"Who?" said Shrini.

"Doug-Bob and Dilly-Bob. They're identical twins, kinda eccentric, but you'll like 'em, once you get used to their sense of humor..." Carrouthers glanced at the wall clock, "You'd better get going, they told me they'll be taking off in about ninety minutes' time."

~ ~ ~

Monday April 18, 5:30 am:

They pulled up to the hangar in a cloud of dust. Donohue stuck his head out the passenger window. "Hey" he said to a skinny man with an aquiline nose and a tangled shock of curly hair, "I'm looking for Doug-Bob..."

"That's *me*," said the young man, staring at Perry through very dark sunglasses, despite it still being half an hour before sunrise. "Who sent *yuh?*"

"Guy named Carrouthers, you know him? Said you could fly us to New York."

"We can fly yuh to *Jersey*," said Doug-Bob in a distinctive nasal rasp. "Yuh might have tuh hitchhike the rest of tuh way to New York." The man had a strange habit of drawing out the last word of every sentence, "If yuh're *coming*, you'd better get your things and *go*. My *bro's* warming up the *plane*."

Shrini quickly parked the van outside and they grabbed all their stuff. Donohue turned as she was locking up and said, "Hey, what're we gonna do about the van? We just can't leave it here!"

Shrini yelled back as the plane's engine roared to life nearby, "There's a car pick-up service..."

Dilly-Bob yelled from the plane, an ancient DC-3, "Hey, you all gonna stand around for *fun*? Maybe you ain't going nowhere, but we gotta *run!*"

Donohue muttered, "I can't believe that thing still can fly..." He hurled their bags through the open cargo door anyway.

They clambered on with difficulty as the plane taxied out to the runway. There were only two seats, one for each Zimmerman, and the back was stuffed full of cargo.

Perry and Shrini were forced to wedge their suitcases between some heavy mail bags and sit down behind the pilots' chairs, on the cold floor of the interior.

"Hang on, here we go," yelled Dilly-Bob. The plane bounced wildly from rut to rut as he gunned the twin engines.

Within a minute they were airborne.

~ ~ ~

Monday, 7:30 am:

The black van was parked outside the baggage claim terminal, waiting for them to emerge, its coppery-coated windows distorting their oncoming images like a funhouse mirror. "Where'd we get the van, boss?" said Browning admiringly. "I thought we didn't have anybody in the Mountain

284

states."

Donner grinned smugly. "We *don't*. I pulled a few strings with our friends in Utah..."

The side van door popped open. They got in with their bags, and the door slid shut with a 'whoosh'.

Cheshire's eyes widened when he saw the driver. He nudged Donner in the ribs, "Hey, boss!"

"What?" Donner glared at him.

"The *driver*," hissed Cheshire, gesturing furtively, "he's *black*."

~ ~ ~

Cheshire took the van to the top of the hill and parked it. He swiveled the seat and looked at the others in the back.

Donner focused the spy cam on a grey sandstone house in the distance. "Are we sure this is the right house?"

"I'm sure," said Browning. "There are only 20 houses in the whole county."

"This *has* to be the place, boss" said Cheshire. "Those tire tracks are still warm—look at the infrared readings."

"Good enough." Donner leaned back in the driver's seat and stretched his short legs. "Now, if the local yokels in the state highway patrol do their job for once, we'll nab Donohue and that Shrinithan bitch too." He turned and grinned at his henchmen, "But, first it's time for some fun..."

"OK, chief," said Cheshire, a smile creeping across his face. He picked up a baseball bat and shifted it from one hand to another.

"This place is miles away from anywhere" said Browning, who also was holding a Louisville Slugger. "No wonder we couldn't find this guy before."

"Easy, son..." said Donner, "we want to find out if he talked to them, first."

"You're sure he'll talk, sir?" said Cheshire, fiddling with his sunglasses nervously.

"We'll smash up his body gizmos one by one until he *does*," said Donner, his chubby face flush with excitement, "and we'll tape everything he says, before we finish him off. C'mon, let's roll. It's *hamburger* time..."

Browning started the engine. The van rumbled down the street and onto the long gravel driveway.

Chapter 22
THE NEW YORK CYBERPOST
THE MANHATTAN PROJECT II
Bumblefly Bomb to Detonate on Patriot Day!

Finally! All Greater NYC residents are being advised to stay in their homes all day Tuesday and not to open any windows because of the planned detonation of the "Bumblefly Bomb." The device, which is designed to kill only insects is set to be unleashed over the skies of Manhattan at approximately 10am, weather permitting – this despite long-standing Federal laws banning insecticides!

Rumor has it the raw materials for the so-called "Bumblefly Bomb" were purchased in Mexico, who never approved the ban.

City health officials defended the decision, saying the bug bomb was "absolutely necessary" to eliminate the plague and restore life to normal. Local business leaders concurred. "One more week of this paralysis could trigger a state-wide financial depression," said Tyrone Greenspan of the Chemical Bank.

Greenspan declined comment on reports the bumbleflies had entered the family mausoleum and devoured the body of his famous grandfather.

Monday, 3:30 pm:
Donner took the wheel badly shaken. He had just managed to drag Browning and Cheshire into the back of the van before the first sirens echoed through the valley. He knew Cheshire was dead because he'd seen the bullet from Carrouthers' rifle blow out the man's left eye. Browning was still breathing, but it didn't look good, not with an open head would like that.

Donner was himself uninjured, but it didn't look like it with all the bloodstains on his clothes and hands. He fought the urge to floor the accelerator, barely remembering to lift as the van went over the crown at the top of the ridge. Now he had to really concentrate as the road twisted downhill, otherwise the bodies in the back would slide everywhere.

The wind started blowing the smoke in his direction. Donner hoped fervently that Carrouthers' body was already aflame. He pulled over to let the first fire engine blast past in the opposite lane. It was normally against regulations to leave the scene of a shootout without first confronting the local cops and pulling rank on them, but with one agent already dead and one probably dying, Donner knew he had little choice.

That bastard Carrouthers…

How could someone so old shoot so goddamned good?

~ ~ ~

The plane steadied in the gale-force winds. Shrini looked ready to jump out of her skin. Seeking to distract her, Perry attempted to make conversation. He tapped Dilly-Bob on the shoulder, "Say, are you fellas related to anyone famous?"

"*Related?*" Dilly-Bob turned around like a shot, his eyes also hidden behind sunglasses, "Alleged*ly…*"

Doug-Bob muffled a giggle, "*Yessss…* our great-grandfather was Woody *Guthrie…*"

The plane shook horrifically as a big gust caught it.

"Oh …" Perry gamely tried again, "So you fly stuff for the US Postal Service?"

Their heads whirled around as one. "WHO told you *THAT?*"

Donohue was caught off-guard. "Uh… no one…"

"*Nobody* told you?" Dilly-Bob arched an eyebrow, "*Some*body must've told *yuh!* Ain't that right, Doug-*Baawwb?*"

"Damn *straight*," said Doug-Bob, peering at them disconcertingly through his Ray-Bans, "Them loose *lips* are gonna sink great big *ships…*"

Donohue began to get irritated, "Well, what *do* you fly?"

"You *name* it, we *freight* it," said Doug-Bob.

Dilly-Bob nodded, "As long as it's *portable*, our rates are *affordable.*"

"We specialize in Very… Strange… *Cargo*," said Doug Bob, staring at his passengers penetratingly. "Big hairy coconuts bound for Key *Largo…*"

"Odds and *Ends*," shrugged Dilly-Bob, "It all *depends…*"

"Horses for *courses*, stuff for *spies*," said Doug-Bob.

"Great gallon *drums* of multi-colored *dyes*," added Dilly-Bob.

Shrini interrupted, "Why are you flying so low? You just missed that power line!"

"Lady," said Doug-Bob, "I done told yuz, we're flying Very… Strange… *Cargo*."

"And that means *you*," said Dilly-Bob over his shoulder, "We're getting paid *double* to keep you outta *trouble.* We don't wanna show up on no radar *screen…*"

"We're allergic to cops, know what I *mean*?" added Doug-Bob. A thought occurred to him. "What do you folks *do*, anyway?"

"We're New York City poli..." blurted Perry without thinking. Shrini elbowed him in the ribs.

"COPS!" Their identical heads spun round. "We're flying with the Man!"

"Coppers! *Flatfoots!*" said Doug-Bob, "The *fuzz!*"

"The *heat!*" added Dilly-Bob, "You know what that *does...*"

"I'm in *distress!*" said Doug-Bob. "I'm in *shock!*"

"We might be *speeding*," said Dilly-Bob, "but I hope *not!*"

Right at that moment, a huge wave of turbulence caught the plane. Shrini looked out and saw the wings bending like rubber.

Dilly-Bob turned around and put his hand on his brother's shoulder, "Doug-Bob, I... I don't wanna say this, but this is the worst flight we've ever had ..."

Another gust shook through the plane, making panels on the fuselage vibrate crazily.

"No! No! *Noooooo...*" Doug-Bob put his head in his hands and moaned, "Is this the *end*?"

Shrini blanched. "YOU MEAN WE'RE GOING TO DIE?" She started hiccoughing violently.

Silence.

Dilly-Bob looked at his brother, who had gone back to steering the plane, "Did we say anything about *dying*?"

"Not *me*," said Doug-Bob, "Heck, *we* ain't even begun *trying*. Looks like we got someone too *sensitive* for *flying*." He held something out to Shrini, "Here, have an air-sickness *bag*, for your *nerves*."

Dilly Bob giggled, "Try not to spill it when you fill it, whenever the plane *swerves*."

Doug-Bob wiggled the plane's wings in jest, "You fill up *five*, we get a free plane wash..."

"...if we do *survive*," Dilly-Bob snickered once more.

"I don't think I ever want to fly again," whimpered Shrini, clinging to her seat.

Dilly-Bob looked over. "Hey, that could be the name of a good song! Please do correct me, if I am indeed wrong..." He looked in his flight bag and pulled out a harmonica.

Doug-Bob's face brightened, "Hey, I got an idea for a *game*! How many famous plane crash victims can you *name*?" A blast of ice crystals bounced off the ancient windscreen, almost causing the windshield wipers to snarl.

Dilly-Bob's eyes lit up, "Buddy Hol*ly*!"

"Otis Redding and Jim Cro-*chee*!" retorted Doug-Bob.

Dilly-Bob fired back, "Ricky Nelson... uh, Roberto Clemen-*tee*!"

The plane wobbled in another gust.

"Oh *yeah*? Amelia Earhart! John-John Kenne-*dee*!" snarled Doug-Bob.

Shrini grabbed a bag and barely got it open in time.

~ ~ ~

Hayte sat scratching his head. He kept turning Caramond's charred spectacles over in his hands. "I asked the desk clerk how Johnny B slipped past, but he had no idea. He said he just went to use the bathroom during the mid-afternoon lull, but otherwise, nobody matching that description was spotted coming in the lobby..."

"That's irrelevant," said Vaughn, "because Caramond came in the back way, probably because he knew he was being tailed. That's where the service elevator stops. I checked the access, and there's only one way to get to it. I bet Johnny slipped in the elevator just as the doors closed, and Bam! that was it for Dr. Caramond. Oh yeah, I almost forgot..." Vaughn reached for his palmtop, "We finally got some more dope on that Wettington woman case."

"Who?" Hayte looked perplexed.

"That woman blown to bits in that Goodwill. We finally got some follow-up on her. Unfortunately, it's not much. She lived alone, didn't socialize, just kept her TV going full blast at all hours when she was home. She was divorced, the husband got custody of the kids—all six. His last known address was in a Florida trailer park, but all attempts to reach him have been unsuccessful, so far. I doubt seriously that he's a suspect anyway, because there's no evidence of any contact between the two since the divorce."

"No known friends or associates?"

"Nope, she was totally anti-social, like half the people in Brooklyn. All her neighbors said she was famously ill-tempered, especially about the neighbors' kids. Here's the weird part—she spent all her time doing volunteer work when she did go out—mostly at the Goodwill where she bit the dust." Vaughn held out his hands. "And that's all. Nobody has any idea about who would want to kill her."

"Or have her killed. Great." Hayte drummed his fingers on the table, "Any possible link to Scott Bunch?"

Vaughn shook his head, "Nothing so far, unless he bought his clothes at that particular Goodwill."

"Dig deeper," said Hayte, "There *has* to be a connection somewhere, because Bunch was the reason *I* was attacked—there is no other possibility. I certainly don't buy *my* duds at Goodwill..." He paused and massaged his forehead. "Hey! Were there any ultraviolet helixes sprayed at the Goodwill scene?"

"Yup," said Vaughn, nodding, "Not identical, but definitely similar."

Hudgins, who had been sitting silently in the corner repairing a frayed dreadlock, looked up, "Have dey done da DNA analysis yet on de Goodwill?"

Vaughn scrolled down the report, "It says here the preliminary findings indicate two bodies were incinerated and vaporized in the blast."

"A blast without noise, right?" said Hayte.

"Yes..." said Vaughn, "That's what really bugs me about all this."

"Me, too." Hayte raised an eyebrow, "Have they compared those DNA samples with the ones I took from the Bunch murder site?"

Vaughn read to the bottom of the report. "There's nothing here about that. It's my guess that they haven't. What do you expect to find?"

"I don't know," admitted Hayte, "but there *has* to be a link, somewhere." He snapped his fingers, "Hey, what about the surveillance cameras?"

"The Goodwill had none," said Vaughn, "And the ones around Bunch's apartment complex were just dummy cameras or weren't being recorded that night. I checked the city ordinances to see if the landlord was negligent, but there's nothing in the law about cameras *having to* be switched on and recording, only that you got to have them for apartment houses for more than 12 occupants. Which reminds me, we need a court order to get the footage from the ones around *your* building."

"It's unlikely those were being monitored either," said Hayte, shaking his head. "The elevator's always broken, so chances are almost nil that the cameras were operational. But, really, the only thing we would probably find out is how Johnny B entered the building. We still wouldn't know who sent him or why."

"Wonderful..." said Vaughn. "So we're going nowhere fast."

~ ~ ~

Monday, 6:30 pm:

Donner had time for a fresh change of clothes and a hasty shave. But the dark circles under his eyes betrayed his frayed nerves. He had barely managed to find a place to dump his bloodied clothes and get to the airport on time.

It was only after the plane had boarded and taxied out that airport security noticed the trail of blood-stained sandal prints leading through the boarding gate.

His mobile began ringing as the airliner took off. He immediately pulled it out, unfolded and put it to his ear. "Donner here,"

From her pull-down seat across the aisle, a stewardess called out, "Sir, you can't phone during takeoff..."

"Sure I can!" barked Donner, cupping his hand over the mouthpiece, "Whattya got?"

"Agent Buschmeier here. We've been tailing that toxicology guy, Dietrich, and he's been making a lot of phone calls from pay phones. We figure he's hiding something."

"Bingo!" said Donner, his eyes lighting up, "Get working on tapping the pay phone server."

Several passengers turned and looked at Donner.

Buschmeier said, "We're working on it right now, boss."

"Who's *we*?" said Donner sharply.

"Agents Lincoln and Marks are with me. We've been watching Dietrich all day. I'm outside his workplace right now and—wait a sec, he's leaving! I gotta grab my fly mask—I'll keep you posted, boss!" The line went dead.

~ ~ ~

Buschmeier shouted to Agents Lincoln and Marks as he ran back in the room, "Hey—he's leaving! Has he got anything suspicious?"

"Just a second!" Marks fiddled with the camera, "Yeah! He's carrying something big!"

Buschmeier hovered over the camera, "What—big enough to carry a head?"

Marks zoomed in, "Uh-huh—it's a large kind of container, looks like it's empty from the way he's holding it."

Buschmeier slapped him on the back. "That's our cue! Let's roll!"

"Just one more second..." Marks tracked Dietrich down the street, "Looks like he's heading to the subway!"

Buschmeier yelled, "Grab your fly masks and let's go!"

"With the van?" yelled Lincoln.

"No time—let's tail him on foot!"

Lincoln grabbed Buschmeier by the arm, "How do you know it's Dietrich?"

"I saw him wearing that coat this morning," said Buschmeier, "and his gas mask don't fit right because he wears glasses under it."

Instantly the room was a beehive of activity. The agents grabbed their fly masks and goggles and scrambled out the door. "Just keep your head down!" yelled Buschmeier through his mask.

The buzzing was everywhere. Lincoln lagged behind because he kept trying in vain to brush the bumbleflies off his goggles, which made the smearing worse.

Half a block ahead, Dietrich disappeared around the corner. The three NPDi men followed, ten yards apart, on opposite sides of the street.

Dietrich looked down, hesitated for a moment, then took the stairs slowly down to the subway.

Buschmeier made it to the stairs and discovered why Dietrich was going so slowly. The huge flies were teeming all over the steps. Stepping on them would cause a smeary mess that could send him tumbling. Buschmeier took a tentative first step and felt the flies squish under his sandals. It was like following footprints in blue-black snow that just happened to be *alive*. He only just managed to avoid slipping on the goo and falling down a couple of times. He looked back and saw Lincoln and Marks were in similar difficulties.

On the platform, the problem was less acute, and Buschmeier could even see Dietrich clearly ahead of him. The train pulled up. He boarded the same subway wagon as Dietrich, with Lincoln taking the car ahead and Marks the wagon behind. Everyone on the train was wearing some kind of gas mask, many covered in duct tape.

The train snaked its way uptown. At the East 96th Street stop, Dietrich got out. He went down several streets and into an alleyway, seemingly oblivious to his tails.

Buschmeier held up a hand to stop the others. "That's the back way into Mount Sinai hospital! I'll stay here, Marks, you take the front—Lincoln, you take the ER. It's time to break radio silence, so use your headsets! C'mon, let's go!" They scattered, leaving Buschmeier to pace the alleyway.

After about fifteen minutes, Lincoln radioed in. "He's coming out, boss! The box looks heavy now, and he's heading toward the ambulances!"

"Shit!" Buschmeier radioed Marks, "He's got the head!! Marks, go to ER on the double—and HAIL A CAB!"

Marks came on. "Boss, no cabs are running until the bumblefly epidemic goes away—it kills the motors..."

Buschmeier thought furiously. He keyed his mike again. "Lincoln—you gotta steal an ambulance!"

"What?"

"You heard me—GO STEAL AN AMBULANCE! They're the only vehicles with anti-fly mesh on 'em! *Don't* argue—I'll meet you at the ambulance bay!"

Buschmeier took off running back to the street. One Birkenstock came off as he skittered around the corner. He came up, huffing and puffing, his mask steaming up, just in time to see an ambulance pulling out slowly.

He thought he caught a glimpse of Dietrich in the passenger seat, but he couldn't be sure. He started running to the other ambulance, desperately hoping to find his men.

Another ambulance pulled out. Buschmeier limped toward it on his one sandal, hoping against hope. He reached out and grabbed the passenger door handle as the ambulance went past.

The door opened, sending Buschmeier swinging crazily with it. Gloved hands reached out and pulled him in. "There's a seat in the back, boss! Buckle up!" yelled Marks from behind the wheel.

Lincoln yelled, "Shit! I think he's seen us!" Marks floored the gas pedal, sending Buschmeier tumbling into the back.

~ ~ ~

Donner folded up the phone, just in time to see a man in a uniform coming down the aisle towards him.

"I'm Air Marshal Felding. What seems to be the problem?"

"No problem," said Donner, with a faint smirk.

"He was telephoning during takeoff," said the stewardess, "There are several witnesses."

"Sir, that's against regulations," said Felding, "Give me your phone."

"*No.*"

Felding's tone grew sharper. "I said, give me your..."

"I heard you the first time," said Donner. With exaggerated motions he put the cell phone in his inside jacket pocket. "The answer is still *no.*" He saw Felding taking out a pad.

"Go ahead and report me," said Donner evenly, "It won't make any difference."

"That's a strange attitude," Felding started writing. "What's your name sir?"

"Donner, Agent Donner of the National Protection Directive. I wouldn't bother writing anything, if I were you." He smiled smugly, "It'll all just go in the shredder."

It was then that Felding saw the bloodstains Donner had tracked down the aisle. He reached for his headset, "I think I'd better call air control,"

~ ~ ~

"Look—he's stopping!" yelled Lincoln.

Marks screeched to a stop just as Dietrich ran into a loading area in back of Beth Israel Hospital. Marks pulled the ambulance onto the sidewalk, and they got out. The bumbleflies continued to swarm everywhere, making it difficult to see properly.

They charged towards the loading dock, guns drawn. "HALT!" yelled Buschmeier through his mask. Gun shells exploded around Dietrich's feet. Startled, he whirled around. Marks and Lincoln stuck their gun muzzles between Dietrich's face and gas mask, breaking the seal. Buschmeier yanked the mask off, taking Dietrich's glasses with it.

"You're under arrest!" said Marks.

Dietrich opened his mouth and instantly regretted it. "Under what charge?" he spluttered, between spitting out bits of bumblefly.

"Transporting stolen property," said Lincoln.

"It's not (phut) stolen," said Dietrich between gritted teeth. He had to blink furiously to keep the flies out of his eyes, "The head belonged to a homeless woman..."

"What?!" barked Buschmeier, "Agent Marks! Open the thing!"

Marks looked at him. "But boss, it's deep-frozen..."

Buschmeier thundered, "I don't care! OPEN IT!"

Lincoln kept his gun in Dietrich's face while Marks fumbled with the heavy lid.

"What's the problem—hurry up!" barked Buschmeier.

"There's a vacuum inside, holding it shut!" Marks yelled back.

Buschmeier pushed Marks off and yanked the container lid off, oblivious to the liquid nitrogen seeping out. Inside, a metal box was visible. He upended the container and pried the hasps on the metal box open with the butt of his gun and stood over it to get leverage to split the two halves apart.

He yanked off the plastic covering and started swearing when he saw the long hair and the remains of a woman's face.

Dietrich said out of the side of his mouth, "I believe her name was Noelle..."

Flies swarmed over the exposed head and froze instantly to it—and to Buschmeier's thoroughly frostbitten fingers. He let out another loud series of expletives, but his hands remained glued to the head. He danced around in a fit of agony, hands stuck, like he was engaged in some sort of bizarre wedding dance with the dead woman's head, under a veil of bumbleblies.

Lincoln shoved the gun barrel up Dietrich's nose, "Where's Chesney's head?"

The pain kept Dietrich from laughing out loud, "Maybe... you... should... ask... Chesney."

"You're lucky I don't blow your face off, dildo-face," snarled Lincoln, grabbing Dietrich in a headlock. "Now, *where* is he?"

"Let go of *my* head, and I'll *tell* you."

Lincoln slowly loosened his grip. Dietrich stood back up and brushed the flies from his face.

"I was just about to tell you," said Dietrich, putting a hand over his mouth, "The Virtual Vice-President exhibit opens next week..."

"The virtual *what* exhibit?" demanded Buschmeier, rubbing his hands in agony.

"I wouldn't do that if I were you," said Dietrich, pointing to Buschmeier's hands, "Your skin will come right off and get infected with fly goo. As I was saying, go to the Bodily Universes exhibit at the MOMA."

"Bodily Universes?!" Lincoln and Marks looked at Buschmeier, "What do we do now?"

Buschmeier grabbed Dietrich's ear and twisted it. "So we go to Bodily Universes, then."

~ ~ ~

11:59 am, Eastern Daylight time:
At the remote terminal at the back of the massive airport, the van door opened and Donner got in. "What've you got for me, Agent Beria?"

An unpleasant grin creased Beria's pocked features, "Some excess baggage, boss." He jerked a meaty thumb towards the back. The air marshal and the stewardess lay tied up on the floor. The air marshal's face was bloody. The stewardess's mouth was open and drooling. Their pupils were like pinpoints, despite the darkened windows.

"Good." Donner nodded with satisfaction, "Hopefully we'll soon have a couple more to keep them company."

The van sped off and headed into Manhattan.

~ ~ ~

Tuesday, April 19– Patriot Day, 7:00 am:

The small plane took off again behind them. A light rain was falling. Shrini sat down on a nearby bench. "I'm so thankful to be on solid ground, I could kneel down and kiss it."

"Better not," said Donohue wryly. "We're in Jersey, I *think*…" He looked around at the barren field. "Man, this is in the middle of nowhere. Any idea where the nearest town is? I forgot to ask."

Shrini pointed across the field. "There's an access road. Let's see where it goes."

Donohue shrugged and hoisted their bags.

Forty-five minutes later, they came to a divided highway that led to what looked to be a small town ahead. They trudged along the meager shoulder towards the city limits sign.

Burnt Torch, New Jersey, pop. 1020.

They came to a row of tacky motels. Shrini stared longingly at them. "Perry, I'm exhausted."

"Me, too." Donohue set the bags down and brushed the damp hair out of his eyes. "But I don't see any vacancy signs—I just remembered today's Patriot Day."

Shrini shielded her palmtop against the drizzle, "We can't try them anyway. We'd have to show a driving license—the NPDi would track us down instantly."

"So none of these are run by expats from India?"

"No," she closed the palmtop and shook her head, "The nearest one on the Nehru Net is 20 miles away."

He leaned against a phone pole, "What about calling Dietrich?"

She grabbed her bag and fished out her mobile. She shook her head grimly, "No luck. The number's been disconnected. I can't even get voice mail."

Perry glanced across the road and saw a group of homeless men. "I wonder if *they* know something…" He crossed the road and headed towards them.

~ ~ ~

Donohue lay down on the smelly cot and fell asleep immediately.

Across the hall in the women's wing, Shrini was having a more difficult time, despite having the whole section to herself. The stench of urine and body odor from the previous occupants was more than she could bear. She tried using the starched white sheet as a filter over her mouth and nose, but the sheet kept slipping off just as she drifted off to sleep.

She gave up and went to open a window. She struggled to get it open. Finally, she wedged her hands between the windowsill and the hasp and yanked up. The window yielded with a big groan.

Startled, she heard explosions outside.

She stuck her head out and saw the volunteer clerk standing below her. "Ah, you got that open, did you? Bet you're the first one in ten years to manage that!" A fresh series of pops echoed off the brick building 20 yards away.

Shrini whipped her head around, "What's that noise?"

She pointed to the sky. "Fireworks, honey. Didn't you know it's Patriot Day?"

"Oh…" Shrini looked up just in time to see a huge multi-colored rocket explode and fill the sky.

"Guess that's the last of 'em," said the clerk. She squinted up at Shrini. "You're alone up there, right?"

"Yes."

"You picked a good night to come. It's a warm night. All our regulars are probably down by the lake, watching the fireworks and drinking 'till they drop."

"I think I'll leave the window open, if that's OK."

"Sure, honey," The desk clerk started to amble off, "Hope you don't mind a few 'skeeters, though…"

She looked at the woman uncomprehendingly, "What are skeeters?"

The clerk laughed, "Mosquitoes, honey. Good night!"

Shrini groaned to herself and trudged back to her cot.

~ ~ ~

There was a loud knock on Hayte's door. He stared through the peephole and was startled to see Stanley Bialystok.

He opened the door. "Stan!"

"Hi…" Stanley averted his eyes, as if embarrassed.

"Don't just stand there—come in!" said Hayte. He closed the door and offered Stanley a chair. "How did you find me?"

"Uh…" Stanley stared at his shoes. "Well, I… kinda followed that nurse of yours… I saw her in the hallway a couple of weeks ago, leaving your place, back when you were still staying there and stuff, I passed her when I was bringing in groceries and saw the name tag on her uniform, so… I went and found out what hospital she worked at."

Hayte let out a laugh. "You're a regular detective, you are…"

"Well," Stanley shifted his bulk self-consciously, making the chair creak. "I got real lucky… You remember Verona? We ain't been filming much lately, so I got her to track your nurse for a couple of days. This was the only hotel she stopped off at, so I kinda figgered you were here."

"Well, I *am* impressed." Rich raised an eyebrow, "So where is Verona?"

"She's off working for somebody else. Business has been kind of slow lately. I'm waiting for a big deal to come through."

"Where *do* you get your money, Stan? I saw your get-up and everything... that doesn't come cheap, those surround sound sequencers and stuff. You can't be earning that much from rental royalties, can you?"

"You're right, I don't," Bialystok absently tried to bore his toe through the threadbare carpet, "I got outside help. Most of my backers come from Hollywood. You know, the rat and the rabbit..."

Puzzled, Hayte looked at him, "The rat and the rabbit?"

Stanley tore a piece of foolscap off Hayte's notepad and sketched two cartoon characters. "You know, *these...*"

Hayte's eyes widened, "You *can't* be serious..."

"I *am* serious!" Stanley shook his head, "Studio heads are sick fucks—especially the ones who cater to children. I dunno what it is, but those are the ones who consistently fork over the big bucks to back all my fetish flicks, every fuckin' time." He waved a pudgy index finger, "But I'll tell ya something—I draw the line at any kind-a kiddie porn. I'd rather chop my own wanger off than do that."

Too late, he noticed Hayte's pained expression, "Oh, *sorry*—poor choice of words..."

"Forget it," Rich held up his hand, "It's just something I gotta live with."

An oppressive silence descended.

Hayte watched Stanley fidget and gnaw on a stray cuticle, "Why did you come see me, Stan? I know you got something else on your mind. Nobody takes the time and trouble to track down a cop unless there's something wrong."

Stanley flashed a slightly chagrined smile, "It's nothing really. I just wanted somebody to talk to."

Something about his answer left Richard unconvinced, "I don't buy that. You didn't come visit me in the hospital, Stan."

"I'm really sorry about that—I meant to, really."

"Sure you did..." A trace of irritation crept into Rich's voice, "But that doesn't explain all the time and trouble you took tracking me down. What is it, Stan?"

Bialystok continued to squirm in his seat, "It's just that I'm between jobs, really. But the run of bad luck has got to stop sometime."

Something about Stanley's demeanor made Richard even more suspicious, "That ain't all that's on your mind. Come on, spill it."

Stanley got up and started pacing. Hayte patiently let the silence drag out.

Finally Stan stopped and turned. "I know you and that nurse ... well, I know about that kind of therapy she specializes in..."

"Uh-huh..." Hayte cracked his knuckles noisily. "What are you getting at, exactly?"

"It means I heard about you two bumpin the uglies."

"No, not..." said Hayte. He cut himself off, angry for saying so much.

"Not *yet*! Uh-huh—that's *good*!" Stan's voice took on a note of triumph.

"What's good?" said Hayte sharply.

Stanley arched his eyebrows suggestively. "Remember, you owe me a favor for putting your dick on ice in the first place."

"It wasn't completely severed and you know it!" snapped Hayte. A light went on in his mind. "What—you want to film us... in action?"

"Bingo!" Stanley clapped his hands excitedly. "Don't answer yet—just *think* about it!"

"So that's it—the whole Frankenpenis thing," Hayte looked away in disgust, "You want to turn me into a freak porn star like whatshisname? that Bobbitt guy? My dad used to talk about that..."

"No... I mean, not really... I'd like to make a documentary of your therapy, you know, chart the progress—no, don't answer now, just think about it!"

"No."

"Don't answer me yet—just let it..."

"*No.*"

"Come on, *think* about it!" Stanley took a bottle of orange juice out of his bag and popped the top. He set the bottle down, empty, "Why not *do it* on camera for once? *Think* about it—it could be fun."

Hayte rolled his eyes, "Why are you bothering, Stan? Porn actors must be a dime a dozen! You just want some kind of freak show."

"No, that's not it at all! You got me all wrong!"

Hayte got directly in Stanley's face, "*Do* I, Stan?"

Stanley met his stare, "Yes, you *do.* " He chewed on his lower lip in frustration. "Damn it all! I screwed up the whole thing!" He got up suddenly and slammed his fist into the wall. "Ouch! Goddamnit!!" He bent over double, clutching his hand.

Hayte looked at him like he was mad, "What is so god-damned important about filming me screwing?" he said quietly.

"Sorry, I got overexcited..." Stanley slowly wiggled his fingers, "I don't think anything's broken..." He resumed his pacing.

Hayte watched him and shook his head. "*What is your deal*, man?"

Stan stopped again and pointed at himself, "Look, I got a confession to make, I...I'm artistically frustrated."

"Artistically frustrated, Stan? You direct porno flicks!"

"They're not *just* porno, OK? There's a hell of a lot of hard work that goes into making them! *Any* idiot can film somebody having sex—but it takes a *pro* to make it *erotic*!"

"So where's the frustration?"

He finally looked Rich in the eyes, "I've never gotten *the real thing* in any of my movies."

"What is this 'real thing' you want, Stan?"

"*Love.*"

Hayte snorted derisively, "Say *what?*"

"You heard me. I've never shot a hardcore sex scene where the people are actually *in love*—it would be something so... *different.*"

Richard stood up to his full height and looked down at him, "Well, you *won't* get that here. She's a *professional*, Stanley. Nothing else."

"Oh yeah? Wake up, Richard! She's *hooked* on you—I seen her leaving your apartment with that special kind of smile..."

Hayte shook his head emphatically, "No dice, Stan. Once my therapy's over, she'll be *gone.*"

"You're *wrong*, Rich—she was even humming to herself!"

Rich started getting annoyed, "Look. The most we could ever be is friends who *fuck*. That's *all*. And the answer is NO. You wanna make a *breakthrough* in porn, Stan? Go film *ugly* people having sex."

The doorbell chimed before Stan could respond again.

Hayte went to peephole and saw it was Dietrich. He quickly opened the door, "Hi Paul, thanks for coming. Oh, *nice* haircut..."

"Thanks," Dietrich came in with a freshly-shaved head. "And thanks again for letting me house-sit for you. You got the keys?"

"Here you are," Hayte handed them over. "You look like you're in a hurry."

"I am. I got no place to stay at the moment."

"Why not? You get kicked out of your own place?"

"Not exactly. The NPDi chased me all the way to Beth Israel Hospital. They wanted the severed head. If I go back to my place, there's bound to be trouble. So here I am."

Hayte laughed in spite of himself, "Those NPDi guys never cease to amaze me..." He looked curiously at Dietrich, "Well, did they get what they came for?"

"Nope!" said Dietrich triumphantly, "but I got marched all the way to the Museum of Modern Art at gunpoint..."

"Are they still tailing you?" Hayte peered down the hallway and closed the door.

"No, I left them gawking at the Bodily Universes exhibit, looking like little boys whose ball just rolled down the sewer. I snuck out and made a beeline for the nearest barbershop." He rubbed his bald pate, "Not only did it get them off my tail, it also was the only way to get those bumbleflies out of my hair." He stared intently at Hayte, "Hey! How do you keep them out of your 'fro?"

"I got these," Hayte held up a plastic hair net and a fencing mask, "Looks weird as hell when I go walking out on the street, but it works all right."

Dietrich noticed Stanley in the corner, still nursing his wounded paw, "And who's this?"

"Ah! This is Stanley Bialystok, adult entertainment director *par excellence,"* grinned Hayte sardonically. "Stan, meet Paul Dietrich, our resident toxicologist and stand-in coroner…"

"Oh." Stan took Dietrich's proffered hand reluctantly, "Pleased to meet ya."

"Stanley lives in the same building as me, so he can show you the way there," Hayte ushered them both to the door. "Now, if you two will excuse me, I've got two days left to cram before my bar exam. I'm sure you two have a lot you can talk about!" He closed the door behind them.

As they headed toward the stairs, Dietrich looked at Stanley with curiosity. "So… what's it like to work with *live* bodies?"

~ ~ ~

Wednesday, April 20, 5:30 am:

They sat in a Waffle House on the edge of town. Shrini wobbled, then steadied herself on the stool.

Donohue looked over, "You OK?"

She had deep circles under her eyes. "Not really. Once this sugar buzz wears off, I'm going to collapse."

"Me too. I know it won't last long…" Perry sipped his coffee.

"We gotta get out of here, Perry. I can't take another night in the homeless shelter—the stench and the mosquitoes kept me awake all night."

"I slept OK," said Donohue, "I was too tired to notice. But now I got all these flea bites." He reached for his wallet. "We only got 30 bucks left. I don't know how we're gonna get back…"

A faint but familiar sound reached their ears. Shrini got up and ran out the front door.

She came rushing back and flagged down the waitress. "Excuse me, Miss? Is there a commuter train stop in this town?"

~ ~ ~

An hour later, they were sitting in the second class compartment, on the first train bound for Grand Central Station.

Shrini nudged Donohue, who was just about to doze off, "How come we didn't see that before?"

"Because yesterday was Patriot Day," grumbled Donohue, "No trains were running. I thought you needed to sleep."

"I do…" said Shrini, "but after we get back, where can we go? We can't go back to my apartment."

Donohue let out a long sigh, "Well, let me think…" He stared out the window for a moment. "I wonder if Rich is out of the hospital?"

Her face brightened "That's a possibility—we could go over to his place and see if he's there."

"That might be a problem." Perry's smile faded, "I don't know his new address. Do you?"

"No."

"Do you have his number programmed in your cell phone?"

"Nope. This is Todd's phone, remember?" She pulled it out, "See?"

"Didn't you program *anybody's* number in it?"

Shrini started to open her mouth, then thought better of it. She switched the tiny phone on and started scrolling down the menu, "Ah! Yes, I did! I got Clint's number!"

"You're not gonna call him now—it's 6:30 am!"

"What other choice do we have?" said Shrini, "Besides, his answering machine will probably pick up..."

"Hey! That gives me an idea! Does he know any television people?"

"Let's try!" She selected the number, "What do you want to ask?"

"I'll write it down..." He started scribbling a list of questions.

~ ~ ~

Miss Clint was sitting on sitting on the sofa eating breakfast. He had just put on his oversized slippers shaped like cans of Campbell chunky crawdad soup when the phone rang.

He picked up on the first ring. "Hello, hello, *hell*-oh!"

"Miss C—it's me, Shrini! I can't believe you picked the phone up!"

"I can't believe it either, but I got the early shift all this week, thanks to that *schlemiel* Shabazz... How are you, girl—we heard you were out sick..."

"Not sick—just a little emergency," Shrini looked over at Perry, then shifted the phone to her other ear, "but that's over now, I'll be back to work in a couple of days. Listen, can you do me a big favor?"

"Sure, ditty, what's the deal?"

"Do you know Rich's new address?"

"Oh sure, girl! I got everybody's! You want it now? Of course you do!" He read it out to her. She scribbled it down on the margins of Perry's list.

"Anything else, girl? I know this ain't a social call, not at this hour."

"Yes." She held up the list and squinted at it, "Do you know any television people? We—I need an eyewitness account or two from one of the TV crews who covered the last Phantoms robbery..."

"No problem at all! I know the G & I teams at VNN, NBC, E! and MurdochVision real well..."

"G & I? What's that?"

"Gossip and Innuendo, girl—it's industry talk for the Entertainment divisions." Miss C. popped another bon-bon in his mouth and continued talking. "They always talk about news anchorpersons behind their backs—what egomaniacs they are, the shit that's in their contracts, who's shagging who, and so on... Give me three days, ditty, I'll have enough news to fill a New York City phone book!"

"Thanks so much, Miss C! Bye!" She folded up the phone, "He says to give him three days."

"Great!"

Shrini tapped the waterproof bag full of Carrouthers' files, "In the meantime, we need to get a hearing with the grand jury."

"I sure wish Rich could handle that—I *hate* Grand Jury stuff..." Donohue looked out the window, "And we got to set aside time to find out who murdered Carrouthers' granddaughter..." His voice trailed off, "Trouble is, once we find a place to stay, our number one priority has to be the Phantoms case. My—*our* jobs may depend on it."

"Any ideas where we should start?"

"Now that we know the Phantoms are using one or more examples of 'our friend' Johnny, one thing we could try is to set up the facial recognition software at 911 Central to trigger an alert whenever his ugly mug enters a bank, no matter how many of them show up."

Shrini shook her head, "I bet Johnny comes in with a mask for the next robbery."

"Maybe so, but that won't matter," said Perry. "You can set up the software to also react to ski masks, stockings over the head, Richard Nixon masks, anything strange like that—right?"

"Yes, *but...*" Shrini sat deep in thought. "There's only one problem with doing an alert about robbers in masks."

"What's that?" Perry stifled a yawn.

"If they rob a bank in New Bombay, there could be problems. We have a large Moslem population, and many women wear full head covering."

Donohue shook his head. "Not a problem. The Phantoms won't hit any banks there."

"Why not?" She fished an apple out of her bag. "Want one?"

"Nah, I'll just eat a hamburger later." He rubbed his razor stubble thoughtfully. "The Phantoms will hit another Manhattan bank—I can just feel it. There's some serious egotism in that ring..."

"You think so?" She bit into the apple.

"I *know* so." Perry began to smile. "They have a real flair for showbiz. They know exactly when to alert the TV networks—and it's always before *we* arrive on the scene...

Shrini began choking on the apple. Perry began slapping her on the back. The apple came back up, but with it came the hiccoughs. Again.

"Serves you right for eating too fast..." said Donohue unsympathetically. He closed his eyes.

Chapter 23

Wednesday, 8:10 am

The familiar skyline of Manhattan appeared in the distance. A bleary-eyed Shrini downed another cup of coffee, spilling some on Perry as the commuter train rounded a long curve.

"Hey, watch it!" he grumbled.

"Sorry." Suddenly, she smiled, "Hey! They're gone!"

"What, the little green men?"

"No, you idiot! My hiccoughs!" She punched his upper arm.

"Ow! That hurts!"

"Good! That'll wake you up—just in time for the break-out."

"Shh!" Donohue looked nervously around the compartment. All the other seats near them were empty. He turned back to her, "And that's break-*in*, by the way." He stopped and looked at her. "You want to do *it in the morning?*"

"Yes," she said flatly, "In the rush hour. Nobody will notice then—especially if it's a Noise Day."

Donohue groaned, "Oh *great*. You mean the big condom didn't work?"

She shook her head. "Nope. It blew off last week."

"Wonderful. Donner confiscated *my* earplugs," Donohue rubbed his eyes.

Shrini grinned, "All the better. People who see us will think I'm helping you to get back in to your apartment to get yours."

The train pulled into Grand Central Station. As they stepped down to the underground platform, Shrini took Donohue's hand, "Don't get any ideas, Perry. I'm only doing this because you're short and I'm short and I don't want to get separated in the crowd."

"*Yeah*, I like *this*…" grinned Perry. "Like newlyweds."

"Try and kiss me, and you'll get a kick in the balls."

"I might have to, if it keeps us from being picked up by the security cameras…" His other hand began inching down her shoulder.

Shrini glared at him, "Lay one hand on my tits and you're history."

The departing throng plodded up the stairs and emptied out into the main lobby. No one paid any attention to the disheveled couple as they made their way, arm in arm, to the side entrance.

Outside, the first strong rays of sunlight poked through the morning fog. Something bothered Shrini. The city was strangely still. She stopped and peered out, "What is all this?"

Donohue peered intently through the glass, "Beats me. Looks like everything's covered in ashes."

"Was there a big fire?" Shrini looked around. "I don't smell any smoke…"

Before Perry could reply, the automatic doors in front of them opened and the noise hit them full force. Shrini grabbed frantically for her earplugs. Perry clutched desperately at his ears.

Earplugs in, she waved at a passing cab. It stopped and the back door opened. They got in hurriedly.

"WHERE TO?" screamed the cabbie.

Shrini scribbled the address on her palmtop and showed the screen to the driver. The doors shut automatically. The cabbie started to pull out.

"No, wait!" said Donohue, "We need to stop at this address first." He took her palmtop and wrote on it.

"What for?" said Shrini.

"I'm overdue for my therapy with Dr. Jacobson."

"*Therapy*? That'll take all afternoon!" protested Shrini.

"No it won't," Perry showed the address to the cabbie, "It'll only take a minute or two—I just need a booster shot and to set up an appointment for next week. Come on, I've missed almost a whole month."

Shrini let out an exasperated sigh, "Can't that wait?"

"Nope." Perry shook his head, "Look, I *need* this. I've been under a lot of strain, it'll just be something to help me *concentrate*."

"All right," Shrini said resignedly, "If it only takes a few minutes."

"Thanks," Perry leaned back and looked out the window. A few 'ashes' floated past, stirred in the wake of a tanker truck. His eyes bugged. "Holy Elvis—they're dead flies!"

"Oh *gross*!" Shrini cringed when she saw them. "They're *huge*!"

"You bet your ass they're huge!" said the cabbie, "They dropped the bug bomb yesterday! We had to stay in all day and seal all doors and windows! Some national holiday *that* was!"

Perry and Shrini were too stunned to reply. They stared out the windows like horrified tourists.

The dead bumbleflies covered the street like a carpet, stretching as far as the eye could see. Traffic was proceeding slowly, creating two sticky ruts in each lane. Perry looked up and noticed fly carcasses spilling off window ledges and fire escapes. Every now and then a gust of wind would send a few more tumbling down. A few pedestrians, some with galoshes, tentatively started venturing out onto the streets and sidewalks.

"Amazing, innit?" The cabbie waved his arms animatedly, "The most unbelievable thing is the air smells like *flowers*! The Big Apple smells like friggin' orchids!"

A few manhole covers burped steam, sending small clouds of dead flies scattering like withered leaves.

The cab went up Park Avenue, then drove over to Lexington and past several brownstones.

"Here you are, pal," said the cabbie, "You want me to wait? It'll cost you."

"That OK with you?" Donohue looked inquiringly at Shrini, who rolled her eyes, "All right, Perry, but only this one time." She fished out a chip card and handed it over. "Charge this to the NYPD, OK?"

Perry opened the door, plugged his ears and raced up the stairs.

After five minutes, he came racing out and got back in the cab.

"That was fast," said Shrini.

"He was waiting for me. I called yesterday from the homeless shelter."

"Where to?" said the cabbie.

"West Houston Street," said Shrini.

Fifteen minutes later, the cab pulled up and disgorged its passengers. Donohue was still plugging his fingers in his ears as they got out. They ran to the front door of the slab-sided building. Shrini fiddled with the key card and the slot while Perry danced about from foot to foot in sonic agony. Finally the front door opened. They raced in, and it shut behind him.

Donohue let out a sigh of relief as he unplugged his ears, "Thank Elvis we got in. I couldn't take much more of *that*."

Shrini glared at him, "You mean, thank *Shrini* you got in."

"Hey, you can't go acting like my wife unless I get bedroom privileges," said Donohue with a leer.

"Oh god, no!" She started hiccoughing again.

"Forget it. You and those damned hiccoughs are spoiling my mood, anyway." Perry read up and down the row of mailboxes, "*There*. On the top floor."

Shrini glanced at the out of order sign. "Uh-oh. Doesn't look like (hic) the elevator is working." They started up.

They emerged, bleary-eyed and out of breath, at the top floor. "Jesus, I never thought six floors would have so many goddamned steps," wheezed Donohue.

Shrini leaned against the wall. "Old apartments and high ceilings equals extra (hic) stairs."

"Which Rich usually takes three at a time..." said Donohue. "Long-legged motherfucker!" A look of concern crossed his face. "Do you think you can decode his PIN for the front door with those hiccoughs?"

"I'll (hic) be OK (hic)" She stuck two tiny prongs in the slot. The tiny hand-held device flashed red, then yellow and finally green. The door popped open with a buzz.

Morning sunlight filled the room. Shrini shielded her eyes.

Dietrich came out of the bedroom in his undershorts, "Morning, guys. Nice of you to knock..."

"Uh, sorry," said Donohue. "What the hell are *you* doing here?"

"In case you're wondering, Rich is taking the State bar exam somewhere in Upstate, and hiding from the NPDi and some Johnny Bs as well. I'm house-sitting for him—want some eggs?"

"No thanks," said Shrini, "I'm still wired from that Waffle House food."

Dietrich rearranged his shorts, "So why did you folks come by? This can't be a social visit—you both look way too beat for that. Besides, today is another Noise Day..."

"We were hoping for a place to crash," said Donohue.

"Help yourself. Rich's got two couches here, and there are extra blankets and pillows in the hall closet."

Without another word, Shrini selected the blue couch and stretched out. Perry took the beige one and followed suit.

~ ~ ~

Shrini woke up first. Her mouth tasted like something evil had died in it. She went immediately to the bathroom to brush out the taste with one of Hayte's spare toothbrushes.

Perry began to stir. He opened a bloodshot eye and groaned, "Man, I feel like I've been almost beaten to death in my sleep..."

"Blame it on the (hic) Zimmerman twins," said Shrini, who was already dressed. "I still (hic) haven't recovered from that plane ride."

Perry looked at her and noticed the black circles still around her eyes, "Jesus, Shrini, can't you stop hiccoughing?"

"No (hic), Perry, I can't." She giggled, "I can't help it, when I get nervous, it (hic) happens sometimes."

"You think *you're* nervous..." Donohue rolled his eyes, "We got the NPDi after us, we're badly in need of weapons, and *you* can't stop hiccoughing. And I feel like I've been in another train wreck..."

"You *both* look like you've seen a few train wrecks," commented Dietrich, who was ambling out of the master bedroom.

"What time is it?" said Donohue.

"7:30. You both slept almost 24 hours."

"Meaning it's about time I got a shave and a bath," Donohue trudged off to the bathroom.

Shrini yawned and stretched. "So what's been happening at the White Elephant?"

"Well, Shabazz is back."

"Back from what?"

"The NPDi took him away for a while."

"What did they do with him?" asked Shrini, "Did they make him sign a contract and undergo training like Perry had to?"

"I don't know," said Dietrich. "But they must've scared him good. I haven't heard a peep out of him since they brought him back."

"So he hasn't been threatening to fire me or Perry for being gone?"

"He hasn't said anything, period." Dietrich lowered his voice, "His door stays closed. You can see him inside, doing stuff on his computer, but nobody knocks on his door and he *never* leaves his office. I swear, he must crap in the waste basket..." He paused, "So, that's what is new on my side—did you get anything out of that Carrouthers guy?"

"More than we bargained for..." She started to relate the highlights of his testimony.

"God damn it!" yelled Donohue from the bathroom. There was the sound of something plastic being thrown against the wall.

Dietrich went and opened the door, "What's going on in..."

A small plastic ball bounced out and bounded off the walls. A totally naked Donohue chased it as it rolled under a coffee table, "Fucking roll-on deodorant!"

Shrini shielded her eyes, "What did you do, Perry?"

"The ball got stuck, so I thwacked it and the ball popped loose!" He fished the ball out and went back into the bathroom.

Shrini rolled her eyes, "Looks like the 'old' Perry is back..." She turned to Dietrich. "He wasn't at all like this when we were on the run. Anyway, Carrouthers gave us tons of stuff to give to the Grand Jury..."

Half an hour later, she finished relating the details.

Dietrich made a wry face, "Now I know how Sisyphus feels."

"Who?"

"Sisyphus. In Ancient Greek mythology, he's the guy forced to push a stone up the mountain, only to have it roll back down, time and again. Seems like anything weird and sick hits the streets, it turns out to be one of GeniTech's 'little screw-ups'. It'd be really great if they relocated, somewhere far away, like Salt Lake City."

"Why there?"

"Because, the Mormons and GeniTech deserve each other," Dietrich scratched his ear with a pencil. "No, wait—that would just mean we'd have to deal with cloned Mormons..." He made a face and sat down, "That doesn't even bear thinking about... cloned bank robbers is bad enough."

Donohue re-emerged fully dressed, "Good news!"

"Let me guess," said Dietrich with a crooked smile, "you just had your first bowel movement in 72 hours." Shrini threw a bundle of socks at him.

"How'd you know?" Donohue looked surprised, "But that's not all—when I opened the window to let the stink out, there was *no noise.*"

Dietrich made a Groucho face, "The noises usually happen before the stink, Perry." Shrini threw another bundle of socks at him.

"No, I mean there was no piercing whistle—today's not a Noise Day. That means we can go and get some work done."

Dietrich frowned, "You want to go back to work? That might be a problem—I was just telling Shrini that the NPDi is swarming all over the White Elephant. They even took Chief Shabazz away for a while."

"Great..." Donohue threw up his hands, "That means I can't get my gun. I left it there in my locker when I flew off to Italy."

Shrini arched an eyebrow. "What about Rich's guns?"

"He probably has them with him, wherever he is," said Donohue.

Dietrich sat up. "No—he didn't! He only took his shock stick with him 'coz he's headed Upstate to take his Bar Exam next week. He left them for me in case the NPDi tried to break in again..." He paused and started to blush. "Uh, trouble is, I forgot where he stashed them."

"Can we look around?" said Shrini.

"Sure, be my guest..." Dietrich started towards the bedroom, "Maybe he tucked him under his pillow..."

"Jesus..." said Perry, pointing to the bloodstains leading from the bathroom. "Lucky thing that Rich didn't bleed to death... I thought they would've cleaned this up by now."

"Who's *they*? The same people (hic) who do the elevator maintenance?" grumbled Shrini.

"I don't know..." Donohue shrugged and began rifling through closets and desk drawers, "Now, where the hell would a guy like Rich keep his guns?"

"No idea. Rich is a strange kind of guy," said Shrini, glancing around. She

"No kidding..." Donohue looked around and noticed the garishly colored room décor for the first time. "If it weren't for that pile of books on his desk, I'd think we'd stumbled into the love pad of a 1970s Superfly..."

"I wouldn't know about that. But he needs a cleaning lady," Shrini looked round the kitchen, "And he *has* been here at least once since he went to hospital, I can see it."

"What do you mean?" Donohue looked doubtfully at the large stack of books in Hayte's in-box.

She pointed under his desk chair, "See all that?"

Perry bent down. "What? That little pile of shredded bits and plastic wrappers?"

"Yeah. That's his latest fad—fortune cookies. The guy eats them like there's no tomorrow."

Donohue shook his head, "The heartwarming story of a man and his hypoglycemia..."

Shrini frowned, "Yes, but it's weird—he *never* reads the fortunes... I watched him go through a whole box once, without reading even *one*." She held up the trash can, "Look at them all, wadded up in little balls. It's like he's afraid of what might be written there."

"He ought to hang out with pregnant women—they could compare notes on weird cravings..." Donohue began going through all the desk drawers, "Nothing here."

Dietrich walked into the kitchen. "*Aha!!*"

"What?" Shrini looked up from the desk.

"Come here and find out!" called Dietrich, now leaning into the refrigerator.

She looked in. "What on earth?!"

Dietrich grinned lopsidedly, "Only Rich would stash his guns in the meat compartment." He took out a .555 Magnum and handed it to Shrini, then gave the other to Donohue.

Perry rubbed the cold barrel on his brow. "Ah, that feels good on a day like this..." He indicated the wall clock. "Not even 9 am, and already it's hot in here."

Dietrich shut the fridge door and sat down on the couch heavily, "Glad that's out of the way. Now the pressure's off for a while..."

Shrini turned the unfamiliar gun over in her hands, "Know any way we can access the NYPD data files on the Phantoms? We need somewhere the NPDi would never think of."

Dietrich sat up, "What about the Transit Manhattan Borough Command?"

"Huh? Where's that?"

"I'll take you there—it's at the Columbus Circle subway station."

~ ~ ~

The posse stood in front of the Museum of Modern Art. An ugly scowl was etched across Donner's plump features. He looked at Lincoln, Marks and Buschmeier in disgust, "So where is the head?"

Agent Marks looked down at his feet self-consciously. "In here, boss..." he said in a tiny voice.

"Well, what are we standing here for? Let's go in and grab it!"

"W-we can't," stammered Lincoln, "Boss, it's got alarm protection and, and-an..."

"What the hell are you blabbering about, Lincoln? Of course *we* can! Follow me," He put his sunglasses on. The others reluctantly followed suit.

They moved in a phalanx to the ticket window. Donner flashed an ID. "Open up. We're confiscating stolen property."

"Not without a ticket, you're not," said the cashier acidly through the loudspeaker.

Marks, Lincoln and Buschmeier drew their guns.

"I wouldn't bother if I were you," sniffed the cashier. "The glass is bulletproof." She reached for the button under the counter.

Donner flipped her the bird and vaulted the turnstiles. The others followed suit. Marks lost a sandal in the mechanism.

Pushing aside onlookers and waving their guns, they followed Marks to the exhibit.

"Here it is, boss," said Marks in a tiny voice.

"Where?" Donner looked around, "All I see are bodies hacked apart and..." He made a face, "...spread out like... like... oh, this is DISGUSTING!"

Buschmeier had an ashen pallor. "I can't believe they unraveled that man's dick like that."

"Here's the head, sir..." Marks pointed to the platform.

Donner's mouth dropped open. He read the plaque. "Dissection of a *Vice-President*?!" He bellowed, "Jeee-sus Christ on a Pony! They hacked off the skin and..." His voice died.

Chesney's entire face had been removed from the skull like some kind of fleshy ribbons and spread out with rods and pins. The tongue spilled out of the neatly slit throat and drooped almost to the floor. The eyes were on a separate pedestal. One was slit open in cross-section. The skull itself was cut in half, with the twin hemispheres of the brain place at 90° angles, with illustrations showing the various regions and functions.

Donner looked up and noticed with a start that a crowd had gathered.

"You press the button, boss it goes through his whole career..." Marks said meekly.

"SHADDUP!" Donner stepped over the ropes, "Come on—we're taking it with us—NOW!" The alarms went off.

"*How?*" said Lincoln helplessly. "I don't have a big enough bag for all the parts..."

~ ~ ~

Friday April 22:

They walked out, Dietrich closing the door carefully behind them. They made their way around the corner to the stairs-and almost ran into a large, sweaty man, very red-faced, bending in front of his door. Dietrich recognized him and nudged Perry with her elbow. Puzzled, Perry gestured back. He put her finger to her lips and winked.

Dietrich snuck up on tip-toes behind the man and said in a loud voice, "LOCK YOURSELF OUT, STAN?"

Stanley Bialystok leapt back as if stung, his bulky frame bouncing off the wall. A lock pick flew out of his hand. "SHIT! I... ah... Oh, hi. Yeah, I locked myself out." They noticed he was perspiring heavily.

Shrini reached in her jacket and pulled out her thin leather pouch. She began thumbing through several thin silicon circuit strips, "Let's see..." She pulled out a thin electronic probe and inserted it in the door slot. The door popped open with a 'whoosh!' sound.

"Oh man, thanks a million—you helped me outta a jam there." He motioned to them, "You guys wanna come in for a moment, grab a cup of good java? I got some real good gourmet stuff, just in this week!"

Dietrich looked at Shrini, who nodded. "Sure, why not?"

They went in. Stanley motioned them over to the padded bar stools.

Dietrich took in the surroundings. "Looks like a hotel bar, Stanley. I like it."

"Thanks. It *was* a hotel bar—I knew the guy who was running the renovation of the Waldorf, he gave me a real good price on all the old furnishings."

"Must be pretty good money, doing 'adult entertainment' films..." Dietrich winked surreptitiously at Donohue and Shrini.

Stanley began fiddling with the coffee maker, "It *was*, but things are not so good any more." He sat down heavily on a stool behind the bar and poured the coffee, "I gotta tell ya, I ain't been doing so good lately. You're the first lucky break to come my way in a while..."

Dietrich suppressed a grin and nudged Donohue with his elbow, "Another bladder infection epidemic hit?"

Stan handed them their cups, "No, not this time. Pardon my French, but that fucking Supreme Court ruling..."

"Supreme Court?" interrupted Dietrich, "I don't remember any recent obscenity cases..."

"Naw, not that. That new directive banning film-makers from using insecticide foggers outdoors on location shots. With all that global warming shit, the insects are getting bigger all the time, 'coz there's almost no winter to kill the fuckers off now." He took a napkin and wiped sweat off his bald head, "It's killing me, big time! We've been doing a lot of scenes in Lake Placid and..."

Donohue wrinkled his nose, "Why in Lake Placid?"

"You gotta adapt, the whole world's changing!" Stanley started waving his fleshy arms expansively, "It's a hell of a lot warmer than it used to be, and the Lake Placid area has a nice low population density. Believe me, you don't want a pack of rubberneckers when you're filming adult movies. The guys get spooked, big time."

Shrini and Donohue started kicking each other's legs to keep from bursting out laughing. Dietrich started biting his lower lip.

Stanley continued, "Upstate's perfect—it's got lots of subtropical forests all tucked away from prying eyes! Now that Viagra and all the other erection drugs are banned, we gotta lotta problems with limpdick, believe me. All our porno guys ain't getting any younger..."

"Why not get some Village studs to service the ladies?" said Donohue, with a big smile.

"Because, no-fucking-body wants to look at torsos and dicks covered with tattoos and body-piercing—and those are the *only* types that show up for auditions around here! Those freaks, they come up and whip out their dick, and it *clanks!* Man, none of my ladies wanna mount a goddamn porcupine prick! And besides, I got a *suburban* audience—that's where the money is—and they get all grossed out by all that piercing shit, know what I mean?"

"A *respectable* audience..." Dietrich bit down on his tongue, hard.

"*Exactly.*" Stanley took another drink, "Anyway, where was I? Oh yeah—we had this hot-ass outdoor shoot going—a Garden of Eden orgy scene—and we was in the last part, the very *last* part, the big orgasm scene, with my male lead, Roy Jamstock..."

Perry reached over and pinched Shrini's leg. "The one with the fourteen inch..."

She kicked him back and tried to stop sniggering.

"That's him," nodded Stanley, "Don't laugh—it *ain't* funny! Right as he was about to come on Cissy, IT happened!" He slammed his fist on the bar.

A solitary tear rolled down Shrini's cheek as she bit her lip. "*What?* *What* happened?"

Stanley chewed on his lower lip, "The BIGGEST goddamn bumblefly I ever seen came buzzing round—and fuckin' Roy INHALED the bugger right up his nose. Medic told me later, the guy must've been sucking air in like a goddamn Electrolux to suck in a fly that size up his honker..."

Donohue began choking on a mouthful of coffee.

"Oh sorry, man, didn't mean to make you choke!" Stanley reached over and slapped Donohue's back. "That's just what happened to Roy! And he's *still* in the goddamn hospital—the doc says it'll take a couple more days to get all the bug parts out of his system!"

Perry stopped gagging and set his cup down, "Owwww! My mouth's *burnt*..." Tears ran down his face.

"Look on the bright side—would you want to change places with Roy? This could end Roy's career—and take me down with him!" Stanley handed him a napkin.

"For swallowing a fly?" said Shrini. She mistakenly took a big gulp of coffee.

"It's the psychological damage I'm worried about," Stanley put his head in his hands. "What if Roy can't ever work again? Good thing I got enough erection insurance..."

Shrini's eyes bulged and drips of coffee began shooting out of her nose. Dietrich blurted, "*Erection* insurance?!"

Stanley responded indignantly, "Yeah, *erection insurance.* I wouldn't be in business without it! You ever think how much an epidemic of limpdick can *cost?*"

Donohue and Shrini slammed down their cups and raced each other to the door. Dietrich was hot on their heels.

"Hey!" yelled Stanley behind them, "What's the matter?"

They slammed the door and ran down two flights before they collapsed in a giggling fit. Shrini started hiccoughing again.

~ ~ ~

Once they were able to walk again, they took the remaining stairs down to ground level. "We can take my car," said Dietrich. They walked across to where the squad car was parked.

Shrini took one look at the Merc. "You mean *my* car, don't you?"

"Hey, as long as I got the key, it's *mine*..." said Dietrich, tearing up the parking ticket. "Seriously, if I had to use my car, the NPDi would be all over us."

"I'm amazed they aren't, anyway," said Shrini.

"Shows they aren't as competent as they like to think they are," said Perry with a grin. He took the key chip out of Dietrich's hand and slid behind the wheel.

"Hey, but it's *my* car!" protested Shrini.

"But it's *my* turn to drive." Donohue started the engine, "Hurry up, we're wasting time!"

They got midway down Canal Street before everything stopped. "*Great.* Another traffic jam," groaned Donohue.

Shrini glared at him. "Why are you even going this way?"

"Sorry—I wasn't thinking." Donohue looked over at Shrini. "Can you hand me a gun now?"

"What for? We're just going to the Borough Command station."

"I feel naked without it."

"All right." She handed it to him.

Suddenly the windshield was covered with soapy fluid. "What the fuck?" Perry rolled down his window. A long-handled squeegee swished the fluid across the windshield.

"It's a squeegee man," said Dietrich, "It started last week. They're all over the place now."

"But that's illegal!" Donohue stuck his head out the window. "Hey asshole—get away from the car! Don't you know the law?"

Shrini tapped Perry on the shoulder. "*He* wouldn't know the law— look at his face!"

Donohue's eyes widened, "Holy Elvis! It's a Johnny B!"

Shrini pointed behind them. "And there's two more behind us!"

Donohue opened the car door and stepped out. "Come here, you!" He stuck the gun in the Johnny's face. Perry grabbed him and leaned him over the car hood to cuff him. The Johnny started clucking in panic.

"Shrini—let's grab the other two!"

"I only got one more set of handcuffs!" she protested.

"Well, let's nab one of them anyway!" Donohue opened the back door and shoved the Johnny down on the car floor, as Dietrich got out the other side to watch.

"Got one!" yelled Shrini, prodding another Johnny with her gun.

"Hey—let him go!" yelled a fat cabbie, "He hasn't finished my windshield!"

Donohue ignored the cabbie. "Here—I'll cuff him," He grabbed the Johnny's wrists and shoved him across the hood. The Johnny made loud clucking noises in protest. Perry dragged him over and opened the back door. He shoved him on top of the other Johnny and slammed the door shut.

Dietrich squeezed in beside the Johnnies. A chorus of car horns started up behind them, drowning out the clucking noises in the back.

Donohue yelled at the traffic, "Fuck off, you dicks!"

"Do you think it's safe with them back there?" said Shrini. "This is my car, and I don't want them tearing holes in *my* upholstery."

"We'll take 'em to Borough Command—they gotta have some holding cells there!" Perry restarted the engine and found an alley that went through to the next block. He zigged and zagged his way through several alleys, shoving trash bags aside as he went.

Shrini glared at him, "You owe me a car wash!"

"Do you take rain checks?"

"Huh?" Shrini looked mystified. "Rain check? What's that?"

They were just about to pull up to the Transit Manhattan Borough Command center when several uniformed cops came dashing out. Perry recognized one and yelled out the car window, "Hey Fielding! What's happening?"

Fielding's head whipped around. "Hey Donohue!" He ran over to the car and stuck his head in the driver's side window, "We got an anonymous phone tip that the Phantoms are going to hit the Chemical Bank!"

Donohue's eyes widened, "Which one?"

"The one across from Grand Central Station!"

"Holy shit!" Donohue turned to Shrini, "We're going!"

"Not so fast! We gotta dump those Johnnys!" said Shrini.

"I'll handle that," said Dietrich. He opened the back door and grabbed the first Johnny by the handcuffs. He reached in and grabbed the second Johnny and lay him next to the first.

Several teenaged bystanders looked on admiringly and took photos. "Cool! Twin criminals! Awesome!"

Perry stuck his head out the window and yelled to Dietrich, "Thanks Paul!" He hit the door close button and rolled up the windows.

They took off behind the first patrol cars, but Perry took his foot off the accelerator and made a quick u-turn in the nearest alley.

"What are you doing?" demanded Shrini. "We'll be late!"

"We need a videocamera," said Donohue. "I want documented proof this time—otherwise I'll have Shabazz all over my ass, just like last time. I'm just gonna run inside, see if they got anything we can use."

Without waiting for a reply, he slammed the door and raced down the subway stairs.

Chapter 24
THE NEW YORK CYBERPOST
Franken-Chickens!

Scientists are reporting a disturbing trend: a mutant gene is 'infecting' certain breeds of chicken. "We've ascertained that the gene affects wingspan size" said Dr. Linus Wheeler of the FDA. "We suspect the gene was triggered by genetically-modified feed. The gene probably attached itself to embryo cells and transformed them, producing an adult chicken with the ability to fly."

"Now that we know of the problem, it should be no problem to erect roofs over chicken pens" said Wheeler. "The first chickens that ate the feed weren't directly affected, but their gametes were. This led to the mutant gene showing up in the following generation." As a result, all chicken farms in the state of Indiana have been quarantined and the National Guard has been called in to enforce the emergency measures passed by the FDA on Friday.

Some of the mutant chickens escaped and are believed to still be at large. "It's not such a big deal," said Dr. Wheeler, "With all the environmental catastrophes recently, it's unlikely they will survive. They weren't bred in the wild."

A New Jersey poultry farmer, Mr. Bolus Snopes, 49, told reporters, "It sure was a surprise to see half our prized flock roosting in the big oak tree behind our house." Added Snopes, "They was building nests and everything—and it sure was a hell of a hassle to climb up and get all the damned eggs."

~ ~ ~

Donohue and Shrini were standing outside the Citibank. "Why are we here?" said Shrini impatiently, "The robbery's happening at the Chemical Bank..."

"Come on—since when do the Phantoms give anonymous phone calls announcing robberies?" said Donohue, "I say we check out all the other banks around Grand Central." She shrugged in response.

They walked towards the Citibank branch.

A group of commuters came past, forcing them to step aside. "I sure wish we had the surveillance van," grumbled Shrini.

Perry fingered the gun in his waistband apprehensively, "Well, we *don't*, so get used to it."

"Is anything happening in there?" Shrini looked around tensely, "I feel *very* conspicuous…"

"I don't know—I don't see anything unusual. Tell you what, you hold the camcorder," Perry handed her the C-size-battery shaped device and pinned the tiny lens tube to her collar.

"What will I do with the cable?" she complained.

"Put it inside your blouse," shrugged Donohue.

She quickly looked around, unbuttoned her blouse and slipped the tube inside between her cleavage. "A *gentleman* would've looked the other way…" she said sharply.

"Sorry. I'm too nervous to have manners." Donohue looked up and down the street. "Too much is at stake. There's a bench—go sit there and watch the front. I wanna have a look round the block." He walked off, trying to act casual.

When he turned the corner, his eyes widened. He raced back to Shrini and hissed in her ear, "We gotta get inside the bank NOW!"

They raced back and wedged themselves into the revolving door. "I hate these fucking doors" said Donohue.

"Come on—what did you see?" snapped Shrini.

"No time—just get in the longest iine—yeah, that one there. I'll be next to the safe door—I wanna talk to the guard—just do it!" He walked quickly over and flashed his badge at the guard, "Hi, I'm Capt..."

Right then, four men barged through the fire doors. "ALL RIGHT, THIS IS A ROBBERY!" blared an amplified voice, so loud it distorted, "EVERYBODY HIT THE FLOOR!!"

Donohue recognized one of the four. He and the guard ducked behind the open safe door. Perry pulled out the .555, crept his way round the door, aimed carefully and fired—blowing a huge hole where Johnny B's face used to be.

Perry ducked behind the door, cursing under his breath.

"What the hell did you do that for?" hissed the guard, "Now we got to shoot them *all* or we're dead meat!"

"Sorry—I forgot this ain't my gun. *Mine's* got rubber bullets."

~ ~ ~

The red light on Shabazz's console flashed ominously. He pressed it, "Chief Shabazz here-what's the deal?"

Chambers' voice was distorted by intermittent blasts of static. "The

Phantoms—Citibank—200 Park Ave..."

"What?! I thought it was the other bank!" Shabazz sat straight up in his chair, "I'll send in the SWAT team..."

More static crackled in the background. "Already called them in, sir, but..."

"But *what*, Chambers?"

"Sir, we understand Captain Donohue and Lieutenant Shrini are in the bank. Shots were heard a moment ago."

"Oh, *great*..." Shabazz gritted his teeth. "Where are you now, Chambers?

"Outside, sir, trying to get a look inside... but all the TV vans are in the way..."

"SHIT!" Shabazz slammed his fist on the desk, "How is it THEY'RE *already* in position every FUCKING TIME?"

Chambers had never heard the chief swear like that. "Uh... I don't know, sir. Maybe someone phoned in a tip to the press too," he said lamely.

~ ~ ~

The employees were scattered across the bank lobby, some weeping behind overturned tables and desks, others grimly stretched out on the floor, face down. Perry stuck his head around the safe door to look.

One of the robbers was sneaking up behind him. The man raised his gun to fire—but across the room, Shrini shot him in the chest.

Perry whirled around just in time to see a gush of red. He kicked the gun out of the man's shaking hands and got a quick look at the robber's face. *Round face, terrified expression. Afraid of death.*

Another bullet whizzed past, missing Perry by inches. He dove back behind the safe door, busting his chin wide open in the process. He wiped the blood away and cursed silently.

He looked up just in time to see a thin, wiry attacker climbing around the top of the safe door and taking aim at him.

Perry shot him in the groin, and the body fell on top of him.

Donohue rolled free and slammed the butt of his gun in the man's temple as a precaution.

He risked glancing at the man's face. Small, wiry build, thin face, aquiline nose. He dove back inside the safe, though he knew he had to go back out to cover Shrini.

He looked around. The bank employees were all huddled at the back of the safe. Perry motioned to one. "Can you help me? I need someone to hold this guy—make sure he won't wake up and cause trouble..."

The 300 lb. bank manager got up and waddled over, "I'll sit on him." He sat on the robber's legs, "There. He won't move now."

"Thanks."

Donohue edged his way back through the safe entranceway. He backed up several steps, then dove behind an upturned desk a few feet away, as several shots just missed him.

He peered cautiously around. Nothing.

Several minutes passed.

Perry's pulse started racing again. Only wind noise.

A tiny rustle of cellophane behind him. Perry whirled and shot, silently hoping it wasn't an employee.

The body spun around. Blood gushed from an open wound in his neck. Perry went to it. Relief. *Not an employee. Another Johnny B.*

Static in his headset. Perry yelled out in the room, "You OK, Shrini?"

She yelled back from behind him, "Yes—LOOK OUT!"

Donohue dove to the side, just before another Phantom fired. Perry fired back, just missing.

More shots followed Donohue back into the safe.

"GOT HIM!!" Shrini yelled from the lobby.

Another shot.

Then silence.

Inside the safe, Perry cupped both hands to his face, "YOU OK, SHRINI?"

Nothing.

He yelled again, "SHRINI!"

Silence.

Gun extended, he crawled on his belly until he reached the edge of the doorway. He slowly craned his neck until he could see out. There were two more corpses, both Johnny Bs. Somehow, the image made his flesh crawl.

He jumped out and scrambled back to the overturned desk. Shots followed him. *How many more? One? Two?*

Donohue heard a loud scream. He inched his way around the base of the desk.

Another Johnny B had grabbed a bank teller and was holding her hostage, gun in her mouth. He glanced at the safe, but there was no movement inside. *She must've been hiding under a desk.*

Perry yelled at the Johnny, "WHAT DO YOU WANT?"

The Johnny opened his mouth, but only clucking noises came out.

That gave Donohue an idea. "What's the matter, can't talk?" he sneered.

More clucking noises from the Johnny. His face became contorted.

Outside a police bullhorn crackled to life, "THIS IS THE POLICE— WHAT ARE YOUR DEMANDS? REPEAT, WHAT ARE YOUR DEMANDS?"

Shabazz's voice.

Donohue had no time to think about the implications. The Johnny yanked the woman by the hair until her face was inches from his. He kept the sawed off shotgun in her mouth with the other hand. Perry heard the shotgun click. In one fluid motion, Perry aimed his gun laser at the Johnny's face, tensed and pulled the trigger.

The Johnny's left ear disappeared in a splatter of blood. The woman fell down, screaming. Perry put two more shots in the clone, and heard a shot behind him. He felt a pain in his side.

Oh shit! Am I hit? He tensed and felt queasy.

It was suddenly very quiet.

He looked down. He didn't see a puddle of blood at his feet.

He turned around slowly.

He saw Shrini get to her feet and motion for him to listen. She pointed at another dead Johnny between them. "I hope that's the last one, Perry. It was sneaking up behind you." She held up her gun and said in a low voice, "I'm out of bullets."

He nodded, "I *think* that's all of them." He walked slowly to the safe entrance and peered inside, "All of you OK in there?"

A few heads looked up. "We *think* so..." said one.

Perry walked to where the manager still had the first henchman pinned. He bent down to look, "He ain't breathing."

The bank manager rolled his bulk off the corpse and looked sheepish as he struggled to his feet, "Oops, didn't mean to do that. Sorry..."

"That's OK—you immobilized him, and that's what counted." Donohue kneeled down and looked at the body more closely. The man's features were clearly different than the others. A light went on in Perry's mind. He remembered the TV interview from the Broadway robbery. He looked over at Shrini, "This guy must've been the spokesman from the last robbery—remember?"

"I'm not so sure." Shrini looked at the man's face, "He looks thinner than I remember. Speaking of spokesmen..." She pointed to the lobby, "We'd better get the area secured before the press descend."

Donohue didn't reply. He suddenly felt a rumble in his gut. He looked around desperately. "Which way is the john?"

The bank manager pointed to the back of the lobby. Donohue dashed in that direction.

As he did, the SWAT team funneled in through the glass doors, guns at the ready. Shrini stood in front of the safe and waved them off, "Hold your fire. The Phantoms are all dead."

Chief Shabazz came strutting in, feet crunching on the broken glass. He stared incredulously at first the dead robbers, then at her. "*You* shot them all?!"

"Half. I shot three, Perry shot three."

Shabazz looked around, "Where *is* Capt. Donohue?"

"Relieving himself," She pointed to the rest rooms.

Shabazz heard more crunching behind him and turned around. His eyes looked like two moons, "HEY! STOP THOSE REPORTERS..."

~ ~ ~

Perry pulled out a fresh clip for Shrini's gun as he sat doing his business. "Ow!" The old clip burned his fingers as it came out. He popped the new one in.

With his free hand, he peeled the last tissue off the roll, spit on it and wiped. He was about to flush and pull up his pants when he heard a commotion.

The men's room was suddenly crammed. The stall door flew open and a boom microphone was shoved in his face. "Capt. Donohue, is it true..."

Enraged, Donohue started firing at the ceiling. "GET THE FUCK OUTTA HERE!!!"

Outside, Shabazz walked up just in time to get knocked down by the reporters stampeding out of the men's room.

~ ~ ~

Sitting in his loft on the Lower East Side, Miss Clint switched off the TV in disgust. "Oh gawd..." He put his hands on his hips disapprovingly. "Why can't they follow someone *cute* into the toilet?"

Chapter 25

THE NEW YORK CYBERPOST
HENNY'S 500th!
VNN-Wiener Bros. Celebrates

"Who'd a thunk it?" Henny the Hyena, the controversial, lice-ridden cartoon character from Wiener Brothers Studios celebrates his 500th episode this week. The "gross-out" series that caused widespread sponsor boycotts nationwide proved mightier than right-wing fundamentalists from coast to coast, especially after the cartoon star became a multi-platinum-selling rap star. Currently, three of Henny's releases dominate the upper echelons of the charts.

"Kids identify with Henny" said child psychologist Dr. Earnest Benway, "because he seems so real. You can't get much more realistic that a character that locks girlfriends in the trunk of his car and writes graffiti with his own offal."

The yellow-spotted "mongrel with a bad attitude" won the hearts of teens worldwide with his incessant foul-mouthed diatribes against churchgoers, the police, multinational corporations, telemarketers and especially parents. "You can hear that high-pitched squeal playing everywhere" said Wiener Bros. CMO Fiona Bundy, "It's become a trademark of the 'in-crowd'."

When asked if it bothered her that Henny rants against globalized companies, Ms. Bundy replied, "Oh no, not at all. Our shareholders couldn't be more delighted. Profits are sky-high!"

~ ~ ~

Morbid curiosity won out. After listening to the police chatter about the robbery shootout, Lt. Pierce made a point to be down at the Morgue in time to see the carnage, right after the ambulances unloaded everything. He poked his head, freshly shaven except for the long pink ponytail on top, through the double doors and gaped at the bodies neatly laid out on the morgue tables. "My gawd, Donohue killed identical triplets!"

"Artificial ones, Miss Clint." Dietrich pushed his glasses back up his nose, "They're clones..."

"That explains their tacky outfits," sniffed Clint acidly, "that practically scream '*I am a criminal*'. There's probably some cheesy clothing store on St. Marks for wannabe hoodlums." He started probing the first Johnny with a latex-covered finger. He suddenly recoiled in horror. "Yee!"

Dietrich smirked. "What's the matter? Can't handle dead bodies?"

Miss Clint started scratching furiously. "Dead bodies are not my problem!" he snapped, "Body lice are! And I just saw one leap into *your* shirt!"

"SHIT!" A scalpel clanged on the floor as Dietrich started pawing frantically at his tunic.

Chief Shabazz picked that moment to walk in. "Oh *chraa*, I don't wanna know..." He immediately made a U-turn through the doors.

~ ~ ~

Ninety minutes later, the fumes were slowly blowing out the open window. Dead lice littered the morgue floor. Dietrich and Miss Clint were covered in red skin welts. Dietrich muttered, "Thank God I stashed that bug bomb before they were all confiscated."

"Normally I'd have to report you for that," Shabazz shook his head at all the carnage, "but I'm willing to make an exception this time..."

"Why the hell didn't you sanitize the corpses?" Clint snapped at Dietrich.

"No time—the bodies were still warm and I needed to get temperature readings." said Dietrich.

"And regulations prohibit that until the clothing is removed and fiber analysis is complete," added Shabazz.

"Well, let's get the clothing *off*," said Pierce impatiently, "and let's see what their equipment is like..." He started unbuttoning the first Johnny's shirt.

Suddenly he stopped.

Shabazz peered over his shoulder. "What's wrong?"

"My glove's caught on something in the collar." Clint gingerly pulled, to no avail. "I don't want to risk breaking a nail—they took me months to grow this long and..." He bent down for a closer look. "What the..." With his free hand he motioned to Dietrich, "Hey, Moose-face—get the magnifier—quick!"

"Okay, Miss Dracula..." said Dietrich nonchalantly. The video screen zoomed in on Clint's snagged finger. "Here?"

"Yes, darling, right there." Clint gave him a look. "*And* I'll overlook that cheap crack about Dracula—for *now*..."

Shabazz squinted at the monitor. "Looks like..."

"A micro-cam!" A triumphant look crossed Miss Clint's rouged face, as he pulled his hand free of the snagged glove. "Aha! Saved my nails!

This..." he pointed to the tiny camera on the Johnny's collar, "...is the break we've been looking for! Can you zoom in on the serial number, dear?"

"How do you know it has a serial number?" said Shabazz.

Clint turned around. "They *all* do. It's microbe-etched in the circuit sliver. Time for me to call the G&I girls and find out who owns it!"

A puzzled expression crossed Shabazz's face. "What's G&I?"

Miss Clint put his hands on his slender hips and rolled his eyes. "Do I have to explain it to *everybody*?"

~ ~ ~

Saturday, April 23, 7 am:

The main office area was still mostly deserted. Hayte, Shrini and Donohue sat in the cramped conference room below the Chief's office, comparing notes. They all looked tired.

Hayte also looked worried. "So you think this Carrouthers guy is on the up and up?"

Shrini nodded, "The files he gave us look authentic. At least the ones I looked at—there were a lot."

Donohue paced the room, "Gawd, I hope so, considering all the hell we went through to get them."

Hayte drummed his fingers on the tabletop, "Well... the stuff about the Johnnys fits in with what I saw at Scott Bunch's place. There wasn't anything left of Bunch except a hand that was cuffed to a bed frame. If that wasn't the result of a suicide bombing, you might as well start talking about space aliens." He shifted uncomfortably in his seat and winced. "Ow!"

Perry cringed. "Uh, Rich... how are things... down there?"

"I'm fine, Perry—OK?" Hayte rolled his eyes, "Man, I'm getting tired of people asking me that."

"You know what I'm getting tired of?" said Donohue, "Going around the squad room and seeing all those telltale bulges around everybody's pant legs."

Hayte flashed him a puzzled look, "What are your talking about?"

"Parole boxes, Rich. That's what the NPDi strapped to my ankle to keep me in line. It took a train wreck to set me free. You, me and Shrini are about the only ones I know who don't have one."

Rich blanched, "Holy Elvis, I *have* missed a lot of shit between being in the hospital and studying for the bar..."

"Dietrich doesn't have a parole box either," added Shrini.

"Good. That means the NPDi has nothing to blackmail him with," said Donohue soberly. "It's scary as hell to think that those bastards have enough on everybody else... Melchers, Champion, Chambers, O'Neill, hell, even Patrovsky's got one."

"So what can we do?" said Shrini.

"Well, they probably can't touch you and me," replied Donohue, "We're heroes, thanks to that Phantoms bust. If we can find the ringleaders, that would ice it. Dietrich' gone back to the Westchester County Coroner's office, which *might* let him off the hook. That just leaves..."

"Me..." said Hayte quietly, "Means I gotta be real careful. Not just on account of the NPDi, either. I still got to worry about another Johnny coming my way. I sure would like to know why I was targeted..."

"I might be able to answer that, Tree-Top," said Shrini, "From what I saw in Carrouthers files, it's no mystery why the Johnny Bees came after you."

"How's that?"

"Do you know what the B stands for?"

Hayte looked perplexed. "No. Is that important?"

"B as in '*Bunch*'. They're certainly Scotty's offspring—sixteen of his chromosomes, anyway, according to the documents I saw."

"Oh, *great*. So I basically signed my own death warrant by meeting with Scotty at the Pickled Ape that night."

"Yes. The Johnnys probably tagged you the same night they were tailing him back to his home. Bunch probably knew that, but he didn't tell you. You did say Scotty was acting very nervous, didn't you?"

"Yes. So I just happened to be in the wrong place at the right time." Hayte slapped his forehead with the palm of his hand, "Serves me right for getting curious..."

~ ~ ~

Monday, April 25:

Down in the Evidence Room, Donohue was cataloguing the Phantoms' equipment. "Ten vials of an unknown liquid substance in mini-jars, five sawed-off shotguns..." He held up a tiny diskette to the light, "One computer micro-CD—we'd better get this over to the Software team for analysis... Hmm, and that is all." He shook his head, "No car key-chips, no subway tokens, or anything else that would show how they planned to escape..." His voice trailed off.

His headset started ringing. "Donohue here."

Dietrich's voice. "Come to the morgue, Perry. Now!"

"OK." Donohue hung up.

Five minutes later he walked through the swinging double doors. "What's up?" He felt a warm hand on his ass. "Hi, Miss C."

Clint was disappointed, "How did you know it was me?"

"Nobody else has hands that big..." Donohue pried Clint's hand off his buns, "...or has a vice-like grip like that. So what's the news?"

Clint leaned over and whispered in his ear. Donohue's eyes widened, "We gotta get Rich in on this." He reached for the transmit button for his headset.

~ ~ ~

Hayte knocked on the Chief's door. The door swung open.

"Come in, Captain. I've been expecting you."

"Hi Chief..." Hayte walked in a froze dead in his tracks.

Shabazz gave him a questioning look. "What's wrong with you?" Following Hayte's gaze, he looked down. "Oh..." He started making a deep gurgling sound in his throat, then his shoulders started heaving. "Eh-eh- eh-ah- ah- ah-hah-hah!" Soon he was laughing so hard that tears rolled down his cheeks.

He plopped a Birkenstock on his desk. "They're just *shoes*, Captain!" The laughter started again in his belly, "You didn't *really* think I'd eh-heh-heh ah-hah-hah..." He doubled over, making choking noises in his throat, "Oh *man!*"

Hayte wasn't amused. "Didn't you, *Chief?*" he said quietly.

Shabazz couldn't stop grinning, "You think I'd embrace Violentology at the drop of a hat? Hayte, for crying out loud—I'm a *Moslem!*" He retrieved the Birkenstock that had fallen off, "I just like the sandals because they're *comfortable!*"

Hayte was about to say something, but thought better of it. He pointed at the Chief's feet, "It'll take me a while to get used to you wearing them."

Shabazz shook his head, "You *do* know they're prejudiced against Blacks, don't you?"

"Oh yeah," Hayte nodded, "but they still wanted my ass real bad."

"Sure. Forgive me, Captain, but the NPDi likes slaves who are big and strong. Tall is even better. Let me tell you something—when they took me in, I got stuck with all that virtual video voodoo mumbo-jumbo about terrorist this and terrorist that, but you know what?"

"It's bullshit," said Richard quietly.

"That's right, Captain. I can't even remember the last time we had a *successful* terrorist attack—must've been six or eight years ago *at least*. Ever since we mounted the big guns on our skyscrapers, we've shot down every hijacked jet any terrorists have tried to ram us with." He sat back, "They just like having power over us. And they wanted *me* to be their Uncle Tom. They kept saying shit like, 'We trust you, in spite of your race'..."

Hayte's jaw dropped open, "Did they really say that?"

"They *did!*" Shabazz nodded emphatically, "I kept waiting for one of them to pop the *N-word*, you know, like we were bosom buddies or something..." He looked at Hayte out of the corner of his eye.

They both burst out laughing.

A sudden thought occurred to Richard, "So... what kind of shit *did* they have on you?"

"I..." Shabazz was clearly startled. "I don't follow you, Captain," he struggled to regain a firm tone in his voice.

"You know, information they could blackmail you with, so you'd join."

Hayte returned Shabazz's stony stare, "That's what they always *do*."

The chief looked away for a moment, "It was personal. Certainly no crime, Captain. I can assure you."

"Can they still nail you for it?"

"Oh Hell. Might as well come out with it," said Shabazz slowly. His voice dropped almost to a whisper, "It was a *mixed* relationship I once had. They said it could get me thrown out of the Church of Islam."

Hayte arched his eyebrows, "Could it?"

Shabazz's eyes bored into his. "*No.*" He chewed his lip, "But I can't really be sure that's not just because I am the police chief right now..." He paused, "Things might change, if the mayor re-instates the position of police commissioner, like she's threatening to do..."

Hayte shook his head, "They *are* bastards."

"The NPDi? Yes they are..." Shabazz pursed his lips. "Captain, frankly it makes me shudder to think those..." He lowered his voice again, "...*Crackers* are in charge of Homeland Security. I'm sorry, but there's no other word that describes them."

Hayte let out a heavy sigh, "Speaking of them, Chief, there's something I've been meaning to ask you."

"What?"

"How do you feel about the NPDi taking over your—our police force?"

Clearly startled Shabazz looked up, "I... I don't know what you mean, Captain."

"I'm talking parole boxes, Chief." Hayte watched the chief's face closely, "You mean to say you haven't noticed all the tell-tale bulges in the pant legs? Word has it that over half of Plainclothes has been to the NPDi training camp."

Shabazz avoided Hayte's stare, "Captain, I am satisfied that our men can carry out their job duties satisfactorily," he said stiffly.

"I see..." Hayte made a face and crossed his legs gingerly.

"Oh..." Shabazz flinched, "I totally forgot—how's your uh... *health*, Captain?"

Hayte rolled his eyes. "Man, does *everyone* have to ask me that?"

"I was only asking for professional reasons," said Shabazz, with a slightly offended air. "If your mobility is restricted, we could transfer you to the City Prosecutor's office, now that you've done your Bar Exam."

"We can wait on that—I'm OK," said Hayte quickly, "I started jogging again last week."

"Good." A mischievous grin spread across the Chief's face. "...And how's your *Johnson*?"

"Chief! That's way out of bounds!"

Shabazz's chest heaved, "Eh-he-heh-eh-heh!" It sounded like he was choking. He wiped the tears away and smirked wickedly, "Sorry, I couldn't resist. I heard about you and that nurse!" He started snickering again, then caught himself, "Oh! I almost forgot. Internal Affairs wants you to get in touch."

"What for?"

"I believe it concerns the ongoing investigation into those three murdered reporters and Captain Donohue..."

"Man, that story's bullshit," said Hayte, "Perry couldn't have been seen with those reporters— the estimated time of death for all three was March 3rd, when Perry was in Italy, and he was still flying back across the Atlantic when their bodies were found."

"Well, you can go and tell them that. It's just a formality, I believe..."

Hayte's headset started beeping. "Oops, forgot to turn it off—sorry."

Shabazz shrugged, "Go ahead and answer it."

"Hello, Capt. Hayte speaking. Yeah?" His eyes widened, "Chief, it's Perry! We got a break in the Phantoms case!"

The Chief leaned forward, "How big?"

"Yeah? The Chief wants to know. Yeah? Something about tracing a micro-cam! Thanks! Bye!"

Shabazz nodded eagerly, "That's big, all right!"

"Perry wants me to go with him tomorrow to make the arrests."

"*Yes!*" Shabazz clapped his hands in delight, "You do just that, Captain. You bust the Phantoms, I'll hold the jail doors open for you!"

~ ~ ~

Tuesday, April 26:

The next morning, Hayte wasn't so sure, "Are you absolutely convinced they are the ringleaders, Perry?"

Donohue looked visibly annoyed. "*Yes*, Rich, *for the umpteenth time*, I *am* positive! Come on! Now's the perfect time—they're all meeting today and we got them dead to rights!"

Hayte looked up at the towering skyscraper and chewed his lower lip. "You'd better be right, Perry..."

A whole line of SWAT vans carved their way through traffic on Broadway. They screeched to a halt around the corner, a few feet away from where Donohue and Hayte were standing in front of the Wiener Comm Building.

Donohue went over to Melchers and held up five fingers.

Through the passenger side window, Melchers gave him the thumbs up.

Donohue and Hayte went to the security guard in the front entrance. Perry rapped on the wire-reinforced glass, "Sir, we have an arrest warrant..."

"For who?" demanded the guard with a big scowl, "The building's closed today to the public. Can't you come back later?"

"No, we can't," said Hayte, "we have authorization from the First District Court of Manhattan."

The guard's expression didn't change, "Look, I'm under orders not to let anyone in. There's an international shareholders' meeting with the company board members..."

"That's who the warrants are for," said Donohue, tapping his magnum on the glass for emphasis.

The guard looked disconcerted, "Do you have the names?"

"Yes sir, we do..." Hayte pulled out a document and started reading the list of names.

The guard's face went pale, "I, uh..."

"Just open the front doors," said Hayte, folding up the warrant and putting it back in the envelope, "and point us to the right floor."

"...or we'll be forced to bust our way in. The SWAT team is behind us," added Donohue.

The guard threw up his hands. The front doors opened with a pneumatic pop. The SWAT teams rushed up the steps. They descended on the lobby and snaked their way into the stairwells.

Donohue turned to Hayte. "I don't know about you, Rich, but I'm taking the elevator." He walked over and pressed the button. The far elevator opened.

The raced toward it.

Hayte had to duck to get in. "Do you know which floor?"

"Has to be the top one," said Donohue, as the doors shut. "E-G-O." The elevator shot up.

"Speaking of..." said Hayte, "Where did you find a judge willing to sign the arrest warrants?"

"I didn't," grinned Perry. "Miss Clint apparently frequents the same bath house as one of the State Supreme Court justices, and he called the First District Court..."

"Say no more," said Hayte, drawing his magnum. The doors opened and they stepped out. Hayte looked down the hall. "Now, which room?"

"Shh." Donohue put a finger to his lips. "Listen..."

They heard eerie high-pitched laughter at the end of the hall. Donohue motioned for Hayte to follow.

Perry stopped again. A minute passed.

Again, the creepy laughter. Donohue put his head to an oak paneled door and listened intently. "It's *here*!" he whispered.

Hayte nudged him, "We'd better act fast—the security cams have spotted us for sure..." He pointed towards the ceiling.

"OK." Donohue opened the nearest door, startling the receptionist, who blurted out, "Sir, you can't..."

"Oh yes we *can*!" said Perry, "Show her the warrants, Rich."

Hayte reached in his coat pocket and flashed the papers at her as Donohue went ahead and opened the double doors behind her.

"Come on, Rich! We got some arrests to make! Shit!" Perry suddenly tripped over an empty champagne bottle.

Hayte walked in and saw more bottles on the boardroom table, most empty.

Down the hall, the SWAT teams burst through the fire doors and started swarming all over the premises.

Perry got to his feet and went up to the boardroom table. "I hereby arrest all of you in conjunction with..." He suddenly broke off. "Why are you all wearing dog masks?"

"It's not a dog mask!" said the chairman indignantly, staggering to his feet. "It's Henny the Hyena, and today is the 500th episode of the Henny the Hyena show!" A chorus of hyena yells ripped through the room.

"Uh... uh," Donohue looked totally confused. Adding to the confusion, the SWAT team entered the room, encircling the table with their weapons drawn.

Hayte steeled himself and started reading out the list of names. "James A. Cheney, Edward H. Bronxmann, Susan Whitney Bush, Harvey Delaney..." He noticed the laughter dissipate as he continued down the list. "...You are hereby charged with running the Phantoms bank robbery ring, with gross vandalism, with hiring illegal aliens to perform the actual robberies, with interfering with police business at seven crime scenes, with illegally monitoring police frequencies and with embezzlement of bank funds. You have the right to remain silent..."

Behind their masks, all the board members started doing the sinister Henny cackle.

"*STOP* THAT!" yelled Donohue. "And TAKE OFF THOSE MASKS!"

The board remained defiant, keeping their masks on and continued their cackling.

Donohue turned to Hayte and whispered, "What *the fuck* are they doing?"

"They're making fun of us," Hayte leaned down and muttered in his ear. "With a war chest like theirs, they can afford to..."

The board members started clapping in rhythm and chanting, "*We got better lawyers, we got better law-yers!*"

Perry looked like he was about to explode. "CAN IT OR WE'LL SHOOT!"

"*Cool it*, Perry," said Hayte, putting a hand on Donohue. "They *want* you to lose your temper!"

"ALL RIGHT!" Perry turned to the SWAT team leader. "TAKE THEM AWAY!"

The SWAT cops stepped forward and nudged the board members with their Bushmaster AR-55 rifles to get up on their feet. "MOVE—OR WE'LL DRAG YOU!!!"

One by one, the board members stood up and defiantly continued their chant. "*We got better lawyers, we got better law-yers!*" They walked out in a line, chanting all the way to the elevators.

Hayte looked at Donohue as the sound of the chant faded. He let out a long sigh and sat down. "That has to rank as *the weirdest* arrest I've *ever* made."

Donohue looked out the window at the spectacular view. "Man, was I tempted to throw a few of them through these plate glass windows…"

"Probably bulletproof Lexan, Perry." said Hayte. "They'd just bounce off, and you'd be in more deep shit."

"Yeah, Rich, I know. I can't believe their arrogance. They *honestly* think we can't touch them." Donohue pulled up a chair and sat down heavily. "What the fuck?!" He rolled off the seat quickly

"What are you doing?" said Hayte.

"I just sat on something!" Perry picked up the object and his eyes widened. "It's a palmtop!"

"Oh yeah?" Hayte peered eagerly over his shoulder, "Can I see it?"

"Sure!" Perry handed it to him.

Hayte de-activated the screen saver and fiddled with the tiny mouse, "Whoever this belongs to, it's still logged in!" He held it in his hand and chuckled, "Which means it's fair game! We gotta rush this into IT Analysis—on the double!" He handed it to Perry.

They both sprinted out of the room and down the hallway. Hayte slowed and stopped, clearly in pain, as Donohue continued on without him.

Chapter 26

Wednesday, April 27:

"DO YOU KNOW WHAT YOU JUST DID?" Shabazz was livid. "YOU CAN'T JUST WALK IN AND ARREST THE ENTIRE BOARD OF VNN!!!"

Donohue and Hayte sat cringing. They both knew the entire performance was visible to everybody in the open-plan squad room below.

"Wiener Comm, Chief," said Hayte quietly, "It's the parent company..."

"WHATEVER!" Shabazz lunged across the desk, knocking over his coffee, "ARE YOU *NUTS?*"

"Look," protested Donohue, "You can't just say that—Lieutenant Pierce found that micro-cam on..."

"I KNOW WHAT LT. PIERCE FOUND!" Shabazz pounded his desk again, "I WAS THERE WHEN HE FOUND IT—REMEMBER?" He mopped the sweat off his forehead with an ebony handkerchief, "But that DOESN'T mean the BOARD is guilty!" Do you REALIZE what a WASP'S NEST you've unleashed?" He turned to Perry, "Donohue, 24 hours ago, the Mayor's Office wanted to knight you for busting the Phantoms, now they are screaming for your head!" He turned to Hayte and rolled his eyes, "And *you!* You have a law degree, *for crying out loud!* That means you're *supposed to know better!*"

"Chief, I hate to point this out, but you're the one who sent me with Perry to do this bust," blurted Hayte.

"And you gave me the verbal go-ahead," added Donohue, patting Hayte on the shoulder, "I got a witness..."

The chief looked about to explode, "ARE *YOU* TRYING TO *BLACKMAIL* ME?"

Donohue looked shocked, "No..."

"...AND I sure as HELL didn't give you approval to bust the *whole* board!" Shabazz fished out another handkerchief and wiped his face, "What are you, *suicidal?*"

"All we're saying," said Donohue "is that we'll have your proof—just give us 48 hours..."

"WHY in HELL'S name should I give you 48 hours?" demanded

Shabazz, "*Waj ab zibik!!*"

Perry smiled tightly, "Because we got a very good change of getting a confession."

"What?!" Shabazz looked startled, "We *do*?"

"We do." Donohue folded his arms and waited for the chief's reaction.

An unnatural silence descended as Shabazz sat and deliberated. The chief's face was impossible to read.

Hayte fidgeted in his chair.

Finally, Shabazz stiffly got up and walked around his desk. He stood looking at Perry for several moments.

Donohue looked up, "Well?"

Shabazz jabbed Perry in the shoulder with his finger, "You'd better be right, Donohue. That's all I got to say."

Before Donohue could react, Hayte grabbed him by the arm, "Come on, Perry—let's *go*." Perry found himself being dragged down the stairs before he could register it.

When they got to the bottom of the steps, Donohue let out his breath, "Thanks, Rich."

"You're welcome." Hayte glanced up at the chief's windows, "I just hope you're right about getting a confession."

"Ask and ye shall receive. Follow me, Rich," Donohue headed to the door to the underground interrogation rooms.

After the stairs, they went down a long colorless corridor that ended with a series of one-way glass panels. "Here, this room," said Donohue, peering at a roster.

"Who's the suspect?"

"Delaney, Harvey. The Chief Financial Officer, I believe," Perry opened the door.

Delaney looked up apathetically. He was a thin, twitchy man with a thick thatch of mustard-colored hair and bushy eyebrows poking over his black-rimmed spectacles.

Hayte took the initiative, "Good day, Mister Harvey Delaney, I presume?"

Delaney nodded weakly. Hayte noticed dark sweat circles on Delaney's orange prison coveralls as he stood behind the man.

Perry sat down. "I'm Captain Donohue, and this is Captain Hayte. We have a few questions for you."

"I demand my attorney," said Delaney. He said it defiantly, but Donohue saw fear in the man's eyes. "I don't have to say anything until I get one."

"That's correct," said Hayte. He read Delaney his rights, "You do understand these rights?"

Delaney nodded, "I do."

Donohue said, "We just want some general information, Mr. Delaney. You work for Wiener Comm, right? As CFO?"

Delaney nodded stiffly, "That is correct."

"How long have you held this position?"

"Seven years."

Donohue continued in a quiet, soothing voice, "Has the network benefited from your services as CFO?"

"Yes." Delaney began sounding more confident, "I helped turn everything around. Before, things were a bit of a mess, I'm afraid."

"Very impressive," said Donohue, smiling. "So you're an essential part of the Wiener Comm team."

"I am indeed." said Delaney, also smiling.

Standing behind Delaney, Hayte nodded to Donohue to continue.

"How old are you, Mr. Delaney?" said Perry.

"Thirty-six."

"Are you married?"

"Yes. Happily, I might add."

"Good." Perry drummed his fingers lightly on the table top, "Do you have kids?"

"Yes. Two girls, seven and ten."

Donohue changed his tone slightly, "Mister Delaney, do you own a Locus XP-11 handheld computing device? Serial number DX-3-1129-Q7?"

Delaney looked down and said nothing. The sweat circles under his arms grew bigger.

Donohue studied the man intently, "Is that *yours*, Mr. Delaney?" He held up the device for Delaney to see. The power light showed that it was still on.

Delaney said nothing.

"It was left on a chair in Wiener Comm boardroom," Donohue leaned closer and lowered his voice, "Mr. Delaney, when we arrested you, this computer was still logged in to your user account." Donohue leaned closer, "Some very interesting websites in your personal browser history..."

Sweat rolled down Delaney's face. "What do you want from me?" he said in a tiny voice.

Donohue and Hayte exchanged smiles.

~ ~ ~

Donohue's throat felt raw. He filled the flimsy paper cup full of spring water and downed it in one gulp. He glanced over at Hayte. "OK, Mister Legal Expert, are we in the clear?"

"Well," said Rich, glancing at the written confession, "Let me think..." His eyes widened, "*Oh!* Perry—we gotta call and find out if Delaney *has been formally charged yet!*"

"Will do." Donohue activated his head set and dialed the central switchboard, "Hello, Captain Donohue here—get me Records. OK, I'll wait. Yeah, I'm calling to find out if Harvey Delaney has been formally charged yet..." He nodded, "Uh-huh..."

Hayte watched anxiously. "Has he?"

Perry motioned for silence and listened intently. "No, he hasn't. What do we need to do?"

"We need to change the paperwork on the double!"

Donohue covered the microphone, "To what?"

"Criminal possession of child pornography."

Donohue handed him the headset, "Here, you do it."

"OK. Hi, Captain Richard Hayte here—what's that? Yes, we need to change the charges on a Mr. Harvey Delaney. Yes, we need to change that to possession of child pornography. Right. You'll do it now? Thanks!" He gave Perry back the headset and let out a long sigh of relief.

Donohue looked perplexed, "Why aren't we changing him with planning the Phantoms robberies?"

"Trust me on this, Perry," Hayte paused to rub his eyes, "We will charge him for that, but only on the basis of this written confession. It has to do the 4th and 14th Amendments, and the presence of an attorney."

"Lord…" Perry rolled his eyes, "I just go by instinct."

"Your instinct was right, in this case," Hayte almost giggled with relief, "I had a question on the Bar Exam that dealt with this—if a suspect confesses to a crime other than the one he's been charged with, the confession is admissible, even without a lawyer present. Which saves our butts from a hell of a lot of legal trouble."

"I get it. It's admissible because we were questioning Delaney on something unrelated to the Phantoms," Donohue started to smile, "Surprised you, didn't I?"

"You did. Second reason, we didn't explicitly tell Delaney which crime he should confess to, so the plea bargain should be legal. And the hand-held computer was left lying on a chair…"

"And it was still on *and* online."

"Right, so you could call it abandoned, which means you had every right to check its contents."

Perry worked the crick out of his neck and let out his breath, "So this *should* get Shabazz off the warpath."

"It should." Richard filled up his own cup with water. "I got a question for you. When you found the palm-top, what made you suspect Delaney could be into kiddie porn?"

"I saw his resume on file, and it said he was once in charge of children's programming on one of the Big Three networks." Donohue flashed a weary smile, "You did say that's where Stanley Bialystok got most of his backing, didn't you?"

Hayte started laughing, "You got a memory like a steel trap, Perry."

"Have to, in this business…" Perry looked at his notes cursorily. "Ready for more, Rich?"

"How's that?"

"We got other board members to question—you know as well as I do that one confession does not a case make."

Hayte nodded wearily. "If you don't mind, I'll just be Good Cop Silent again."

"That's OK. Just look big and intimidating." Donohue looked at the roster. "Now it's Bronxmann's turn. Let's see if Delaney's confession loosens this guy up."

~ ~ ~

By the time Hayte left the White Elephant that night, he felt like he couldn't see straight.

Six interrogation sessions was really too much for one night…

He tried to remember some of the particulars and found he couldn't.

He drove slowly and took extra time at each light to make sure he really was driving carefully and obeying the traffic signs.

He inadvertently almost drove past the intersection leading to his street. He made a u-turn and was surprised to find an empty parking space, under the big tree where Stanley usually kept his van.

He got out of the car and looked at the apartment building apathetically.

With a sigh, he shut the car door and reluctantly walked up to the key card reader. He was surprised that he still remembered his PIN code. The front door popped open. He looked around in both directions before going inside.

He silently watched the door shut behind him. The elevator was still broken, so he took the steps, stopping at every floor to check that he wasn't being followed.

He didn't really feel safe here, but there wasn't much choice.

Anywhere he moved, he would have to notify the NYPD, which meant Donner and his crew would immediately know where to find him.

In any case, there would be no hiding from the Johnnys. He was tired of running away. Time to confront them, but on his own terms. As he plodded up to his floor, he silently hoped there weren't any more of the suicide bomber ones left.

He opened the fire door and walked down the hall.

As he did, he noticed something odd, but he didn't know what. He started to reach for his gun.

Then he recognized that it was Stanley's door. It was partially open.

Against his better instincts, curiosity got the better of him.

He pushed on the door and it swung away. It revealed an empty living room.

Even the carpet was gone.

He went through all the rooms.

Empty, all of them. A few pennies scattered here and there, and a small pile of trash under the bay windows.

He walked out, shaking his head. He tested his own door and saw it was still locked. He opened it and walked in. The red light on his answering machine was flashing.

It was from Stanley. "Hi Rich, didn't get a chance to say goodbye, you can call me at 383-5620..."

Richard dialed the number. "Hello, Stan?"

"Yeah, hi Rich! How ya doing?"

"I'm fine. Why'd you move?"

"Aw, I'm getting out of the adult entertainment business and have to cut costs, ya know? So I just moved in with my brother. We're starting up a new business venture—I'm really excited about it!"

"Oh yeah? Doing what?"

"We're photographing weddings! Drop us a line if you and that nurse— hello? Rich, are you there? *Hello?*"

Epilogue

Thursday, April 28, 8:30 am:

Hayte barely made it to the Grand Jury hearing on time. "Sorry, I overslept. Perry kept me up late doing interrogations."

She flashed him a worried look. "You didn't have any time to prepare for the GeniTech inquiry!"

"Nothing to prepare, I'm afraid," said Hayte wearily. "The recorded evidence should speak for itself. All you have to do is state how you got the testimony and that the witness was of sound mind and body when he recorded it."

She looked around the lobby, "Where is Perry?"

"I told him not to come. He's way too over-exposed at the moment."

"What do you mean, Tree-top?"

"Didn't you see all the photos in the paper after the Wiener Comm bust?" Hayte made a wry face. "I'm glad I went out the back way…"

Shrini reached up and straightened his necktie. "Here, you can't walk in to a Grand Jury hearing like that. Are you ready?"

"Ready as I'll ever be…" said Hayte, with a sigh, "but I already don't like the vibe around here …"

~ ~ ~

12:30 pm:

"I can't believe that just happened," said Shrini, sitting down heavily on a plastic chair in the oak-panelled hallway. She looked exhausted.

"Grand Juries are extremely hard to convince," Hayte sat down next to her. "And they're very anal about certain issues like the legality of obtaining evidence. Unless we can find a way to *conclusively* prove that Carrouthers didn't steal that evidence, we don't stand a chance." He started to massage her shoulders, "GeniTech *always* has the best lawyers."

Shrini smiled a little, "But we have *you*, now."

"*Maybe…*" Hayte continued massaging. "But I still lack courtroom experience. They'd eat me alive. If we could ever get even that far..."

Her eyes met his, "Do you think the Grand Jury took *any* of it seriously?"

He looked up at the ceiling for a moment, "I hate to say it, but... I don't think so. When I run through the details myself, it does have a certain resemblance to wacky conspiracy theories. You know the best thing that could happen?"

"No. What?"

He chuckled in spite of himself, "If Johnny Bees started popping up *everywhere*, on the streets, on the subways, all over the place... I guarantee that would change their minds in no time flat!"

Shrini gave him a baleful look, "Be careful what you wish for, Tree-Top."

~ ~ ~

When Shrini opened her car, the dashboard display beeped. "Got a message, Tree-top. Do you mind if I read it?"

"Go ahead," shrugged Hayte, clambering in the back seat, "We got all the time in the world after that fiasco."

Shrini pressed the screen and opened her mailbox. "Oh no!"

"More bad news?" Hayte rolled his eyes.

"Carrouthers!"

"The guy who gave you all that GeniTech stuff? What happened?"

"It says here that he's gone missing. His house is empty but riddled with bullet holes. And there were bloodstains on the driveway..."

"Who sent the message—is it a reliable source?"

Shrini scrolled down. "Dilly-Bob."

Hayte wrinkled his nose. "Huh?"

"One of the Zimmerman twins. They deliver mail to him."

"So they would know." Hayte rubbed his eyes.

"Yes." She started the engine. "Where do you want me to drop you off? Back at the Chelsea?"

"Nope. I've moved back to the Village."

"You're kidding!"

She saw him shake his head in the rear-view mirror. "Nope. It dawned on me that I'm going to be hunted, no matter where I go. So I might as well stay there—at least until my lease expires." Seeing her worried look, he added, "I'll be careful—I got no choice." He pulled back his coat to reveal his holster. "I got my .555 loaded and with me at all times. I even put in a request with the department for night vision glasses."

"All right, Tree-top, " Shrini still looked doubtful as she dropped him off at the corner, "Better get some sleep tonight. We have that meeting with Shabazz tomorrow at..."

"...eleven O'clock. Our 48 hours are almost up. See ya there," He rubbed his eyes again and stepped out of the car.

~ ~ ~

Friday, April 29:

The Chief's office was open when Hayte, Donohue and Shrini walked up the stairs.

Hayte poked his head in first. "Hi Chief, got something for you. You're not gonna believe this," He held up a printout and read from it. According to their official statement to the NY State Grand Jury, GeniTech 'is only engaged in the cloning of human organs, but never with cloning an entire organism.' They go on to claim Bunch, Caramond and their team were engaging in an illegal 'rogue project for their own material gains.' The material gains were of course *not* specified."

Shabazz had a wry smile. "So your cross-country odyssey was for nothing," he said, looking at Donohue and Shrini as they walked in. "May I suggest that next time, you share your findings with *me*, so that we can avoid such a wild goose chase in the future?"

Donohue opened his mouth but thought better of it after Hayte flashed a warning look. They all took a seat.

"The case with Zane Lewis and the other murdered reporters is still open, Chief," said Shrini. "Carrouthers' testimony about that still might be useful in the Wiener Comm case."

"Speaking of..." Shabazz swiveled around in his chair and looked squarely at Donohue and Hayte. "What have you got on Wiener Comm, Captains? Your 48 hours were up about 12 minutes ago."

"We got a full confession from Delaney, the CFO at Wiener Comm," said Hayte. "He admitted the Phantoms ring was being run at the board level. Personally, I suspect it isn't the first time news has been artificially, uh, *created* to stimulate ratings. They called it something like a 'News Stimulus' package, and it was one of their off-the-balance sheet things..."

"What about the other board members?" interrupted Shabazz.

Donohue shook his head, "The others didn't bite. Guess they still think they have better lawyers..."

Shabazz flashed them a worried look, "Are you sure the confession will stand up in court? This Delaney guy could be some kind of flake that would wilt under cross-examination. We're staking our reputation on this bust."

Hayte shook his head, "I don't think so. First of all, although he's only 34, he's the CFO, which carries a lot of weight in court. Secondly, the info he gave us was far too detailed—and revealed a lot of insider knowledge."

"I'm still worried," said Shabazz.

"Why?" Donohue frowned.

"First, we could still get nailed for extracting the confession under false premises—what if you have to produce a list of kiddie-porn websites the guy is accused of hitting? Second, any mention of child pornography will instantly discredit Delaney as a witness."

"Hey, wait a second!" Perry shook his head, "The confession is about the Phantoms—not the kiddie porn. True, we officially charged him with possession of kiddie-porn, but those charges will be dropped..."

"...as part of the plea bargain," added Hayte. "His counsel agreed to it, too, once we confronted her with the evidence. No mention of child pornography will be admissible in court."

Donohue continued, "Anyway, he *volunteered* the info about the Phantoms while we were questioning him. Rich did read the guy his rights before we started..."

"And he indicated he understood them,'" confirmed Hayte, "After that, we couldn't have shut the guy up if we'd tried. He was just plain *scared*; you could see and smell it—he damn near pissed on himself. As far as he's confirmed, it'll save him from all sorts of embarrassment—I seriously doubt he or his council will pursue the matter any further. Certainly not enough to check his log-in time from his server's records."

"That sounds better," Shabazz nodded thoughtfully. "One question, though—you said they were having a party in the boardroom. Why was Delaney online at all?"

Hayte spoke up. "I bet I can answer that. He was transmitting pictures to an absent board member. I noticed a couple of empty seats."

"Speaking of being absent," Shrini raised a hand, "I need to visit the ladies room."

"Go ahead, Lieutenant." Shabazz pointed to a chair in the corner, "We'll save you a seat."

"How hard is the D.A.'s office going to hit them?" said Donohue.

Shabazz's smile faded, "Not very. Unless we can find documented— hard copy—proof that explicitly shows that they were planning heists from the boardroom, the most we can go for is facilitation of a crime or aiding and abetting, which carries just one year in jail as its maximum penalty."

"Is that *all*?" said Donohue, visibly shocked.

"That's all," said Shabazz resignedly, "We have to be realistic. They really do have better lawyers." he said with an apologetic glance at Hayte, "or at least, more experienced ones."

Shrini walked back in and poured herself another cup of coffee.

"Wow, that was quick," said Hayte.

"Professional secret," smiled Shrini, sitting back down again. "I got a question," she looked at Donohue, "What made you suspect VNN-Wiener Comm was behind the Phantoms, Perry?"

"When I took the time and thought about it, it became obvious that the press had inside information about the Phantoms. I also know there was no leak inside the NYPD."

"Your proof is?" said Shabazz.

Perry stood up and poured himself a coffee, "The other cases we had were just as newsworthy, but none of those made any headlines."

"True," agreed Hayte, "so we managed to keep a lid on those cases, at least."

Shabazz nodded, "But how does that relate to the Phantoms and VNN?"

Donohue took a sip and grimaced. "It's quite simple, really. We all know a story about clones with a suicide bombing angle would've been front page news everywhere, especially since cloning humans is still banned in the USA. But neither Bunch nor the Wettington murder merited more than a tiny column on page five of the local news. There were no reporters hassling cops around those crime scenes. That should've set off some alarm bells, but I was too distracted with all that NPDi shit. It wasn't until I was sitting in a cold, dark holding cell in the NPDi's basement that I actually had time to think things out—it was the only way to keep my sanity."

Shrini raised an eyebrow, "Did it work?"

"Nope..." Perry playfully feigned throwing her a punch from across the room, "The other thing I noticed was the other news providers were much nicer about giving out their footage of the robberies. For example, the people at the CyberPost were downright cooperative. VNN, on the other hand, even had the nerve to threaten to take me to court. And yet, every time they were involved—meaning at every Phantoms heist—the place was a circus, more press than police. As soon as I figured out someone was importing the robbers on a rotating basis, I started looking for a ringleader. Then I started thinking some more about VNN's reaction. And getting a hunch that their involvement in this was rather personal in nature."

"But VNN has unlimited capital," protested Shrini, "Why would *they* go around robbing banks?"

"Ratings. Ad revenues soared after the first robbery and have only gone up since then. And they did it because they *could*," said Donohue, "And to amuse themselves by making us cops look like a bunch of idiots."

Hayte shook his head, "The egos involved..."

"Speaking of *egos*," said Lieutenant Pierce, peering round the door, "Hello everyone! Hope I didn't miss too much..." He tossed the end of his pink feather boa over his shoulder with a flourish, "Hope nobody said anything too awful about *me*... I just got back from a Gay Squad meeting that ran *way* over. Coffee, coffee, have we got any coffee here? This is supposed to be a *proper* meeting!"

"Coffee's over there, Lieutenant," said Shabazz, pointing to the canister in the far corner. "There, under the picture of Mecca."

"Oh! How appropriate!" said Pierce, clapping his hands. He rushed over and filled his oversized mug to the brim, "Ahhhhh! Manna from heaven!"

Shrini leaned over and whispered in Hayte's ear. "Have you noticed Shabazz is so much nicer to me since I shot those robbers?"

"Yeah..." nodded Hayte. He whispered back, "And he's being positively civil to Miss Clint too. Maybe he's actually *mellowing*..."

"All right, can the chatter!" said Shabazz, tapping his desk, "We were talking about..."

"How the Phantoms were making us all look like *fools*," said Pierce, seating himself in the middle. His feather boa's color started turning purple.

"But this time they tried to make us look a bit too stupid," said Shrini, "That anonymous phone tip..."

"And the micro-cam?" interjected Hayte, "What was the deal with that?"

Miss Clint rolled his eyes, "The micro-cam was so VNN could show the Phantoms robbing the Citibank and getting away scot-free..."

"While the NYPD was supposedly staking out the Chemical Bank a short distance away," said Donohue, "Because they all knew we'd be so desperate that we would trample over each other rushing over there, just because we couldn't afford *not* to..."

"Even for a lousy anonymous phone tip," Hayte grimaced, "They really do hold cops in contempt, don't they?"

Perry nodded, "They're arrogant bastards all right, you saw that in the boardroom. When Miss C. told me about the micro-cam, I decided to roll the dice and bust 'em while they were supposed to be celebrating the anniversary for that hyena cartoon of theirs—I was hoping there'd be alcohol involved..."

"How did you get a Grand Jury indictment?" said Hayte.

"That's what I'd like to know too," interjected Shabazz, "I'm still in shock about that."

Pierce smiled cryptically, "That's my contribution, girls. A few Grand Jury people frequent the bath houses on my beat." He winked, "That's part of why I was late."

Hayte groaned, mostly to himself. "I knew there was an angle we should've tried with the Carrouthers case!"

"We'll discuss that later," interrupted Shabazz sternly. "Let's get back to the Phantoms—how did they get away from those other crime scenes? It's like they vanished into nothing."

"Delaney divulged that little detail," said Donohue, "Four were outside, working at their day gigs as TV reporters but really functioning as spotters for the three gunmen inside. The gunmen then herded all the hostages into the safety deposit box safe, and then the four 'reporters' created a diversion by breaking through the police barricades and starting a stampede with all the other reporters. You remember the big revolving doors at the Broadway bank's entrance?"

Everyone nodded.

Donohue continued, "Once the reporters got the revolving doors moving, the three gunmen, now also disguised as reporters, joined the free-for-all. We didn't see them changing outfits in the video because we were busy shutting the power on and off. We couldn't see them out front because of the mirrored windows. Delaney really filled in the rest. Turns out, the real robbery happened right at the very beginning—*electronically*. The bag men were already in the bank, at the cash machines when the robbers came in. They took advantage of the diversion to go to the employee terminals, which were still logged in. They then introduced deep viruses into the system. These viruses later accessed the largest corporate accounts and transferred large amounts to a long series of self-destructing dummy accounts that eventually took the cash offshore."

"But what about the bag men? How did *they* escape?" said Shabazz impatiently.

"I'm getting to that. The robbers—the ones *posing* as robbers, I mean— herded the hostages into the safety deposit vault at the very beginning, so nobody would notice the bag men going to the terminals. The master stroke was that the bag men *joined the hostages inside once they were finished.* They were herded in at gunpoint and treated just like the other hostages. They even carried stuff into the safe. While the real hostages were freaking out while the safe was being shut, the bag men discretely placed the potassium bombs in the corners. All they had to do is wait for us to open the vault back up. Afterwards, the bagmen simply went home, like all the other freed hostages. The hostages were not required to give us their names, so that was that."

"And *none* of this was on the security camera footage?" said Shabazz, with disbelief.

"Nope, because most of the time we had the juice switched off, which is standard procedure when hostages are being held. But they had their own safeguards against us seeing anything from outside. All security cameras operate using frequencies. Some of the VNN TV vans were there to jam their signals—but only while the bag men were going about their business. Once they went inside the vault, the signal returned, and that's when we started getting ransom demands on the air."

Shabazz frowned. "But left the bag men in danger. What if you hadn't gotten the vault back open?"

"They took a risk, all right. Guess they had faith in the NYPD after all. We sure obliged them by blowing the safe wide open." Donohue shook his head in wonder.

"And when Melchers and his crew herded all the reporters back behind the barricades, there had to be at least 75 reporters in all, too many to haul downtown," added Shrini.

Perry nodded ruefully, "Right. We were expecting to haul bank robbers, not a whole pack of press people—so we let 'em go—just like that..."

"I assume we are going after the robbers themselves—the ones who did the other robberies," said Shabazz.

"How?" retorted Shrini, "We forwarded their mugs shots to Interpol and have heard nothing since. We killed all of the ones in the Park Avenue Citibank. And as far as going after the Johnnys that were involved in any earlier robberies, how do we know *which ones* were involved?"

"I don't like it, but... all right, I see your point..." Shabazz drank some more of coffee and made a face, "But why go to all that trouble? Wouldn't have been far easier to just steal the money electronically during off-business hours?"

Shrini shook her head, "Even wireless dialups are traceable. There are so many cyber-cookies that a computer sends out, there's no way of disguising or eliminating them all. If you try and delete all of them, your access gets automatically denied. The only way to plant deep viruses without it being traceable is to do it on-site."

Dietrich poked his head around the door and knocked. "Can I join you? Sorry, but I just heard about the meeting a few minutes ago."

Hayte looked at Shabazz inquiringly. Shabazz nodded, "Sure, if you bring another chair."

Dietrich grinned lopsidedly, "I came prepared." He turned around and rolled in an office chair.

"Getting back to the Phantoms," Donohue drummed his fingers, "The whole Broadway robbery was amazingly well planned, a totally sophisticated exercise from the beginning. But the Citibank one *wasn't*— they had all their dirty tricks ready, but I got the feeling they did it on the hop."

Hayte raised an eyebrow, "How so?"

"Well, they didn't scout the premises beforehand. They expected all the police to be around the corner. They definitely didn't bargain on Shrini and me already being inside."

"Oh! That reminds me!" Shrini interrupted, "Did they bring stuff for another diversion? I didn't see any vials of potassium on the robbers we shot."

"Yes, they brought something else..." Perry paused for emphasis, "What the coroner found on their bodies were seven small vials of *some*thing—and those vials were hooked up to *tiny timing devices*. Toxicology says the contents look suspiciously like some kind of nerve agent, but we'll never know for sure..."

Shabazz interrupted, "And *why* not? *We* have the vials in our possession, right?"

"Yes, but there's a problem. Spectral analysis indicates it's something new. Toxicology doesn't have the capability to analyze whatever it is— we'd have to send it to the FBI, and *then*, because it could be a Homeland Security issue, *they* would pass it on to our friends with the Birkenstocks..." Donohue suddenly spotted Shabazz's footwear, "Oh-oh..."

Shabazz gave him an annoyed look, "Will you *stop* looking at me like that? I only wear these *because they're comfortable*, dammit!"

Hayte cleared his throat demonstrably, "Uh, Chief—there are some other things I'd like to clear up, now that we're all here."

Shabazz set his coffee mug down. "All right."

"Can I say something?" Shrini tapped Dietrich on the arm, "Paul, I've been meaning to ask you—why did all the Inter-Police ID searches turn up nothing when we did searches with the Phantoms' mug shots?

"As far as I can tell," said Dietrich, "the algorithm for the iris-recognition software had a basic error—it checked the mirror-image of the composites, so the left eye became the right eye and vice versa. Of course, it didn't help that some asshole hacker introduced a virus into our network that transposed big red clown noses on all the mug shots..." His trousers rode up his legs as he sat down.

"I notice you're not wearing Birkenstocks, Paul..." said Shrini, pointing at Dietrich's feet.

"They didn't take me in, 'coz they had nothing on me," Dietrich smiled broadly. "I disposed of Chesney's head properly."

"Where, if I may be so bold to ask?" said Hayte.

"I donated it to the Bodily Universes show. Go check it out."

"No thanks," Richard made a face, "if I want to see mutilated flesh, I just need to unzip and look down..."

"Rich!" Shrini winced. "I thought you were making a good recovery."

"Oh, I am," admitted Hayte, "but I'm still not wild about going to see cut-up corpses." He glanced at Dietrich, "I heard Donner's boys had you nailed just outside Beth Israel the other week."

"Oh that? I knew I was being tailed," said Dietrich, "so I took Miss Noelle's head with me to throw Donner's goons off the scent. I left instructions with the second ambulance wait 20 minutes and then to go to the exhibit organizers for the formal donation. They were thrilled to get it."

"But what about the stolen property charges?" said Donohue. "That's how they nailed me in the first place."

Dietrich shook his head, "I hate to tell you, Perry, but they were bluffing. It never would've stood up in court. The VP's head was never officially reported as stolen, so the whole thing's in the clear."

Pierce stood up and spread a printout on the table. "One question, girls—why aren't the news sites reporting the Wiener Bros. bust? I scanned all the dailies this morning—nada! What's the deal?"

They all looked at each other. "Hmmmm."

Shabazz reached for the phone. "We'll have to change that..."

He pressed a few buttons, then hung up with a look of satisfaction.

"What was that?" asked Hayte.

"My own version of G&I..." Shabazz smiled enigmatically. "You'll see..."

"Anything else we need to discuss?" asked Hayte, looking around.

"If anybody cares, I have some pertinent info about the three murdered reporters," said Miss Clint. "It might even be what you call so *endearingly* term a 'smoking gun'..."

Everybody sat back down. "Well, do tell, Miss C." said Hayte, "That's the one thing I could never figure out."

"Well, if Mister Donohue and Miss Shrini had come to me sooner, you would've found out that much quicker." Pierce crossed his legs in one elegant motion and flung his now-lavender tinted ponytail over his shoulder, "Put your trust in G&I, it never fails. Anyway girls, listen up!" Pierce clapped his hands, "There was a little get-together at that infamously overpriced little bistro on the top floor of Prada, the night after the Phantoms robbery on Broadway a couple of months ago. The group consisted of VNN newscasters Bernard Duncan, Barbara Delacroix and Zane Lewis..."

~ ~ ~

Barbara Delacroix in particular still seemed hyper. "Wasn't it wild how we got past all the police barricades and almost to the robbery scene itself?" she said.

"Yeah," said Zane, a telegenic slim dark-skinned woman with short hair, "three more steps and we would've entered the crime scene itself!" Her face was also flush with excitement.

"It was a real zoo!" added Bernard, taking off his wire rim spectacles. "It sure wasn't normal..." He nervously lifted his brandy snifter to his lips. "I mean, we should've shown the police more respect..."

"I was too busy trying to keep upright," commented Zane.

Barbara nodded, "I've seen riots that were more disciplined."

"And did you notice all the top brass?" said Zane, "I mean, I saw Clive Jetnikov *and* Ted Eisner, Juanita Rayburn, and even Dick Helmond there— it was like a *Who's Who* of mass media!"

"Wait a minute!" said Bernard, tapping heavily on the table, "I *saw* them too—*and* in the same pack as us. I remember now, one cop was waving a nightstick in Eisner's face as we broke through!"

"I saw that," Barbara poured herself another glass of sangria. "He didn't look too pleased—imagine Mister Hard News with bloodstains on his Brooks Brothers suit—*that* just *wouldn't* do!"

"I don't get it," said Bernard, "I can understand a bunch of rookie reporters getting carried away, but Jetnikov and Eisner? They're seasoned professionals. This whole thing really makes me wonder if we're finally getting as bad as the police say..."

Zane added, "Yeah, but it's really down to having so much competition- there are way too many reporters now, every time I do a remote broadcast, I feel like my ribs might get crushed. I feel like I'm in the middle of a stampede."

"It *was* a stampede," said a voice behind them.

Startled, they all turned, "Dick Helmond!"

"Hi guys!" Helmond flashed his famous grin, "And I agree with you about crowd control—that last episode was disgraceful! The police really should've done more," he shook his head, which momentarily revealed plastic surgery scars under his jawline. He smiled again. "I saw you come in and thought you three might like to join us," with a sweep of his arm he indicated the far booth where Jetnikov, Eisner and Rayburn were sitting.

Barbara's mouth dropped open. "Uh… yeah, *sure!*" She fumbled in her purse for her compact. "Can I touch up my lipstick first?"

Helmond smiled again. "Of course."

Equally star-struck, Zane asked "Was it true that you were there in Havana when the Cuban Civil War broke out?"

"That's right!" beamed Helmond, "Say, why not come over and join us! I'll be glad to fill you in on all the gory details. Just follow me." He guided them over to the booth where the other senior reporters were clustered. Soon the discussion became quite animated and the drinks flowed late into the night.

~ ~ ~

"Anyway, that's what Boris saw, and he swears it's true…" sighed Miss C. "That was the last time anyone saw the three alive. None of them went home afterwards, none of their beds were slept in, nada."

Shabazz said sharply, "Is this fact, or just a bunch of useless gossip?"

Lt. Pierce put his hands on his hips. "These are *eyewitness* accounts!"

Shabazz rolled his eyes, "From a bunch of gay waiters and flakes in the entertainment biz? What kind of police work is *that?*"

"Well, Mister Holy Man, in *this* town, it *pays* to hang out with *deviants*. Specifically, the designer B&D crowd, the ones with leather masks by Gucci and anal pain thongs by Atrocità of Milano. I can get testimony on video if you need it. Confession night is every Tuesday at the Limelight—I'm one of the bartenders there. The cover price is $25 and drinks are free, and I *guarantee* I can get enough to put half the VNN board behind bars for accessory to murder. The Limelight's one of my best sources of hot street info, especially among the Wealthy and Influential. You ought to loosen up, Chief Holy Man and lose that clerical hat of yours—or whatever they call it in Arabic—you'd learn a lot more and make a lot of influential friends! *You might even get to keep your job…*"

The room went deathly silent.

"It's called a *Kufi*, by the way," Shabazz whispered icily.

Hayte, Shrini, Donohue and Dietrich quickly excused themselves and went quickly downstairs.

Rich and Shrini went out the back way. Donohue snuck back to his cubicle to type an e-mail.

~ ~ ~

Venice, Saturday April 30:

Henri Brezzi saw Perry's message the next morning. His hand trembled too much when he tried to click on it to open it. He grunted in annoyance and said "Basta!"

The message opened. He read the first line and let out a long sigh of resignation.

> Hi Henri,
> I'm really sorry, but there's no reward for catching that Albanian man. Although I still think he intended to be one of the Phantoms henchmen, there is not enough evidence to link him to the robberies. The FBI only pays out rewards for domestic (U.S.) criminals and/or terrorists.
> BTW, we did break the Phantoms case. We arrested the entire Wiener Brothers board—it seems the whole thing came out of a boardroom bet about raising viewer ratings! I bet the other networks were involved too, but we haven't found a "smoking gun" pointing to anyone else.
> Pretty soon everything will be done in the name of ENTERTAINMENT. Is nothing sacred? Maybe we should re-name Madison Ave. as Hype Boulevard…
>
> Again, sorry about the bad news.
> Perry.

Brezzi started typing out a reply immediately.

> Hi Perry,
> That's all right about the reward money. My brother-in-law is a mason. He came up with a cheap way to stop my wine room from collapsing and taking my house with it. Tomorrow we start filling the whole room with bricks, with cement all the way to the top. That should keep the ocean out!
> Maybe we can leave a little hole for a few wine bottles, for your next visit.
>
> Ciao,
> Henri.

Murano said, "That seems like a good solution…"

Startled, Brezzi's head whipped around. "Franco! Don't startle me like that!"

"Sorry." Murano shrugged, "I thought you'd like to hear more about our mysterious head. I've been doing a little digging in my extra free time."

Brezzi laughed. "So you couldn't stay retired, eh?"

"It's my hobby now. Much better that way…" Murano pulled out a cigarillo, then stopped. "I really must quit these things." He sighed and put the pack back in his pocket. "So what do you want to know?"

"Well," Brezzi shut off the screen. "Why did the head end up here, of all places?"

Murano laughed. "Oh, Henri, you gonna love this. It was shipped to Locarno for a top-secret conference on cloning, but was stolen by a dedicated gang of eco-terrorists who wanted to sabotage the event, which was to present human cloning as a full-blown fait accompli to the scientific community, even after all the bans. They planned to set international guidelines for it."

Brezzi looked dumbfounded. "So why was it dumped in our canal?"

"I guess the eco-terrorists wanted maximum exposure, but it backfired. Once the paparazzi found out no murder was involved, nobody cared about whose head it was. After all, with all the unidentified body parts being discovered daily by police in the former Soviet Union, a head that's been dead at least 40 years is hardly worth mentioning."

"But... how did it end up with the lipstick and shit?"

"Unfortunately, you sent it on at exactly the wrong time of year. Remember all those wild bats that caused all incoming planes to France to be diverted elsewhere? Well, the same thing happened in Lyon, so the transport plane was re-routed to Düsseldorf. There it got misplaced by a junior postal worker and, instead of being sent to the German *Bundeskriminalamt* in Wiesbaden, it was mistakenly sent to a *Karnival Sitzung* at a local police station, where it ended up as a prop during a long night of drunken debauchery. That's also why the head smelled so funny—I didn't realize it was leaking *Altbier* all over the place..."

Brezzi looked even more puzzled, "What the hell is *Altbier?*"

"The local beer in Düsseldorf." Murano made a face, "Not to my taste, but my friends at Harry's insist it is better than the Americano stuff. When I go, I would prefer to be soaked in a vat of Valpolicella."

Brezzi reached under his desk and produced a bottle, "Franco, we can start right now, if you like..."

~ ~ ~

Wednesday May 4, 5:30 p.m.:

The round-faced sergeant from reception tapped Hayte on the shoulder. Richard turned around. "Hey, what's up, bro?"

The sergeant looked distinctly unhappy. "You got a minute, Cap'n?"

"Sure." Hayte leaned back in his chair. "Whatcha need, Mathers?"

Mathers let out a heavy sigh. "I need to show you something."

"No problem, I got all the time in the world—I just found out I passed the state bar exam." grinned Richard.

"All right!" Mathers's face brightened momentarily. "That means you're now a bona fide legal expert, right? Well, I got a possible test case for you..."

"Oh yeah? What?"

"Come with me, Captain. We gonna take a lil' ride on the A-train to Harlem."

"To Harlem? What for?" Hayte stood up, dwarfing the pudgy sergeant.

Mathers beckoned with his finger. "You'll see."

As they passed, Shabazz poked his head out of his office. "Captain

351

Hayte, could I have a word with you?"

Before Hayte could reply, Mathers spoke up, "Hey Chief, come along with us—you don't want to miss this."

"How so, Mathers?" said Shabazz stiffly.

"Come on," Mathers waved emphatically, "Trust me, you'll wanna see *this*, Chief. It's like a page straight out of Babylon."

Shabazz shrugged and grabbed his jacket. He came trotting down the steps.

They walked out of the White Elephant and down the street to the nearest subway station. They descended the stairs to the subway platform.

Mathers said in a low voice as he fed tokens into the turnstile mechanism. "You remember the phenomenon of 'White Flight'?"

Shabazz flashed him a puzzled look. "Sure..."

"Well, this is almost the opposite."

They got to the subway platform just as the A-train pulled up. They got in the middle wagon. "Let's grab the seats in the back—they'll give us the best view..." said Mathers enigmatically. He sat down heavily and slid over to make room for the two of them. Hayte let his legs stretch out into the aisle.

Shabazz looked at Mathers, "So what's this about 'White Flight?'"

"Well, Chief, it looks like we got some kind of returning flock. Or two. Or twenty. And this time, you really can say they *do* look alike..."

Hayte raised an eyebrow. "I don't like the sound of this."

The train slid into the first Harlem stop, and Richard's jaw dropped open. Shabazz just stared.

In every corner of the platform, huddled in dirty rags, were groups of Johnny Bs, scattered like festering clumps. No one got out.

"You see what I mean?" Mathers shook his head. "But that ain't the worst of it by far."

The doors shut and the train rattled its way to the next stop, which was the biggest subway station in all of Harlem. "Here's where we get off." The doors opened. Shabazz looked horrified. "*No!*"

"Oh yes." said Mathers, as they stepped out into a vast cacophony of shrieks and guttural clucking noises.

The entire area, a vast cavern of concrete and steel girders, was filled with Johnnys. Rich wrinkled his nose in disgust at the smell.

"You see? Mm-mm-*mm!*" Mathers grimaced as he waved his hand. "I been getting phone calls all day from folks coming out of the Apollo and from the Bayou restaurant, all complaining about aggressive panhandling and..."

A tossed lit cigarette barely missed nailing Shabazz in the eye. "Motherfucking shit!" He looked around in a rage.

He advanced on the nearest bunch of Johnnys—and got a hailstorm of more lit cigarettes and quart-sized malt liquor bottles for his trouble, before the Johnnies scuttled up the support girders and out of reach.

"Fucking-ass *monkeys!*" Shabazz's voice echoed down the tunnel.

The Johnnys made mocking faces and clucked at him defiantly from above.

"Calm down, Chief!" Mathers grabbed him by the arm. "They *like* it when you get mad. You can't catch 'em!"

Shabazz gave up trying to find a foothold on the girder. "Aw FUCK!" He looked at the filth on his hands.

Hayte tried to hide his amusement. "Look on the bright side—at least these ones don't have the explosives..."

"How do you know that?" demanded Shabazz angrily.

Hayte handed him a Kleenex. "Otherwise, they'd be blowing up folks instead of just crapping on them." He pointed above at the Johnny a few feet to the left. "You can see the difference. No pull rings on their belts—hell, they ain't even *got* belts."

Mathers shook his head. "They ain't housebroken, Cap'n, that's for damn sure. C'mon, we better go upstairs before we *really* get shit on."

They got to the top of the steps. Hayte glanced back down. "I can sure understand why folks have been complaining."

"That ain't the half of it, Cap'n, womenfolks been sayin' that they're being accosted."

Shabazz blanched. "*What*—attempted rapes too?"

"No, not *that* bad..." Mathers made a face, "...*yet.* But they been whipping out their tiny weenies and walking right up to women—hell, I even got *prostitutes* complaining to me."

Shabazz wiped his hands with a black handkerchief, "So these are the ones that *don't* blow people to bits?"

Rich nodded, "Right. Only a few were 'properly' trained to carry out their intended suicide bombings."

Shabazz folded the handkerchief neatly and put it in his pocket, "So why did the bomber ones go after you?"

"Well, I'm guessing here, but once a few Johnnys got loose and started reproducing, GeniTech went into damage-control mode. The real kicker was when one Johnny ended up as a Phantom—that's when the shit must've really hit the fan. After that, they probably started sending out the trained ones—to kill off anyone who could connect them to the project. The woman at the Goodwill was an egg donor, so she obviously had to go. Scotty was about to spill the beans to me, so he had to die too."

Mathers broke in, "Can I ask something? I read the case file—what about the handcuffs at the Bunch murder scene?"

Shabazz's head whipped around, "You *read* the file?"

"Yeah," said Mathers defensively, "I read them all—when you get weekend duty, there ain't *nothing* to do, most times. Would you rather I do crossword puzzles?"

Before Shabazz could think of a reply, Mathers turned back to Hayte, "So what's the deal with the handcuffs and Bunch's hand?"

"Scott was a deviant—I'd bet anything those were *his* own cuffs. Chances are, there were more than one Johnny, they overpowered him, cuffed him to the bed frame, then one lay on him and detonated. There were two different blood types among the samples we collected. But locating Bunch family DNA has been a real nightmare, so we never got any further with than that."

"OK," Mathers nodded slowly, "And the helix swirls—what was the deal with those? Why put up graffiti after murdering someone?"

"The helixes were done *before*—to mark a victim for 'extinction'. That follows standard suicide bomber patterns—first they do a recon mission or two, to plan out the explosion, then they come back to finish the job." A rueful look crossed Hayte's face, "Too bad I didn't pay more attention to that last detail…"

"But the swirls were done with a special ink…"

"Right. It's only visible under UV light. That's one thing about the Johnnys—they can see way beyond the normal spectrum—that's one of their non-human genes."

"Which means the ones down there can also see in the dark." Shabazz let out a groan, "Which means we're gonna have a hell of a time getting rid of them." He looked around, "Well, at least they aren't on the street level."

Mathers looked grim, "That's only 'coz the local fire brigade came down and opened the firehoses on them. But the hoses don't reach down into the subway stop, and we can't shut off the third rail without disrupting service anyway…"

Hayte looked up and down the street. "Is it only happening here on the main line through Harlem?"

"No, man—they's everywhere—I've gotten calls from Jamaica-Queens, the Bronx… Hell, the only place I ain't heard from yet is Manhattan."

"So all the other precincts are aware of the problem?" said Shabazz.

Mathers nodded emphatically. "Not yet, but it won't matter anyway, 'coz they can't do shit about it."

Shabazz looked disconsolate, "There ain't enough cops, and there sure ain't enough jail space."

Mathers nodded again, "From what I been hearing, most of the local precincts in the boroughs ain't even bothering to answer calls any more, that's why folks from all over been calling us now."

"There ain't much we can do, either, even if we open up the underground cells in the White Elephant." Shabazz despondently kicked a can into the gutter, "This is just *wonderful*—a humanitarian crisis in the making, caused by packs of non-humans! They've just invented a new type of redneck—the new Jukes family!"

"Except these turn *brown* in the sun…" said Hayte.

Shabazz gave him a poisonous look.

~ ~ ~

Friday, May 6:

The ringing of the phone jarred Brezzi from his dreams. He fumbled around in the darkness. "Ciao, Brezzi," he grumbled.

"Murano here. I have some bad news, Henri."

"What is it?"

Murano told him. Brezzi sat straight up in horror, banging his head on the bed frame. "*No!* It can't be—*another* severed head? *Where?*"

"You're not going to like this. It was floating right next to the Baglioni."

"Minge Morte!" Brezzi put his head in his hands.

Murano's voice crackled in the receiver. "Why did you say that, Henri? You're not from South Italy!"

"Right now, I *wish* I was. I think I'll move—*to Africa.*"

~ ~ ~

Later that same day:

"You're making excellent progress. Have a good weekend, Captain." said Dr. Max Jacobson IV, looking up briefly from his notes. "See you in a fortnight."

"Thanks, doc. See ya." Perry closed the door behind him. He stepped outside and squinted in the bright sunshine. He fished around for his sunglasses.

Unusual shadows floated by. He looked up. What the hell? Those can't be pigeons...

White feathers wafted down and a familiar clucking noise reached his ears. Donohue took a step back and almost fell down the stairway to the cellar. "That can't be!"

He turned around again as a little old lady came past. He pointed up, "Excuse me, ma'am, are those..."

"Chickens, young man. Haven't you ever seen one before?" she replied evenly.

"But not *flying* chickens!" protested Donohue.

"Where have you been? Haven't you been reading the dailies?" She picked through a guidebook and fiddled with her glasses. She pointed to an illustration. "I believe that one there is a Plymouth Rock Blue. See? The plumage is very distinctive." She turned to another page, "I hear there's a pair of Gold-Laced Wyandottes nesting on the Empire State Building—young man, where are you going?"

Perry up the steps and began ringing Dr. Jacobson's doorbell incessantly.

~ ~ ~

Saturday, May 7, 4 am:

As they got in the car, Hayte was still shaking his head, "I can't believe how many guys were there! There must've been four hundred!"

Condilee smiled and arched an eyebrow, "You were expecting *women*? At a Cut Manhood therapy group session?"

"No, what I mean is..."

She looked at his profile silhouetted in the street lights, "You didn't think there were so many others in the same boat as you."

"Yeah." He paused as they came up to the blinking red light. "I can't believe none of those crimes—they must've been crimes—got reported."

"Can't you?" She reached over and ran her fingers over his arm. "Think of the tabloids and all the funny looks people give you, once they *know* your 'masculinity' has been cut..."

"I see your point," Hayte sighed. He looked over, "I'm sure glad we had *our* therapy session before we went there..."

She looked away. He felt the mood chill. He wanted to ask if he said something wrong, but there were too many cabs to maneuver around.

Finally the traffic cleared as they got past Central Park. Hayte looked over. "You OK?"

"I'm not sure..." Condilee smiled wanly. "I just feel funny about riding in a police car, that's all."

Hayte laughed, "Well, it's not like you're in the back seat."

"That's true." She pointed down the street. "You can drop me off here."

"You sure you'll be OK?"

"I'm sure." She turned to open the door, then stopped. "I should say something. About us..."

Rich looked over. "Yes?"

She pulled the collar of her coat around her ears. "I... I don't know, Richard. If we did, you know... get serious, I'm not sure it would work."

"Oh."

"It's not *you*, Rich that's the problem—it's *me*... my situation. I'd have to change careers. It's not just quitting *a job*, it's a lot more permanent than that." She chewed her lower lip. "It would mean a *lot* less money for me."

"I could transfer to the D.A.'s office. Their pay isn't too shabby."

"I know, but..."

Hayte reached for her hand. "You don't have to decide now, you know."

She sighed. "I hope you're patient, Rich. It might be a while before I know, myself."

"Yeah, I know." He awkwardly shifted his hand in hers.

She took her hand away and gave him a quick peck on the cheek. "You're so nice to me." She turned to get out of the car. "Sometimes, *too* nice." She got out and closed the door.

Hayte watched her walk away, past expensive townhouses and gentrified condominiums. She walked around the steps of the last one on the block.

He sighed to himself and started the engine again. The fuel tank was full, and he halfway intended to use it all up before dawn. He drove up through Harlem and saw all the trashcan fires and clusters of Johnnys grilling chickens. More trashcan fires all along Martin Luther King Boulevard. He shook his head.

Hope the chickens reproduce as fast as the goddamn Johnnys...

Before he knew it, he was past Central Park and moving south. He went down Broadway into the heart of the Village.

After a while the scent of her perfume dissipated.

A new odor began to take its place. It started to bother him, but he couldn't place it.

Ahead on the street, a bar called the Big Cahouna still had its sign going, flashing an exotic blend of purplish and UV hues to highlight its exterior, which was smeared with glow-in-the-dark graffiti.

Rich detoured around some sawhorses and briefly went over a curb, right in front of the club.

Suddenly, his windshield was covered in symbols.

In shock, he backed up again.

All the car windows were covered in symbols.

His heart raced. Nowhere to hide.

He drove numbly through the backstreets heading for Canal Street. He had to get to his gun, and quick. He cursed himself for leaving it home.

Traffic was very light, virtually empty even, except for all the debris blown in by the hurricane. He had to slow down to steer round some piles of garbage in the road.

A movement in his periphery caught his eye.

He didn't consciously register seeing the wiry, black-haired pedestrian at first. But... something about the way he moved...

Hayte knew instantly who it was. Before he realized what he was doing, he switched off the driver's aid sensors and floored the accelerator.

The Johnny B's body slammed into the grill and flowed onto the hood in a slow-motion pirouette. Rich slammed on the brake and gas pedals at the same time, spinning the Merc in a neat 180° arc and knocked the Johnny down again just as he was crawling. Hayte quickly backed over the body with a satisfying crunch and then went back and forth three or four times to make sure.

It was then that he made the mistake of opening the door and checking out his handiwork, which by now bore little resemblance to anything human—or humanoid.

The body was on its side, revealing the ribcage. But it was the arms, red but devoid of any flesh, that got to him, especially the bony fingers grasping at the flood grating.

He got back in the car and tried to drive off.

A white van came round the corner and blocked his path. He hit reverse and did a 180°, but another van blocked his path.

The lead van stopped and the passenger side door opened.

Hayte's heart sank when he saw their footwear.

Birkenstocks and white socks.

One had bloodstains.

"We remember you, Richard." said Donner. "Now we meet again—*finally*. T.I.N.A."

"Tina?" said Hayte.

"It's an acronym *you* should know," Donner grinned like a shark. "*There Is No Alternative*. Margaret Thatcher said it. She was right, and *I* am, too. Time to join us. Hit and run is a pretty *serious* crime..." Donner flashed his torch up at Hayte's eyes.

Hayte walked up to him, as close as possible so he could tower over Donner. "It's a *clone*, Donner and you know it."

"I know and you know, but District Attorney's office *doesn't*," smirked Donner. "And you know there's no legal distinctions yet. Besides, we can *make* the crime fit the *punishment*..."

More sirens echoed between the towering buildings.

Donner started moving the Johnny's limbs.

"What are you doing?" snapped Hayte.

"Making it look a little more convincing. It's your call, Captain. Either you come with me and finish off your training—or your ass will be nailed *and* jailed for vehicular manslaughter and attempting to flee the scene of the crime—my agents will be glad to testify against you. So, what'll it be, Captain?" He moved Johnny's corpse over to where the biggest bloodstains were.

Something metal clinked on the asphalt. Donner shined his torch on it. "What the hell is that?"

Hayte said, "Don't touch that, Donner."

"Whaddya mean, don't touch?" Donner shined the torch back in Hayte's eyes and clicked on the bright beam. "Your ass is *mine*, not the other way round!"

Hayte dove behind his car, bashing his face hard on the curb.

An intense white flash reflected for an instant on all the windows, following by a hissing sound. The other van suddenly gunned its motor and took off down the road.

Hayte rolled over. He felt blood trickling down his forehead. He sat up.

There was only a charred lump and the remains of a pair of sandals.

Hayte kicked them down into the drainage vent in the curb just as the first squad car came round the bend.

He walked slowly to the driver's window and flashed his badge. "False alarm, looks like a gas leak caught fire—but it's out now."

"OK, Captain, I'll take your word for it," said the woman, reaching for the intercom. "False alarm, repeat, false alarm." She drove off, leaving Hayte standing.

He let out his breath slowly and silently gave thanks that she hadn't seen the bloodstains. He decided to get in his car and get the hell out of the area before anyone else got curious.

Monday, May 9:

THE NEW YORK CYBERPOST
BANKS PULL PLUG ON VNN!!
Guilty Before Proven Innocent?

Enraged investors have 'convicted' VNN months before the company's board members are scheduled to go on trial! In an unprecedented move Monday, every major investment bank worldwide has been selling their shares in VNN parent company Wiener Comm. The shares, which one peaked at $ 250, closed yesterday at $.005 in "extremely heavy trading."

The domino effect hit markets worldwide, as stock indexes plummeted, some by over 1000 points in the space of hours. Hardest hit were entertainment and media sector stocks, with Disney and Universal/Vivendi share prices halved in the minutes after news of the VNN board arrest broke.

"Now might be a good time to invest in alcohol and pharmaceutical firms," commented one analyst, who asked not to be named.

CLONE PLAGUE HITS MUSEUMS!!

All museums in Manhattan were forced to close yesterday as a safety precaution after security officials at the sold-out Bodily Universes exhibit were overwhelmed by packs of the mysterious clones seen popping up everywhere over the past few weeks. The clones, allegedly the product of GeniTech (although company spokespeople deny this), have been populating metropolitan subway tunnels and "turning them into some kind of underground ghetto," according to one health official, speaking on condition of anonymity.

"Now they're camping out amongst the Bodily Universes exhibits themselves," said a Met spokesperson. "And we cannot get rid of them. Every time we clear them out of one section, more pop up. We're currently petitioning the exhibition owners to let us use tear gas."

FBI Raids GeniTech

GeniTech HQ became a massive crime scene yesterday after "at least 100" FBI agents raided the premises. Local authorities refused to comment.

The End

About the Author

Walter von Wegen currently lives near Bonn, Germany. He teaches English at various locations in Europe.

He is currently working on a historical novel—his third—one which takes place in Germany and in the USA.

Printed in the United Kingdom
by Lightning Source UK Ltd.
104677UKS00001B/307-318